STOCKMAN'S SHOWDOWN

THE STOCKMEN SERIES

MEL A ROWE

Also by Mel A ROWE

ELSIE CREEK SERIES:
The Art of Dust
Diamond in the Dust
Caked in Dust
Xmas Dust
Muster in the Dust
Rolled in Dust
Written in Dust
Doctoring Dust
Buffalo Dust

OASIS OF THE OUTBACK DUOLOGY:
The Station, Volume One
The Station, Volume Two

THE STOCKMEN SERIES:
Stockman's Sandstorm
Stockman's Stowaway
Stockman's Stormcloud
Stockman's Showdown

THE STOCK SQUAD:
Rough Stock
Cold Stock
Wild Stock
Prime Stock

STANDALONE STORIES:
Avoiding the Pity Party
Unplanned Party
The Football Whisperer
Winter's Walk
Run Beautiful Run
The Sister Trip

Receive exclusive insights, and news on upcoming releases by joining:
https://melarowe.com/newsletter/

COPYRIGHT

***Caveat: As a courtesy, since there may be some sparse language choices in this story that may represent an obstacle for the reader, I am offering this warning. Please note this language and cultural references are purely for fictional purposes only and not designed to offend any individual persons, culture, or religions implied.*

The following is written in Australian English

For those who wouldn't mind a bit of
Bree's Outlaw Attitude in their life…

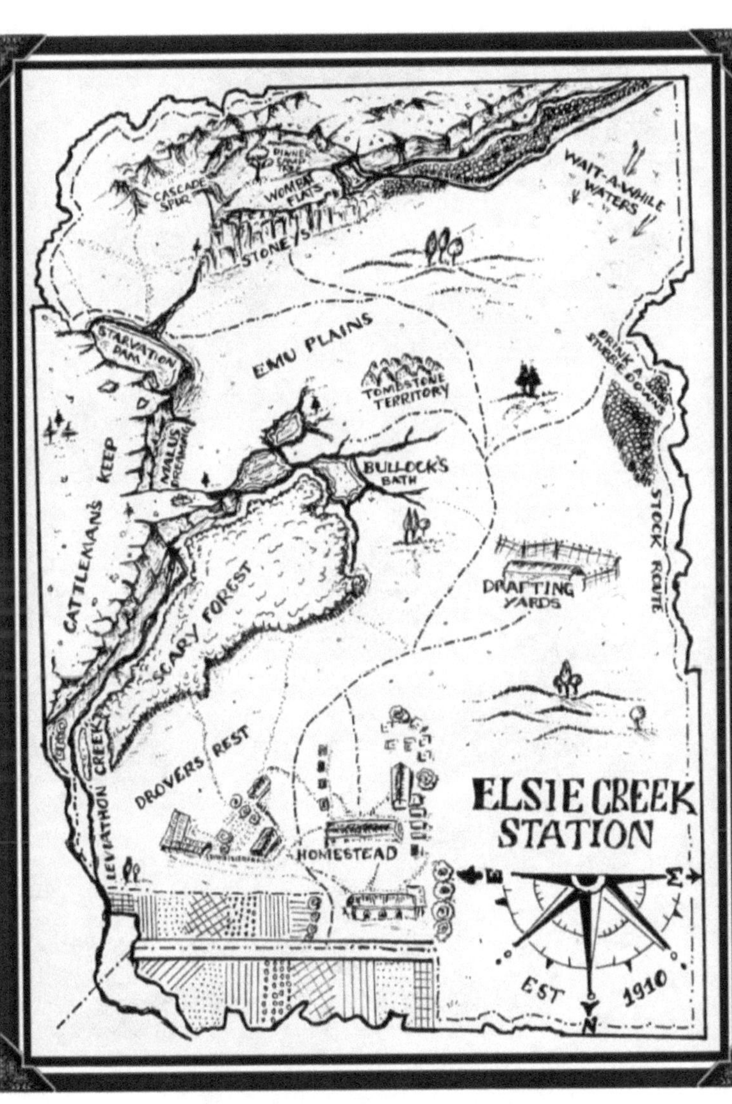

CASCADE SPUR
DINNER CAMP TREE
WOMBAT FLATS
STONE'S
WAIT-A-WHILE WATERS
STARVATION DAM
EMU PLAINS
TOMBSTONE TERRITORY
DRINK-A-LITTLE STURSIE DOWNS
MALLUS DREAMING
CATTLEMAN'S KEEP
BULLOCK'S BATH
STOCK ROUTE
DRAFTING YARDS
SCARY FOREST
DROVERS REST
LEVIATHON CREEK
HOMESTEAD
ELSIE CREEK STATION
W
E
N
S
EST 1910

Zero

Elsie Creek Station—September 1962

This place was soulless. A place in the middle of nowhere, where a girl had to depend on herself while not die from boredom or loneliness. Forcing Penelope Price to repair her handbag, which was on its last legs, like her marriage, and pretty much everything else in her life.

Welcome to purgatory. Trapped with no means of escape in the stark remoteness of this outback cattle station, where red dust lazily swirled under a scorching sun. Months without rain had left the soil dry, cracked and brittle, tempting the thought of finding somewhere to swim despite the risk of getting cosy with crocodiles.

A sturdy set of boot steps coming down the stone path of the cottage drew Penelope out of her thoughts. When she looked up, the sun was in her eyes, distorting the shadow of an approaching stockman in an enormous hat.

Oh no, was her husband back already?

Her eyes darted to the table where her handbag was in the middle of major surgery gone bad. Jack Price hated to see her playing with his tools or having any mess on the dining table except for food. Heaven forbid he finds out she'd been daydreaming about a new handbag, one like Audrey Hepburn's in *Breakfast at Tiffany's*.

There was a knock on the door, and the clunk of a heavy toolbox. 'Hello, Mrs Price?'

'*Harry*?' she squeaked. 'When did you get back?'

'Yesterday. Finished my linesman contract, got a few footy games in, and...' Head lowered, his eyes met hers through the flyscreen door. 'You know I couldn't stay away long. Not from you.'

It made her step back deeper into the cool shade of the cottage, anything to get away from his heated stare. 'You can't be here.'

'Your husband sent me over.' The screen door opened, no longer shielding her from the cheeky smile that only served to define his firm jaw, dusted with stubble. His dark blond hair was long enough to escape his hat where the ends curled at his ears. Along with his eyes that were such a pretty summery blue, it made up the man who had stolen her heart—who was supposed to stay away from her for good.

Hand to her throat, she swallowed hard to push down the emotions she'd thought she'd buried. Months had passed, and in those months before he went away, they'd only flirted a little. Until he'd kissed her so passionately, they fell into each other's arms. But then the musters finished, leaving her both sad and glad he'd gone to work for the telephone company, so she could be the dutiful wife again, always careful to never be one on one with any man, especially Harry Splint. 'Why did my husband send you here?' Was this a test?

'I'm here to put in a new telephone.'

'Really?' Her eyes lit up at the thought of having something so modern in such a foreign and forgotten part of the outback.

'I've just finished putting one up at the farmhouse. I even got you the latest model on the market.' He grinned, holding up the chunky black phone with a rotary dial for numbers. 'I said I'd do it for the boss man.'

Harry brushed off his boots on the doormat, removing his hat as he stepped inside. 'Where do you want it, Mrs Price?'

'Harry...'

His grin was positively sinful. 'I'm here on official station business. And we all know how much your husband hates anyone not calling you Mrs Price.'

Closing her eyes, she took a deep, shuddering breath, longing to reclaim her own identity—even though her husband still owned her. 'You can put the phone on my husband's desk.' Her voice was colder than she'd intended.

'It's okay, Pen.' Harry offered her such a tender smile, as if he understood or could see that thick layer of loneliness she'd tried so hard to hide.

Yet, it was both exciting and terrifying to have someone see her, as if she was a person of flesh and blood and not some property belonging to a man who controlled her entire life. But with Harry, he'd left her a heartbroken mess, even though she'd told him to go.

But now he was back.

She dragged away her husband's office chair as Harry began pulling out the large desk to get to the wall. The thick edge of the desk clipped the side table, knocking over the vase of flowers.

'Oh no.' She barely caught it, as did Harry, both of their hands holding the vase. The heat and warmth of his strong fingers were a stark contrast to the water leaking out all over the wooden floor, along with her pink grevilleas.

'I'm so sorry, Pen. I didn't mean to do that.'

'It's okay.' Removing her apron, she used it to mop up the water. 'So, I'm assuming you're back on Charlie's couch up at the stockman's shack.'

'I am.' Harry picked up the flowers and put them back into the vase.

As she tried to mop up the water, she noticed it trickle under the large cabinet and disappear. 'That's strange.'

'What is?'

On hands and knees, she peered under the cabinet. 'The water disappeared.'

Harry arched an eyebrow at her.

'I'm not being silly.'

'I didn't say you were.' He crouched down beside her. 'You might have a hole made by pests.'

'White ants?' They were everywhere, wood-eating monsters no bigger than her sewing needle, that built enormous nests. Some were impressive pyramids of red mud, others were like thin gravestones for giants. Along with the snakes, scorpions, and spiders bigger than her head, Elsie Creek Station was a terrifying place for a girl who'd come from the city wanting a home and a family.

'Want me to take a look?'

She shrugged.

'I'd hate for you to fall through the floor.' He looked at her with concern. That's what Harry did, always watching out for her welfare, always checking on her. How she'd missed that, and him.

Together, they slid the heavy dresser aside to expose the line where the water had disappeared between the floorboards.

From his toolbox, Harry pulled out a small fencing crowbar and jimmied the floorboard free. 'Crikey, that was easy.'

'What do you mean?'

'By rights, it should have been harder to shift.' He pulled the board back to reveal two metal military tins wedged in the space above the concrete slab.

'Careful.' She grabbed Harry's arm. 'My husband stores his dynamite in those types of army tins.'

'Was Jack in the Army?'

'Jack doesn't like to talk about it.' Her husband told her nothing these days, and she'd stopped asking questions a long time ago. She'd been so dead inside, until Harry entered her world like he was the sun. 'Do you know where Jack is?'

'He's with the rest of the men out at Starvation Dam. They're blasting today... But would your husband keep his dynamite in the house, under the floorboards?'

'Jack keeps his dynamite in the shed in this special wax paper I make for him.' It had her curious though, using her apron to mop off the water from the lids. 'Do we have to look inside?'

'Do you want me to?'

She gazed into his beautiful blue eyes, his tan only enriching their colour, and noted the level of kindness. It was that same expression he'd worn, the first time they'd met, over a year ago now, when the young stockman, Charlie Splint, introduced his older brother, Harry, to her at the local Elsie Creek Rodeo. She'd never expected Harry to become a stockman at the station, where he'd tip his hat to her with a smile.

At first the cordial conversations started in the sheds, the chicken coop, even the laundry house. And then she'd catch him leaving flowers for her in the washing basket, in the cleaning cupboards, or on the windowsill by her kitchen windows. Places only she would find them.

Slowly and surely, Harry Splint had wormed his way into her heart. Despite the fact that, as a married woman, she'd done everything she could to drive him away.

But here he was, back in the flesh. And once again her heart was being a traitor to good common sense. 'We should put the floorboard back and forget those tins exist.' A flare of panic had her heart hammering. What if Jack came home?

'You're not at all curious to see what's inside?'

She gnawed on her bottom lip.

'I promise I won't tell anyone, especially your husband.' Harry scowled at her wedding photo. 'You have to know you're the reason why I came back, Pen. I hate how he treats you. No woman deserves to be treated like that, especially by their husband.'

'It's none of your business.'

'But it became my business when I fell in love with you.'

'Stop saying that, Harry.'

'I know, I know.' He shook his head, his shoulders sagging under his deep sigh. 'But at least I made sure I got you the best telephone I could find, so that if you do decide to chase me away again, you can call me any time to come and get you.'

'You haven't even connected it yet.' She went to move, but

he grabbed her wrist.

'Penelope.' The way he said her name, as if letting each letter dance on his tongue, while he gently tucked her hair behind her ear, had her shivering.

Lord help her, she was a fool when it came to Harry Splint.

'Can you open those tins?' She needed him distracted and his hands busy away from her.

He gave a cheeky wink, then dragged the two tins from their hidden grave beneath the floorboards. He flicked down the latches and lifted the lid. 'Crikey.'

It was cash. Oodles and oodles of cash, all wrapped into neat bundles that only made her scowl.

'I don't believe it! Jack told me he had no money to buy me a new handbag.' Penelope pointed to her broken purse on the kitchen table. 'And he has all of this cash hidden under the floor.'

'Maybe he's saving for a house.'

'Jack has never once mentioned a house to me. Ever. Saddles, saddlebags, stockwhips, spurs, boots, and stockman's hats, sure, but nothing that resembled a home or anything for me.' Instead they were in the head stockman's house, which some called the caretaker's cottage, that they only lived in because of Jack's job. Because that's what Jack Price did, he was a stockman first, and a husband last.

The sight of all that money was so infuriating, she grit her teeth. 'What's in the second tin?'

Harry unclipped its sturdy latches and pulled off the sticky lid. The tin was filled with paperwork and more cash.

'Stop.' She grabbed Harry's hand as it was about to dive into the paperwork. His fingers were so much bigger than hers, and how easily they shifted to hold her hand, giving it a tender squeeze.

'It's okay, Pen.'

No, it wasn't. 'Jack always knows when something is out of order. Look at how he's packed that cash, it's all in denominational order. To go through that paperwork, we'd have to be methodical.' It would take time, because her husband was notorious for setting little traps as telltale signs of where she'd been. And she knew them all.

But this, this was different.

She gazed at the tins full of cash. It was enough for her mind to whirl from panic to suddenly pin her hopes on a preposterous plan. 'Harry, I need your help.'

'To do what?'

She gripped his wrists, shifting to face the only man she'd ever loved, as hope filled her bloodstream. Once again she'd come alive, and she only did that with Harry, who had now come back—it must be for a reason. It must be for this. 'Help me escape from my husband!'

One

Elsie Creek Station—Present Day

Ryder Riggs hadn't meant to fall for Bree Wilde. It just happened. That feisty redhead with curves and curls, had become such an enormous influence over his life, she was impossible to ignore, no matter how hard he'd tried, even when they practically argued with each other on a daily basis.

With an outlaw attitude, Bree only ever looked at Ryder with pure disdain. Not that he could blame her, when he'd not only cut those logs to burn, but he'd also poured the fuel to start that fire.

But beneath her fearlessness, he'd seen her fierce protectiveness for those she cared about. He'd seen the extraordinary lengths she'd gone to for his brothers, and his nephew, trying to help them turn Elsie Creek Station into a home. And for that she had his respect.

But when Bree turned this old tack room, which she'd called the *murder room*, into his office, it pretty much sealed the way his heart felt about her.

He could blame Bree for it, blame it on the details she'd put into remodelling his office space—which they'd renamed *the boardroom*—as if she understood him. And very few people knew who Ryder Riggs was. Not even his brothers could say they did, not after a ten-year absence.

Ryder swung open the heavy door to the room that used to be Bree's hideaway for her illegal gin still. Now the reinforced walls were lined with custom-made gun racks, and ammunition, creating a private arsenal. The door shut whisper quiet behind him, the locking mechanism—hidden under a panel giving the appearance of just another wall—clicked into place. Inside the main room it held workbenches, his desk, and a long boardroom table the caretaker, Charlie, had made by hand.

Under the bright industrial lights, on the shiny steel workbenches Bree had built perfectly for his height, lay his latest job: Bree's shotgun.

He'd snatched it off the wild woman a while ago, back when she was going to shoot Mia's ex. Somehow Bree had a huge cache of shotguns stashed all over the station, and she'd already shot one guy, so she wasn't afraid to use them, which made him pause about giving it back to her.

As an army-trained armourer, a firearms engineer, and a gunsmith in the civilian world, Ryder had completely disassembled the 1960 Winchester Model 12, with no serial numbers on it. And that was rare.

After cleaning it, he'd inspected the components for signs of wear and tear. Lubricants ensured a crucially smooth operation before it was reassembled. He didn't have a firing range yet to test it out, but as he looked down the barrel, the line of sight was perfect. And his job was done.

He spread out a dark green blanket, soft from many years of use, and used it to wrap up Bree's shotgun like a present.

Then his watch pinged with an alarm.

It was time.

Tucking the wrapped shotgun under his arm, he turned off the wall of monitors that ran their surveillance cameras. He silenced the widescreen playing the business channel, then watched the large industrial lights dim. Since Bree had handed him the keys, he'd spent all his after-work hours here. He rarely went to the farmhouse anymore, except to sleep—if he slept, because his mind never stopped.

Ryder let the heavy door shut with a click behind him and pulled the key from the lock. Tucking the key into his denim pocket, he passed Bree's latest remodelling project, which had all his brothers involved this time. It was their very own outdoor bar that ran along the back wall of their office, right next to the workshed that was Dex's mechanical workshop, and where they parked their cars. It even included a watering trough for their horses.

The new bar was where they'd meet, drink beer and discuss work like they always did. Except they'd shifted from crowding the farmhouse's front verandah to watch the sunrise and sunset, to one of best views of the open paddocks.

It's where everyone was going to meet shortly as they were going on a muster to Emu Plains, and he was looking forward to it.

But first he had to deliver his gift.

Silently he jogged across to the far side of the homestead and down the long run of corrugated fencing that shielded two sides of the caretaker's cottage, to meet the wire fence line that he effortlessly hiked over.

On his right, the lights were on in the stables where the well-trained stockhorses were waiting to be saddled. On the left stood the silent sheds that Charlie called the smithy's workshop. In the middle, through the wooden fence rails and garden, he caught a glimpse of the open back door of the caretaker's cottage. Bree and her grandfather's voices carried outside on the slight pre-dawn breeze, which was perfumed by the assortment of flourishing fruits and vegetables that cleverly disguised the scents of the stables.

Ryder could have dropped off Bree's shotgun to her, but he didn't want the rejection or the lecture he'd cop for taking so long in returning her gun, considering he'd pinched it from her in the first place.

He liked being unseen when it came to watching over Bree, and his days in the military had trained him well. If Bree ever caught him, she'd have him for stalking while probably aiming a shotgun at him.

A surprising grin forced his lips to curve.

Only Bree did that to him. She'd make him angry, only to make him smile when he didn't want to.

But he was doing this because he had a lot of bridges to repair with Bree, who had the knack of bringing out the worst in him, and Ryder was pretty sure the woman he loved hated him.

Two

'Come on, Pop.' Bree slung her saddlebags over her shoulder as she pushed open the back screen door to head for the stables.

'Have we got everything?'

'Yes.' *For the thousandth time.* 'The food and swags are ready to load onto the horses. We just need you.' She stopped to wait for the old man who was hesitating by the back door, when normally Charlie would be leading the charge to the stables, telling her to hurry.

'Are you sure we need to camp out overnight? We could just drive out to Emu Plains.' She'd been riding out there daily to check on the herd, while checking her various fishing spots before breakfast.

'Nah, I want this, kid. There's nothin' like sippin' on a fresh cup of billy tea while laying on your swag watching a sunrise over the ranges.' Charlie decisively closed the back door of the stone cottage, sliding on his old Akubra with the crocodile headband from the beast that had dared to bite him. He scooped up his saddlebags and swaggered towards her. 'I'll be teaching them girls how to make a proper campfire damper this time, so there'll be less cooking for you.'

'I don't mind camp cooking over the coals. Just don't tell those boys I said that, Pop.' Otherwise, they'd be begging her to be their permanent muster cook, when she'd graduated from that job way back when she was a teenager.

Illuminated by the lights from the open stables, they

followed the stone path through the vegetable garden where the heavy dew made the leafy vegetables seem shiny. Bree slowed down to match her grandfather's gait, which was slower than normal. Was his heart okay?

'I want you to let that mob cook this muster.' Charlie paused to take a deep inhale of the air before resuming his stride. 'They've gotta learn.'

'We don't even need to do a campfire.' She should be calling off this overnight camp and bundling him back inside to rest.

'Come on, kid, you can't tell me you don't enjoy it out there as much as me.'

That was true.

'That last saddle-pack muster to Wombat Flats,' he continued, 'reminded me how good it is sleeping out under the stars, and how we'd tell stories sitting around the campfire. It won't be long now, and the build-up's weather will crowd our sky with clouds, making it too hot to camp out.' Again, he peered up at the stars highlighting the night sky with that same look he had when he'd carry his cup of tea to this very same back fence to raise his tin mug to salute the sun as if to say, *I made it another day*. And Charlie had a ticking clock, because his poor heart was long past its expiry date.

Every day was a gift to Charlie, making their time together all the more precious, which is why Bree always gave in to him, like agreeing to go on this overnight muster.

She unlocked the back gate and swung it open. 'Have you got any spooky stories to scare the tourists with, Pop?'

Charlie gave a wry grin, patting her shoulder as he walked past. 'You've heard 'em all, kid.'

'Well, I promise to not spoil the ending.' The gate clicked back into place and through another gate, they entered the stables. 'Hello, my lovelies.' The horses nickered, as some stamped their hooves with excitement. 'Ready to earn your horse feed?'

'They're more than ready.' Charlie's bandy-legged

swagger seemed more pronounced this morning as he went to greet his favourite stockhorse, Slim. 'Mornin', young fella. You ready to chase some long tails under the sun?'

The grey horse nickered as if it understood.

Bree wanted to help the old man saddle his horse, but Charlie would only get mad at her for interfering. Instead, she brushed down her favourite horse, Black Hand. Grandson to her first stockhorse, Black Mamba. He was as black as midnight and such a bad-arse. 'Ready to do this, trouble?'

The horse rubbed his long nose against her arm. Black Hand was clever, fast, and fearless, all the traits she admired in a horse.

Bree reached for her saddle. 'What the...'

She paused at the blanket, the wool coarse but so soft and thick, its colour a deep emerald green. She followed the edging, discovering a few small patches where the hand stitching was rough, but it held. On the underside, it bore the worn label: *R. Riggs.*

The blanket was old and worn, yet incredibly soft. It was gorgeous. She lifted the heavy weight of pure wool to reveal a shotgun. 'No way.' It was her old shotgun, smelling of gun oil, the barrel polished and clean, and the wooden handle incredibly smooth. She cocked it open, checking it was unloaded, but it looked and felt as if brand new. No, this was better than new, the trigger action was like listening to the precision of a Swiss watch tick.

'What's that, kid?'

'My shotgun.'

Charlie poked up the brim of his hat, before taking the gun. 'Where's it been?'

'Ryder pinched it.'

'When?'

'Months ago.' When she'd aimed it at Mia's ex-boyfriend. Back then, Ryder had snatched it out of her hands and stripped it down to parts in a matter of moments, while telling her off for breaking the rules to some *murder club*. He'd been so quick it had stunned her into silence—only for a few moments—before she argued with him to give it back. But he never had… Until now.

Hmm, what did Ryder want from her now?

'The lad's done some work to it.' Charlie peered down the shotgun's barrel. 'Straight as a pin, that.' He levered the pump action a few times. 'That's smooth as butter. What did Ryder do wrong to give you this?'

Bree shrugged. 'Do you need me to write a list?'

'You've forgiven him for calling you a cattle rustler, right?' Charlie rested the shotgun against the pole. 'Ryder's put a lot of effort into that gun. It looks like a peace-offering to me, kid.'

Only until Ryder started their war again.

'You'd better thank him when you see him. He is the boss.'

'Not my boss. I don't work for those boys.' She frowned, hoisting her saddle onto Black Hand. No one was her boss. Yet here she was, mustering for the Riggs brothers, *again.*

Individually, they'd each taken a shot at trying to convince Bree to come on this muster, where she'd flatly told all the Riggs brothers *no.* But those four sneaky boys knew how to manipulate Charlie, telling the old man he was the head stockman for this muster, which meant Charlie demanded Bree be on his team. And she was only doing this for Charlie.

Even though the Riggs brothers were getting under her skin, they shouldn't. She wasn't part of their staff as a muster cook, or a stockwoman. Yet here she was hoisting her arse into the saddle before dawn, clipping on her stockwhip, and sliding the newly returned shotgun into its saddle holster. Slipping on her riding gloves, she checked the tether of her four-horse train, which would follow her, then nodded at her grandfather from beneath the brim of her stockman's hat to make a start on this long day ahead.

A stiff cool breeze blew down from the escarpment, it was always coldest before the dawn. She grabbed the gun's blanket and wrapped it around her shoulders like a long shawl. It smelled like him. Gun oil, polished wood, leather, cigar smoke and bourbon, blending with a rich man's smell, the one of a boss. Just not *her* boss. No one lorded over her— even though Ryder Riggs tried to.

'Ready to greet the dawn, kid?' Finally, her grandfather had that spark in his grey eyes again. Sitting proudly in the saddle, Charlie was more than ready to greet the day. This is what the stockman lived for.

'Always.' Nothing beat riding a horse towards a spectacular sunrise on this cattle station she called home— but only for as long as the caretaker's caveat remained in place.

Three

It was a freaking circus! Gathered by the new bar near the boardroom, Ryder could only shake his head with embarrassment at how his younger brothers were acting like fools, completely unorganised as they attempted to get their women onto their respective horses.

'You keep clicking away on your camera like that, Soph, and you won't have any battery left.' Dex checked over the saddle straps of his new lady's saddle.

Typically, Sophie ignored Dex to aim her camera at the ground, the cobwebs, even the horse's eyelashes. 'But this is my first muster.'

Ryder groaned, barely containing his frustration. The fact that his brothers insisted on bringing along these inexperienced women had his eyeballs wanting to roll back in his head for good. Come on, this wasn't a tourist trail ride, it was a muster. It was a job. Simple.

But his younger brothers couldn't bear being one night away from their ladies. They'd even brought along a toddler and that much extra baggage they had to borrow some stockhorses to carry it. Come on, this was for just one night— he'd hate to see how much junk they'd pack for a weekend at the pub.

'Will we be doing any scary riding like the Stoneys trail?' Harper slid on her new stockman's hat. The woman had more hats than they had space in the farmhouse's hallway, which was overrun with kid's toys and pampered house dogs.

'I dunno?' Ash peered back at Ryder.

'Doubt it. It's all flat country.' Ryder had spent days in the chopper, pushing the cattle closer, with his chatty passenger, Charlie, who'd predicted they'd all be heading for the waterholes.

'No muster chopper today?' Again, Sophie zoomed that camera at him.

Ryder scowled at the blonde. 'You take another photo of me, and I'll snap that lens off.' Sophie was as annoying as a buffalo fly.

'Touchy.'

He narrowed his eyes at her, his voice deep and laced with warning. Ryder only ever gave one warning shot. 'Dex.'

'Yeah, I know.' Dex rode up beside Sophie. 'Hon, I'm agreeing with Ryder. Put the camera away. You've only had a few riding lessons, and you need to concentrate. And none of us appreciate a camera in our face.'

'I'm sorry, I'm just so excited.' Sophie slipped the camera band from around her neck to slide the camera into her backpack.

'Where's the cat?' Cap asked, helping to hoist the tiny Mia into her saddle. Mia was a farm girl who worked hard, was good with the dogs and their land, and she made Cap happy. Cap deserved it.

Ryder didn't mind Mia, and he was getting used to Harper, who was an excellent mother to Mason. The bonus was Harper was helping Ash become a man to be proud of.

As for Dex, he had Sophie, as the latest addition. Even if she irritated Ryder, Dex was smitten by the blonde in the most embarrassing way. The once-fierce fighting man was whipped.

'Mr Purrington is happy hogging the couch,' said Sophie. 'Don't worry, he's got plenty of food and water to last him a year. And Dex left the TV on for company.'

'For a cat?' *What the hell?* Ryder arched his eyebrows at the ex-bare-knuckle champion pandering to a cat. Even

Charlie loved that big ginger cat, walking it around like a dog on a lead.

'Mr Purrington likes watching the fights as much as I do. The animal.' Dex grinned as he settled into his saddle.

'Babe, are you ready?' Ash tapped Harper's denim thigh.

'I am.' She flexed her fingers in her riding gloves.

'They're new?'

'I learned my lesson on the last muster. Gloves and neck scarf, just like Bree wears. And this trip, Charlie's going to show me how to use a stockwhip.'

'Lord help us all,' muttered Ryder. Dex nodded in agreement.

'As Charlie would say, it's good to see you having a go, Harper.' Cap climbed into his saddle, steering his horse next to Mia. His entourage of a dozen cattle dogs shook the dust off their coats where they'd been lying. The kelpie, Willow, was the newest addition to Cap's muster-dog pack, who was about to be broken in on her first muster.

'Well, don't you look like a mob of trouble?' Charlie trotted up on his grey stockhorse, with Bree behind him, bringing up their packhorses.

Ryder just froze, staring at Bree who had the gun in her saddle, with the blanket—that damned green blanket— wrapped around her shoulders like a shawl, highlighting her red hair. When she nodded with those green eyes locked on his, he was sucker punched.

'So, what's the plan?' Dex asked.

Ryder dropped his head to focus on his boots, the dirt, the job. 'Charlie, you're the man with the plan.' They'd already discussed it at length. But having Charlie in charge allowed them to have Bree on board, and she was a better stockwoman than all of them put together. Plus, she knew the land, and the cattle knew her, because of Charlie's clever little concept of stock school.

Ryder also had the sneaky suspicion that his brothers were going to be too busy watching over their women to do the job when Ryder was counting on them.

Did he need to drag them back to the drafting yards for another meeting to remind them of the job they were all investing heavily in to create a lifestyle and a legacy for generations to come?

Charlie clambered off his horse, leaving Bree to hold the reins. He dragged out a map from the back pocket of his worn jeans, and spread it over their new bar where everyone could view it from their saddles.

He loved their new bar, catching the grin from Dex, who too enjoyed the fact they could ride up with their horses, open the fridge to steal a coldie, and give the horse a quick drink, then ride off again.

Bree was a genius with her plans, dragging up furniture and metal sheeting, even slabs of wood from one of the back sheds to cleverly repurpose materials, saving Ryder thousands.

'We'll ride out to Emu Plains, where we'll make our stock camp this side of Koala Creek. It's a pretty place on the plains.' Charlie pointed to the map. 'We'll then muster up those stragglers from One More No More Corner and Scary Forest, pushing them towards Koala Creek. Then tomorrow we'll begin the long walk to the fencing channel to the drafting yards.'

'Are there any crocodiles in Koala Creek?' Mia asked.

'Always.' Bree sat on her fierce black horse like an amazonian warrior, with her thick red plait trailing over her shoulder. 'Unless you want me to start writing your obituaries, treat every waterhole, every creek, and every river as a hunting ground for those sneaky river puppies.'

'So why are we camping near that creek, if there are crocodiles?' Harper held out a small hat to Ash, who put it on their son's head, Mason, who was strapped to his father's chest in his carrier, ready and raring to go. That fast-growing boy was a future stockman in the making.

'For Rijidij Dugout, of course.' Bree let rip a playful grin that sparked in her eyes. If anyone knew how to play it was Bree.

'The what?' Dex asked.

'Pop, you like telling stories.' She nodded to her grandfather, always letting the old man take the lead.

'Well, lemme see…' Charlie pushed back the brim of his well-worn hat. 'Darcie's dad gave those hot springs the name, Rijidij Dugout. And it's a good one too. Over the years, the stockmen of Elsie Creek Station kept digging it deeper, while building the small wall of river rocks to surround the natural hot springs where we'll be camping. Darcie's dad swore by it, whenever his arthritis played up.'

'So it has healing properties?' Sophie reached out to hold Dex's hand. 'That might have helped you, and me, after that last fight?'

Didn't that remind Ryder that even though Sophie may be irritating, she'd earned her place at this station. In fact, all of his brothers' ladies had helped save this station, one way or another.

'After being in the saddle all day, Rijidij Dugout's hot water is the best place to wallow while cracking open a cold beer, with Emu Plains spread out before you showing off the sunset.' The old man sighed wistfully as if picturing it in his mind.

'It gives the term being rock bottom new meaning,' said Bree with a devilish grin, 'it's like a heated spa under the stars you won't regret.'

'Oh, I'm in. I love spa days. Good for the skin,' said Harper, who was flawlessly dressed as always, having turned their farmhouse bathroom into a make-up studio. Their shower was filled with shampoos and conditioners, while assorted painful-looking electrical hair gadgets congested the bathroom bench. It was safer for Ryder to use the outdoor shower, because if he moved the wrong way inside the farmhouse bathroom, he'd cause an avalanche of hair care products and make-up.

'But I'm going to cook, right?' Harper may be politically savvy, and good with the books, but she couldn't cook to save herself. She'd try, but it always ended up as muck that only the pampered house dogs would touch. No wonder they were getting fat.

'I've told Bree to let you lot cook for a change,' announced Charlie.

'Aww, really?' Dex screwed his nose up as Ryder frowned at the news. 'That's the only reason we wanted Bree to come, for her cooking.'

Sophie thumped his arm. 'I can cook.'

'You can't camp cook like Bree, babe.'

'How do you know?'

'Can you cook on a campfire?'

'I don't mind learning. Like Harper is always having those cooking lessons.'

Ryder rolled his eyes, groaning at the mess he expected, knowing those *cooking lessons* were just a codename for long liquid lunches attended by Bree, Mia and Harper. He doubted any cooking got done, but lots of cocktails were consumed using Bree's homemade gin.

'Bree, please tell us you'll be cooking?' Or Ryder was going to drag out his army ration packs.

'For you, cupcake? Never.' Her eyes were like fire, and that grin was just as evil—together it was as sexy as sin, it sent his heart into a rat-a-tat spat of gunfire in his chest.

'Play nice, Bree.' Charlie folded up his map, before climbing back onto his horse. 'The lad did fix your gun.'

'That he pinched like a pickpocketing professional at the Paris Olympics.'

Ryder didn't expect a thank you. After all, he'd done the wrong thing. Not when she'd done more for him just by wearing his blanket, and she didn't even know it.

Giving his horse a slight nudge, he rode past Bree, barely catching a whiff of her scent—warm vanilla and pecans complemented that hint of something intoxicatingly spicy underneath.

'Thank you for cleaning my shotgun, Ryder.'

Ryder, huh? Bree rarely called him by his name. It was always *cupcake*. Cap had the nickname tiger, or kennel master. Dex was stormcloud. And Ash was snowflake. The girls had their own nicknames too, none of which Ryder cared to remember. But he vividly recalled the day Bree had called him that ridiculous pet name—*Cupcake.* It made him grit his teeth that someone dared call him that. But that redhead did it with all his brothers, as if poking and prodding to see what they were made of.

Beneath that outlaw attitude and brassy sass was a clever woman who challenged him daily—if he was lucky to see her daily. And if he did, it was rare she stayed longer than ten minutes at a time, passing through to drop her bomb of information and leave.

The only time they'd spent any real time together was when they'd mustered a herd at midnight after a wild dog attack. They didn't talk much, but listening to Bree sing a soft lullaby to the herd under the glow of a full moon had been truly magical.

Then there was the time when they were sitting in the hospital room watching over Dex, who was strapped to a breathing machine. Bree had been there, holding Dex's hand as he struggled to breathe, with the noise from the in-and-out raspy machine pumping oxygen into Dex's lungs to keep him alive. Ryder had never been more grateful to Bree, who had stood by his family—and by him. It was during those moments he'd felt a shift, opening a space in his heart just for her, even if he hadn't realised it at the time. And after finding someone who had seen him through the darkest of nights, was it any wonder he wanted to hold on to her?

So, this muster he had a plan. Ryder had purposely chosen to park up his muster chopper, leave the satellite phone home, and ride in the saddle in hope of connecting with Bree, while keeping her in his sights. And she was worth the watch as a third-generation stockwoman.

Funnily enough, Bree was the only one Ryder wasn't paying to work this muster. Originally, he'd paid Harper to be the nanny, but now she did a day in the office as their bookkeeper. Mia was their full-time employee as their nursery manager. Sophie had originally been paid to nurse Dex back to health. Now he was paying for their time on this muster. And he paid his brothers and Charlie wages as stockmen. The only one who refused was Bree, repeating that line: *I don't work for you boys.*

Sure, it annoyed him, but he had to respect her for that. Even so, he always made sure he'd given Charlie double the wages, plus a bonus for Bree's help.

Bree was also the only woman he'd ever handed his credit card to so she could shop for their musters. Not only did she stock up their farmhouse pantry, but she ensured they all had proper equipment, providing the receipts, and not ripping him off once, when he'd given her plenty of opportunity to do so. Without knowing it, Bree had ticked all his boxes.

Now, he was hoping by the end of this muster she realised how much he cared for her—even though he was expecting her to fight him.

With a military past, it's a good thing he was used to fighting because she was worth the fight, as the only woman fiery enough to melt the ice in his veins.

Four

'This place is amazing.' Sophie clicked away on her camera, while swivelling in her saddle.

With mild amusement Bree grinned at Sophie, who was riding her horse like a drunk stockman leaving the pub long after last drinks had been called.

'Welcome to Emu Plains.' And what a glorious morning it was, where the sun had yet to breach the escarpment that made up Cattleman's Keep, extending its shadow across Emu Plains. The sweet scent of sunrise made Bree lift her chin to the clear cobalt-blue sky as a salmon-pink haze chased the last of the night beyond the horizon.

This wide-open valley held some of the richest grazing grasses and was now home to a small herd of buffalo wallowing in the nearby billabong. Spread like a crochet carpet over the water's surface, small wild lotus opened their white petals to greet the new day. Groups of ibis, a few ducks, and even some long-legged jabirus stalked along its edges. Elsie Creek Station was certainly putting on a show this morning—no wonder Sophie kept clicking away at her camera.

'Are they buffalo?' Dex rode alongside Bree, nodding at the beefy herd.

'They're not feral, if that's what you're thinking.'

'Charlie never mentioned them.'

Bree shrugged.

'But I bet you know the plan for having them here?'

Of course she did. It was her idea. 'We brought the buffalo in when Darcie's son took all the cattle. They're good for keeping certain grasses down that would otherwise become a potential fuel for bushfires.' Once this valley used to be filled with cattle, like snowdrops across a painter's canvas, now it was just a sea of grass.

'So they're there for a reason?'

'Gold star to you, stormcloud. Don't worry, we monitor their health, so they don't become a pest.' Remembering herself and her position, she shifted in the saddle to check on the four horses trailing behind her. 'It's something you'll need to discuss with your brothers if you decide to keep the buffalo.'

'Do you think we should?'

'It's not my place to say.' Not anymore, that's for sure.

'Come on, Bree…'

She sighed, wiping her mouth with the back of a riding glove. 'Perhaps you can use them until you get cattle grazing in this valley again. Then you could move them closer to Scary Forest to keep the edges clear around some of the billabongs, and as bait for any crocs lurking there, instead of them pinching your beef. They do fight against those snapping handbags, especially when they're kept to a small herd.'

'Good to know.'

She could practically hear Dex thinking from his horse. But would they do it?

So far they'd taken on most of her sneaky suggestions, dropped as part of a conversation. But lately, Dex and Cap were more forthcoming, as if they'd noticed her plans all along—which were always for the welfare of Elsie Creek Station.

She might not own Elsie Creek Station, but she couldn't switch off her deep level of care for this land and all its inhabitants, which had been the only true home she'd known.

At the entry of Emu Plains, the dirt track wove through the flat and smooth structures, as tall as her while on horseback, yet they were barely as thick as her open hand. They looked like giants' tombstones, a large cluster of grey ant mounds that followed the curve of the land like a graveyard.

'What is this place?' Again, Sophie played tourist, watching the world through her camera lens.

'Tombstone Territory.' Bree led her four horses, with Dex riding along her right side, leading the Riggs brothers' much bigger horse plant overloaded with gear. What were they carrying for one night's stay?

'They're magnetic ant mounds,' replied Dex. 'Looks like a graveyard for giants, doesn't it, hon?'

'Can we stop? I'd love to take photos.' Sophie swayed in her saddle, barely holding the reins, confusing the horse.

'You'll have to speak to the boss.'

'Ryder?' Sophie asked.

'Dex, you are part of management, aren't you?' If Bree could nudge him, she would.

'I hate this part,' he muttered quietly to Bree. 'You tell her.'

'She's wearing your engagement ring, you tell her. Sophie and I are only acquaintances who live on the same property.'

'You're not friends yet, like you are with Mia and Harper?'

'In case you hadn't noticed, stormcloud, the only thing we have in common is you. So how about you put on those big-boy britches and act like the boss by telling your lady to get a grip of those reins.'

'Um, hon…' Dex cleared his throat as he adjusted his hat. 'We're on a deadline to get to the stock camp —'

'Before Christmas 2031.' Bree rolled her eyes. Seeing Dex like this was painful to watch.

'But I'll only be five minutes.' Sophie didn't even bother to look at them, with her eyes glued to her camera, zooming in on some scrappy wildflower.

Bree had to do something for the sake of Sophie's poor stockhorse.

'Dex? Why not make a date with Sophie and bring her out here with a basket of goodies and some wine, to watch the sunset? You could then let Sophie set up her tripod to take a trillion photos while you cook a barbecue, kicking back, drinking beer.'

Since when did she make romantic plans for stockmen? Especially when she'd unsubscribed from romance, cancelling her membership to the love library long ago. Yet here she was, playing Doctor Love for another one of the Riggs brothers.

'That way, Sophie won't have to worry about which termite mound her horse is going to headbutt first.' Bree pointed to Sophie's stockhorse.

'Oh, sorreee.' Sophie briefly looked away from her camera to grab the reins. 'They don't come with cruise control, do they?'

'That's a good idea.' Dex nodded at Bree that pretty much said thanks for having saved his arse again. 'What about we make it a date, hon? Camp out for the night in the ute.'

'Oh, okay.' Sophie put her camera away into her backpack—for a whole thirty seconds—before lifting it up again to take more photos of the rocky red escarpment rising from the earth.

'Did you hide her camera batteries?' Bree muttered to Dex.

'I did. In Ryder's saddlebags.'

They both chuckled, knowing the ever-gruff Ryder would tell Sophie no, and probably growl at her to get back to work. Sometimes it was handy having Ryder as the grumpy boss, who had ice water in his veins.

'Did you hear?' Dex said, 'Ryder picked a paddock.'

Bree shrugged. The younger three Riggs brothers had each chosen a paddock as a place to work on their own unique farming trials and techniques, before implementing them on the rest of the station. Ash had turned his paddock into a clever place to test out his tech, managing his paddock and herd all from the comfort of his gaming chair. Cap had turned his neighbouring paddock into a revegetation experiment that had the cattle in Ash's paddock straining the fence to chow down. And Dex's paddock was now a reservoir. 'How is Dead Dog's Swamp going?'

'Good. It's not a swamp anymore.' Dex's lips barely shifted, but his eyes shone with pride from beneath the brim of his stockman's hat. 'Hemp is the easiest thing I've had to grow.'

'Do you have any real weed amongst those weeds?'

'If you tell me where you've hidden your gin still, I'll tell you where my stash is.'

'You know I can just take our resident drug dog, Scout, for a puppy dog playdate. She'd love the adventure.' The loppy-eared beagle had played scout a few times for her. In fact, she'd borrowed many of Cap's dogs for a job now and again, taking them for a spin in the Razorback. But she'd always given them back. After losing her own dogs in one cruel act, she didn't have the heart to adopt another one.

'So, um…' Dex shifted his saddle. 'I'd better tell you about the paddock Ryder's chosen.'

'Do I look like I care?'

'I think you might.' Dex rode closer as his voice lowered. 'He chose Drover's Rest.'

Bree didn't respond, keeping her focus on the ride ahead.

'Which includes Scary Forest. And he's told Ash and Harper to do what they want with the farmhouse to make it their home.'

So where was Ryder going to live? The boardroom?

'That farmhouse will end up being one big hat rack, you know that,' complained Dex.

'Harper wears hats for a reason.' It hid the scar Harper had from a car-bombing incident in Belgium. You couldn't see it, now the hair had grown back, but Harper was still conscious of it, fuelling her love of stockman's hats to suit her stylish wardrobe. 'Come on, you can't tell me that Harper doesn't look cute in her hats. Plus, she's setting a great example for your nephew, always ensuring little Mason has his hat on, too.' The small boy, riding in the harness strapped to his father's chest, peeked around to wave at Bree.

Of course she waved back at the little big man.

Dex rubbed the back of his neck. 'I'm sorry, Bree, but I think Ryder's looking at taking the cottage when the caretaker's caveat is over.'

'When was this decided?'

'Yesterday. Ryder's going to tell Charlie today about using Drover's Rest.'

Of course, that calculating businessman had waited to choose his paddock, just to make sure he had the best one on the property. 'Do you know what Ryder plans to do with Drover's Rest?'

'No idea. But we all know Ryder would have some clever market strategy worked out.'

She shifted in the saddle, her hands gripping the reins a little tighter, as if trying to rein in the temper that was bristling under her skin. That prick was going to take control of her backyard, and her home, is what he was doing! And she couldn't do a damned thing about it.

It's why she refused to call herself a stockwoman anymore. And why she refused to work for the Riggs brothers. Especially when she'd been successfully running this place for years, while caring for an ageing Charlie and Darcie—who used to not only pay her but give her a share of the profits.

It had been heartbreaking when Darcie had died, only to watch Darcie's son strip this station of all the cattle she'd helped raise.

She hated how her grandfather had never found the courage to leave and start somewhere fresh. Leaving her to battle with the neighbour, Leo, to protect her grandfather over the caretaker's caveat. And then she had to bite her tongue when Elsie Creek Station was sold to strangers—and she couldn't do a damned thing about it.

It was like everything she had ever loved was being taken from her, piece by piece. It was just another reason to despise

Ryder Riggs, who'd set his sights on Drover's Rest, as if boldly declaring his intention to take over the cottage—the only place she called home.

Five

Rijidij Dugout was such a well-hidden spot, you wouldn't know it was there until you were practically on top of it. Wisps of steam rose from the shimmering surface of the large rock pool, creating a natural spa. The water was so clear you could see bubbles slowly rising between the smooth river rocks, mingling with a soothing mix of sand and the softest mud.

After a long day of chasing cattle, Ryder was looking forward to kicking back in that spa, beer in hand, while taking in the view of Emu Plains. An open valley filled with sun-drenched grasslands that rippled like a sunlit sea, it stretched endlessly to meet the sinking sun on the horizon. As that great ball of orange and red fire bathed the valley in golden light, each blade of grass seemed to reflect that fire. The hazy horizon blurred softly into the distant ridges of the Stoneys that stood like silent soldiers, yet somehow crafted a seamless tapestry of ochre gold and amber, it truly was the land of the big sky.

Still in the saddle, Ryder tried to work out where to set down his swag for the night, which was proving a challenge when the girls had marked out most of the territory with tents!

Ash and Harper had a big tent to help contain little Mason. Meanwhile, the toddler was having a fat time with the stash of yellow rubber ducks Bree had emptied into the rock pool for the kid to play with, while the adults discussed swimming lessons.

As for the other adults, Sophie had Dex so whipped it wasn't funny, by building Sophie a tent city. They had a tent for sleeping in, a tent for changing in, and a tent to shower in, with no clue what the fourth tent was for. It was an eyesore.

Mia and Cap simply had their swags set up together with their dogs surrounding them, well back from the campfire.

Charlie had his bed-roll near the campfire, the camp cookers were set up, getting ready to give a lesson on camp cooking, while their usual muster cook was nowhere to be seen.

Ryder craned around in his saddle to peer at the wide-open plains. 'There you are.'

Bree was leading her group of horses towards the rocky escarpment that made up Cattleman's Keep. What was she up to now?

Bree had been avoiding him all day. First, keeping to the back of their convoy, and then taking no time in riding out to begin the muster. By the time Ryder and his brothers had caught up with Charlie, Bree was bringing in the first lot of stragglers from Scary Forest.

There, plans were made, where Dex and Ryder took Bullock's Bath and Ash and Cap had Station Dog Cemetery, meeting in the middle to muster their cattle into one large herd of over a thousand head of prime beef cattle. It was so much more than he'd realised.

Once again, they'd practically been gifted another healthy herd, cleverly hidden by Bree, that he knew she checked regularly, as part of her morning horse rides.

But then that clever concept of stock school had the cattle following that redhead like pets who didn't need coaching, they just followed Bree like she was the Pied Piper, leading them to the promised land.

Charlie was right, with this group of cattle it was like gathering them up with a butterfly net, mustering them closer to the other side of Koala Creek. While on this side, his family had set up their stock camp like an unorganised bunch of squatters.

To escape the rabble, Ryder rode after Bree, where she'd disappeared under the tree line that spread below the verge of the rocky escarpment. The towering red rocks had created a drip line that fed into a creek he followed upstream to catch up to Bree.

'Go away.' Bree scowled at him over her shoulder as she led the horses along the creek bed.

'Where are you going?'

'To water the horses.'

'Why not here?' They were walking through cool fresh water as it was.

'If you like it so much, cupcake, stay here then.'

He scowled with such a hate for that nickname. He was no bloody cupcake.

But he wasn't going to stop following her. Bree was up to something.

Bree led her team of horses deep within the cool thicket of trees where the creek wound alongside the rocky walls that hid the sky. The air was damp with the rich smell of wet earth, along with the sharp scent of eucalyptus leaves lingering in the background. He could almost taste it on his tongue, along with gritty dust from a long day mustering on horseback.

With no fear of crocodiles, Bree led the way on her fierce black stallion, as the sturdy stockhorses splashed through the shallow creek to meet the white sandbar that they used to cross over to the far side. Up the riverbank, they plodded along a rich dirt path that muffled the sound of their hooves, where soft ferns brushed against the horses' lower legs like feathers. The movement stirred up dozens of hidden blue-winged butterflies, rising from among the fronds to flutter gracefully around them. Even Bree paused, holding out her hand and smiling as the curious, soft-winged creatures landed delicately on her fingertips.

All he could do was sigh from the saddle, as she took in the moment of the world around them, that was part of this land he called home.

'You shouldn't be here.' She scowled at him for being in her space.

'I live here.'

'Hmph. Why don't you act like a middle-aged hairline and start disappearing back to the stock camp.'

'No.' Even if he felt like he was intruding, he wasn't going anywhere.

Again, Bree kicked on, pushing her horse uphill, the stockhorse's hooves clashing against the rocks, only to disappear around a massive boulder.

Ryder spurred his horse on to catch up and was led into a large brightly lit rock cave.

'No way...' Ryder ripped off his hat to stare up at the open circular ceiling of blue skies surrounded by high rock walls to create a cave, where fresh water spilled over its smooth rocky ledges to create an indoor waterfall. 'What is this place?'

'The Veil.'

'How did it get that name? Come on, Bree, every place on this station has some sort of story to it.' Finally, this was his chance to hold a conversation with her that lasted more than two minutes.

'There's no story to the name...' Bree got off her horse and pointed to the waterfall. 'Because that's The Veil.'

Ryder climbed off his horse and peered at the fall's watery curtain, which shimmered like a veil, cleverly shielding a primitive rock painting of a kangaroo that stretched across the entire back wall. 'Will I have a problem with this Indigenous rock painting?' Land claims were tricky things.

'Relax. It's not a sacred site. That was painted in the seventies, back when the dot painting technique was first taught to them by a white English teacher. Charlie told me the artist who painted that mural was one of her students.'

'I know all about the history of dot paintings. Remember, I'm from the Territory, too. One of our local Elders told me when I was a kid that the original purpose for dot painting was to paint dots on their bodies for ceremony only. It gave them a shimmering appearance when they danced. So, this…?' He pointed at the rock art.

'It's just a painting by a guy who liked to paint on rock. He was an Aboriginal stockman from lower New South Wales.' She sighed at their somewhat cosy surrounds, before stretching her neck to greet the skies. For once she seemed at peace.

One of the horses nickered, breaking her trance, and she turned to unsaddle Black Hand, and lead the horses to the watery edge where they eagerly waded into the chest-deep water.

With her saddle resting on an altar-like rock, Bree removed her boots, shirt, and jeans. 'Staring much.'

How could he not? Her figure was all curves of creamy skin, with plump breasts perfectly cinched by a sports bra that made him want to inhale that cleavage, and the way her smooth-fit matching briefs cupped her arse, she was good enough to eat. 'What are you doing?'

'I'm wearing a ball gown for dinner, so I'm searching for a tiara to match my outfit. What do you think?' Pulling a beer bottle from her saddlebag, she waded into the water and began washing down her horses.

He peeked into her saddlebag to find a sixpack of icy cold beer. 'That's my girl.'

'Hey! That's mine.' She paused from washing down a horse to scowl at him.

'I'll pay you back later.' Popping the cap, he took a deep mouthful of beer. 'Ahh. That hit the spot.'

He then quickly unsaddled his horse, stripped down and waded into the crystal-clear water where soft sand and smooth pebbles made up the floor. 'This is a good idea.'

'Who invited you to my private pool party?' Something had ticked her off so much it made her eyes glow.

'Is this the part where I tell you I own this land?' Again.

She scowled at him with such heat, it was a struggle to

not grin at her.

Then he realised why she was so angry with him. *Dammit.* 'Who told you?' They were now wearing matching scowls, which was normal these days.

'Who do you think?' Her sneer was lethal.

'Dex.' *The dick!*

'You've got over a million acres to choose from. You could have picked another paddock. Why there? Drover's Rest is Charlie's. I'm pretty sure it's still covered under the caretaker's caveat.'

'I told Charlie I'm not doing anything with it.'

'And the caretaker's cottage?'

'Charlie told me he's got a spare room at the cottage.' Her scowl deepened, making him grin wider.

'You have the farmhouse.'

'That's getting crowded with a toddler and a younger brother determined to break the wall or his bed. That couple need their space.'

'Get a caravan and park it next to the boardroom where you spend all your time.'

'How do you know that?'

'I know nothing.'

'I don't believe that, Bree, you know everything.'

'Do not.' She swam away from him to the far side of the falls.

He had to follow.

'This place reminds me of the waterfall at Grass Tree Creek.' That waterfall was only a shallow rock pool. This place was a massive brightly lit cave with a hole in the roof where the water filtered down into a deep pool, to become part of Koala Creek.

'Have you ever climbed to see where the water comes from?' He pointed his beer to the ceiling that was raining sweet, fresh water that sparkled like diamonds under the dying sunlight.

'It's part of the run-off from Cattleman's Keep.'

'I haven't been back, not since the day Charlie first

showed us this place.' He leaned back against the rock wall that was surprisingly smooth. The waterfall's turbulence massaged his legs, as he sipped on his beer. Now this was living.

Bree said nothing, but he could feel her watching him.

'I never take time out to do things like this.'

'You get that when you're busily stealing land to increase your empire.'

Smart-arse. 'I'm not doing anything with Drover's Rest. I just said it was mine because my brothers were harping on about which paddock I was going to choose. I'm not running any new experiments, I'll leave that to my brothers. But I do want the concept of stock school to continue, if Charlie is willing. Maybe he can talk to Cap about using the guardian dogs?'

'We don't work for you.' Laced with heat, her words were very controlled, skimming across the water.

He should have stopped and heeded her warning. But he couldn't resist. Even if she might be a pretty package of poison—one who should clearly wear a warning label about her outlaw attitude—but she was also an attractive temptress who'd somehow melted this man's heart of ice.

'Your grandfather is stoked it's still allowed to continue. And I will not say no to the old man, and I know you don't either.' It was just another reason for respecting her, even if he wanted to be disrespectful with her body.

'I do, too.'

'No, you don't. But you sure as hell tell me and my brothers *no* all the time.' How could he ever get her to say *yes*?

Unexpectedly, her upper lip curled and a twinkle appeared in her eye.

'Why do you always defy me? When I'm trying to be the good guy here.'

And didn't the sweet little outlaw arch her eyebrows at him. 'You called me a cattle thief.'

'I'm sorry.'

'Is that why you gave my shotgun a makeover?'

He couldn't say the real reason why.

'Fine...' She rolled her eyes dramatically. 'Thank you, again, for cleaning my shotgun. And I liked the blanket.'

'I'm sorry, what?' He blinked at her.

'It's a nice blanket.'

'It's old.'

'So? It's wool. Do you know how rare it is to find a hundred per cent woollen blanket in a part of the country that has no sheep. Where did you get it?'

'You'll think I'm dumb.'

She faced him fully, completely, with her green eyes locking on his. 'No. You are not dumb. Maybe a bossy workaholic who's put his emotions and empathy on ice, but dumb you are not.'

'Is there a compliment in there?'

'What's with the blanket?' Her eyes narrowed at him.

'You tell me the story of Drover's Rest first.'

'I'm surprised Charlie hasn't told you already.'

'Me too. But it means a lot to you guys.'

'It's our backyard, of course it does.'

'But...'

She huffed. 'Drover's Rest was where the drovers would return first with the cattle in the early days of the station. Of course, it was hand-seeded by Granny Darcie back in the day. Ask Charlie to give you the tour.'

'No, you can.'

'Why me?' She shrugged her creamy shoulders above the water line, causing ripples to spread across the surface. 'Charlie is happy to show you guys everything.'

'Why aren't you?'

She glared at him. 'What do you want from me, Ryder? I don't work for you. Is that it? You hate that you can't control me? Like you're the boss of everyone else around here?'

'Hell, no. If you were my employee, I would have sacked you on day one for your smart mouth and outlaw attitude.'

Swimming away from him, her laughter tinkled around

the cave.

'I want to know — what does Drover's Rest mean to you?'

'I already told you, it's my backyard.' She leaned back against the rock wall, allowing her tiny toes to float to the surface.

'Go on, Bree, there has to be more to the story. There always is.' Bree saw things from many different angles and Ryder appreciated her opinion, when she did share.

'None of the ringers were allowed near Drover's Rest. It was the first rule Charlie made when he became head stockman.'

'How come?'

'Because he had a little girl — my mother — who he wanted to protect from the men.'

Damn. He wished he hadn't pried, stirring up thoughts of her deceased mother. But underneath he had this need to know everything about Bree, and it was rare to have one-on-one time with her like this in an open conversation.

Bree wove her slender fingers through the crisp water that rippled softly, reflecting the golden hues of the late afternoon sun, and for a moment, it seemed as though time stood still, her connection to the earth quiet and unspoken, but deep. 'Back then, Charlie would sack anyone if they dared come near our sanctuary without permission. Drover's Rest is where the girls got to play. I flew kites, learned to ride my pushbikes and motorbikes, made cubby houses, played chasey with the calves and the stockhorses out there. You know, kid stuff.'

'I wouldn't know about that kind of stuff.' He sighed heavily before taking a deep pull of his beer, feeling the responsibilities weighing heavily across his shoulders.

'So you were an instant adult straight out of the womb, hmm?'

'Pretty much.' He rubbed the bridge of his nose, the falling water the only other noise in the cave, yet it felt like the silence was deafening if he didn't answer her. 'As the oldest of seven, I didn't have much of a childhood. I was busy washing bottles or babysitting, always stuck carrying a kid on my back or on my hip like some ape.'

Bree didn't laugh as he'd expected her to. She just watched him with a look that could crack open his bones to peer deep into the marrow, to go beyond the shadows hidden within his skeleton, to the places that hid his deepest, darkest secrets. It was a place where he'd tucked away his nightmares.

'You never played games?'

Why did that feel like there was some hidden meaning to her question? 'Monopoly.'

'Figures.'

'Cards occasionally, with my father and grandfather, if I wasn't washing the dishes or putting the younger ones to bed as chief babysitter.'

'So you're still babysitting your brothers. Buying this property for them, in your role as the big brother who doesn't like to play.' She swam closer to where the water's reflection highlighted the colours in her eyes. With her hair wet and slicked back, knowing she was just in her underwear had his mouth watering.

'I didn't say I don't like to play, I just...' He shrugged, sipping on his beer.

'Are you saying you don't know *how* to play? When you live on one of the biggest adult playgrounds?'

'I know you do.'

She laughed, and it was as light as her smile that echoed around the cavern as she swam away from him like a water sprite playing games with his soul.

Finally, he was alone with her, and he wasn't going to let this opportunity get away from him—even if it copped him another stinging slap in the face, he was prepared to take his shot.

Six

Ryder Riggs was crowding her space. It sucked. Especially when Bree had come to this waterfall to get away from everyone, hoping to let the pounding water massage her shoulders and neck with the hope of drowning out her thoughts. But even as the water fell from the sky, it still didn't switch off her mind, because Ryder was far too close.

How could anyone not know how to play? Jeez, his inner child must have retired by the time he was ten.

Then something touched her shoulders, and a set of strong fingers began kneading her skin.

'What are you doing?' It was Ryder, of course.

'I can do a better job at massaging your shoulders than these falls can. Stay there and don't complain.'

In shock of sorts, she was helpless to stop those strong hands that held her shoulders, pushing her into position like a doll of clay that was melting with his touch. The kneading of her flesh, the movement and easing of her muscles, the falling water and she was under his spell, relaxing deeper and deeper until she copped a face full of water.

'Are you okay?'

She wiped over her face. Her beer was gone.

'Did you fall asleep?' He chuckled as he plucked her beer bottle from the water.

'Gotta go.' It was time to bolt from this guy now. Because her body was giddy for him, and there was no way she'd let the enemy win.

She sloshed out of the pool.

'Where are you going?'

'I'm not riding through the creek in the dark.' She dried herself off at her saddle.

But when Ryder walked out of the lagoon, the sun's dying rays sparkled against the cavern to highlight his hard body. Built like a machine, Ryder had broad shoulders, packed with muscle. Everything about him was hard. Especially that one part of his body that jutted out from his wet boxer briefs, slick against his skin.

She couldn't take her eyes off him as rivulets of water dripped down his wide chest and over the hard planes of his stomach. She curled her hands into fists to stop herself from reaching out to trace the same path with her fingers, as droplets trailed down his pecs and over the ridges of his abdomen to that torturous treasure trail.

'Bree?'

She raised her eyes to meet his, the colour of warm toasted hazelnut. They were such a contradiction for a man with ice in his veins. But they were dark and hooded, and locked on to her like she was prey.

There was no denying his presence, or the trimmed beard along his jawline that only made him sexier. It highlighted his lips, that had found a neutral position short of an actual smile.

His gaze dropped to her body, then back up to her face, dropping again to her lips where they lingered, making her flush from her fingertips to her toes and everywhere in between.

No. This was not happening. Not with Ryder Riggs.

She gritted her teeth, trying to focus on her shopping list, her ABCs, some song, something, anything, to get control and not look at Ryder Riggs standing in nothing but a pair of wet boxer briefs that showed off the gloriously masculine shape of his body.

Dear lord, he was equipped. In fact, he'd doubled up in

that department, that he had her mouth watering as the heat just bloomed inside her.

He reached for her, his biceps rising like some Hollywood movie star. There were a few scars on his pecs, but no ink work, nothing but a whole load of hot, wet skin.

What was worse, he was going to kiss her.

Ryder Riggs—her enemy—wanted to kiss her. There was a fine line between can't, won't, and *what the forge are you doing?* And it was fast becoming a step too far into hellfire, a place she never wanted to revisit. Yet, he wanted to play?

Hold the phone, Ryder didn't play. Everything he did was for a reason. It had to be some strategy because he was always ten tactical steps ahead of her. She couldn't trust this. She needed to step away from him, but where was she going to go when her back was pressed against the rock wall?

Then his lips brushed hers. It was like igniting a wick, sending sparks to scurry across her nerve endings. She was powerless to stop him.

Ryder should never have this power over her. Ever. He should not have even been allowed to get this close to her or find her alone! She'd made a tactical error.

Refusing to close her eyes, his dark brown eyes were glimmering slits of intensity solely focused on her. She'd never forget how they looked at her with hunger, even though her brain had switched off, leaving her mind completely numb. This was not happening.

Unquenched desire briefly coated her tongue as she tried to fight the rush in her bloodstream that competed with the buzz in her brain.

He pulled back, his eyes crawling over her as if admiring all her curves and bumps. But then he gripped the rock ledge above her and leaned towards her, stretching that beautiful body in an arch, showing off the ridges of his perfectly defined abs, where somehow the air got heavier and thicker that she struggled to breathe.

He dipped his head closer. Her lips parted as she leaned towards him like he was a magnet. One kiss. She could do one kiss. Right?

Somehow that magical cord snapped, pushing her towards him. Or was it his hand on her hip pulling her closer? But when his fingers cupped her head, and his lips met hers—it was as if her entire world had zoomed in on this one moment, where time had stilled.

With a groan, he gathered her closer, sweeping his tongue across her lower lip. While she responded with a tiny sigh of surrender, allowing her tongue to slide against his while melting against his naked torso.

Her hands skimmed hungrily over his muscular arms that were warm, wet marble that ignited a primal appreciation, that soon started a scorching blaze in her lower belly, especially when his thick thighs pressed against hers.

A breathy, choked cry emanated from her throat, it echoed in the cave to come back and haunt her, followed by the neigh of her horses.

That's when reality hit her. That's when she pushed back. Her breath was ragged as he grunted in her ear. Oh, hellfire, it was a harsh and sexy sound that had her struggling to get away.

'I have to go.' She couldn't look at him, even if her lips tasted of him. She quickly dressed and saddled her horse for the ride back to camp.

In her time, she'd kissed plenty of men. At one time, she'd thought the only man who could kiss her properly was her ex-husband, Finn.

At no time had any man ever kissed her like Ryder Riggs. The delicious high he'd elicited from her with the power of his lips from just one kiss had her shivering with temptation.

That's when she knew she was in trouble.

She may crave the closeness of Ryder—but he was the type of man who'd want to own you. He may own her home, her property, and all she held dear, but he would never own her soul.

Seven

That kiss had surpassed anything he'd ever imagined. Now Ryder wanted more.

Following Bree back from The Veil to their stock camp, it was like landing back into a land of chaos, reminding him of how home used to be when he was growing up. All his brothers and their partners were gathered around the campfire where the aroma of fried onions had his stomach grumbling.

Pity the rest of the feed wasn't up to snuff. The damper was dry and burnt. The spuds were crispy on the outside and raw on the inside. And he couldn't decipher what they'd done to the other vegetables.

'Bree, help us. Please?' begged Ash.

'What did you do now?' Bree, all clean from her dip beneath the waterfall, peered at the mess.

'We've stuffed up somehow.' Harper held up the egg flip, wearing white flour on her cheek with her hands covered in clumps of glue. 'I followed the recipe, but a campfire doesn't come with a temperature dial to control the flame.'

Bree giggled. It was a sweet one.

She had so many laughs and spoke differently to each family member, as if curving to their personalities.

Charlie waved his hand at his granddaughter. 'Have a gecko's gander at saving dinner, or we'll all be havin' a dingo's dinner, kid.'

'What did he say?' Harper gathered the dirty dishes

together. 'I need a dictionary just for your sayings, Charlie.'

In a matter of minutes, Bree had something cooking on the campfire where they'd gathered around as the sun left tangerine-coloured streaks across the sky, before it sank deep beyond the plum-coloured horizon.

This is what Ryder loved about being a stockman, the great outdoors where the views were better than anything money could buy. For a billionaire, it was humbling to enjoy moments like these that didn't revolve around wealth, just time spent with family and friends, and for the rarity when his mind became still, as he watched Bree effortlessly prepare their meals. The entire moment felt like a slice of heaven under the stars.

Of course, Bree ignored him as she bantered with his brothers. But he preferred to sit back and watch over them. Ryder didn't need to talk. They talked enough that he didn't need to add to their fray of nonsense. But they were all having a good time.

Maybe it wasn't such a bad idea bringing the other girls along after all, when it was rare they all got together like this.

'I'm thinking of going for a walk under the stars later,' said Sophie. 'To take some photos.'

'I wouldn't do that, girlie.' Charlie pushed up the brim of his stockman's hat that had seen many Sundays under the sun. 'We're in Travellers' country. Home to the Mimih spirits.'

'Whose country?' Sophie peered back at the old man.

'They go by many names.' Charlie's voice was low and serious. 'Some call 'em Travellers. Others reckon they're shadow folk, spirits that walk the land when the sun's down. You must've heard the stories.'

'Are you for real?'

'Well, you'd better listen and learn, missy, if you're gonna live out here, 'coz we're in Travellers' country. It's best to show respect.' Charlie plonked himself down on one of the logs that were set out around their campfire, where sparks crackled and popped to float towards the ceiling of countless stars. With his scuffed-up tin mug in hand, the steam from his billy tea curling above the rim, you could tell he was brewing another story.

'What are the Travellers, Charlie?' Harper asked.

'They're a dark spirit of sorts. Some stockmen used to say you could sense them or get that funny feeling that you're not alone. Or that feeling of something out of the ordinary. It's difficult to explain, and impossible to forget when you do come across one of 'em.'

'Have you seen them?'

Charlie nodded. 'Plenty of times. And it's best to always be polite, nod your hat at 'em and move along.'

'What are they?'

'Some say they're from the spirit world trying to warn you about something. Mostly, they just protect the land.'

'No way.' Mia hugged her knees tighter like a child, wriggling closer to Cap on their blanket. Before them, their working dogs stretched out in the dust, with their shadows lengthening before the campfire. 'Where did you see them?'

'They usually take a stickybeak when we're out hunting or camping in this area. It's a tradition now, that we call out whenever we enter Emu Plains to let them know we mean no harm. So never build here. Leave it for the cattle to graze. They don't mean no harm, coz they're like the unseen guardians of the land keeping an eye on you.' Charlie leaned closer to the three females, the newcomers to their family, and said with wide eyes, 'And you wouldn't even know they were there.'

Harper swallowed, clutching her necklace. Mia moved closer to Cap, with Sophie doing the same to Dex.

'W-w-what can we do to avoid them?' Harper asked, with Mia nodding with wide eyes.

'If you are being peaceful and respecting the land, they'll leave you be, sure enough. Some will come out to warn you if you're about to enter a place that's not meant for you—especially around them Aboriginal ceremonial grounds. And some play tricks to lead people astray in the bush at night.'

'What do they look like?' Sophie's voice was so frail.

'Shadows. Tall and slender, with no faces. They're fleeting—dark figures you catch moving out of the corner of your eye.' Charlie tapped the corner of his eye, then pointed out to the darkness that hung heavy around them with no sign of civilisation, just the vast and empty outback that had the knack of making a person feel infinitesimal.

'I don't worry about them, because we're not here to harm the land. But sometimes…' Charlie's voice was hushed, yet loaded with warning, as he leaned in closer and said, 'they trick you. So, if you ever hear your name being called in the dark and don't see anyone, it's a Traveller calling. And…' Charlie leaned back, as the girls' leaned forward as his voice lowered even more, 'if your dog or your horse stops on you for no reason and refuses to move, it's because a Traveller is nearby warning you to stay away from that space.'

'But-but-but…' Sophie sat huddled with crossed legs. 'What if I need to pee?'

'Take someone with you, just never go on your own in case they pinch you. Heed the warnings of an old man who's lived his life in the outback, where many spooky things happen after dark. Be mindful of the Travellers, I'd hate for you to get on their bad sides because—'

'BOO!' Ash jumped out from the shadows with his son Mason, also doing the same. The girls screamed, with Charlie and the rest of the brothers laughing.

That's when Ryder noticed Bree was gone.

Eight

Bree grinned at the squeals coming from around the campfire, caused by the same story she'd first heard when she was seven years old. Charlie was going to be smiling pretty for the rest of this muster. Goal achieved.

'What are you doing?'

'What the hellfire?' She pointed her shotgun at Ryder. 'Didn't your mother ever tell you it was rude to sneak up on someone in the dark while they're carrying a loaded shotgun?'

'I wasn't sneaking up.'

'Pfft. You sneak. All. The. Time. Is that an army thing? Which is odd when you have such a heavy footfall around the farmhouse.'

'Maybe I do that so I don't catch my brother Ash and his partner in a compromising position.' Ryder paused to stroke the nose of her horse. 'What were you doing?'

'Checking the horses, keeping them calm.'

'Because you knew the screams were coming?'

She'd spotted Ash sneaking along the edges and could read what was going to happen next. 'Not my first scary campfire story, cupcake. I bet you'd have some tales to share.'

Again, he shrugged.

'You know what? You're always telling me to talk to you, but you won't talk either, which is annoying. It's as annoying as that kiss.'

'Excuse me?' Sliding his hands into his jeans' pockets, he

rocked on his boot heels like Dex. 'You liked that kiss.'

'Pfft. Whatever gave you that impression?' As if she'd tell him the truth!

'Baby, you melted into me.' The smugness of the guy, it was as if he'd conquered the Roman Empire.

Even if it was true, that kiss had been wrong on so many levels. 'Let me be clear here...' She tried to push him back from her personal space—but he was solid stone—so she took a step back, in need of cold air and distance. 'You just did that because A, you're male.' A darned fine-looking but broody specimen of a male. 'And B, I just so happen to be the only single female around.'

'Is that what you think?'

'Duh. It's pretty obvious it was just a convenience thing. Oh, and that I'm the only one you can't boss around, because I'm not on your payroll, which must be some sort of game to you.'

His lip curled, and that sinful shine of amusement danced in his eyes. Which was rare and sexy all at the same time.

Nah-ah, cowboy. Not gonna happen. Bree narrowed her eyes as a warning for him to not push it.

'So, you didn't like the kiss?'

She snorted, tightening her grip on the shotgun. 'Fine. It was a hot kiss.' But the picture of her having hot hate sex with Ryder wasn't exactly the best thing to have flash before her eyes while alone, in the dark, with this man, when she was trying to put out that scorching flame of heat that kept flaring up between them.

'Want to see what a second kiss will be like?'

'No.' She even held her hand up like a traffic cop, hoping to stop the testosterone-loaded bull charging at her. 'I'm here for Charlie, and not for your amusement. Good night, Ryder.'

Bree could feel his eyes following her when she'd never been this aware of any male. Not even her ex-husband had affected her like this.

She just couldn't understand how—after being immune to him for so long—her body and mind were suddenly consumed with all things Ryder.

It wasn't fair.

It wasn't going to happen.

They were so incompatible it was a joke.

Or was this part of some master plan of Ryder's, or motive to his actions? There had to be a reason. Because Ryder wasn't the type to sneak kisses in the dark for fun.

She wasn't having a bar of that, and it only made her more determined to avoid being alone with Ryder for the rest of this muster — which might be harder than she realised.

Nine

T he smell of sizzling bacon and fresh outback air had Ryder inhaling deeply as the stars dimmed above him in a deep, maroon-coloured sky, while on the distant horizon, a ribbon of red began to glow across the rugged landscape. Ryder sighed heavily, because nothing beat an outback sunrise. All he needed was a coffee and he'd be set.

He peered at the top of his swag that seemed heavier, only to discover his blanket. It was the green one he'd given to Bree.

He scowled at it, instantly engaging in a foul mood.

Not only had she snuck up on him while he was asleep, but she'd also given his gift back. And that was a big no in his book, especially when he knew how much she'd liked it.

Dragging on his boots, raking fingers through his thick hair, he grabbed his jacket.

'Morning, Boss.' Charlie poured him a cuppa. 'Here, you look like you need one.'

'Thanks.' He sipped on the brew, trying to simmer his temper. His brothers were still asleep. It was almost five. Sunrise wasn't due for an hour, but they had a stock camp to pack-up and a muster to finish. It was going to be a long day.

'Here's the water you wanted, Pop.' Bree came into the camp light carrying a bucket, only to huddle closer to the fire, warming her hands up. 'The dew is thick out there.'

'Here.' Ryder flung the blanket around her shoulders, scowling at her. 'I gave you this for a reason. Don't you dare give it back?'

'Well, didn't you wake up on the wrong side of the swag, cupcake?'

He didn't care. 'You need to stay warm.'

'I can look after myself, thank you.'

'I know that. But you're always looking out for everyone else, so who looks after you?'

She stared at him with her green eyes widening to reflect their campfire.

Look out, he must have hit a sore spot. Which made sense. Bree didn't think of herself, only everyone else. Was that because she too had ghosts that chased her in the dark? Considering Bree's background was filled with horrors that would've had bigger men crumbling, that it was remarkable how Bree still got up and kept on swinging, he admired her for that.

Watching her wrap that blanket—his blanket—around her shoulders and cinch it securely into her belt satisfied some deep, primal urge within him. Something raw, almost savage. It was like seeing a woman in his T-shirt, with her legs bare and messy bed hair on full display, only this was so much better

'Here, take this.' She passed him a plate with seared sandwich steak, crispy bacon, hot fried bread, and some good old-fashioned beans and greens to make a bushman's version of bubble-and-squeak, topped with eggs sunny side up. Just the way he liked it. She remembered from their first muster to Wombat Flats, like she remembered the details of conversations. There was a clever woman behind that sly smile. 'Now sit down over there and eat your brekkie, and stop annoying the cook.'

He took the plate, grinning to himself. Now she was looking after him.

There was no way his attraction to Bree was because of the convenience of her being the only single woman in the area. He'd had plenty of gold-diggers pursuing him, only too willing to burn through his cash. All of them had failed to meet her standards like it was a test. Only one had passed, and she didn't even know she'd been trying out for the position.

Yet trying to approach the redhead with a temper of fire was tricky, where he'd been biding his time to find that right moment. Yesterday's kiss had proven his patience was finally paying off.

Ryder sat beside Charlie as they ate breakfast and drank the best billy tea Charlie had ever made.

With daylight breaking, he packed up his swag and approached the horses where Bree had already saddled Charlie's horse, and their packhorses, now working on her tough black horse that was a beast he wouldn't mind riding one day.

'Do you have much left to pack?' Ryder dropped his swag beside his saddle, picked up a brush and chose a horse to ride for the day.

'Nope. Our gear is already on the horses.' Bree patted the nose of one of her sturdy stockhorses. They were well-trained animals.

'You're efficient at this,' he said, brushing down a strong mocha-coloured mare. 'My old sergeant would have approved.'

'Wait, let me turn up my hearing for a second.' Bree stopped brushing down her stallion to poke up the brim of her stockman's hat with the hatband made of contrasting strips of cloth, lace, twine and leather, making it as unique as the stockwoman, wearing his blanket like a poncho, tucked securely into her belt. 'You know, that's the first time you've actually mentioned something about your time in the military.'

'I can't tell you my missions, but I can tell you anything else you want to know.'

'Riiight.'

'Hey.' He grabbed her arm. 'This is me trying to hold a conversation with you. So...' He inhaled deeply. 'I was a captain in the Australian Army in charge of an ordnance specialist team, before I retired.'

'Is that something to do with weapons?'

'I was responsible for the safety, security, and accountability of my unit's weapons and ammunition.' It was the word-for-word textbook response he still remembered from his days in basic training. 'I found, after growing up in a junkyard repairing junk, that I had a knack for weaponry as a First Class Lieutenant. I made captain when I was recruited into the Special Forces. I'm no grunt, I was an officer.' Leadership came easily to him, so said his superiors. Guess that's what happens when you order around a tribe of siblings by the age of five.

'Were you working on the super-secret squirrel stuff?'

He chuckled. 'Yeah. The secret stuff.'

'But it's more than that. I've seen what you did to my shotgun. It's a passion for you.'

He nodded, quietly pleased that she'd noticed.

'And...?'

Dammit, if he didn't speak, the redhead would get mad at him, and he wanted to talk to her, when normally he didn't talk. He had to say something, because Bree was waiting for a response. 'It's how I made my money.'

'Excuse me?'

'I sold the patents for certain weapons I'd designed for the military.'

'So, you didn't steal from some diamond mine?'

'No.' The chuckle burst from his lips. She amused him so effortlessly, always surprising him. 'After I retired from the outfit, I saw an opportunity and went to work on a diamond mine, and I did some offshore oil rigging, too.'

She arched an eyebrow at him, before flinging her saddle onto her horse. 'But you were an officer.'

'Getting my hands dirty never bothered me.' He slid on his gloves, well-worn from being a stockman, not like some overseer. 'And those places came with uniforms, meals and accommodation—just better pay.'

'Yeah, but...' With her playful green eyes sparkling, she

wiggled her finger at him as if peeling back his shields. 'There's more to that story, isn't there?'

He adjusted his stockman's hat, fighting the temptation to brush the fine stray hairs from around her face, that had worked free from her thick plait. 'I worked at the mines while waiting for the patents to come through. I made more money out of the department as a civvy, selling them the patents on the weapons I'd designed, which I learned to reinvest.'

'Which is how you knew all about the patents for Ash's tech gear.'

He nodded.

'Clever.' She turned her back on him to tighten her saddle straps.

'Any other questions?'

'Oh yeah, stacks. But I've got horses to saddle, and a dust-stirring muster to start. But I'll have all day to think about the questions I want to ask.'

A full wattage smile broke the seal of his steel facade, and his chest felt so light and free as it filled with crisp morning air.

'Wow, look at you, cupcake. You look like you've swallowed the sun.'

He felt like it too. Only Bree did that for him. 'I've told no one, not even my brothers, how I made my money.'

'I won't tell anyone.'

'I know. That's why I told you.' He kissed her cheek, then whispered in her ear, 'By the way, if we're opening a dialogue and being truthful, I hate being called *cupcake*.'

Her abrupt laugh rang out like a melody, clear and bright, filling the air with a contagious warmth that made him smile. 'I know. That's why I say it.'

Together they saddled all the horses they'd need for the day. Working in silence alongside Bree was both comfortable and companionable. He was hoping today was the day they didn't argue with each other. He also wanted to continue the conversation with her, and yet he couldn't think of a damned thing to say.

'We were coming to help,' said Ash, approaching with handheld radios tucked securely into their halters, along with Dex, stuffing his face with the last of his steak sandwich.

'All done. Thanks.' Bree took a radio from Ash and clipped it into her shoulder holster like a cop with their gun. Her stockwhip on her hip, sliding on her riding gloves, she was ready to ride. 'I'll go help Charlie.' It was so typical of Bree to walk away. Normally she'd keep her interactions to a strict ten-minute limit, where she'd dump some information bomb then leave.

'You can unsaddle them when we get home,' Ryder said to his brothers, as he clipped on his radio and stockwhip, watching Bree share a joke with her grandfather, 'if we make it to the drafting yards today.' The other women were slowing them down by playing tourists, while he was ready to climb into the saddle and take advantage of the cool morning before the outback's hostile sun blazed down on them like the wrath of a thousand firestorms.

Suddenly, a scream pierced the air, making the hair on the back of his neck stand on end.

'SNAKE! SNAKE!' It was Sophie running through the tall grass while trying to pull up her jeans with one hand and holding her camera in the air. But her scream was so high-pitched it was as if a dozen banshees were howling in the air, the noise echoing as if it was coming from all directions.

'*Sophie!*' Dex ran after her.

'At least it's not bird spiders this time, like Harper,' said Ash with a chuckle. 'Was Sophie taking photos while peeing?'

'Looks like it.' Ryder tilted his head as Sophie tripped over her jeans to roll in the grass, with Dex chasing after her. Surprisingly, her screams still shattered the morning air, like a sonic boom, ricocheting everywhere across the open plains as if surrounding them.

'Oh, no.' Bree's voice instantly set off alarm bells for Ryder.

'What?' He approached her.

Bree dropped her head, looking at the ground. 'Can you feel that?'

Ryder felt the ground rumble beneath his boots and the rise of dust. It only meant one thing. 'Aw hell, no.'

'STAMPEDE.' Charlie climbed onto the log and waved his hat in the air.

The earth rumbled like an earthquake as over a thousand head of cattle pounded the red soils to stir the largest cloud of red dust to stain the sky. And it was heading straight towards them.

Ten

'*Get on your horses, now.*' Bree swung into her saddle. She unsheathed her bushman's knife from her belt and sliced though the rope to safely release the horses, knowing they wouldn't run far. Right now, she focused on her grandfather where he stood in the path of the thunderous herd of cattle heading straight for their campsite.

Bree let her stockwhip crack as she urged Black Hand to leap over their campfire and gallop straight for the herd that had yet to cross Koala Creek. She had to protect her grandfather and the others, that included little Mason. 'Pop?'

'Cap and I will hold 'em off. You get in front, kid.' Charlie swung his stockwhips in the air, their crack like a thousand guns as Cap, and his team of muster dogs, created a barrier between the creek and their small stock camp. It was enough to force the cattle to head upstream.

Aw come on! Why couldn't they have gone downstream in the direction of the drafting yards?

Gritting her teeth, she nudged her horse, aiming to cut off the stampeding herd.

'BREE!' Ryder's voice shouted over her radio. '*Don't you dare get in front of them.*'

Ignoring him, she rode hard, doing what Charlie had taught her. Her stockwhip's long length whirled like a helicopter to *CRACK!*

The cattle closest shied away, pushing against the others to turn the tide of thundering beef.

Before her the ancient sandstone formations rose from the horizon like a battalion of soldiers guarding the front line. They were impassable. And if the herd didn't slow down, they'd crush themselves in their panic, with nowhere to turn.

'Come on.' Black Hand's hooves pounded as they raced for the front of the herd, with Bree driving him hard in the saddle as the deafening noise of a thousand bellowing cattle filled the air. A gritty dust storm stirred against her eyes, nose, and ears, but she blindly pushed forwards with Black Hand, powering fearlessly through the dust cloud to finally break through.

Ahead of her was a small rise, and she raced towards it. There she turned the horse and stood fast and pulled out her shotgun.

KABOOM!

Its sound echoed like thunder bouncing off the massive wall of sandstone that rose behind her like a rock giant facing down over a thousand head of Brahman, with their white, wild eyes and sharp horns, barrelling towards her. With the reins in her teeth, whirling the stockwhip in one hand, *CRACK*, she gave a well-practised pump of the shottie with the other, then squeezed the trigger.

KABOOM!

The first row of cattle stalled. Then the next. And then the next, starting a wave of white-coated cattle slowing down to a stop.

Only then did she breathe, letting the reins fall free from her teeth, to slide her shotgun away. 'Well done, Black Hand. Well done.' She slid off the saddle and patted her trusty horse, who stamped his hooves and snorted with fire, raring to go again.

But her legs were shaky, and so full of adrenaline right now, with her heart beating a bazillion beats she could only laugh at what they'd just done.

Ryder rode up in a fury. '*Are you freaking crazy?*' Jumping off his horse, he was all in her face. '*Do you have a death wish?*'

'Bit harsh, cupcake. When all you had to say was thank

you.' Considering she'd just stopped his herd from hurting themselves while also protecting his family. But, no, Ryder typically had to go and ruin the moment with a lecture.

'I just want to protect you. Don't you get it?' He ripped off his hat, roughly raking fingers through his thick hair.

'I—'

'No.' He pointed his hat at her. 'No, you are not some convenience. You are not some urge or itch to scratch. And you are not something I want to own, like a possession I bought from a store. You are someone I truly care about, and when you go and do dumb crap like this—'

'I was helping you.'

'Stop it.'

'No. You stop it. You don't control me.' She sneered, raising her chin in defiance. So what if he was all tall, hot, and broody. With his tousled brown hair, chiselled jaw, and trimmed beard. He never scared her.

But then he slapped his hat back on his head, shading the look in his eyes that were a warm toasted hazelnut—it was such a contradiction for a man with ice in his veins. Especially when arguing with the a-hole!

'I don't want to control you, Bree,' he said, so close their hat brims were touching. 'All I want is to take care of you, because you mean so much to me.'

Her eyes flared wide as she stepped back from him. 'You can't.'

'I can't help it. Believe me.' Again, he removed his hat, to wipe away the perspiration on his forehead, using the upper sleeve of his shirt that tightly showed off his muscles.

'I'm all wrong for you.'

He shook his head as he readjusted his hat. 'No, you're perfect.'

'Are your ears full of bulldust or something?' Giving him her best dramatic eye roll. 'I just told you I'm all wrong for you. Because if I was right for you, we wouldn't be *screaming at each other!*' Her own voice echoed to blend with his, while the cattle watched them like spectators in a shopping mall.

'Remember, you and your brothers conned my grandfather into coming, knowing of course he'd manipulate me into playing stockwoman. So here I am, doing that job—that you already told me you would've fired me for! You ungrateful—'

Beneath their feet the ground rumbled again, and something cracked on the hill behind them. 'What was that?'

It was enough to make the hair stand up on the back of her neck.

They spun around to search for the source, as something else cracked like ice being broken but a thousand times bigger, coming from above them.

The horses nickered and started pawing at the ground, with the cattle once again stirring, heading back the way they'd come.

Get out of here, Bree. Go.' Ryder threw her into the saddle.

She struggled to grip Back Hand's reins, managing only to grasp his mane, as the horse hurtled down the small hill and bolted towards the back of the rising dust cloud caused by the shifting herd.

A massive rumble began from behind them.

Bree peered over her shoulder as the entire side of the rock wall fell. She knew the escarpment's height was only half the size of Uluru, but still taller than the Eiffel tower, sending tons of rubble, rock, and sheered sandstone powder to wash over them in an explosion that hurt her ears.

As the dust scattered, and the exhausted cattle slowed down, Ryder and Bree pulled up their horses to turn and gape at the damage. The air was filled with a chalky haze blended with the gritty dust coating her sweat-soaked skin, which she could taste on her tongue. She dragged out her water bottle, taking a deep drink to wash out her mouth, swallowing hard to stop the ringing in her ears. 'Here.' She passed the bottle to Ryder.

'Thanks.' He took it, splashing some over his face, before guzzling deep.

The landslide had transformed the lower section of once-solid rock face into a jagged pile of rubble, resembling a beach left bare by the retreating tide. It was catastrophic.

'Did Bree do that?' Dex asked, riding up to meet them.

'It's sandstone. Crumbly stuff, that's always falling off the escarpment.'

'With some help from cattle and redheads with shotguns.' Dex grinned at her.

'Are you two, okay?' Ash rode up fast to join them.

'We're fine.' She brushed the dust from her clothing, where that green blanket was now red. The good thing was, as she removed the thick dust-encrusted blanket from her shoulders, it had saved her clothes and her hair from the brunt of the dust.

She really liked this blanket. Taking the time to roll it up and securing it to her saddlebags, even copped a nod from Ryder.

What was the story behind this blanket?

'Bree, you're a nut case and a hero all in one,' Ash said, with Dex chuckling beside him. 'You're the only woman I know who'd race to cut off a herd and end up starting a landslide.'

'Is everyone at the camp, okay?' Bree couldn't see them through the dusty haze. But the cattle were calming down and drinking from Koala Creek, which was a good sign.

'Charlie, Cap, and his dogs protected them. What the heck happened?' Ash poked back the brim of his hat.

'Sophie is what.' Ryder scowled at his brother.

'Flipping hell.' Dex dropped his head, rubbing his forehead. 'I'm sending her back.'

'Don't worry, brother, I'm sending Harper and Mason home, too.' Ash patted Dex's shoulder.

Ryder scowled. 'Good. A muster isn't a summer camp for teens, which is what you two were turning this into. This muster isn't—'

'What is that?' Bree turned her horse away from Ryder's lecture.

'Will you stop rushing into danger?'

'I want to see the damage.'

'And cause another landslide.'

'I didn't cause that. It was coincidental. And I'll find a geologist I can pay to back me up.' When she was really hoping to skip another one of Ryder's lectures.

'Why? Do you have one in your pocket?'

'At the pub. You can find all sorts there. Or, I can be like Ash, who found his nanny at the supermarket in town.' She cheekily winked at Ash, before riding closer to the edge of the rubble, spotting the dark shadow, like a hole. 'Look. It's a cave.' She jumped off her horse and shared some water with Black Hand who seemed keener on sniffing around, as Ryder and his brothers rode up.

It was as if nature had peeled back the lower quarter of its rocky curtain to reveal a secret cave, the wide entrance framed by loose rocks and rubble scattered across the ground. Dust hung in the air, swirling lazily in the beams of sunlight to shine into the cave's mouth, exposing rough and irregular walls of red and orange sandstone that faded into darker, more ancient tones that were lost deep in the shadows.

'You are not going in there.'

'Watch me, cupcake.' She didn't care what Ryder said, kicking herself for not packing her torch in her saddlebags. 'Stay, Black Hand, I'll be right back.'

'You are the most—'

'Will you lighten up?' She scowled at the broody a-hole barking in her face. 'Stop being such a buzzkill. And stop ranting at me like some nattering, no-fun nanny. You're not my parent, you're not my brother, and you are certainly not my boss. So stop ruining the day's adventure.'

Ryder's jaw dropped as if she'd slapped him.

It was enough to make her pause and inhale deeply to temper herself. 'Look, cupcake—' The nickname always elicited an annoyed scowl out of him, which was a much better look than before. 'We've just survived a stampede and a landslide, so let's catch our breath, and let the herd do the same, while we take a peek inside this cave.'

'It could be unsafe.'

'I'm willing to take my chances.' She entered the mouth of the cave where the floor was strewn with loose rocks and debris. Dust lingered, but the air inside was cool and free from any humidity, it only heightened her curiosity at this unearthed mystery.

Certain sections of the cave's walls had been cut away with straight, deliberate lines. The ceiling bore deep gouges, while some were faint but visible under the layers of dust and dirt. In some places, even though aged, sturdy wooden support beams braced the interior, unmoved by the landslide.

Leaning against the wall was a sturdy hammer and some shovels, a sight that made her shudder, as if an eerie ghost were scraping its nails across her scalp, sending a ripple of goosebumps to squirrel down her spine. 'It looks like an old mine.'

Ryder grabbed her forearm. 'Careful. Please?'

'Well, since you asked so nicely.' Matching his pace, they entered together.

'You two are as crazy as each other,' called out Ash, well clear of the main entrance. 'I'm not going in there.'

'Good. You can watch our horses.' Dex rummaged through his saddlebags. 'I've got a torch, so don't start without me.'

The temperature dropped as they entered the small cave where old planks of wood braced the roof and sides. It was surprisingly sturdy enough to survive that landslide.

'Did you know this was here, Bree?' Ryder asked.

'No. I knew they did some fossicking deeper in the Stoneys, and they'd panned for gold in the creeks, but not this...' She stopped, her hand instantly reaching for Ryder's solid chest.

His large hand squeezed hers. 'What is it?'

She pointed with a trembling finger. 'That.'

The torchlight swept across the cave's uneven floor, illuminating a large wooden crate where two skeletons, clad in tattered clothing, were huddled together, their yellowed bones eerily well-preserved in the cool, still air.

Beside them stood two old suitcases with the leather remarkably intact, although their metal clasps were tarnished. Beside them sat a smaller wooden box, with the words *Charlie Splint* etched in the weathered grains.

Bree took a step closer towards the skeletons. They were holding each other like lovers. One wore a dress, the other wore pants and a shirt that was rolled up at the cuffs, with an old stockman's hat pushed back against his head. Beside his skeletal fingers a chisel lay in the dirt, below the wall, where the words *TOGETHER FOREVER* were scratched in the stone.

The message hit Bree like a sledgehammer, leaving her nauseated. When Charlie had re-launched the search for Harry, she'd always feared it would end in heartache. But nothing could have prepared her for this. She struggled to breathe, to speak, her voice trembling, barely above a whisper: 'I think that's Pop's brother, Harry, and the woman he ran away with.'

Eleven

It wasn't Ryder's first body. As the others took a step back, Ryder patted down the trouser pockets on the male skeleton, wearing an old-style Akubra.

He found a wallet and flicked it open.

'What's the name?' Bree was pale.

It made his stomach churn to see her like that, so he hesitated.

'Don't you dare.' She went to grab the wallet.

'It's your great-uncle. It's Harry Splint.'

Dex wiped his mouth with the back of his hand. He'd turned the torch into a lamp, its beam highlighting his wide-eyes as he stared at the skeletons. 'So, that'd be her. Penelope Price.'

Dust particles drifted through the beams of sunlight streaming from the mouth of the cave, never quite reaching the skeletons huddled together in the shadows.

Bree unsheathed her hand-forged bushman's knife, as she kneeled down to the box bearing the label: *Charlie Splint*. 'Do you have your satphone on you?'

'No.' Ryder wished he did. But he'd agreed with Charlie to have a phone-free muster. 'Hey, that could be evidence.'

'It's got my grandfather's name on it.' Using the blade, she jimmied open the lid of the wooden box to reveal a pile of rocks and an envelope.

Dex peered over her shoulder, holding the lamp higher so they could all see. 'It that gold?'

'Raw gold ore. I've seen enough of Charlie's paydays to recognise it.' Bree passed out some stones.

Surprisingly, the gold wasn't what had captured her interest, it was the envelope hidden inside. 'Pop knew it. He always said his brother would leave him a note.' She held up the envelope that said: *To my baby brother, Charlie 'Splinter' Splint.*

Dex ran his fingers through the rock pile, shifting its weight. 'That's a lot of gold.'

'It's raw,' Ryder said, tossing the rock he was holding back into the box. 'It'll need to be smelted down.'

'Yeah, but it's still a lot, right?'

Ryder nodded, knowing his brother was already calculating the fortune hidden in those rough chunks. 'Bree, are you okay?' She didn't look okay.

Pulling her hat free, she used the sleeve of her shirt to wipe away the dust covering her forehead that was now shiny with sweat, as she glanced back at the skeletons.

'Did you know him, Bree?'

She screwed her nose up at Dex. 'My mother wasn't even born when Harry went missing. Oh, Charlie.' She sighed, with her hand covering her heart. 'I owe that old man the biggest apology.' Slapping on her hat, she headed for the entrance.

'Where are you going?' Ryder followed.

'To get Charlie. He'll want to see this.'

'Bree, no.'

'You can't hide this from Charlie. For sixty years, he's been wondering what happened to his brother.' She stopped and faced him. 'Once I've returned with Charlie, I'll lead the herd to the yards.'

'Why?'

'Because you'll need them out of the way to bring the police here.' Her mind was ticking over already with a plan.

'Send the girls back home, too,' he said.

'Good idea.' She actually agreed with him for the first time that day. It was enough for Dex to cock his eyebrows in surprise. 'Can you go back with Charlie? He'll show you the shortcut through the Scary Forest.'

'Why?' Ryder wasn't a babysitter.

'Because you're the boss, it's your land, and you know the town's top cop well. I know when Charlie sees this he'll crumble or go into shock. He'll need someone strong—like you—by his side.' She even squeezed his hand, without any of her usual sass. It was impossible to say no to the redhead when she was like this. 'You'll know what to do. You'll help Charlie back to the cottage, you'll call the police, and help him unsaddle the horses, before fuelling up the Razorback. By then, the girls should have arrived at the homestead, having taken the long way around, because they're not confident enough to race the horses through Scary Forest, and they would only slow you guys down. I estimate they'll show up not long after you guys have done all your other tasks to help them unsaddle, keeping Charlie busy until the police arrive.'

It made sense. 'And what will you be doing?'

'Helping your brothers finish this muster. But that's *after* I've brought Charlie here. It's better coming from me than you, Ryder.' For once, she'd said his name and not the nickname. 'Hey, why are you looking at me like you're about to spit nails?'

He wasn't angry at her, but at this whole stupid situation. 'What if I say no?'

'Really? You're going to argue with me now? Unless you've got a better idea?'

She was right. He'd want to be there to meet the police, because this was his land.

'Well then, I'd better go break the news to my grandfather.'

'Hey...' He gently gripped her arm. 'Are you okay?'

'I'm more worried about Charlie and how he's going to react, which is why I'm asking for your help. Please?'

This was a whole new side to Bree he hadn't seen before. The vulnerable side that slammed into his heart to ignite something deep into his soul.

Her ex-husband, Finn had advised him that if Bree ever asked for help to do it. Without question. Because it was rare for her to even ask. And in the entire time he'd known her, she'd asked nothing of them. Ever. Yet the rest of his family were always seeking Bree out for her opinion, and to work on the musters. Now, here she was, volunteering to step up as head stockman for the good of his family's station. 'Okay, I'll wait here for you and Charlie to return.'

'Thank you.' She gave a nod and left the cave.

'What's going on with you two?' Dex asked, coming up beside him.

How could he answer that when Ryder didn't know himself? Instead, he grabbed Dex's torch. 'Let's check out this cave.'

'What do you think happened?'

Ryder shone the beam of light over the structure. The cave itself was solid, with sturdy beams that had survived a cave-in. After sixty years, they still stood strong as ever.

Guessing by the condition of the suitcases' leather, the cave had somehow preserved them from the outdoor elements. Although covered in dust, even the clothing on the skeletons was in fairly good condition. 'I'm guessing they got trapped behind a landslide that buried the entrance, cutting off their way out. They must've run out of oxygen.'

'Brother, the escarpment's wall is strong,' said Dex, tapping on the sides of the cave. 'It survived a landslide.'

'And?'

'It's not natural.'

Ryder paused to watch his brother go over the load-bearing beams. Dex had a mechanical engineer's brain, was a whiz with maths and could have gone places, but as a kid who'd gotten expelled from school, he was content to play with the tools on the station. 'What are you trying to say?'

'I went through those devastating earthquakes in New Zealand and other places to see those landslide aftereffects. But for a shotgun and a herd of cattle to cause that much damage?' He shook his head.

'We all felt the thunder of that racing herd back when the stampede began.'

'But for that amount of rock to fall, it doesn't seem right. Not when this cave is still intact like this. In theory, it should have collapsed in on itself.'

Dex had a point.

Ryder crouched down beside the skeletons, that were holding onto each other. Those words: *Together Forever*, would have been the last thing they saw, if they had light. But there were no signs of a campfire, obviously to conserve the oxygen.

'It'd be a horrible way to die.' Dex's torchlight swept over the skeletons, causing their shadows to stretch over the cave's walls.

'It's every underground miner's nightmare.' Ryder felt sorry for them. 'I'd say the couple would have lost consciousness and eventually succumbed to hypoxia.'

'What's that?'

'Oxygen deprivation. They would have become dizzy and suffered with a shortness of breath.' He pointed to the shovels and the old mallet and pick leaning against the wall, where they'd tried to dig themselves out. 'Eventually they would have passed out.' Which they did in each other's arms. 'At least they weren't in any pain.'

'Do you think, that if they died trapped in here, was this some sort of cosmic karma, as a payback for murdering Penelope's husband, Jack Price?'

'That's for the forensic team to decide. But at least Charlie will finally have his answers.' But how was the old man going to react when he discovered his brother had been trapped inside this cave, like a tomb, for sixty years?

In desperate need of some fresh air, Ryder exited the cave with Dex right beside him. He faced the sun, inhaling heavily to peer up at the sky, and the sheer wall that towered above them that made up Cattleman's Keep.

Ash stood nearby, holding the horses' reins in the shade

of the stone wall. 'What did you find? Bree said little.'

'We found Charlie's brother Harry.' Dex dragged out his water bottle from his saddlebags.

Ryder took the reins of his horse. 'Ash, can you ride back and help the girls pack up camp, and send them home. Tell Cap to get his dogs ready to finish this muster, then follow Bree's lead.'

'Fine by me, I'm not one for stirring up ghosts in dark caves.' Ash quickly flung himself into the saddle and adjusted his reins. 'I'm glad we're sending the ladies home. That stampede reminded me how dangerous mustering can be.'

'It's the wake-up call we all needed.'

'It's what I was warning you about.' Ryder scowled at his two younger brothers.

'What's up your nose? Bree stopped the stampede and the way the cattle are, they'll follow her.'

'Bree nearly got trampled by the cattle—and then almost crushed by the landslide. This is our job, our herd, not hers. Remember, Bree isn't even on our payroll, yet she's about to lead the muster.' The memory of how close she'd come to disaster, and how much she was already doing for them, had him so angry that if he gritted his teeth any harder, they'd crack.

Ryder saw through Bree's need for being overly independent. It was a defence mechanism for being constantly let down—and he did not want to let her down. Yet there was nothing he could do to help Bree, who was about to give her grandfather the kind of heartbreaking news no one ever wants to deliver to someone they love.

Twelve

Ash caught up to Bree, helping her round up the stray stockhorses with their saddles and packs still in place, forming a long horse train as they headed back to camp. Ahead, she spotted her grandfather, sifting through the remnants of their stock camp.

It was enough to make her guts twist into hot knots of lava for what she was about to do.

'Hey, Bree, well done on stopping the stampede. I took some awesome photos.' Sophie grinned, holding up her camera.

Bree scowled at Sophie. 'Pack up camp. You girls are going home.'

Mia froze, her eyes wide, side-glancing at Harper, who looked just as stunned. 'On our own?'

'You'll be fine.' Ash jumped off his horse, to stroke Harper's cheek tenderly, giving her a gentle smile. 'I trust Shortbread to take you home, no worries.' He pointed to the cream-coloured stockhorse he'd bought his partner as a gift.

'But?' Harper hoisted the toddler Mason higher on her hip.

'You can do it. Just stick together and keep at a steady pace.' Bree gave an encouraging nod to Harper and Mia. It was Sophie who might need some coaching. 'Cap, can you and your muster dogs help me, and Ash, muster the cattle towards the yards?'

'Sure.' Cap nodded, as he approached them.

'Cap and I will take care of the horses, we'll wait for your call, Bree.' Ash nodded at her with sadness in his eyes. 'I'll find some torches and put them in your saddlebags.'

'Thanks.' For once she didn't think ahead, her mind was all muddled.

Ash nodded at her. 'You do what you need to do.'

She'd rather do anything but this.

Dismounting, Bree removed her hat as she approached her grandfather. 'Pop?'

'You looked good out there, kid.' Charlie swaggered up and patted Bree's stallion. 'Black Hand, you're a beast, you are.' He held out some sugar cubes for the horse, who lapped them up as Charlie rubbed his nose.

Bree licked her dry lips, with her throat so tight. 'Um, Pop, I...'

'What's wrong, kid?'

She swallowed hard, pulling the envelope from her back pocket. 'We found him.'

'Found who?'

'Your brother. Harry.' She pointed back to the edge of the escarpment. 'There was a landslide.'

She inhaled deeply, searching for the strength, hating that she was about to ruin her grandfather's day. This was so freaking hard! 'Pop, um, we found your brother. We found Harry's remains. He died alongside Penelope Price.'

Charlie's jaw fell as he sat hard on the nearest tree stump, scattered around the cold campfire like chairs. 'Where?'

'In this old mine.'

The many wrinkles shifted across his brow. 'There are no mines out here.'

'Well, there is now... Pop, you were right all along. You said your brother would leave you a note, and I found it. Here...' She held out the letter. 'I'm so, so sorry I never believed you.' The guilt was enough for Bree to drop to her knees in front of her grandfather, her hands trembling as she held out the letter that he'd been searching for.

'That's Harry's writing.' Charlie's voice was frail, as he

blinked at the envelope. 'Where is he?'

'Back at the cave. Ryder and Dex are there. I'll show you.'

'Er… yeah…' Charlie stared at his name on the envelope with confusion strewn across his face. She just hoped he wasn't going to go into shock.

She helped Charlie with his horse as he slowly climbed back into the saddle, with Bree doing the same.

'This way, Pop.' Salty tears blurred her vision. As if the guilt wasn't enough for not believing her grandfather, along came that old familiar feeling of grief laced with a lashing of fear to wash over her sinking stomach once again. She may have never met Harry Splint, but he was Charlie's brother—a reminder that her grandfather was the last family member Bree had left.

Thirteen

'I'm so sorry, Charlie.' Ryder held his hand over his heart, with Dex doing the same, as they stood before the cave.

'Do you know what happened?' Charlie dismounted, his legs shaky, with Bree quick to help him. 'I've got it, kid. I'm okay. Stop fussing.' He slapped her hands away.

Bree glanced back at Ryder. Now he understood why she'd asked him to watch over Charlie.

'I've got him, Bree.' Ryder approached Charlie.

'Ash grabbed us some extra torches.' Bree dragged them out of her saddlebags and passed them around. 'Do you want me to come with you, Pop?'

Charlie stood at the cave's opening, his neck craning back to face the escarpment. He looked so small standing before the towering wall of red rock that had yet to reflect the sun. 'Would you?' Even his voice was frail.

'Absolutely.' Bree hooked her arm through her grandfather's, their boot steps heavy with Charlie's spurs clinking against the rock hidden under the dust.

'Aw bugger, Harry.' The old man ripped off his large hat exposing his grey-white hair. 'There you are, ol' mate. Still in that snazzy hat you scored from Sydney that you said the ladies would love.' Charlie slowly lowered himself to his knees and gently patted the skeleton's shoulder as if greeting an old friend. 'All this time you were right here, mate, when I'd thought you'd done a runner.'

The cave was eerily quiet as Charlie took a moment of silence, while Bree, Ryder and Dex removed their hats and waited.

Then Charlie cleared his throat as he stood, sliding on his hat to face Ryder. The grief had already begun, worn in the deep crevices belonging to a man who'd lived a long life under the sun.

'Any guesses what happened?' Charlie asked.

'There was a cave-in. Hypoxia—which means they didn't suffer in pain,' replied Ryder, copping a nod of gratitude from Bree at that part. 'The police will find out more. Harry left you that box of gold there. It came with that letter.' Ryder lifted off the lid from the crate.

'Struth. Gold, huh?' Charlie rested his hands on the hips of his jeans, where his stockwhip was attached, and peeked inside the crate.

'And that suitcase is full of old cash.' Dex tapped at it with his boot.

'How much cash?'

'Dunno. Heaps.' Dex pulled back the lid on the hard suitcase, where amongst the lady's vintage silk underwear were thick wads of cash. 'Did they rob a bank?'

'Dex!' Ryder scowled.

Dex shrugged. 'Bree would've asked the same.'

'That's true,' mumbled Bree.

It made Ryder pause, considering Charlie's brother Harry was wanted for murder.

'Is that cash still legal tender?' Bree asked Ryder.

'Sure. But right now, we need to leave it for the police. This is all evidence.' Even though they might get into trouble for it, it hadn't stopped Ryder and Dex from poking through everything, finding a few shotguns and a duffel bag with Harry's clothes in it. 'Have you read the letter Harry left you?'

Charlie shook his head, patting the envelope tucked into his shirt pocket. Taking in the scene, he slowly shifted his boots, their thick Cuban heels and spurs clinking against the rocky floor, to face the wall where the words *Together Forever* were etched in stone.

Bree rubbed her grandfather's shoulder. 'Are you okay, Pop?'

'Um, I...' Charlie looked lost.

'Listen up, Pop.' She stood right in front of him, getting really close as if to force her grandfather to focus on her. 'Ryder is going to ride home with you. You need to show him the shortcut.'

'Yes. Right. Um, we'll cut through, cut through the—the...'

'Scary Forest. Ryder will call the police. You'll then unsaddle the horses and get the Razorback ready.'

'Why not the chopper?' butted in Dex.

Ryder would love to, but he couldn't. 'The dust and rubble is too fresh for the helicopter to come anywhere near this place. It'd cause a dust storm and may disturb this—' He couldn't call it a crime scene, or could he? 'I'd hate for it to start another landslide.'

'Yeah, yeah.' Charlie nodded as if his mind was trapped in a fog. 'I'll get more torches, water.'

'There's food in the fridge. You need to eat when you get home to keep up your blood sugar levels. And I packed a couple of snack bars in your saddlebags if you need it.'

Dammit. Did Charlie take his pills this morning?

They all knew the caretaker had a tricky heart, flatly refusing heart surgery. But it never stopped the old stockman, that at times Ryder forgot Charlie was in his eighties. But grief was a tricky beast that made people react in different ways. And this, well, this was something entirely different. How do you describe the shock of finding something so completely unexpected, when they all knew Charlie had hoped for a happy reunion when he found his brother again.

'Pop, look at me.' She held her grandfather's cheek, lowering herself to meet his eyes.

'But—'

'Right now, you need to go get the police. You need to focus.'

'Yeah. You're right.' Charlie nodded, blinking the grit out of his eyes as if to clear his head. 'Where are you going, kid?'

'To finish this muster. Or do you want me to stay with you?'

'Yeah—nah. There's a muster to finish. The cattle are spooked enough as it is. Just be home in time for supper, eh?'

'I'll try, Pop.' She hugged her grandfather. 'I love you, Pop, and I'm so, so, sorry I ever doubted you.' With a nod, she was gone.

Ryder wanted to go with her. 'Dex, keep an eye on her.'

'You don't need to ask. I was going to anyway. My condolences, Charlie.' Dex shook the old man's hand, slid on his hat, and followed Bree into the sunshine.

'Ready to go, Charlie?' The sooner Ryder called the police the sooner they could get some answers.

Charlie paused to look back at the skeletons frozen in their embrace. 'Harry didn't deserve this.'

'No one does.'

By the time they left the cave, the first cracks of the stockwhips echoed through the air. It was Bree, with Dex on the other side of the large herd of cattle that stirred the moving dust cloud away from Cattleman's Keep. A place that had finally revealed its secrets.

Climbing back onto his horse, Ryder scoured the area to work out the best way to bring their vehicles in. That's when he noticed the channel in the back, like an old forgotten track hidden by the small hill. 'Charlie, how far away was it where you found Harry's car in the Stoneys?' The old Holden Bree called Pandora.

Charlie paused, high on the saddle to narrow his grey eyes back at the Stoneys that stood like stone soldiers on the outer edge of the valley. 'It's just on the other side of that gap. I didn't think to look this side. We were working inland.'

'You wouldn't have found this cave, not before the landslide.' A cave cleverly hidden behind the small hill Bree had used to make her stand against the stampeding herd. The silly woman! Damn, it was hard to get angry with Bree when he had to admire her grit at the same time. 'What was your brother's job on the station?'

'Boundary rider.'

'So he had a horse?'

Charlie nodded from the saddle of his stockhorse, Slim, which was steadily picking its way through the rubble and onto the grassy plains. He craned around in his seat, his grey eyes shadowed by the brim of his stockman's hat. 'Do you reckon Harry drove out here with Penelope to stash their gear in this cave, hid his car in the Stoneys to avoid attracting attention, and then pack or something?'

Ryder followed on his own horse, which he had yet to name. 'That would've taken some planning—leaving the car in the Stoneys.' Which was miles away. Yet from his preliminary search with Dex, it looked like the couple had been preparing their escape for a while considering they had suitcases, a handwritten letter, and a box of gold.

'But does that make my brother and Penelope murderers for killing Penelope's husband?'

Ryder shrugged. 'I'm not familiar with the case.' It was a sixty-year cold case, after all.

'Well, I know the murder involves weapons, and Bree told me you're good with guns. I saw what you did with her shotgun—you understand them in a way most people don't. And you've got Dex there,' he said, nodding toward Dex, who was mustering the herd. 'That boy's good with numbers. Look, I know you and Dex are clever lads. D'ya reckon you could take a gander at that murder file for me?'

'Haven't you read it?'

'Policeman Porter won't let me. I know the lad means well and all, but aren't you good mates with his boss, Sarge?'

'Marcus, yeah.' Ryder had helped Marcus a few times since coming to Elsie Creek, they became friends who shared a liking for top-shelf bourbons.

'Do you think you could ask him?'

'I won't promise anything, Charlie, but I'll try.'

'Thanks. That's all a fella can ask.' Charlie nodded, digging his heels into his grey horse's flanks and they began the trek across the plains.

As the massive herd shifted like a sea of white coats, their horses galloped across the open range, eating up the grassy plains beneath their beating hooves. They wove their way through the large thicket of paperbark trees that was part of the dried-out swamp, where rich terracotta soils contrasted against the pale trunks of the peeling paperbarks that stood beneath a pale blue sky.

The track wove across the plains until it approached a wall of trees. The red rock escarpment towered over them on the right, as the track dipped steeply to meet the creek. The temperature dropped, and the sky was hidden above a blanket of trees.

'We need to walk through here for a bit.' From his horse, Charlie led the way down to the small creek. 'You can only get through here in the dry. In the wet season it's all under water, making it prime croc country.'

Didn't that make Ryder peer keenly from his saddle, scanning the rocky creek beds for any telltale drag marks and other signs of the man-eating predators.

'Have you been through the Scary Forest yet?'

'No.' Ryder removed his sunglasses to crane his neck at the monsoon forest's thick clusters of trees with their interlocking branches, tangled with vines, as swooping groups of colourful parrots screeched like an in-house alarm system.

With the jungle hemming in from all sides, it triggered a memory of slapping at mosquitoes with a team of men wearing camo gear. He did not want to remember. He did not want his mind to start playing tricks on him as he peered into the shadows of a thick monsoon forest. 'Why the name Scary Forest?'

'Bree's mother named it Scary Forest when she was four. Beatrice was so small then, she'd sit on the front of my saddle with me, and we'd go check on our cherabin pots, or go to the waterhole to do some fishing, and check on the cattle.' Charlie's soulful sigh had his shoulders folding over to slouch heavily in the saddle.

Their horses sloshed through the creek, happy for the change of pace. Yet the air was thick over what Charlie was going through, finding his long-lost brother in a cave, and being reminded of how he'd lost his daughter to murder, it was enough for Ryder to try for a change in conversation — which he wasn't known for.

He'd grown to respect Charlie since they'd bought the station. In that time the caretaker had become a friend you could ask anything, and right now, they desperately needed a change of conversation, so Ryder blurted out the first thing he could think of… 'Do you know why Bree gave us our nicknames?'

What the hell was he thinking, asking Charlie that?

'Pretty obvious, don't you think?' Riding side by side along the shallow creek bed, Charlie glanced at Ryder, his eyes heavy with sadness. Yet, the old man gave a nod of approval for trying to lighten the atmosphere on a day that was about to get heavier. 'Stormcloud is for Dex because he was a walking storm of thunderous rage—until he met Sophie.'

'The woman who started the stampede?' It was enough to make Ryder scowl.

'That young girlie is green, she's never been out here before. She wouldn't know the rules to mustering. Which is my fault.'

'None of this is your fault, Charlie. I shouldn't have let them come.'

'But I wanted them all to come.'

'Why?'

'Because I don't know how many musters I have left in me. I wanted them to feel the joy of camping out under the stars, to be in a place where people talked around a campfire and not stare at some small screen in their hands. I wanted you all to be in a place where people bonded like a family. Trust me on this, young fella, in a year or two, you'll all laugh about how Sophie started that stampede. Mark my words.'

Ryder didn't feel like laughing today.

'Anyhoodle, Bree nicknamed Ash snowflake because he was a bit of a snowflake, always dodging his responsibilities and being a whiny man-child.'

'That he was.' Ryder chuckled, surprised to hear it echoing back at him from the thick forest, where all the trees had started to look the same. 'But my little brother has grown up.'

'It's good to see, right?' Charlie peered back at the high riverbank, thick with exposed tree roots, showing how deep this creek would get in the wet season. It was taller than Ryder, sitting on a horse that sloshed around in the ankle-deep creek.

'I never got that chance with my brother to see him grow, like you do. To see Harry have his own family, like I had.' Charlie's voice was thick and hoarse as if the grief was cracking across the man's shell. He cleared his throat, sitting straighter in the saddle once again. 'Is that why you bought the place for your brothers?'

'I needed a home. We all did.' Ryder also needed to feel again, and not see the world as the enemy.

'Do they know you bought this station for them?'

Ryder frowned as their horses climbed out of the creek bed to follow a leaf-littered track where soft ferns feathered along the sides. 'Is that what you thought?'

'No, I didn't. I saw a group of brothers trying to make a home for themselves, which is why I said yes to you lot buying this place. It was Bree who pointed it out to me. She said your brothers would spend the rest of their lives trying to pay you back to become equal partner, but you didn't care, you did this for them. Bree's right, isn't she?'

Ryder barely nodded.

'Bree reads people well.'

'I noticed. So why did she call me cupcake?' He scowled

at the thick jungle that hid the world from the sun. He hated that name.

'You don't know?' The old man widened his grey eyes with something between surprise and amusement.

Ryder matched it with a scowl. 'I'm asking, aren't I?'

Charlie gave a devilish grin.

'What?'

'Cupcakes are Bree's favourite food.'

Ryder cocked an eyebrow.

'Everyone knows Bree loves her cupcakes. Cowboy Craig, Lenny, Policeman Porter, even her ex-husband, Finn, all know if you want Bree to do something for you, or you wanna get into her good books, you just get her some cupcakes. That kid's baking them all the time. She's even got this whole special cupcake prayer.' Charlie's chuckle echoed around them, making the birds pause from their squawking.

How the hell was Ryder supposed to respond to that?

Charlie shrugged, while loosely holding the reins. 'I'm guessing she named you cupcake, coz you're no cupcake.'

'Hell, no.'

'But you are part stockman and part soldier with a truckload of toughness you only get from living a hard life. I've heard them say you've got ice in your veins, but you're also a decent fella underneath it, too. You're a bloke who takes care of his family and for that, I take my hat off to you.' Charlie tapped the brim of his hat. 'It's what I tried to do for my family. But...' He sighed heavily, regripping the reins of his horse as it steadily plodded along. 'All I've got left is my granddaughter, and I'm truly blessed to have her around. Reckon you could do me a favour, Ryder?'

'What's that?'

'When I go, do you reckon you could keep an eye on my granddaughter for me? Wouldn't want her getting into trouble, is all.'

'Isn't Bree planning some holiday?'

'Reckons she's gonna do a road trip to the nearest international airport to catch the first plane out to Tahiti.'

'Why Tahiti?'

'Bree reckons they've got no dangerous animals there. No deadly spiders, snakes, scorpions and other whatnots like we live with. Even though they may have some stingers and sharks in their waters, they've got no crocodiles and Bree plans to do a lot of swimming in between drinking cocktails on the beach.' Charlie chuckled, ducking under a low branch.

Again, Ryder scoured the sides of the creek bed for any sneaky swamp puppies, checking his rifle sitting neatly against the saddle.

He ducked low under a branch as the creek widened, and where the water was barely a trickle. 'Wasn't Bree going to some game's finals?'

'The Stanley Cup. It's the ice hockey finals. Brutal game.'

'How did Bree get into watching ice hockey?'

'I dunno, for sure.' Charlie shrugged his shoulders, readjusting his grip on the saddle. 'She had her reasons for it.'

'Which are?'

'Well, at the end of the day, Bree would fill up her trough with water and ice to make this outdoor bath where she sits in front of the outdoor tellie. There, she'll have her jug of gin in one hand and the remote control in the other, and that's where she'll watch ice hockey. I don't think that kid's ever seen snow or a live game. But, after working in front of that fiery forge in the smithy's shed, hammering hot metals during an outback summer, you need something to cool down from that kind of heat, and them ice baths of hers have proven to be priceless. And then watching men skate around on ice must help her cool down some, too, like some trick of the mind or something?' Charlie shrugged. 'I prefer the footy myself.'

'Have you tried those ice baths?' Because Dex had put in the request for an ice machine in their new bar.

Charlie nodded. 'Oh yeah. Coupla times. Especially after spending all day hammering out a new legacy brand, it did the trick, lickety-split.'

'Which reminds me... How much do you want for our

station's branding iron?' He'd assumed buying this station that they'd get the cattle brand that went with it, yet somehow the crafty master brand maker had ownership of the Elsie Creek legacy brand.

Charlie grinned. 'It's not for sale. But I'll make sure Bree brings it down for the next draft. But there'll be no more pound work for my granddaughter in them there drafting yards. I promised her that. You should send in Ash to man the gates or get a young jackeroo to jump the rails… It's good you've got Harper learning the sticks, and Mia working the muster dogs. Give either of them girls a few years and they could start working on the drafting calls.'

'And you'll be on the top boards, teaching them.'

'Nah.' Again he sighed with his shoulders drooping. 'You'll want Bree doin' them calls. She's got a better eye than me. Always did, from the time she was nine, manning them gates, when she could barely reach the chest height of some of them cattle.' He snorted out a chuckle. 'It fair dinkum used to upset my wife, it did. But not that kid. Bree was fearless in that pound. Still is.' He gave a wry grin, rolling his shoulders that seemed to fill with pride. 'I know the kid lets me think I'm in charge, but she's the one who knows the cattle better. She'd make a helluva head stockman, or a stock inspector, if she wanted. But she likes working as a blacksmith these days.'

'Didn't you say that Bree went away for a while?'

'She did—when she married that devil, Finn.' Charlie's tone sharpened as he continued. 'He'd been working here for a while, and he was a good stockman, too. But, like most men who were starting a family, he wanted to own his own land. Finn's mob were from Queensland, so Bree went with him. First Queensland, then Victoria for a bit, too.' Charlie scowled at the path ahead, his grip tightening on the reins. 'But then I ended up in hospital. And just like that, Bree showed up with her son, telling me she was moving back in with me. She took care of me, Darcie, little Liam, and this station.'

His expression softened as he added, 'Boy, were Darcie

and I glad to have Bree back home, too. Darcie adored her like a niece. He would've liked you and your brothers.' Charlie gave Ryder a firm nod, a glimmer of approval in his weathered eyes.

'Is that why you sold us the station?'

'And that you'd agreed to maintaining the caretaker's caveat.'

That caveat had the caretaker living in the best house, which overlooked the prettiest paddock on the property like it was a separate farm.

'You said Bree came back to run things *again*. Was Bree running the station before?'

'You could say that.' Charlie grinned wryly, patting down his chest, that again seemed to fill with pride. 'Of course, she had us two old fellas mentoring her, letting us think we were in charge. But that clever kid was pulling the puppet strings her way, and everyone prospered.'

'Hmmm…' That sneaky redhead never let on. She refused to call herself a stockwoman, even though she was a bloody good one who never interfered with them running the place. But running a station meant a lot more than just managing men and herd.

All of Ryder's brothers had consulted with Bree more than once when it came to the station—it had irritated him that Bree knew more about what was going on than he did, when he was the one paying the bills!

'Darcie and I figured the reason Bree came back that last time was because she was having marriage problems, is all.' Charlie shifted easily in the saddle as his horse navigated the thick leaf litter along a wallaby track that crossed yet another creek bed. The place was like a maze, with each turn looking the same as the last one. 'We only saw Finn a coupla times, showing up on that noisy bike of his. But whenever he did make an appearance, he always got that big hug and kiss that'd make a grown man blush.'

Ryder had hated seeing Bree kiss another man—only to later learn it was her husband. The sight had put him in a foul mood that lasted a week, until he found out she was actually divorced from Finn. But that still didn't explain the reunion scene he'd witnessed.

'Why do you hate Finn?' Which was rare, when Charlie liked everyone and got on with everyone—except their neighbour Leo, and Finn.

'I never used too... But when their son got sick, Bree left Finn countless messages, that bugger never answered.'

'Some jobs you can't call people or up and leave. I know from my time in the Army, I was restricted from contacting anyone outside the mission.' It was a reminder that he needed to make time away from work to take in the places that his property had to offer. Except jungles. He wasn't keen on jungles. And he had the Army to thank for that.

'Yeah, nah.' Charlie shook his head, wearing a deep scowl. 'Finn wasn't in no Army. He was a Queensland stockman, who was gone for almost a year in Victoria. What job stops a fella from contacting his family for a year?'

'Finn knew Bree is an independent woman who is quite capable of looking after herself. Most military wives are the same.'

'But he left Bree to deal with little Liam's illness all on her own, with no word from him for ages. And when my great-grandson passed away, that mongrel finally shows up three weeks *after* the funeral.' Charlie huffed, his jaw locked as if seething with anger. 'But I saw it that day my granddaughter buried her son, she buried her soul with him, and Finn knew it, too.'

'You know Finn was away for work.' Ryder couldn't help but defend Finn, who'd been working undercover. But because Charlie couldn't keep a secret, no one had told him. 'And sometimes work—'

'No man should ever put their career before their *family*!' Charlie's stern words echoed around the forest, once again silencing the birds and the buzz of insects, leaving only the soft tread of their horses on the leaf-littered path, which released a rich, earthy aroma. 'I understand a man has to work to provide for his family. But they should always remember it's only a job. A man should never put their job, or money, before their family, especially when they needed them the most.'

As a self-made billionaire, Ryder fully understood how money changed a person, having seen it in those around him. It's why he never showed off that he had money, and why he never talked about money or how he made his money with his family. But he sure as hell made sure he provided for them. No matter the cost.

'But then the idiot gets so angry, he punches out this high-ranking copper and ends up in prison for assault. When Finn, that flamin' fool, should've been helping Bree get through her grief, or at least go through it with her.' Charlie wore such a pained expression as he tapped at his chest. 'That's what family does. Even if it's just to put the kettle on to make a cup of tea, while you sit quietly in the corner, you're there. Like Bree is always there for me, tinkering in the garden, helping me to go riding in the mornings, or stoking up the forge for me, or agreeing to come on this muster with me. When I lost my grandson, I know I grieved for that boy, just like Darcie did, because that small boy brought so much joy into our world, but I don't think Bree ever fully dealt with it.'

'What do you mean?'

'Bree never packed up Liam's room in the cottage. She locked it up and went straight back to work, choosing to let our guests crash on the couch instead.'

'So, the caretaker's cottage has three bedrooms?' Even though Charlie had offered him the spare room, Ryder had never set foot inside the place he owned.

But then it clicked—that spare room must've been Liam's!

No wonder Bree was furious at the thought of him taking over the cottage.

'The caretaker's cottage has three-and-a-half bedrooms. The smallest room was a nursery, when I moved in with my wife. I made it into a walk-in storeroom for my rodeo gear.

Now it's full of junk. I think Bree would love to turn it into a pantry and renovate the kitchen.'

Again, Charlie sighed, craning his neck at the leafy canopy where the sun sent down it's rays in between the gaps. 'Not long ago, right before he left, Finn was in Liam's room. You could see the fella was broken over it. Bree let him take what he wanted as a keepsake, then waved off Finn, locked the door to Liam's room again, and went back to work.' Charlie shook his heavy head once more, with his voice softening as he said, 'Bree might be tough, but that kid is worried about me leaving her.'

'Bree is very protective over you.' It was admirable.

'Because I'm the only one who's never abandoned her. That kid got abandoned by her father, who did the most terrible thing to a child. No child should ever witness their mother getting murdered by the person who was meant to show her love and protection. Then, as a grown-up, Bree's husband abandons her for his career and then prison, and then her son. When I go, well…'

The silence was as heavy as the thick humid air that clung to the sturdy tree trunks entangled with vines, as their horses criss-crossed another series of creek beds.

'I'll be there for Bree, Charlie.' Even if Bree wanted nothing from Ryder, he was damn well going to be there if she needed him. He would have done that anyway, without question.

'Thank you.' Charlie gave an affirmative nod. 'It's all a fella can ask.' Their horses climbed a steep sandy track to break through the trees and into open daylight. In the distance the solar panels lining the roof of the caretaker's sheds sparkled under the sun. 'We're home.' And they raced across the field to phone the police.

Fourteen

It had taken all day for the police to conduct their investigation inside the cave hidden at Cattleman's Keep. They had taken photos, methodically boxing and bagging up all the items, before finally zipping the skeletons into a pair of black body bags and taking them away in the town's one and only ambulance.

By the time Ryder drove Charlie back to the homestead, the sun was long gone. The deep rumbling engine of the Razorback announced their return to the sheds behind the caretaker's cottage, where he parked it beside Bree's bright yellow Kombi van.

A rich, savoury aroma of something baking filled the air, releasing hints of butter and herbs that blended beautifully with the subtle smokiness of roasting vegetables. Together, the scents created a mouth-watering medley, that was enough to make Ryder's tummy rumble.

'Smells like the kid is back from the muster.' Charlie grabbed his trusty tin mug and thermos from the back of the old bull catcher.

'They must have finished that muster in record time.' Carrying the esky and water cooler, Ryder followed Charlie down the concrete path lit by a row of solar-powered bollard lights.

'Bree doesn't muck around when she's head stockwoman. Come on, you must be hungry.' Charlie's bandy-legged swagger was heavy, reflecting how tired they both were as they passed the silent blacksmith shop on their right. The stables stood on their left with the grand view of the lush paddock, called Drover's Rest, that lay between them.

Through the wrought-iron gate, they entered the complex vegetable garden, with its crazy paved rock paths that led to the back of the stone cottage's entertainment area, which was lit up with outdoor fairy lights.

Ryder had been lucky enough to score an invitation to their Saturday pizza nights, twice. On those nights, the large pizza oven was ablaze, with Charlie using a long paddle to tend the pizzas, in between stoking its flames like a blacksmith's furnace.

Ryder had heard Bree call that pizza oven Charlie's outdoor oven, and some mornings the aroma of baking bread reached them all the way at the farmhouse to torture them.

It's where they found Bree working with a sizzling cast-iron frypan in the outdoor kitchen, with the large table set for dinner. 'Beer or gin?'

'Beer.' Ryder was grateful for the offer.

She handed them both an ice-cold beer.

Ryder thirstily chugged the bitter-tasting ale. It was just what he needed after a long day.

'Got enough tucker for the boss man, kid?'

'The boss, no. For Ryder, sure. Do you eat fish? Got some fresh barra.'

Ryder nodded. He'd gladly eat anything she cooked. 'I hear you guys go fishing in the mornings.'

'You betcha. That's when we're checking our cherabin pots in the Scary Forest, that's got some red claw, too. But this time of the year, them freshwater crustaceans like to burrow under for a bit. In a few months we'll have feasts again.' Charlie washed his hands at the outdoor sink.

By the time Ryder had washed and dried his hands, Bree had dished out plates of baked sweet potato, a fresh garden salad and thick barramundi steaks coated in garlic butter with a basket of fresh crusty bread. It was a struggle to stop salivating.

'Dig in, we deserve it.' Charlie sat at the head of the table. Bree was on his left, with Ryder opposite her.

As the outdoor widescreen played in the background, dinner conversation was light, as Charlie explained to Bree what had happened with the police. '... And I've asked Ryder to take a gander at the murder file.'

'Why?' Bree delicately placed her cutlery down on her empty plate, to sip from her glass of gin.

'Because I don't believe my brother is a murderer. Harry just never had it in him.'

'Have you read his letter yet?'

'Nah, I was waiting for you, kid.' Charlie dropped his cutlery onto his plate, then dragged the envelope out of his pocket. It was dirty and bent from Charlie staring at it all day, but he'd never opened it. 'The coppers would have wanted it for evidence, so we didn't tell 'em about it, not until we've read it first.'

Fully satiated, having cleaned up his second serving of food, Ryder went to move. 'I should go.'

'Nah, stay, son.' Charlie held Ryder's shoulder. 'It might help you if you're gonna look at the murder file.'

'Do you have the murder file?' Bree narrowed her green eyes at Ryder.

'Marcus is emailing me a copy. And no, I will not show you the pictures.'

'I don't want to see them.' Bree screwed her nose up. 'I may seem cold and callous, but I don't get any macabre kick out of peeking at photos of dead people, thank you.'

'Did I say you were?' Ryder grumbled back at her.

'Says the—'

'Play nice, kid.' Charlie pushed the envelope across the table. 'We should have a port for this. Do you want one, Ryder?'

Ryder hesitated, waiting for that smart-arse response from the redhead seated opposite.

'Even if you might consider it poor-man's plonk, it's a good port. We just don't do sugarcane champagne and cigars like you do, cupcake.'

Was she deliberately trying to get a rise out of him by using that nickname? Wait a second, what had Charlie said about her like for cupcakes?

Hmm, maybe she did like him, if she'd nicknamed him after her favourite food.

Nope, that cunning redhead did it to make him bite.

So he responded by frowning at her.

Of course, she matched his frown with a *don't give me that look!* 'Hey, what's that bottle Dex says only comes out for special occasions or commiserations?'

'The Master's Keep.'

'See…' Bree playfully wagged her finger, giving it a little twist for emphasis. 'Even the name says it's a boss man's drink. So be brave and have some port. It might surprise you.'

'Well, okay then, I'll have some poor-man's plonk.' He liked it when Bree played nice, with her grin barely curling across her lips.

Bree cleared the plates off the table, following Charlie into the house. Ryder grabbed the last of the serving dishes, to follow them inside. He never did this at the farmhouse, but he was a guest here, plus he was keen to see inside the cottage that was over a hundred years old.

Inside the temperature dropped a few degrees, but there were no fans on the low ceiling. The stained-glass windows that bookended the front door were open, allowing in the sweet scent of florals coming from Charlie's flower garden.

To his right stood a large kitchen with deep double sinks and a solid timber countertop. The lower cupboards were old and worn, and the overhead cupboards had no doors, but they were full of assorted vegetable and fruit preserves as if he'd stepped back into some homesteading era.

Ryder placed the serving tray on the impressive island bench made from one slab of timber. 'No dishwasher?' He'd bought one for Harper to use in the farmhouse kitchen because no one wanted to do dishes.

'I wish,' said Bree at the sink. 'It's a lifelong punishment, eh, Pop?'

'You've got two hands, kid.' Charlie winked at her as he grabbed some port glasses. 'Leave them for tomorrow, kid.'

'Don't need to tell me twice.' Bree dragged out a glass jug, which she filled with water from the large water cooler by the door. Above it stood a long rack of assorted hats and coats, that shaded an assortment of working boots.

'What's with you, cupcake? Are you here to do some property inspection as the land baron?' Bree put the water jug on the bench to cross her arms over her chest.

'It's the first time I've been inside.'

'You're kidding.'

'Nope.'

'Well, consider this your quick two-dollar tour of the caretaker's cottage.' She pointed to the open doorway on the right as Charlie rattled around in the kitchen. 'That's Charlie's room. As you can see the lounge and living area commands the centre space, where they used to have a fireplace.' Bree sounded like a real estate agent. 'Oh, and that's the best couch in the world.' She fluffed up some cushions against the long leather couch that ran beneath the stained-glass windows.

'So I've heard. I bet if I sat in that I'd fall asleep after that meal and this long day.'

Finally, she shared a sweet and soft smile that made it all the way to her pretty green eyes. 'I'd do the same.'

He then spotted the branding irons resting high on the wall the way someone would display their swords. 'You know that's our cattle brand, right?'

'Pfft. You need to talk to Charlie about that one.'

'I did. But the old man won't accept any bribes for it.'

Bree knew that, obviously, from her sly smile. The woman had a catalogue of smiles to suit every occasion—from sweet to sarcastic, sly to positively sinful.

Ryder pointed to a large black-and-white image on the wall of a man on a bucking bull. 'Is that you, Charlie?'

Rattling around in the cupboards, Charlie peeked over the counter. 'Yep. That's me and Buckshot. The bugger who made me retire from the rodeo.'

'Pop was the king of the rodeo, especially with bulls.'

'Like local champion?'

'Three times Australasian Champion, thank you.'

Charlie shrugged with a touch of regret, lowering his head and slowly rubbing the back of his thick neck.

'The Station Hand mentioned you were a rodeo champion…' Ryder took another look at the large bookcase, packed with rodeo trophies and shiny belt buckles. A gold-plated set of spurs, were set alongside a set of chaps and a rodeo rider's leather vest, encased in glass and hung like a prized portrait on the wall.

Yet again, it was the legacy brands that caught his eye. The one that belonged to Elsie Creek Station, that somehow Charlie owned. 'Who do the other two branding irons represent?'

'The top one is the Splint family brand. My father made that one for my brother.' Charlie cleared his throat as he wiped over his face. 'And the other one is the Wilde brand. I made that one for my, um, great-grandson.'

Neither of them were alive today.

'Shall we strike while the iron's hot and open this letter, Pop? So you can get some rest?'

'Yeah, let's do it, then we can put this cracker of a day to bed.' Carrying the bottle of port and glasses, Charlie hobbled outside, his weary walk showing his age, as the strain etched in the crevices of his sun-hardened face.

As Charlie poured the port, Bree turned off the TV, creating a heavy silence. Under the glow of fairy lights, a delicate tinkling sound came from a set of wind chimes caused by a soft breeze that carried the inviting scents from the nearby vegetable garden. It was enough for Ryder to sink heavily into his comfy outdoor chair, feeling the weight of a long day.

He sipped on the strong port Charlie passed to him, the

deep ruby liquid coating his tongue. It was rich and smooth, like velvet over his palate, carrying a quiet heat, spreading slowly through his chest. If he wasn't careful, he'd fall asleep here—he hadn't felt this level of comfort in a long time. 'Nice port.'

'Told you it was a good poor-man's plonk,' murmured Bree, as she opened the envelope, yellowed with age, that had long since lost its glue. Yet, the pages of the letter itself were surprisingly well-preserved.

'*Dear brother…*' She gave Charlie's hand a tender squeeze.

'Go on, kid. One clean strike, like you said—get it done.'

Bree lifted the pages and read aloud:

Hey, Splinter, it's Harry.

I've never been much for writing, so I'm sorry that I was left with little choice except to put this down in a letter when I really wanted to tell you this in person. But I wanted to avoid you giving me a good bollocksing for falling for a married woman, Penelope Price.

I didn't mean to fall in love with her. And neither did she. It just happened.

But, mate, that's what love does. It makes grown men do dumb things, and I know this might be the dumbest thing I've ever done. Yet it feels so flaming right.

I didn't expect to fall in love with her, or the amount of trouble that soon followed.

So, I'm just gonna be as blunt as can be…

Jack Price is not who he says he is. Jack Price was actually born Jake Blackwell. A deserter from the Army, who is wanted for stealing a truckload of shotguns.

'Wait.' Ryder lifted his hand. 'Is that why you've got so many shotguns stashed all over the place?' He asked the redhead sitting opposite him. 'That shottie of yours I fixed is a 1960 Winchester M12. Commonly used by the Army in that era.'

Bree barely shrugged.

Ryder tilted his head slightly, pressing his lips into a thin line. 'How many shotguns do you have?'

'Can we hold off on the questions till *after* she's finished reading the letter, please?' urged Charlie. 'Go on, kid.'

Bree adjusted the pages and went on:

The problem was Jack—or Jake—had sold those stolen guns to this mob down south. Instead of delivering them, like he'd promised, the scoundrel kept them and drove north. He met Penelope along the way, before getting a job here at the station as a stockman. He'd been a drover, mustering on various cattle stations in Queensland before he joined the Army. You always said Jack Price was a good head stockman for Elsie Creek Station.

'That I did.' Charlie gave a short nod.

Without missing a beat, Bree carried on:

'The only reason we found out that Jack was Jake was because Penelope and I found this huge stash of cash, inside these old army ammo tins, that were hidden in the floor of the caretaker's cottage. Her husband had been hoarding it from selling those stolen shotguns in the pub.

But now someone is after him.

There are some bad people looking for Jack, and it's got him worried. He's been drinking heavily, pacing the front of the caretaker's cottage with the shotgun at night like an armed guard, waiting for someone or something. And that mongrel has been taking it out on his wife.

Poor Penelope, the bruises he'd leave on her skin, no woman deserves that. So of course, I agreed to help her.

You see, when Penelope found that money, she searched the house for more clues and found Jack's passport. His real one, showing his true name as Jake Blackwell. She showed it to me on her birthday when I got her a special handbag for a present.'

'I bet he's talking about the handbag we found, when we relocated Carked-it,' said Bree, pausing to take a sip of water.

'I was thinking the same thing,' mumbled Ryder.

'I reckon you're both right,' said Charlie. 'Anyhoodle, keep going.' He waved his hand in circles at Bree as if to hurry her up with her reading.

Again, Bree flicked the pages of the letter and read aloud:

That's when we both realised, Penelope had not only married a liar, but if Jack Price didn't exist, then her marriage wasn't legitimate.

But finding that marriage certificate is taking a lot longer than we expected, and it's vital that we find it before we leave.

You see, Penelope believes Jack tricked her into marrying him so he could get a marriage certificate, that he then used to get a driver's licence under his new name. They were married at the courthouse where Penelope worked as a clerk, believing she was in love, looking forward to the adventure of moving north.

It was only later that Penelope realised that when Jack took her to the local police station, soon after they'd arrived in Elsie Creek, he'd used Penelope, unknowingly, as an accessory to help create his false identity, in a new state, before starting his new job at Elsie Creek Station.

So really, Penelope Price isn't a married woman.

But the thing is, if she isn't married to Jack, she'd have no right to any of his property, especially the money she'd found. Whereas I believe Pen bloody well deserves all the cash, just for what the mug put her through over the years.

I don't think Jack ever loved her. Not like I do. So know this, brother: Penelope is the woman I'm going to marry.

Our plan is to head to Queensland. We've got enough to buy a small farm. But first, Pen and I need to go to the police and tell them about Jack. We can't do that anywhere near Elsie Creek—not with Jack too close for comfort. Worse, I fear whoever is after Jack might use Penelope as bait to get to him.

We both know it'll take time for the authorities to work out if Pen's marriage is legitimate or not, and I'm willing to wait for as long as it takes. I've left her before to work as a linesman for the new telephone lines, I won't leave her behind again.

So, I've been working on this goldmine. It's not much, just a cave I've reinforced, but it had a rich vein of gold ore. I found it accidentally, chasing a calf when doing the boundary run. Back then it was only a crack in the wall, and being crumbly stuff, it fell away easily to reveal a cave.

It's where Pen and I would meet in secret. She'd ride through the monsoon forest, and I'd take the long way round. It became our place to be free, and to be together.

But that cave produced enough gold to leave some with you. Don't worry, Charlie, I've got plenty to start my new life with Pen, and well, the lady is loaded. I think she cleaned out Jack's stash of cash.

Anyhoodle, brother, we've got Jack's papers hidden in Pen's suitcase. She's sewn a hidden pocket in there, she's clever like that.

Just so you know, we haven't rushed this, because we found that cash in September, the same week I came back to work at the station, that's when Pen asked for my help to escape. We've had our bags packed since October. We have Jack's passport and all his other paperwork, both fake and real, we just need their marriage certificate. Once we have that, we'll be making a run for it, fast, which is why I'm writing this now to not forget.

We know Jack is a dangerous man and not to be trusted. I pray he doesn't take this out on you. So Pen and I reckon you should tell Darcie everything and stay as far away from Jack as you can, little brother.

As I write this letter, you're out mustering with Darcie, then you said you'll be droving for a while. Hopefully, you won't miss me much, until I can send word of where I am. Keep an ear out for the new telephones I installed at the homestead, as I'll call once we're settled.

Anyhoodle, the crate of gold I've left for you should clear all my debts, even if you wanted none of it back, but you were way too generous, little brother, with your rodeo winnings that you always shared with me. And you did help me buy my car we're using to run away. Just be sure to save some dosh from the gold, because I want you scrubbing up to be my best man, because, mate, I'm getting married.

In the meantime, take care, little brother. I'll be taking the family brand, so you'll always be with me. Keep your chin up, Splinter, and may your arse always sit well in that stockman's saddle, with that stockwhip whirling like the wind, as you keep an eye on an outback sunrise.

From your big brother,
Harry.

Bree folded up the letter, slid it back inside the envelope, and placed it in front of her grandfather. 'I don't know about you two, but that doesn't sound like a letter from a murderer.'

Fifteen

Even though she'd spent the past two days in the saddle, Bree galloped on Black Hand, skirting the far outer edges of Cattleman's Keep. Before her, the hazy horizon stretched out like a summer blanket, where the day's heatwaves had yet to meet the sun. Clusters of trees softly undulated like an olive-green ocean spreading southward, meeting a fortress of soft, custard-yellow ranges that lined up like an uneven row of eggs in a carton. It was the Stoneys.

Out here, there was nothing but pure countryside, void of any man-made sounds this far from the homestead, that somehow served a double dose of loneliness that sat heavily on her shoulders. A person could easily get lost out here.

Normally, Charlie would ride alongside her, but the old man was asleep and in dire need of rest. It had been a hard couple of days for her grandfather, with the muster, and finding his brother. Now all they could do was wait for the police, and plan Harry's final resting place.

Nudging the ever-energetic Black Hand forwards, Bree continued to check on the aftermath from yesterday's landslide.

So far, they'd been lucky enough to find it hadn't interfered with any of the creeks or the many free-falling waterfalls.

The last time they'd had an explosion of some kind—that led to a landslide—was when their neighbour, Leo, and his cronies had destroyed the wall of Starvation Dam. It's why she was visiting this man-made abomination today.

'Whoa up...'

Black Hand slid in the soft rubble. He loved to slide and had to be her best horse yet.

Leaving Black Hand in the shade to pick at the greenery, she scrambled up the dam's walls that efficiently captured the run-off from the extended limestone escarpment. From here, it channelled to other areas of the station to water the many troughs and crops.

Just shy of the height of a three-story building, the wind danced around her, as a lone, white-bellied sea eagle flew over her, its shadow stretched across the rocky ridge that made up the top of the dam's wall that was wide enough to drive the Razorback around.

The Riggs brothers had done a good job in repairing the dam. They'd made it twice the size and height, effectively capturing an area of water the size of a football field, while also allowing for the overflow to feed through to the Stoneys, just like it had always done.

As she walked around the top edge checking for any damage or telltale cracks in the dam wall, it gave her a grand view of the area. In the hazy distance lay Emu Plains, where a dirt track ran like a thick red ribbon through to the drafting yards, telling the story of yesterday's muster.

Bree was waiting to see which brother was going to ask her to be part of the cattle draft, which was silly when they all knew she'd say no. Not even her grandfather could talk her into spending another day in the drafting yards, not now that she'd officially retired from sucking up yard dust.

Ryder was also getting a little too cosy for her tastes, claiming Drover's Rest as his paddock, and then his sneaky house inspection on the cottage last night. Asking about a dishwasher as part of his plans to move in. Bah!

Even though she was grateful for what Ryder had done for Charlie yesterday, she'd also noticed Charlie had stopped calling Ryder *lad*, like he did with the other brothers, and had started calling him *son*.

Not even Cowboy Craig—who was like a son to Charlie—ever got called that. Charlie said *lad, fella, mate, bloke,* and so on, but never *son.* Yet, it came so easily to her grandfather that maybe Charlie hadn't noticed it. Had Ryder?

Bree didn't work for the Riggs brothers, and only saw them if she had to. The thing was, Ryder was getting harder and harder to avoid, that she hadn't expected Ryder to stay for dinner, like she hadn't expected that kiss at The Veil. And she hadn't expected to warm to his company, with that level of respect growing for a man she did not want.

Bree wanted no one.

She had her grandfather, who she was hoping would outlive her, and that was enough.

Bree couldn't be bothered with the graceless dance of dating. A long time ago she'd unsubscribed from the love library, because she didn't have the patience to go through that clumsy phase of getting to know someone new, suffering through that self-conscious time of working out boundaries, which meant a lot of awkward polite talk—like Dex and Sophie were going through now.

Falling in love, then falling out of love, made a woman deal with a lot of healing, loathing, alcoholic soul-searching, along with a decent bout of self-sabotaging just to survive the tragedy of love. Bree should know.

That's why she deliberately gave Ryder a hard time, hoping to drive him away.

Yet, if she was honest with herself, the first time they'd met—when Ryder and his brothers had arrived in their convoy of utes and trailers of boxes—she'd found the tall and broody a-hole attractive. His tousled brown hair, chiselled jaw, and untrusting icy stare were a potent combination, especially when he effortlessly exuded the unseen power of a man who could hold his ground. He was battle-worn, tough, and clever. And if she had a checklist to tick for rare alpha males, she was pretty sure Ryder would top that list, and he'd fight every other bastard to keep the title, too.

With his well-groomed beard framing a granite jaw, solid

square shoulders, and lips good enough to bite, Ryder was every one of her fantasies come to life—which was exactly why she had to keep her distance. Since then, she'd done everything to avoid getting within six feet of him, and never for longer than ten minutes at a time, if that.

She just hadn't expected Ryder to become attracted to the brutal ugliness of her smart mouth that never held back.

Was he like Leo? Who, no matter how much lip she gave their nasty neighbour, Leo, with his lethal mobster vibe, still kept asking her out. For Leo, it seemed like a game, a form of amusement. For Ryder? Well…

She kicked over a rock, and it rolled down the side of the dam wall, where it hit against something, giving an unnatural clunking sound.

She skidded down the rocky sides to where the dam wall met the open terrain to reach the spot where the rock she'd kicked had landed. And there she found a hidden PVC pipe, about four inches in diameter.

Grabbing her bushman's knife from its sheath on her belt, she hacked at the hard soil and dug around the black pipe that was deeply embedded inside the dam's wall.

'Black Hand?' She whistled for the horse, and it obediently trotted towards her. 'Good boy.' She patted his nose, and dug around in her saddlebags, to find his raisins as a reward. She also dragged out her phone and took a photo. Then, with the tip of her knife, she pierced the pipe and water spurted free. The pipe was running water directly from the dam.

Again, with her phone, she videotaped the scene. She then dragged out the thick gaffer tape she always kept in her saddlebags, along with other tools and equipment, repairing the hole to not waste any water. She then re-covered the pipe with dirt in case this was one of the brothers' projects.

But she was pretty sure she knew about all their projects.

After all, they'd each sought out her opinion at one time or other. And Charlie could never keep a secret, replaying his conversations with the boys nightly over dinner.

Bree's shadow spread over the red soils as she followed the channel of dirt that was well concealed. Every ten metres or so, she'd dig at the crusty soil to locate the irrigation pipe. With her horse behind her, she tracked the pipe's trail, until her heart dropped, as heated anger bristled across the back of her neck. 'You prick.'

The pipe ran under the fence to disappear into Leo's land!

Sheathing her knife back onto her belt, she loosely looped Black Hand's reins over the fence post, preparing to jump the fence and follow that pipeline.

BANG!

It was gunfire.

Her horse nickered, tugging on his reins.

'Yeah, I heard it.' It was enough for Bree to swing back into the saddle.

A red plane, with a straw broom painted on its underbelly, flew overhead, as another gunshot rang out: *BANG!*

Bree ducked from the looming shadow of the plane that was so close it sent a cascade of falling leaves, stripped from the treetops, as if suffering the turbulent wind of a massive dust devil.

The black stallion's sleek muscles rippled as it reared up, his nostrils flaring wide. Dust billowed up from the dry ground beneath its thrashing hooves, as Bree yanked the reins, trying to steady the panicked beast and held fast in the saddle. 'It's okay boy, it's okay.'

With her heart hammering, she wiped away the sweat from above her top lip, trying to soothe the horse. Bree recognised the red plane, heading in a north-westerly direction towards the homestead.

Repositioning her hold of the reins, she peered back at the dense scrub that made up her neighbour's land, but didn't spot anyone. But they had guns, were stealing water, and they weren't shy about shooting at planes, which meant only one thing.

It was too big to handle on her own.

'Dammit, I'm going to have to talk to Ryder, aren't I?'

Sixteen

Spread out over the boardroom table was Ryder's copy of the murder file. He'd re-read each interview, each witness statement, and the officer's investigation reports while making his own notes. But what held his attention the most were the various images of the actual murder scene itself. Together, it just didn't add up.

Through the open windows, Ryder heard loud rock music as if it were coming from the clouds.

'Do you hear that?' Ryder called out to Dex, who was working on the harvester inside the mechanical workshop.

'Yeah.' Using a rag, Dex wiped the grease from his hands as he walked out to meet the sun. 'You won't believe who it is, brother.' Dex pointed to the air, his cheesy grin growing, as a red plane skimmed above the shed's roof with a straw broom painted on its undercarriage. 'It's the *Wicked Witch of the Westerly Winds*.'

It was their cousin, Monet.

'Where's she going to land?' Dex asked, as rock music bellowed out of the plane as it circled wide over the homestead.

'On our driveway.'

'Since when is our driveway an airstrip?'

'Since you graded it. Apparently, our driveway doubles up as an airstrip when Leviathan Creek floods in the wet season.' Ryder couldn't imagine the dust bowl turning green and the dry Leviathan Creek flooding. But he was looking forward to it.

'Who told you that?' Dex asked.

'Monet did, when she flew in our parents, while you were having that brief vacation in the hospital. Our cousin has the wet season contract to make mail deliveries to remote cattle stations and said we're on the list.'

'Seriously?'

'Both Charlie and Monet have warned me that Leviathan Creek gets big and it's notorious for flash flooding. You remember Leviathan? It's where I picked up your car where you got that lift into town with Bree, in the Kombi van you said you'd never get into.' Ryder grinned at Dex, who scowled.

'The monstrosity that Bree had lacquered into my wall.'

Ryder chuckled. Only Bree would take a photo of the one and only vehicle his rev-head brother hated and use it as wallpaper to cover an entire wall in Dex's house. That woman knew exactly what she was doing, always stirring up his brother in their game.

'I've told Sophie to cover that picture of the Kombi with something else. Wish I hadn't. Every night there's over a hundred photos she wants me to look at.'

'How long do you think it'll be before Sophie stops playing paparazzi?' It was irritating.

'Listen, brother.' Dex stopped and faced Ryder. 'Sophie is just so excited over everything, and I don't want her to stop doing what she loves. In such a short time, I've seen how much she's improved. But Sophie is also sorry for what she did on the muster, and for getting into everyone's face with her camera. I know Harper and Mia told Sophie, on their ride back to the homestead yesterday. And well, Bree threatened to punch her out, just like you threatened to destroy her camera. Do you hate Sophie?'

Ryder shrugged. 'No, she's just annoying.'

'Bree said the same thing.'

Which would have to be one of the rare times Bree and Ryder agreed on anything.

'Bree reckons the only thing she has in common with Sophie is me.'

'That's true.' Ryder patted his brother's shoulder and held it for a moment. 'I only want to see you happy.'

'Sophie makes me happy.'

'I know that.' It's why he put up with the blonde and her camera.

'Enough about my love life, how's yours going?'

'Hmph.' Ryder frowned as they continued walking across the homestead, as the buzz of the red plane grew closer with Monet preparing to land.

'What's going on between you and Bree?'

'Nothing.'

Dex tilted his head at Ryder. 'You sure?'

Ryder said nothing, as per usual.

'I know you like her.'

As if he'd share how deeply he cared for Bree with Dex.

'Brother, I should warn you, Bree doesn't like anyone.'

'Yes, she does. Bree loves Charlie. She's nice to Harper and Mia, even Cap and his dogs. She spoils Mason, and you are like a brother to her. As for me…' He sighed, hooking his thumbs into the belt loops of his jeans as they stood on the side of the track to watch the plane make its descent. 'All we do is argue.'

'It's almost the same as how you used to argue with me until we made our peace.' This time it was Dex's turn to pat his shoulder.

But Ryder didn't think Bree would accept the type of peace he was willing to offer her.

Last night had been his first time sharing dinner with Bree and Charlie. The only other time they were seated at the same table was when her ex-husband Finn and Marcus, the local police sergeant, sat between them as they worked out a way to catch the cattle rustlers. She'd never fully forgiven him for accusing her of being a cattle thief. He couldn't really blame her for that.

The red plane dangled as if by a piece of invisible string

getting lower and lower, to then softly land on the red soil. The propellers created a dust storm that brushed against their skin like sandpaper. As the little red plane whizzed past, its wingspan took up the full width of the driveway, then raced down the length of the driveway, before it slowed down enough to turn and taxi towards them.

The engine silenced, and the twin propellers became still. The plane's door opened and out jumped Monet in her workboots, denim shorts and white workman's singlet. Her blonde pixie haircut ruffled in the wind, wearing her aviator shades that made her look effortlessly cool. 'You won't believe what your mongrel neighbour just did.'

'Hello to you too, Monet.' Dex gave her a hug. 'Jeez, I remember when you were this—Nah, you never did grow, eh?'

'Leave off.' She playfully shoved Dex aside and nodded at Ryder. 'Hey, Ryder. How come you never age?'

'Monet.' He gave his little cousin a brotherly peck on her cheek. 'What did you say about the neighbours?'

'The prick shot at me. I'm taking Leo and his station off my Christmas mail run this year.'

'*What the flip!*' Dex scowled with open anger.

While Ryder's well-trained defence mechanism kicked in, protecting him from feeling the fear and concern that he didn't allow himself to show easily. It's what earned him the title of having ice in his veins. 'Are you sure it was Leo who shot at you?' Leo wouldn't be stupid enough to take pot shots like that, would he? It was so unlike Leo to do this. 'You actually saw Leo raise a weapon?'

'I know Leo Travers. He's the sweet-talking, Armani suit–wearing, black-hatted mongrel who shot at my plane.' Monet tenderly patted the body of the red plane as if walking around a horse. 'I was cutting through on my way back home after doing mail deliveries—'

'And you thought you'd check out the neighbour's yard?' Dex cocked an eyebrow at their cheeky cousin.

Monet ripped off her glasses. 'I knew it.' She pointed to

the edge of the wing, where the shattered carbon-poly fibres splintered like timber. 'That prick shot me.'

'You could have been *killed!*' Dex's voice echoed around the plane.

It was enough for the blood to pump a little harder inside Ryder's chest, while outwardly he remained tightly controlled. Yet his body became tense, with his jaw clenched, to avoid a rare explosion of emotion.

'I'm okay. Don't sweat it guys. I'm just looking for a quick patch up and a cup of tea?' Monet seemed completely unbothered by it all.

It was enough to simmer the edge off Ryder's temper. But it didn't stop his mind from channelling that unwanted emotion into formulating a plan, by leaning into his military training—that was calculated, efficient, and protective. It made it easier to keep his emotions at bay, by focusing on a strategy to defend or attack.

'I've got some epoxy in the shed to fix that,' said Dex, looking at the damage.

'No. It's not a car, it's a plane. Grab the foam gap filler, duct tape, a couple of clamps, sandpaper and that bathroom sealant we used for your place,' ordered Ryder, inspecting the wing. 'We'll patch it up enough to get you home.'

'I'll be right back.' Dex ran back to the shed with the same easy gait. Even though he'd retired from professional street fighting, Dex still trained in the mornings, keeping in fighting shape.

'I'd better ring Tim and tell him I'm going to be home late.' Monet dragged out her mobile phone.

Ryder leaned in closer to check the plane's underbelly. The wing might not have much damage, but they could've hit the fuel tank, or damaged one of the propellers, making her lose control.

On the landing gear, he pulled out a thick bunch of leafy twigs.

'How low were you flying, Monet?' Fully aware of her daredevil antics in the sky.

'Um, you know…' She shrugged. 'And before you ask, I didn't see anything. I heard the shots and got out of there quick.'

'How many shots were fired.'

'Two.'

'A warning shot and then this.' He tapped on the wing. Again, rage bubbled inside, urging him to confront Leo.

But Ryder never allowed his temper to take control. The only time he'd ever reacted with heat that he could barely contain, was when he'd learned Bree had been attacked by a crocodile. In that instance, he was ready to load up his assault rifles and go hunting with a grenade launcher. Even though his brother Dex had assured him Bree was fine, it was then Ryder had realised how deeply he cared for Bree.

Oh, and then there was the time he'd accused Bree of stealing their cattle. He deserved that slap that had stung for hours. At the time, he'd been so furious about losing his stock, overwhelmed by helplessness, and Bree, who'd been out all night, and not knowing where she was, the worry hit him harder than expected, forcing him to realise just how deeply he did care for her. Accusing her of stealing their cattle had been a dumb move. Not telling her sooner how much she meant to him—even dumber. But what really stung was how long it had taken him to figure it out.

'Don't stress, cousin, I'm good. I swear it.' Pushing her sunglasses higher through her short blonde hair, Monet gave him a cheeky smile, raising her phone in the air. 'No bars… Your intranet isn't set up yet?'

'Soon. It'll be fully functioning before the wet season—we're just waiting on the steel to build the towers. Then we'll have internet through the system, but mobile reception is still a no-go out here.' Ryder continued to inspect the red plane's outer shell to ensure there was no other damage. 'Harper has a landline in the house you can use to call Tim. And you're more than welcome to stay for dinner? Or overnight?'

'Is Charlie and Bree home? Charlie makes the best cuppa and Bree's always good for a chinwag and some cake.'

'It might be best to leave them be for a bit.' Ryder peered back to the silent cottage. No smoke filtered from the blacksmith's forge.

'Why? What's going on? Are they okay?'

He slid his hand into the pockets of his jeans, and sighed, successfully putting a lid on his temper. 'We found Charlie's brother yesterday.'

'Is that the one who murdered this station's head stockman over sixty years ago?'

'You obviously know the story.' It didn't surprise him, because Monet knew all the gossip in this region. 'We found his remains out near Rijidij Dugout.'

'Oh, man, that's rough. How is Charlie taking it?'

'He's pretty upset.'

Monet sighed. 'Well, according to Mickey, the master of all things mechanical, his number one hobby is listening in on the airwaves at the town's airstrip, and he told me he'd heard the cops had been called out to Elsie Creek Station.'

'Which is why you're here to find out what's going on.'

'No.' But her cheesy grin said *yes*. 'Your mother said for me to keep an eye on you guys.'

'Monet, I'm pretty sure we're big enough and ugly enough to look after ourselves.' He messed up her hair like the little girl he remembered.

'Hey, I'm not six, you know.' She straightened up her hair. 'I honestly was on my way back from making deliveries, and ever since Jonathan told me how your neighbour was after your water, I make a point of doing a fly-by whenever I can. I guess this time I got a bit too close, eh?'

'If I were you, I'd take photos of the damage before Dex repairs it.'

'It's just a scratch.'

He frowned at his petite cousin. 'Monet, the prick *shot at your plane*. If you don't make a report, I will.' She was family.

'Okay, okay. I usually only take photos of my plane for my social media accounts, not this. But hey, I'm sure this will generate some public interest, right? Not every day I get shot at.' With camera in hand, she took selfies of her and her plane. Nothing like crime scene shots at all.

After scouring the police murder file all morning, he was learning fast how they liked to keep it all neatly compiled, so he took out his own phone, to take detailed photos that included the date and time for evidence. 'Please tell Tim about the plane being shot at *before* you post those images to social media.'

'Aw, yeah…' Monet screwed up her button nose. 'Tim got cranky at me last time. Hey, how did the muster go?'

'How did you know about that?' *Nice change of subject, cousin.*

'I spotted Charlie in the pub with Bree the other day when they were getting supplies. Charlie was excited. I like how you take Charlie with you. You know he's got the best stories.'

'I've noticed. Bree and my brothers finished the muster yesterday.' While Ryder spent the day with Charlie and the police. He'd felt bad for Charlie, who'd been quiet all day at the cave, watching the coming and goings of the police, while standing guard over his brother's skeleton.

'So, you'll be doing the drafting next, huh?'

Ryder nodded. 'Do you know of any kid who wants a job as a station hand. We need someone to help in the drafting yards. You know the usual jobs of cleaning troughs, fencing, and looking after the stockhorses.'

'You should ask Bree. She's always getting applications for station workers emailed to the official Elsie Creek Station email address.'

'The what?' It's the first he'd heard about this.

'It's the one Bree uses to get included in my wet season mail runs when the front creek gets flooded. Don't you talk to Bree?'

Not as much as he'd like to. 'I talk to Charlie, or should I say Charlie's always talking to me?'

'You should talk to Bree.'

'And how do I keep Bree still long enough for a

conversation, that doesn't involve gin? Where Bree then says she's off the clock and won't talk about work.'

'Cupcakes. Everyone knows Bree likes her cupcakes.'

He hated that word!

Dex roared towards them on the quad bike with assorted tools sitting in the crate strapped to the back. 'Ready to give this plane a bit of a tickle?'

'I'm so sorry, Gertrude.' Monet tenderly stroked the wing of her plane as if it were an injured animal.

'Don't worry, Monet, your plane is in good hands,' said Ryder. 'I'm going to call Harper.'

'What for?' Dex dragged out the orbital sander.

'I want her to bring something back from town. Monet, I'll also be calling the police and emailing them my photos of this incident.'

'Say hi to Marcus for me and tell him not to stress.' Monet was so casual about the shooting. She was more interested in assisting Dex patching up her plane.

'Do you want to talk to the police?'

'No. You can. Then you can tell me what they want me to do. If I need to make a statement, I'll email them, or Marcus can meet me at the town's airstrip later in the week.'

At the farmhouse's front steps, the large shepherd eagerly greeted him. 'G'day Sarge.' Ryder patted the staunch soldier who often kept him company long after the others had gone to bed.

As he opened the front screen door, the pitter-patter of another ex-police dog greeted him. It was the beagle traipsing down the corridor. 'Hey, Scout.' He patted the friendly beagle.

Nearby, the fat cream labrador thumped her tail from her fancy dog bed. 'Ruby, I see you're off the clock.'

Scout and Ruby had become pampered house pets, with Harper giving them fancy-smelling shampoos, leads, and collars, probably as a reward for enjoying Harper's regular gastronomical failures.

But not the shepherd. Sarge never came inside, dutifully

manning his post on the front corner of the verandah. He wasn't a pet. He was a soldier.

The screen door shut behind him, the childproof latch clamping down in place. The lounge room was free from the boxes that used to crowd this space, now held a lounge suite, a large mat, along with a set of dog beds, Dex's old TV, and a big box full of toys for the toddler.

The kitchen had a dining table Bree had found for Harper. The old kitchen table, which they'd pinched from day one, still sat out the front of the house, even though they rarely used it now, preferring their new boardroom and bar space in the shed.

Unlike the caretaker's cottage—where the walls were covered in various historical images, rodeo paraphernalia and branding irons—the farmhouse didn't have a single painting or a picture hanging on the faded walls to show it housed a family. But they had a hallway lined with assorted wide-brimmed hats. All of them were Harper's.

With the large kitchen on his left, the bedrooms ran along the right. At the end of the hall was Ryder's room.

Inside, his large bed was made every day, a habit from the Army. A desk stood in the corner, but he rarely used it now that Bree had made him his office. He only came in here to sleep—if he slept—or to use the spare cordless phone. He didn't know where the other handset was, and didn't want to spend the next hour looking for the thing.

He dialled a number, as he uploaded his images of Monet's plane.

'Elsie Creek Police.' The deep voice over the phone's speaker was stern, as if prepared for bad news.

'G'day, Marcus.'

'Hey, Ryder, thanks for emailing me that letter last night. We found the paperwork inside the suitcase's lining, just like it said.'

'How is the investigation going?'

'I pulled Porter off road duties to work on the case full-time. He's got a lot of evidence to crawl through.'

'Why? It's not an urgent matter.' It was a sixty-year-old cold case in some ways. And the only reason Porter had reopened the file in the first place was to gain experience for his detective's qualifications.

'I'm doing it for Charlie and Bree. They're good people, who've helped me and my family plenty of times over the years. Porter is a family friend of theirs, and I know he's keen to give Charlie some answers.'

'I'm calling on another matter…' And he explained to Marcus about Leo shooting at Monet's plane. 'Monet isn't upset about it, but that prick clipped her wing.' Outwardly he may not show any emotion, inside it ticked him off big time. 'I'm emailing you the photos I took of the damage. Monet has her own, that I think she's going to post to social media.'

'Monet would. She's become an online influencer, and she never really takes things seriously.'

'I know. Which is why I'm calling you myself.' Ryder doubted Monet would take it any further, but her partner, Tim, wouldn't hesitate to load up his guns once he heard about this and confront Leo—which is probably why Monet was playing down the incident.

'You're a pilot. Is that plane safe for Monet to fly?' Marcus asked.

'Dex is fixing the wing now. It's mostly cosmetic damage. It won't interfere with any of the plane's capabilities to get her home. Otherwise, I'd ground her myself. But our little cousin is in good spirits, keen to get home.'

'Well, I learned a long time ago that Monet plays by her own rules, but she always means well.' Marcus exhaled heavily, and Ryder could picture the no-nonsense senior sergeant rubbing the back of his neck with concern. 'So, I'm guessing you have a request over this plane shooting?'

'I want Monet to file a complaint, but I'd like you to keep it off any official police action just for a bit.' Ryder knew he'd get Monet to comply, but Marcus was another matter.

'Why? You know I have a job to do, mate.'

'I still haven't worked out Leo's endgame, but I know he's

up to something. He's been trying to block us with his lawyers—'

'But he's taking *pot shots at planes!*'

'Bree does it here if Ash's drone gets too close to her backyard.'

Marcus chuckled, defusing the heavy mood. 'Bree would.'

'And Leo could argue he was just protecting his property.'

'Leo doesn't own the airspace.'

'Look, I found some leaf debris twisted around Monet's landing gear, and how she pilots her plane—'

'Pushing it to the limits, you mean.'

'I'd say Monet flew that plane too low, and likely breached some Civil Aviation Safety Authority regulations. Leo could use that against her.'

'Ah. Right. I see...' Marcus paused. Something squeaked in the background, like he was rocking in his chair behind his desk.

Ryder inhaled before broaching his next sentence. 'Have you spoken to Finn lately?' Finn was involved with the Federal Stock Squad and had helped them catch the cattle rustlers and recover their stolen cattle.

'No. Why?'

'Finn mentioned he was going to do some digging about Leo. At the fights he mentioned that he knew who Leo was.'

'I must have missed that conversation. Do you want me to reach out to Finn?'

'If you could.' Not that Ryder wanted to contact Bree's ex-husband, but it's all he had. 'Finn told me that Leo works for some southern gang who smuggled drugs and other goods into the country through the docks.'

Whack! It had to be Marcus, sitting up in his chair. 'I definitely missed that conversation. And you're only telling me this now?' In the background, Marcus shuffled paperwork across his desk, probably looking for Finn's number or an email address. 'What else did Finn say?'

'That Leo had only gained the property from a debt that had to be paid. The thing is, Leo is cunning enough to trick a person into creating that debt in the first place. But Finn seemed to believe that Leo wasn't here for the lithium mine.'

'What do you think Leo is here for?'

'Not sure. But we must be getting close if he's shooting at planes. But it's also not like Leo to be so clumsy like this, by drawing attention to himself. Leo is usually a lot more calculating than this.' Ryder believed it.

'Did Monet see anything?'

'No.'

'I know we didn't see anything when Finn used the drone over the property.'

'You guys were looking for cattle, and you used a heat-seeking drone.' But he was going to get Ash to use his favourite toy to take another look.

'Don't do anything foolish, Ryder.'

Seventeen

At the open doorway of the newly renovated boys' boardroom, Bree hesitated. She couldn't believe she was about to do this. All day, she'd been avoiding the Riggs brothers—helping Charlie, sorting out orders, and trying to figure out why Leo was stealing water from the dam.

She'd assumed Monet had already told them about the gunshots. Letting them stew over that for a few hours had seemed wise, especially if she was about to add fuel to the fire by mentioning the sneaky pipeline.

Even though Bree was used to handling problems on her own, they needed to know.

She leaned against the doorjamb where Dex and Ryder were busy with some paperwork. 'Knock. Knock. Hello, children, and what mischief have we been up to today?'

'Bree?' Ryder was holding a black-and-white photo. He didn't just glance at her, he gave her a full-minute detailed inspection.

She felt positively naked in her welding pants and sweaty work shirt, that he'd made sexy under that glare—until she recognised the man in the photo Ryder was holding.

'What are you doing with my great-uncle's photo? And this room?' It might not be hers, but she'd spent a lot of time and effort creating it for Ryder. They'd pushed the workbenches to one side to clear the floor space. That's when it clicked. 'You're going over the murder scene.'

The last time anyone had tried to map out the murder scene was when she'd interrupted Policeman Porter and Charlie, back when Dex was dragging around an oxygen tank like a puppy.

At that stage she'd been more worried about getting busted for her illegal gin still than a sixty-year-old murder mystery, especially when she'd assumed her Great-Uncle Harry had done the wrong thing.

Oh, how wrong she'd been.

It was enough to make her roll her heavy shoulders where guilt had nestled in for the long haul, for ever thinking badly of Harry like that, and for not believing her grandfather in the first place. It was enough for her to call a truce of sorts, to try and play nice with Ryder so she could get involved in solving this murder mystery, in the hope of clearing her great-uncle's name.

'We are. And I had these brought in for you.' Ryder lifted the lid of a white cardboard cakebox, its edges slightly frayed from being jostled around, but the contents inside were nothing short of perfect: a dozen cupcakes.

Oh, heavenly sweet cakes. 'Are these train station Lucy's cupcakes?'

Ryder shrugged.

She narrowed her eyes at the man who she'd never imagined holding a cakebox filled with assorted scrumptious cupcakes that sang sweet promises full of flavour. Oh, how she loved those dainty, feel-good party cakes.

Hold on. Had someone told Ryder about her love for cupcakes?

'What do you want?' She narrowed her eyes at the cunning male.

'I just want to talk.' Ryder even pulled out a chair for her to take a seat at the table.

'What about?'

'I have a list.'

'You always have a list.' She pointed to his large whiteboard listing out the station's various projects. It was a to-do list that never ended.

'This is a different list.' The ways his hips swayed as he walked with those strong thighs, was a thirst trap as he approached the coffee machine.

Now that's how you wear a pair of jeans.

'Coffee?'

'Sure.' She dropped into her seat, anything to stop looking at Ryder. 'Are you in on this too, Dex?'

'Would you shoot me if I was? But I wasn't.'

'Go on, eat one.' Ryder put a coffee mug down in front of her and dragged the cakebox closer. She could smell their divine sweetness, each one uniquely decorated, promising a burst of flavour.

There was a rich red velvet cupcake, its crimson hue highlighted by a swirl of velvety cream-cheese frosting. Next to it, a chocolate ganache glistened like liquid silk beneath a delicate chocolate curl. There was a lemon meringue, perched atop a zesty lemon base. A coffee and walnut creation stood near the white chocolate glossy glazed cupcake, and so many more. Bree's mouth watered.

The big man then placed one of the fluffy, buttery delicacies on a napkin and gently placed it in her hands. 'Eat.'

No one did that for her. Leaving her to marvel at how gentle Ryder was with his touch.

'If you insist...' She grinned as she used the tip of her finger to taste the butter cream and recited her favourite prayer. 'Dearly beloved, we are gathered here today to join these mixed groups of sugars in the holy art of cupcake heaven. May our cholesterol and blood pressure remain steady for another day.' Bree bit into her frosty cupcake, her eyes rolling with pleasure.

Dex sniggered behind his mug as he rocked on his chair. But it was Ryder's deep chuckle that did something to her insides, especially when his eyes crinkled with amusement.

She washed it down with a mouthful of coffee. They made good coffee. 'Well okay then, seeing as how I'm always up for bribery and corruption,' she said, guessing this was their master plan, 'we'll go question for question. You can ask me something, and then I'll ask you something.'

'Deal.' Ryder said that way too fast, when he usually preferred to answer questions with a question, to avoid spilling the details.

'Do you want a cupcake, cupcake?' Never had she been more satisfied with his *do not test me glare*.

'Do you have the email address for Elsie Creek Station?'

'I do.' She pinched a piece of paper and a pen off the boardroom table and scribbled down the details. 'This is the sign-in, and the password. I used to monitor it for Darcie and Charlie to manage the station's correspondence and bills, and I've been babysitting it at the request of the trust lawyer.'

'Why didn't you tell us sooner?'

'You never asked. And I kept forgetting.' She took another bite of her delicious cupcake. It was a rich and moist carrot cake, made with almond flour and coconut oil that was such a delicious combination, she'd eat a dozen if she wasn't careful. 'My turn. Was Monet here earlier? I saw her plane flying over.'

'She was here.' Ryder's scowl was ferocious, with Dex's just as bad.

Bree used the napkin to brush away the crumbs. 'What's going on, Dex?'

'Leo shot at Monet's plane, clipped her wing. I had to repair it before she could fly home.'

'Is Monet okay?' She leaned forward, full of concern. Not only was Monet their favourite bush pilot, but Monet was also a friend of the family who loved her cocktails and music as much as Bree did. Liquid lunches with Monet had been known to roll into days.

'Monet's fine,' replied Dex. 'She went home.'

'Good.' Bree calmed her fears, licking the icing from her fingers, well aware that the following words were going to push their buttons. 'I heard those gunshots.'

Eighteen

The woman was pure evil, sitting on the other side of their boardroom table, teasing Ryder with her freaking cupcakes.

Cup. Cakes.

Tiny little cakes with creamy icing, made from sweet and floury ingredients to create cupcakes.

But the way Bree was eating them was pure torture. She gave a small sexy moan, with her eyes rolling every time she took a bite of the cupcake. The sound had him shifting in his seat.

But when she started licking the cream from her fingers, his stomach and brain dropped to his groin. He couldn't think of anything else.

But it got worse.

Much. Worse.

That tiny tip of her pink tongue flicked along her luscious lips. It forced him to gulp down his searing hot coffee to try and control a once very calm, controlled, and emotionless person. But not with Bree. He always struggled when it came to Bree. It was like she was defrosting his defences that had once been filled with ice, was now flushed with the heated desire to pick that redhead up by her hips, while swiping the junk from the table, to lay her down and have his wicked way with her.

If Dex wasn't in the room Ryder might have lost control over his emotions—which never happened. But when it came to Bree…

Until she dropped the bomb. Like she always did. 'I heard those gunshots.'

'Where the hell were you?' Ryder leaned over the table, his hands in fists, his heart hammering in fear for the redhead calmly eating a freaking cupcake on the other side of the table.

'Out riding.'

'Give me details, Bree.' He ground his teeth, noting the irony at how some days it was like pulling teeth to get a straight answer out of her.

'I was riding along the east side checking for any damage from the landslide.'

'You were at Starvation Dam.'

'Correct.' For once, it was a straight answer. Even if she used her fingertip to scoop some cupcake cream that she then popped into her mouth and sucked. *Slooowly.*

Ryder roughly rubbed a hand over his face to concentrate. 'And?'

'The last time the station suffered a landslide was when Leo and his band of balding gorilla's damaged the dam.'

Ryder glanced at Dex. They hadn't thought of that.

'Don't stress, boys, the dam is fine. But…' Then those luscious lips parted, her mouth widened to take another bite of her cupcake, where she chewed with shiny eyes.

The dramatic pause was driving him nuts.

And she knew it!

'Bree?' Ryder's scowl got deeper—as did his voice. How in the hell did the simplicity of Bree eating a cupcake become the sexiest thing he'd ever seen on a woman. Who knew there was such a thing as seduction by cupcake!

But then Bree dusted her hands, her humour swapped with the sexy serious side of Bree. And that had him worried.

'What did you find?'

'One very long, industrial irrigation pipe.' She scrolled through her phone to bring up a set of images and, without hesitation, she handed it over. 'The irrigation pipe is embedded deep into the dam's wall, then buried under the topsoil. It was pure luck I found it.'

'And you followed it? To where?' Because that's what Bree did. She was fearless. And that had Ryder worried enough to start giving him ulcers. But at least Bree had come to them first and not gone off on her own — which was a big move for the brassy redhead who was so stubbornly independent. The woman set crocodile traps before breakfast, but here she was doing a show-and-tell.

'I'll give you one guess where it ran to.'

'Leo's.' Ryder raked fingers through his hair.

'Correct, cupcake. Don't you get a gold star for being king of the class?' She grinned, dragging over the station's map that lived on the table. 'I found the pipe here, and it runs in this direction. From the fence line, I saw nothing, no cameras, just yours. But I heard the two shots fired here.' Using the map, she tapped at the station's eastern border. 'Monet flew over me, coming from the same direction where that little itty-bitty irrigation pipe had disappeared into the scrublands. Now what do you boys think Leo's doing in there if he's game enough to shoot at planes?'

'He's growing dope,' Dex said with a scowl.

'Aww, look who gets named dux of the class.'

Not Dex. He may have been expelled from school, but Dex was the underworld's bare-knuckle champion, regularly known for brushing shoulders with the seedier side of life, who didn't mind the recreational weed.

'How big a crop are we talking about?' Ryder asked Dex.

'It must be substantial enough for Leo to steal our water supply like that.'

'Did Finn ever mention anything to you about Leo?' Ryder asked Bree, who double-blinked at him, as if struggling to understand how calmly her ex-husband fit in their conversation.

What would Finn say to Ryder about sneaking in kisses with Bree?

'Finn warned me to watch my arse with Leo and to stay

away from him.' She then sat forward, to play with the handle of her coffee cup. 'But I have a theory, if you want to hear it?'

Hell, yeah! 'Sure.'

'It's about time,' mumbled Dex. 'Don't hold back.'

'Do I ever?' She gave Dex a grin. 'Is it true Leo's lawyers are always fighting you?'

'Correct.'

'It'd have to be costly keeping a legal team on a retainer like that.'

It was costing Ryder a fair chunk, too.

'Out of all the legal matters that Leo is contesting, like the turkey nests and carbon credit scheme, does he have any chance of winning? Or is he just doing it to waste your time and money?'

Ryder rubbed the back of his neck. He was getting daily emails over some trivial matter from Leo's lawyers. But the way Bree was watching him, she was seeing it from another angle. Bree also had the clever skill of reading people, too. 'Do you think Leo is using the lawyers as a distraction for something else? You've known Leo a while—you'd know who we're dealing with?'

The corner of her lips barely curled, subtly indicating she knew a hell of a lot more than she was letting on. 'I think Leo's up to plenty of naughty things—like laundering money to pay for his lawyers while relishing the game of pissing you off.'

'Dammit!' He stood so fast his chair flung back against the wall, gripping the top of his head as all those pieces fell into place.

'What?' Dex stopped swinging, to sit forward with a hard clunk on his chair.

Ryder started pacing the length of the room. 'I can't believe I didn't see it sooner.'

'It'd be nice if you shared with the rest of the class, cupcake.'

'Tell me if this makes sense... Leo is growing a cash crop

and working for another organisation while owning a run-down cattle station. Publicly, he's claiming to build a lithium mine and painting us as the enemy in a legal battle over water and land zoning. He's keeping us distracted while using the so-called mine to launder money—funnelling cash from illegal activities through fake contractors and investments tied to the project. And where's that money going? Some of it pays his lawyers to keep the pressure on us.'

'It makes sense to me.' Bree nodded at Ryder. The intelligence on this woman was just another tick as to why she fascinated him so much.

After this conversation, he was going to buy her a dozen cupcakes. Jeez, at this rate, he may as well find a decent cupcake recipe to get up at sunrise to bake the things when Charlie was baking his bread.

'Here, I can't eat them all.' She pushed the cakebox towards Dex.

'Nah, Ryder bought these for you.'

She arched her eyebrows at him in disbelief.

Hell, yeah. He was definitely going to buy her more just for the conversation.

'Bribery will only get you so many places.'

Oh, honey, if you only knew the places I want to explore with you.

When she took another bite of her small cake, her eyes rolling at the heavenly flavour, he couldn't stop watching.

'The Station Hand's wife, Queen Elizabeth, made this one, I can tell. She's perfected the red velvet cupcake.' Bree washed it down with a sip of her coffee. 'So, who's up for a sneaky midnight visit to the neighbours?'

And there it was. The real reason why Bree was here telling all—she didn't want to do this on her own.

Nineteen

'I'm surprised you didn't jump the fence.' Dex grinned at Bree while rocking in his chair.

It didn't stop Ryder from scowling at her. 'I bet you were thinking about it.'

She hated how Ryder could read her so well. So what if she had contemplated jumping the fence. She normally would have. If caught, she would've made some lame excuse about searching for cattle or her dog had run off.

'But you heard those shots…' Ryder let the obvious hang in the air.

'And got my sweet arse out of there.' It's why she was here. The cupcakes were a bonus she hadn't expected. 'Have you spoken to the police today?'

Ryder nodded. 'They found Jack Price's real passport in the suitcase lining and Marcus has got Porter working on the case full-time.'

'Good. That'll make Charlie happy.'

'How is Charlie today?' Ryder's swapped his scowl for a look of concern. It was obvious how much Ryder cared for her grandfather.

'Charlie is having a rest day, watching black-and-white Western movies in bed, while eating his favourite snacks. I doubt Pop will need dinner, and neither will I if I keep eating these cupcakes.' She closed the lid and pushed the box across the table towards Ryder.

'I'll stash them in our fridge for later.' Ryder got out a

large marker and wrote: *Bree's Cupcakes. Do not touch unless you want to lose your fingers!* The definitive stabbing motion he made for the exclamation mark on the box showed he meant business.

Dammmn, that's hot! 'That's subtle, cupcake.'

'Ash and Cap would wolf them down in a second if they saw them.'

She tilted her head as she watched him put the box into their fridge. The view of his arse in those jeans was delectable.

But this was Ryder. And that was a no-go!

'As we're waiting for the sunlight to disappear, so we can do the sneaky fence hopping—'

'You're staying.' Ryder slammed the fridge shut, as if making the decision final.

'You need me to show you where that irrigation pipe is. Look, cupcake, consider it my reward for actually listening to you for once, by *not* jumping the fence in broad daylight. Instead, here I am, informing management of what's going on like a good little girl.' They'd better not pat her on the head, or she'd have some stern words to spill.

Ryder narrowed his eyes at her. 'If you really want to be a good girl,' he said to the bad girl, 'we'd like you to do the cattle draft calls.'

And there it was. She'd been waiting for this.

'We could really use your help, Bree,' pleaded Dex from the far end of the table.

'That's Charlie's job. I've retired from the pound.'

'We know,' said Ryder. 'But Charlie told me, only yesterday, that you do a much better job at the drafting calls than him.'

She was not taking this away from Charlie. That old man loved being a stockman. It was the reason he jumped out of bed in the mornings, to play stockman on a cattle station— except for today. 'I don't work for you boys.'

'But I'll pay you for your time, and I'm hoping you might know of a young jackeroo to run the pound and do some other jobs around the place.'

She arched an eyebrow.

It was time they got help. A cattle station of this size, when in full operation, should have over a dozen full-time staff—ringers, station hands, stockmen, fencers, bore runners, feed-lot handlers and more. 'That's a really good idea, guys.'

Ryder and Dex looked at her in disbelief at the rare compliment.

'As much as you boys think you're sun-fuelled Supermen, immune to kryptonite, as station owners you have other responsibilities to focus on than dealing with daily menial tasks.'

Plus, if they got someone in, it would save her shins, sinuses, and her sanity from manning those drafting gates.

'Where would they camp?' Dex asked.

'You could lend them your old tent you used to live in. Wait, I burnt that in my cauldron, in some midnight ritual to the gods.'

'Witch.' Dex grinned at her as he rocked in his chair.

'You could use the ringers' rooms.' She pointed to the open door. 'It's the structure at the far the end of the stables.'

'I haven't gone in there yet,' said Dex.

'Me neither.' With hands on his denim hips, Ryder surveyed the area through the open door. His silhouette was strong, his hands even stronger as they rested on those hips.

How could the view of a tall and broody male, simply walking with those sturdy thighs and hips, become so sexy?

'How many rooms are there?' Ryder slid into his seat at the table, directly opposite her.

She had to clear her throat and look away from him, and if those cupcakes were still on the table, she'd be eating her feelings right about now. 'Six. You can bunk two per room, four if you push it. One room has space for six. It'd need a good airing out. But there's a communal bathroom, laundry, and a main dining room where they can cook their meals.'

'Didn't you have a station cook?'

'Only a muster cook. The ringers were only here for the

musters. Most of them had their own horses, which is why they put the ringers' rooms by the stables. I can ask the Station Hand for any recommendations. He gets hit up all the time.'

'But I heard you do, too, with the station's email.'

'That is now under your control.' It was their station, not hers. 'My turn… So, are you going to tell me what you were discussing about the murder?'

Ryder and Dex both shared a look.

'I know Charlie's side better than anyone. I can help.' She had to help.

'Yeah, but…' Dex winced as he looked at Ryder, who was shuffling the papers back into the folder.

'Hey, that's my great-uncle you're discussing.' She pointed to the photo Ryder was putting away.

'You said you'd never met the man.'

She gritted her teeth at Ryder steepling his fingers together. Who put Ryder in charge?

'Tell me the real reason why, Bree.'

'I want Charlie to find those answers.'

'We all want that,' said Dex, sitting straighter in his seat.

But it wasn't Dex she needed to get past, it was Captain Cupcake himself. And if she didn't fess up, Ryder would keep digging until he got the answer he was looking for.

Fine.

She sat back, picking at the lint from her workpants. 'I've been feeling guilty for not believing Charlie about Harry.' It had been eating at her ever since they'd found those bodies in the cave. What's worse, she'd never believed her grandfather, calling it an unhealthy obsession ever since they'd found her great-uncle's car in the Stoneys.

She lifted her eyes and bared her soul to the man seated opposite. 'This is my way of making it up to Charlie for not believing in him, and for my lack of support.' At first, she'd shaken it off as the ramblings of an old man needing to tick some boxes in his sunset phase of life.

How wrong she had been.

Ryder nodded at her. No smirk. No sneer or jeer like she'd expected. 'Thank you for your honesty. But you have to be brutally honest with us.'

'Always.' That was a no-brainer. Even if some people never believed her, she never lied. She just played with the truth.

'It doesn't go anywhere, what we discuss.' Dex dropped his two-cents' worth.

She'd kind of forgotten he was even sitting at the table, interrupting her negotiations with the dark, broody, bearded enemy. 'Does that include your pillow talk with Nurse Kitty? Where is Sophie? Out shooting something with her camera?'

'Night shift at the hospital.' Dex sat back, sheepishly. 'Besides, I'm not telling Sophie anything unless she asks.'

The corners of her lips curved. She knew that game well and played it that way all the time.

'No. I know that smile, Bree, and I am not having any of that.' Ryder stabbed his thick finger at the table. 'If you want to be a part of this, Bree, you'll tell us the whole truth and not keep anything back. I want all your cards on the table.'

'Does that go for you, too?' Because Ryder rarely showed his hand, and he was asking an awful lot of someone who didn't like to share her secrets.

Ryder gave an affirmative no-nonsense nod. 'And I want you to agree to no sneaky side missions where you run off, following some hidden agenda. If we do this, we do it together. Or we don't do it at all.'

'O-kay!' She flung her hands in the air in frustration. 'What more to do you want from me? Do you need me to sign a contract in blood, for you to file at some disciplinary court specially convened for wayward women?'

Ryder grinned at her as if he'd won that round.

She should've been ticked at agreeing to working with the enemy, but she was doing this for Charlie. And Ryder knew it. *Well played, Ryder, well played.*

Twenty

Finally. Ryder felt like he was finally starting to break through the many barriers surrounding the pretty little outlaw. He understood why Bree shielded herself, but she needed to know he wasn't the enemy.

'Would you like us to give you a run-down of where we're at?' This was him putting down the chips on the table, as per her request. 'But I won't show some images, okay?'

'Sure. No icky stuff.' Again, there was that rare hint of vulnerability in her eyes.

His chair scraped across the floor. 'Dex, have you got that measuring tape?'

'Yeah.' As Dex sat forward, his chair legs whacked against the floor. 'You'd remember this scene, Bree.'

'What do you mean?' Ryder's brow shifted as he peered back at the pair of troublemakers.

'Bree interrupted Porter that time.' Shifting to the window, Dex extended the tape measure.

'I didn't see much.' Bree got up from the table with her pretty green eyes dancing with curiosity.

'Because you chased us away to protect your illegal still.'

The sneaky wench. Ryder grabbed the end of the tape measure and paced out the distance from the window as per his own detailed notes, then used his triangular drafting ruler to line up his measurements. 'Can you grab that chalk on the bench, Bree?'

'Sure. Are we going to play hopscotch?'

He shouldn't grin, but at least they were playing nicely together. 'Can you mark a line on the floor here? At the outer base of the ruler. It'll be our starting point.'

'Okay.'

Ryder let go of the tape measure. 'Dex, can you go outside to feed that tape measure to me?'

'You two play nice while I'm gone.' Dex's laughter followed as he left the room.

Ryder grabbed some masking tape and laid it on the floor, where she'd marked it with the chalk. Through the polished steel of the side cupboards, he noticed Bree's head tilting to watch his arse in the air as he taped down the floor. She was perving on him.

Well, well, well. Remaining expressionless, he referred to his notes.

'Which way was the body lying?'

'Huh?'

'I have the chalk, I can draw in the body. You're measuring the gun's—'

'The trajectory of the shot, based on the entry and exit points.'

'Yeah, that. I'm good at drawing stick figures. And I've watched the odd murder mystery or two.'

But this was also close for her.

Bree narrowed her eyes at him, the anger flaring.

He did not want them arguing again. Not when they were finally playing nicely together.

He dragged his boot across the floor. 'Price was lying about here, face down, with his head towards the doorway.'

'Okay. How big was he?'

Ryder referred to his notes. 'Five-nine.'

'So, Cap's height?'

'Yeah, but he had Ash's build.'

'Got it. Were his arms out, in, tucked under? How were his hips? Legs—'

'You know what...' He rummaged through the file. 'I'll show you, but I'll block out some parts of it.'

'No, I can take it. I'm guessing accuracy is the key if we're recreating the crime scene.' She pulled his hand away and inspected the images.

'You don't have to do this, Bree.'

'You don't have to either, but you are. And I'm doing this for Charlie.'

She was so close he could pick out the details of her eyes with their differing greens that contained fine shards of aqua blue. They were beautiful.

'I'm here. Miss me?' Dex called out from the window behind them.

'Pass the tape through.' Ryder laid the photo face down on the table as Bree began drawing a chalk outline across the concrete floor. 'Hey, Bree?'

'Mmm…' Her concentration was amazing to watch, and he marvelled at the level of detailed accuracy she'd created, copying the police taped outline on the floor. But then again, Bree was used to drawing plans for her job.

Ryder grabbed the end of the tape measure from Dex and began pacing out across the floor as per his notes, to double check his measurements. 'In your great-uncle's letter to Charlie, he mentioned stolen guns.'

She stood and faced him. 'Are you asking if my shotguns were Price's? I'm assuming they were.'

'How many?' Dex asked from outside the window.

'Originally, there were six cases. Twelve guns in each.'

Damn. Ryder dropped the tape measure, and it whirled back with a snap.

'What the flip!' Dex shook his hand.

'How many are left?'

'Over the years, Darcie sold a few guns to the ringers.' She shrugged casually. 'As for the remaining shotguns on this station, there are sixteen working guns left. Now that you're working with the police, does this mean I have to surrender them?'

'Good question.'

Dex called out through the window, 'What I'd like to

know is where did you find them in the first place?'

'Where do you think, Stormcloud?' She nodded at the hidden room built behind the wall, which Ryder had turned into his arsenal.

'Did you find them when you set up your still?' Ryder asked.

'I was much younger than that.' The woman with many secrets grinned. 'So, what were you measuring?'

'I'm trying to figure out where Price was standing, but the investigator's numbers are all wrong. It's bad enough they're all in imperial measurements, but this…' It wasn't right. 'Bree, stand right here for me.'

Ryder grabbed the levelling string and handed one end to Dex and the other to Bree. 'I need a stand. Wait there, you two, I'll be right back. Don't move.'

'Where's he going now?' Bree asked Dex.

'No idea.'

Ryder grabbed the stand Dex used for his mobile spotlight for working on engine bays and dragged it back into the room. 'Good girl, you listened.'

'You really think I'm a good girl?' She cocked an eyebrow at him as if in challenge.

'Well, if you're naughty, I can work that out of you later.'

Her jaw dropped.

His eyes flicked over to Dex, who thankfully hadn't heard him. But he had trouble keeping a straight face, especially when he found a reason to grab her hand. 'I want you to grip this pole.'

She gave a choked sound, but amusement was lighting up her eyes. 'How tight do you want me to grip your pole, boss?'

The dirty, flirting, pretty little outlaw! He'd never been like this with anyone.

Then she laughed.

She was toying with him.

He exhaled heavily, dragging his focus back on the job. He used the measuring tape to find the appropriate height on the pole.

'Hold the string right here.' He manipulated her small but strong fingers. 'Don't move.'

'If you insist.'

'Dex, I need you to move to the left. Bree, can you shift the pole slightly to your right… There.' Again, he took the opportunity to touch her soft hips, moving her around the pole. He leaned close to her ear, her soft hair brushing his cheek. 'Don't move.' He loved this game.

'Okay. But—'

'This is where the shot entered the body, based on his height and shape.' He inhaled her soft feminine scent of vanilla, pecans, and something alluringly spicy underneath.

'Way to kill the foreplay, soldier boy.'

This time, his jaw dropped.

'Is this good?' Dex called out from outside.

'Yeah… No. Hold on.' Bree was torturing him, he had to walk away from her.

He emptied the folder out on the table, shifting the images around like a puzzle to create one big picture. 'Dex, you need to go lower. Your end represents the height of the gun's barrel, and where Bree's holding the string is where the shot entered the body.' He tilted his head at the images, then glanced back to the window. 'The crime scene photos show there was a stack of old oil drums stashed along that window.'

'Wait, I'll grab one of them. There's some close by.'

'Do I stand here and keep holding this string as practise for my debut as queen of the midnight infomercials, selling faux jewellery that'd tarnish in a month?' asked Bree. 'Or do I tie it off?'

Ryder leaned one hip against the table. 'You can stay right there, while you seriously consider staying home tonight.'

Plonking her free hand on her hip, she scowled at him. 'I did the right thing telling you first, before I—'

'And I'm glad you did. Just know I'm trying to keep you safe.'

'Pfft, I may be a fine figure, but I'm not made of porcelain, cupcake.'

'Why do you call me that? When you know I hate it.'

'Call you what?'

He dipped his head at her. 'You know very well what I'm talking about. I'm not a cupcake. If anyone else called me that, I would've decked them on the spot.'

Her tinkling laugh was evil. Since when did an evil laugh make his skin tighten with desire?

Bree was filled with the ultimate feminine power of a goddess of war and lust, all wrapped up into one curvy package, who was skilled enough to play the long game of a master strategist. It was the sexiest thing about her, along with her soft hair that he wanted to dive into face first, and those lips he wanted to taste that came with a body he wanted to explore…

Yeah, he was into her more than she realised.

'I'm back.' Dex shifted an oil drum against the window. 'What now?'

Ryder focused on the job, putting Dex and Bree into various positions. He'd given up on the original police report's measurements, written over sixty years ago. But he did work off the images and the coroner's report that showed accurate measurements for the entry and exit wounds on the body, using those as a guide. Once he got the right angle for the shot fired, he'd then use that as a base to work on the bigger picture.

'It makes little sense.' Ryder dropped heavily into his seat at the table, while Bree leaned near the door as if to make her fast getaway.

They'd been at this for a while, working on different scenarios and measurements. Dex had resumed rocking in his chair, swapping out his coffee for a beer. 'We've got the measurements right?'

'Yeah. Mine. Not the police reports.' And he'd checked the images, sprawled across the table, countless times now. 'Whoever pulled the trigger couldn't have been right at the window, not when there were two rows of drums in the way.' He tapped on the picture that had zoomed in on the drums. 'How did they line up the sight to hit the body from that angle?'

Dex turned the various images of the crime scene that were spread across the table. 'Hey, who'd keep an old oil drum like that without a lid, right under a window? The fumes would fill this room in no time. Unless that's common practice for you guys?'

Bree shook her head. 'Remember, this is before my time. But I do know Darcie was very particular about fuels and oils because he had an old burn scar on his leg he'd gotten as a kid. He made sure everyone put any and all flammable things away in particular places. I also remember Pop telling me that Jack Price would lecture the new ringers about everything being in its place when they started here at the beginning of the muster season… What I want to know is,' said Bree, as she pulled out a photo. 'What is that length of elastic string doing there?' She tapped the corner of the image. 'They use that for sewing and it's not something you'd normally find in an old tack room. Not to mention I can't see why or how they could accuse my great-uncle of this murder. It could have been anyone.'

Ryder and Dex both sat back.

'What am I missing? You'd better not be hiding anything from me. Not when I've been forthcoming with you two.'

'Bree deserves to know,' Dex mumbled to Ryder. *The big mouth.*

'Are you kidding me?' Bree wagged her finger at Ryder, her temper making her eyes shine. 'Did you think you could deceive me with your fluffy powdery sugar cakes, hoping I'll be too busy counting calories to notice!'

'Calm down, Bree.' Ryder went to his desk and removed the photo he'd hidden for a reason. 'I didn't want to show you this one.'

'Uh-uh, sugar pants, we had an agreement.'

'Yeah, but this…' Ryder hesitated, because he was trying to protect her.

She snatched it out of his hands. 'No freaking way.'

It was another image of the dead body, taken from a different angle, but it was enough for Bree to become eerily still, and completely expressionless. And they thought he had ice in his veins—not when Bree had a much quicker trigger to shut down her emotions.

She then grabbed the chalk and approached the outline of the body, where the right hand lay in a particular position. There, she wrote the words of a dead man:

Harry Splint did this.

'The chalk was in his hand when they found him,' explained Ryder, taking the chalk and the damning picture from Bree's small hands. He felt the slight tremor in her fingers, but also saw the look of terror in her eyes. But Bree feared nothing. She may seem hard as ice set in a glacier wall, but the cracks were starting to show all from that one image that killed any hope of her proving her great-uncle's innocence.

Twenty-one

Just after midnight, Bree stood at the cottage's front gate. Dressed all in black, with her rifle in one hand and a small cooler in the other, she was ready to play commando with Captain Cupcake and his offsider, Sergeant Stormcloud. And she was looking forward to it. Hello, it was sneaky, illegal, and everything that made her pulse tick that little bit quicker, as she waited.

Dex had suggested they take the Razorback, but Ryder said it was too noisy. Surprisingly, Ryder was using his fancy ute, that was worth more than most people's houses, so said her grandfather, who'd hammered away on their PC's keyboard to learn more about the car Ryder drove when the Riggs brothers had first arrived.

She had taken great pride in teaching her grandfather how to use the internet, where Charlie was now part of a stockmen's chat group that shared stories in the region. It was amusing watching Charlie type with two fingers, while cussing under his breath, complaining about some silly sod's comments, in between gulps of his beer. She'd learned to walk away in those moments.

Now she couldn't stop thinking about how she was going to tell Charlie that all the evidence was pointing to Harry being a murderer.

Charlie must have known about Jack Price accusing Harry in such a damning way. And with Bree not believing Harry's innocence in the first place, Charlie may have kept that piece of news to himself.

Poor Charlie.

Doing this sneaky raid on their nasty neighbour was the best thing for taking her mind off her family dramas—because so far, her murder-solving skills just sucked!

She gazed up at the stars that seemed extra bright tonight without a moon. On the other side of the large compound stood the farmhouse with its pantry light barely casting a soft glow inside.

To the left of that, the boardroom lights had just switched off.

They were coming.

She cocked her head, straining for the sound of a vehicle starting.

Then, in disbelief, she watched the ute's taillights disappear down the back of the property, leaving her behind.

'That a-hole!' A surge of anger had her slinging the rifle strap over her shoulder as she marched towards the back shed to take the quad. She wasn't getting dressed up like a plus-sized Catwoman for nothing.

When the ute spun around, its bank of powerful spotlights shone over her when she was halfway down the fence line.

'Were you going to saddle a horse?' Dex asked, with his head out the window as Ryder stopped the car beside her.

'You were going to leave me here.'

'I contemplated it,' Ryder said, his deep voice tinged with amusement as he climbed out of the vehicle. 'But we both knew you'd either take a quad or saddle a horse. Which one?' He walked around the back of his ute, all dressed in bad-arse black. No hat, but a black beanie.

Oh, lordie!

'Quad.' Wait, she was supposed to be mad at him, not perve on him!

Ryder opened the back door. 'Get in, cupcake.'

'That's not my name.' Wow, the guy opened the door for her.

'I'll have to find you one. Please excuse Dex for hogging the front passenger seat. He wanted to play shotgun.'

Nope, she was not going to ease up on him for his gentlemanly actions. Okay, maybe a little. 'That's fine by me. I've done my fair share of opening and closing gates, and I know how many there are between here and the eastern boundary.' She scooted into the middle of the back seat.

'Damn, I didn't think of that.' Dex swivelled around from the front passenger seat. 'Do I smell food?'

'For the drive.' She opened the small cooler, revealing foil-covered burger rolls, and let it rest on the middle console. 'Or does the driver have a no food policy?' It did have that new vehicle smell to it.

'Too bad, I'm starving.' Dex peeled back the foil to unleash the aromas of beef patties, with her special barbecue blend. 'Yum, hamburgers. When did you make these?'

'It was supposed to be dinner, but Charlie wasn't hungry, and I always cook when…' When she was thinking, or worried, because yes, she was a girl who ate her feelings—then drank her gin to not feel.

'Thank you, Bree.' Ryder took his burger, peeling back the foil. 'Have you eaten?'

'If you count the cupcakes.' She had to do something with her hands, taking the smallest one.

'This vehicle is huge.' It was so smooth a ride, she couldn't believe they were driving down a dirt track filled with potholes and corrugations even at speed, thanks to Ryder's lead foot. With a steel bull bar on the front, this twin-cab ute was a tank on wheels, that came with air conditioning and an actual windscreen, where she didn't cop bugs in the face, or suffer with windblown knots in her hair, like she did when hooning around in the Razorback.

'It's fancy.' It was also a big reminder of how rich Ryder was. While she was nothing more than the caretaker's granddaughter, hustling for pennies as a smart-mouthed blacksmith.

'It's not as fancy as my ute.' Dex grinned with his cheeks

full of food. 'And it's a thousand times better than that monstrosity you drive.'

She grinned, sitting back in her seat. 'Don't knock the Kombi van, stormcloud. It can go anywhere, and it's reliable.'

'It runs on elastic bands and sewing machine oil.'

The mention of elastic bands had the one in the crime-scene photo playing on her mind. How could it be part of a murder scene? 'Go on, admit it, you like the Kombi. You've got it plastered on your wall at home, that I bet you worship it every night.'

'I've put Sophie in charge of getting a new picture for that wall. Hey, can you teach her to make these?' Dex held up what was left of his meal.

'Nope. That's your kitchen. Your girlfriend.'

'Have you invited Sophie to your cooking lessons, yet? Like you do with Harper and Mia.'

'Sophie says she's busy with work and knows how to cook.' Not that they ever cooked much at their cooking lessons at the cottage.

Ryder peeked back at her, one hand on the steering wheel, the other holding his half-devoured burger. 'Did you explain to Sophie that your cooking lessons are code for long liquid ladies' lunches?'

'I'm sure Harper or Mia have told her.' It wasn't Bree's place—well technically it was, because they held it at the cottage. 'I hardly see Sophie.' No, she kept right away from the blonde who had started a stampede. And Bree was not apologising for getting up Sophie either.

Poor Dex was stuck in the middle. *And* Dex was her buddy, *and* he loved Sophie, *and* Sophie did make Dex truly happy, *and* he deserved that. Which meant Bree should be playing nice to the straitlaced nurse for Dex's sake.

Ugh! The things she did for people.

She sat forward and tapped on Dex's upper arm. 'Next time I'll be sure Sophie gets word to come.' But she doubted Sophie would come, because Sophie had never warmed to Bree, after assuming Bree and Dex were a couple.

How could Sophie ever think that? Not when Bree's broken dial for attractive males was swinging only in Captain Cupcake's direction.

'Thanks, Bree.'

Ryder didn't say anything, but he was watching her through the rear-view mirror.

She wasn't used to this much attention while in such a small space, he was too close. Especially when she had no exit and was truly exceeding her ten-minute limit of breathing the same air as Ryder. 'What's the plan?'

'You show us where you found the pipe.'

'Where are you hiding this beast? Now that you've cleared that space along the fence line?'

'Among the trees by the overflow creek.'

'Then what?'

The brothers hesitated.

'You'd better not ask me to stay by the car, like a child stuck out front of a supermarket with the promise of an ice cream. I found the irrigation pipe. I know the direction it's going—'

'Okay, Bree.' Ryder grabbed her waggling finger and held it.

She pulled away, not expecting the warm tenderness of his touch to send tingles up her spine to creep over her scalp, then down the front to her chest. Her chest!

She grabbed her water bottle and took a deep gulp, washing down the desire that had surfaced so hard and fast, all from the simple touch of his hand.

'Is the AC on?' She fanned her face.

'Yeah, there's a vent back there.' He reached back.

'Stop looking, I found it.' Again, their hands met. Only this time she pulled back as if he'd burned her, with her eyes flicking to meet his in the mirror.

There was no way a mere male should have that much power over her, making her body hot and super aware of his touch.

Come on, she'd held Dex's hand at the hospital and that

never bothered her. Cap was a serial hugger, especially when she'd delivered her homemade dog stew to feed his many muster dogs. And Ash, he'd grabbed her hands plenty of times when she'd given him lessons on how to change his son's night nappies, or when she helped him put on the baby carrier for those days he took his son in the saddle. None of them made her react like this.

Had she always been unconsciously aware to steer clear of Ryder, to not get within his personal space, or let him in hers, and most of all, to never touch him? But it was hard to miss the man, built like a machine, sitting behind the steering wheel, giving her the perfect view of his broad shoulders and muscles that went for days.

Honestly, Ryder was so wrong for her, just as she was so wrong for him. It was simple girl-maths really, especially when she was using all her ancestral strengths to live life like a country music song that skipped the happily ever after to a condensed playlist of over 600 songs all about being unlucky in love.

She was quite prepared to end up as a cat lady seeking all her emotional support from her pile of unread romance books shoved to the back of her cupboard.

But this was different.

Trapped in his car, all she could see, smell, feel was Ryder.

But she wanted to be here. She was curious to see where that hidden water pipe was going to lead them. And if it was as bad as Dex and Ryder were speculating, she needed to plan for Charlie's sake.

Maybe she should have taken the quad for her own sanity and put up with the bugs, because this drive was like some B-grade movie marathon—where the opening credits took too long and you just wanted to get to the action—as they drove down the dirt track under the cover of midnight, to go peek at their nasty neighbour's property. And Leo never played by the rules. Good thing was, she never did either.

Twenty-two

In the distance, Cattleman's Keep loomed like a black monolith, its jagged cliffs swallowing the faint starlight, casting a heavy shadow over the still waters of Starvation Dam. The outback's silence seemed heavy as Ryder parked his ute behind a thick cluster of trees that sat on the higher side of the dam's overflow creek bed. It was the perfect cover for tonight's recon of the neighbour's property.

At the ute's back tray, he handed his spare Kevlar vest to Dex, slipping on his own, before handing Dex a handgun. 'Take this, brother. In case things go sideways.'

'I always did like your toys.' Dex checked the magazine of the nine-millimetre pistol. 'Got any spare clips?'

'Always.' He handed over four extra magazine clips then slid some into his own Kevlar vest. He checked their torches, passing one to Dex, then fitted his night-vision goggles over his cap. Topping the ensemble, he slipped the strap for his favourite toy over his shoulder, a lethal M16 that delivered over 700 rounds per minute, nicknamed *The Woodcutter*. Now he was ready to play!

'Do I get one of those?' Dex's white teeth flashed in the dark.

'No.' Ryder frowned. He didn't have to share everything with his brothers. 'Here, put this war paint on.'

'Wow, we're really getting into costume.'

'Leo mentioned he'd spent time in the military. If he's growing a big cash crop out here, he'll definitely have cameras as part of his security.' He dug around his box and pulled out some compact, camouflaged 360 cameras. 'While we're there, let's leave some of our own. These will blend right in with the surroundings.'

'Nice...' Dex tucked them into his small pack. 'But wouldn't the wildlife trigger the cameras?'

'Leo will have his set at a certain height for a man, not a wallaby.' He smeared on the face paint. 'If you need a leak, do it now.'

'Good idea.' Dex wandered off.

'Bree, where are you?' She'd disappeared behind the bushes somewhere.

'I feel so underdressed for this party.' She pointed at Ryder's vest and guns. 'Ooh, make-up looks so good on you, cupcake.'

'C'mere.' He hooked his finger into the waist of her jeans and pulled her close to smear camo paint on her pretty face.

'Are you available for face painting at children's parties too? I want a fairy face, please.'

It was hard to keep a straight face when Bree was like this. She had such a gift of being playful at the worst of times.

'Do you have your weapons?'

'Sure.' She had her bushman's knife sheathed on her belt and her rifle strapped over her shoulder. She also looked hot in skin-tight black.

'As I don't have a spare vest for you, I think you should stay here.' Ryder wanted her safe. Even though they needed Bree to show them where the pipe was, he still had hope of talking the pretty little outlaw into staying on this side of the fence and not entering no-man's land.

'Not now I'm all dressed up, cupcake. It's rude to take a girl out on a date and then make her stay in the car.'

'I wouldn't class this as a date.'

'But look at you.' She flicked at his Kevlar vest. 'I can tell you enjoy wearing this can't-see-me kit.'

'It's been a while.'

'Have you ever tried cosplay?'

He arched his eyebrows at her. 'What?'

'Hmmm… It might be the perfect way to teach someone like you how to play.' Bree purred, and it was the sexiest sound he'd ever heard.

He wanted to bring her close to his chest just to let that sound vibrate against his skin.

'I have this mask fetish for Ghost.'

'Who?' *What?*

'Ask Ash. He'll tell you who Ghost is. You share the same build.' Bree grinned in a sinful way, her eyes all sparkly. 'I think Ghost is a lieutenant in the British Special Forces or something.'

He growled. That's right. A deep growl rolled like thunder in his chest all from some other soldier Bree was swooning over.

'We ready?' Dex came round from the other side of the ute.

'Yeah.' Ryder wiped his fingers free from the camo paint, dropping the container back into the box on the back of his ute full of his specialised gear.

Bree peeked inside the metal box. 'Are you preparing for a zombie attack?'

The surprised chuckle spilled free, as he locked up the metal box.

'Aw, look at that. He's ready to party.' She playfully messed up his cap, knocking his night vision goggles out of place.

It should have annoyed him.

But not when Bree looked cute in her black skullcap that she normally wore in the Smithy's shed. 'Let's go, daylight's coming.'

'Not you.' He tugged on her jeans, pulling her back. 'You stay on my six.'

'Your what?'

'It means you stay right behind me.' He started walking with Dex beside him.

Bree followed, yakking away. 'If I do that, I'll walk on

your boots, and one of us will trip over, then I'd make you blush with my swear words, and then I'll feel worse for being so clumsy and might start a stampede of runaway wallabies to rush through the scrub that'll set off all the alarms.' Bree then did something so unexpected it stunned him to a standstill—she jumped up onto his back.

With arms wrapped around his shoulders in a piggyback, she whispered in his ear, 'You know that saying, save a horse, ride a cowboy...'

'Bree, play nice with Ryder,' said Dex, chuckling. 'The brother is armed to the teeth.'

Her legs had a decent grip on Ryder's hips—pity he was facing the other way. Instead, he cupped her butt with a resounding slap and gave her denim arse a good squeeze.

'Oi.' She jumped off, rubbing her butt as she strolled past him with that sexy swagger of hers and tapped on their barbed-wire fence. 'Now Dex, remember the last time you went through the scrub you got all kung-fuey over a bunch of incy wincy spiders?'

'It was a bird spider that was the size of a freaking dinner plate.' Dex positively shivered with that foolish grin. 'Harper will back me up on that. She said hers was bigger.'

'Will you two behave?' They were like children. Ryder swiftly hiked over the fence, with Dex doing the same. 'Come on.' He held out his hand to Bree.

'I might not play the part of a bunny who can jump tall buildings like Supergirl on steroids, but I can climb a fence.'

As if Ryder was going to miss his chance of holding her, to swiftly lift her over the fence. 'Tuck your hair in.' Even with the camouflage paint on, she was pretty.

Bree stepped back, tucking her hair away. 'Got any wise words of wisdom from the war room, Captain Cupcake.'

Dex snorted in a deep snigger, desperate to stop laughing out loud. 'Dare you to say that three times real fast.' Dex nudged Bree as if they were in some playground.

'Oi.' Ryder scowled at the pair. 'Stealth mode actually means being quiet! This isn't some game. We're now trespassing.'

'Like Leo and his band of balding gorillas haven't done it before.' Bree drew out her hand-forged bushman's knife as she crouched down and dug at the ground to locate the pipe that even had Dex arching his eyebrows in surprise. They both hadn't seen it.

'This way,' said Bree, keeping her knife drawn. 'Don't worry, I heard you tell Dex about staying as low as a wallaby in case of any cameras. Try to keep up.'

'I'd really like that girl if she didn't scare me,' mumbled Dex.

'Yeah...' Ryder followed Bree with Dex at the rear as they silently crept through the deep undergrowth of the scrublands of spindly grasses and low-lying shrubs, punctuated by the twisted trunks of eucalypts and acacias. Without the moon's glow, the clusters of trees created a heavy darkness that made the air feel denser, carrying the scents of parched earth and dry vegetation. There was the occasional snap of a twig, or the rustle of dry leaves made by the wildlife that easily blended into a place where instead of streetlights and cars, there was only darkness, silence, and stars.

Bree stopped to brush the dirt and leaves aside, revealing the pipe's junction.

'What's wrong?' he whispered at her side.

'It splits off into two.' She pulled out the pipe join, exposing the hose running in two separate directions. 'They're not even bothering to bury it anymore.' She removed her glove and held the pipe.

'What are you doing?'

'You can feel the water running through it. Shh... I can hear sprinklers running.' She then inhaled. 'Get a whiff of that.'

A strong, sickly sweet herbal scent carried on the breeze. It was cannabis. Ryder had been around Dex's hemp crop enough to recognise the scent. It also wasn't the first dope crop he had to do recon for, but then he'd had a military team to back him up. Today he had adult children.

Dex inhaled deeply, his cheesy grin growing. 'It smells potent, people.'

'You're not taking any.'

'Brother, at this stage all I have to do is walk through the field and the resin will stick to me. I can roll it off and hot knife it later. I'll go this way.'

'Wait, I'll do a scan of the area first.' Ryder unclipped the detector from his belt and pointed it at the area.

'What is that?'

'An MMTD.'

'Can we use big words for the civilians present, please?' asked Bree.

'It's a combined thermal imaging and RF detection unit. It's to detect people or animals, but it also scans for radio frequencies to identify hidden cameras, audio bugs, or other forms of surveillance equipment.'

'Cool.' Dex leaned in closer as Ryder adjusted the green screen and scanned their area. 'How long is the range?'

'In this terrain,' Ryder said, nodding at the thick vegetation, 'we'd be lucky to get ten metres. In the desert, I'd get two hundred. But the thermal's picking up a large open field ahead.' He watched the small screen for any movement. 'I'm only seeing wallabies, a dingo... and cameras.' He pointed toward the field. 'There's a camera at two o'clock and another at eleven.'

'So it's like swimming between the flags, then?' Crouched low, Dex adjusted his gun. 'I'll follow the pipe this way.'

Ryder grabbed his brother by the arm and slammed an earpiece into his hand. 'Put this in and be bloody careful. Stay low. It looks like there are cameras set every thirty metres, pointing out at the bush, which would give them a range of anything between thirty to one hundred metres.'

'In other words,' said Bree in a hushed tone, 'please keep your arse to the ground as much as possible.'

'You, too.' Dex winked at Bree as he slipped in the earpiece. Crouched low he followed the pipe, disappearing to their left.

'So, I guess we'll take pipe number two.' Bree crept stealthily along the undergrowth, her footfalls incredibly silent, only to pause for her fingertips to brush away the leaf litter to feel the topsoil.

'You can track?'

Bree nodded. 'I've been hunting since I was a kid.'

She went to walk on, when he grabbed her shoulder, pulling her back. 'What the—'

He covered her mouth with his hand. 'Shh.' He then pointed to the thin wire ahead of her, cleverly hidden behind a thick ant mound. 'It's a motion sensor. Dex...' He hissed over the radio, 'Watch for any motion sensors. They're set just on the perimeter of the field. And be careful not to leave any footprints in the mud near those sprinklers.'

'Got it,' whispered Dex.

Ryder pulled Bree back to hide behind the thick trunk of a eucalyptus tree. 'Stay here.'

'Where are you going?'

'To take some video. And don't you dare pull out your phone. The backlight will instantly draw attention to yourself, even on night mode.'

'Talking from experience, are we?'

'Stay put. Please.'

'Okay.' She shrugged, as she stood on the toes of her boots to peer out into the field.

'I'll be back soon.' He activated the camera integrated into his night-vision goggles, then bypassed the motion detector and stealthily followed the irrigation line deep into the crop of mature cannabis. It had to be worth millions.

And that meant it was now a deadly game with Leo.

With plenty of video footage of the area, giving him a clear sense of what he was up against, he set up a few of his own cameras before heading back to find Bree. 'It's one big field.'

Bree shrugged. 'Is that unusual? Sorry, but this is my first dope field.'

'Normally illegal growers have them scattered in smaller crops to avoid detection from the air.'

'You do realise we're in the middle of nowhere, in the most forgotten region of Australia? We're not on any flight path, or near any major roads or even a large regional town. Come on, the only time the Northern Territory makes the national news is for a cyclone or a crocodile attack. Hey, would those satellite pictures have picked up on Leo's field? I know Finn used a drone, but that was set for—'

'Heat. I know.' It's what Ryder would do. 'Come on, let's go back.' He led the way, tapping his comms. 'Dex? Come in.'

'Yeah, bro.' Dex's hushed voice was clear over the headset.

'Where are you?'

'Right in the middle of the field. Don't lecture me, I had to see how big it was. You knew I'd do it, and it's a top place to put in one of those 360 cameras.'

'Good. You can come back. Now.' It was an order. He did not want Dex getting clip-happy with the foliage to have the growers suspicious because of some buds missing.

'On my way.'

Beside him Bree gnawed on her bottom lip.

'You look worried.'

'I am. It's a big crop.'

'I shouldn't have brought you here.' He hated that she was worried, grabbing her hand to try and console her as he led them back to the fence.

Then he heard a vehicle.

'Get down.' He pulled her to the ground behind a row of thick bushes and protectively covered her, as an ATV came over the small rise from the far end of the firebreak that was too far for his handheld detector to pick up. With a sweep of its spotlight, it shone over the boundary, missing his ute, hidden by the trees, but it clearly highlighted their dam's wall.

Inside the open-air all-terrain vehicle, the passenger manned the handheld spotlight. The blend of heavy metal and hip-hop music blared over the speakers to bounce off the scrublands, loud enough to disguise the crunch of the ATV's beefy tyres rolling over the dirt track

'It sounds like Linkin Park.'

'Shh.' Ryder covered Bree's soft lips with his hand.

The smell of coffee, petrol and cigarette smoke reached them as the ATV rolled right past Bree and Ryder.

'Nothing but roos, again tonight. Not exactly the action I signed up for.' The passenger bellowed out over the music.

'Keep it that way. Leo will have our bloody heads if we miss anything, and no stirring up the old bloke next door, not unless Leo says so,' called out the driver, flicking his cigarette butt out on the dirt.

They were the worst night sentries! But Ryder could feel Bree's heated anger growing. She was very protective over her grandfather. 'Don't,' he warned her under his breath.

'Are you sure this spotlight's not losing its juice? Feels like it's barely reaching the trees next door.' The passenger tapped the spotlight, its beam of light shuddering across the dusty fire track.

'It's fine. You're just getting paranoid coz we're this close to harvest...' The ATV slowly cruised past with the men casually chatting as if on a Sunday drive, heading in Dex's direction.

'Dex, they have sentries.' Ryder grit his teeth, his hands on the M16 peering down the scope. 'They're pathetic, just doing the rounds. They won't hear much over the music, but don't draw attention to yourself as they have a spotlight. Meet us at the ute when you can.'

'Righto.'

'We're just a joke to those cowboys. Not only are they blatantly stealing your water, but how they treat Charlie... He's never been a threat to them.' Bree sneered in anger. 'Those arseholes are—'

'Whoa.' Ryder pulled her back down, hooking his leg over her to use his entire body weight to pin her to the ground while covering her mouth. 'Calm down.'

She muffled something under his hand.

'Are you going to be a good girl for me?'

She scowled at him.

He liked this game.

With his hand over her mouth he sniffed at her slender throat, truly inhaling her scent of vanilla, pecans and something seductively spicy deep down into his lungs. His nose nuzzled into that soft spot below her ear, delighted to feel her squirm and the bare outline of goose pimples disappearing under her shirt. 'If I let go, will you remain calm?'

She nodded, her breath ragged.

Slowly he moved his hand away, ready in case she did something, especially when Bree could be reckless and completely unpredictable.

'We'll wait here for a bit until that ATV is out of range.' Hey, he was in no rush to move, staring down at a vision. With his fingertip, he brushed down her cheek, her dainty chin, then across those luscious lips. 'You can't scream, baby.'

Even though she was frowning at him, his eyes locked with hers. He licked his lips, which curved into a smile, as he was filled with a sudden urge to *play*. He pressed his lips to hers, kissing her with an intensity that left no escape, not when he had her pinned beneath him.

Twenty-three

Bree was no stranger when it came to kissing handsome stockmen in the dark, but when Ryder's lips met hers, the electricity that arced between them was positively magnetic. It set every nerve ending alive with desire, forcing her to kiss him deeper, as if he was the only reason she was alive. And she was oh-so very much alive.

His rough fingers tangled through her hair, his mouth crushing hers, his pelvis pushing his hardness against her, making her thighs part. And when they did, he gave a sexy groan of approval, licking her neck, then up to her lips. 'Even though you taste like face paint, you are freaking delicious.'

Before she could respond, his lips were on hers again, pinning her to the ground. She had no choice but to kiss him back, while trying to rake her nails under his Kevlar vest, where his muscles would have to feel like warm marble that fanned the flames of desire. No, this was worse, she had a scorching blaze inside her that wanted skin. All of his skin.

His large hand cupped her thigh, where denim was all that was keeping them apart, tucking her leg over his hip, giving him room to grind into her, while kissing her deeper as his tongue tangled with hers.

A twig snapped nearby, followed by a *thud-thud-thud* of a wallaby hopping away.

She pushed against his chest, their kiss broken, and he stared down at her with nothing but pure hunger.

'Not the place,' she whispered.

'I know.' His finger traced down the side of her face as if memorising the details.

She probably looked a mess, lying on the ground, wearing smudged face paint, with twigs and leaves in her hair.

'But I do know that when you get up, you'll put on that mask again, and I won't get another chance. Not like this.'

He was right.

'Stop fighting me on this, Bree.' With his eyes hooded, the attention and the open desire he had for her were alarming.

Fighting was her default. She always fought. If she didn't, she'd get hurt, and she'd been burned way too many times in her life, where that kind of emotional scarring didn't heal overnight.

Ryder rolled off her, the cool air a welcome reprieve from the heat they were generating between them.

She sat up, trying to assume some semblance of calm, but her lips were throbbing, including the skin around her mouth. He'd kissed her hard.

'Can we go now?' She didn't wait for a response. She knew the way home, even if her legs were trembling, especially her inner thighs that had wrapped around his waist. The desire for him was still a roaring fire inside her, it was unfair.

At the fence line, Ryder gripped her hand. 'Don't get mad, Bree. I just saw an opportunity and took it. Besides, you were kissing me back just as hard.'

That was true.

Ryder held out a cloth. 'You can wipe off the face paint. It's smeared.' He gave her a devilish grin, as if enjoying the fact that he was the one who'd made a mess of her make-up.

She wiped the greasy paint off her cheeks, her chin, and lips, while Ryder watched her carefully. 'Are you the type of guy to watch a woman dress?'

Ryder leaned in so closely, his thumb pressed on her bottom lip and his warm breath brushed against her neck as he whispered, 'And to watch a woman eat cupcakes, yeah. But only with you.'

Before she could respond he scooped her up and dropped her on the other side of the barbed-wire fence as if she weighed nothing. Then he effortlessly leaped over it.

She knew Ryder was all muscle, but it was also the sexiest thing to see him decked out in all that weaponry. And she really did have a weird fetish for masked men in military camouflage—the grungy, get-down-in-the-dirt kind of gear that he was wearing right now. Oh lordy, lordy, lordy did they break the mould with this guy?

How was it possible that the man who'd been her taunting enemy could suddenly be so hot?

Or was she getting high off the dope fumes that lingered in her hair and clothes?

At the car, Dex was waiting for them, frantically pacing up and down. 'Brother, it's twenty acres.'

'Which means?' Ryder opened the back tray of his ute to put his guns away.

'Bush weed yields anywhere between five hundred to two thousand pounds per acre. That,' Dex said, pointing back to the neighbour's property, 'is a twenty-acre crop that could potentially produce ten thousand pounds, easy.'

'What would that be worth?' Ryder asked.

'The street value is anywhere between a thousand and fifteen hundred dollars a pound, depending on the quality. But brother,' said Dex with wide, worried eyes, 'I'm betting Leo's field is worth about ten to fifteen million dollars, easy, with only a few weeks left to harvest. If that.'

Bree's heart fell, as if her entire world was being crushed by the weighty complications of having something that big right next door. No wonder Dex was in a panic. 'Leo is in the big leagues, isn't he?'

Ryder put his arm around her, protectively tucking her against his side. 'Yeah, babe, he is.'

Twenty-four

'**A**re you going to tell the police?' Bree asked. 'I'll have a quiet word with Marcus in the morning. I'll let him sleep, like you should be.' After dropping Dex off at the stockman's shack, Ryder drove Bree around to the caretaker's cottage. It was just after one o'clock in the morning, when Ryder opened her car door.

'What are you doing?'

'I'm walking you to the front door.'

'I'm fine. I know the way.'

A rich and sweet floral fragrance floated up from the cottage's front garden as he rushed to open the front gate for her. 'I'm already halfway there.'

'Why? It's not like this was a date or anything.'

'Normally dating is a boring time for me. And it doesn't involve guns, war paint, and hiding from a drug lord in the long grass.'

There it was, that slight smile.

'What are you doing tomorrow?' He knew Bree wouldn't sit still for long. And that's what bothered him, because he didn't want her rushing off and doing her own thing—not when he had to keep her safe.

'I'm taking Charlie into town. We're going to the morgue to talk about Harry's remains, and Charlie wants to visit Porter at the police station.'

'I'll take you.'

'Why?'

'If I'm going to talk to Marcus, it's better to do it face to face. I can show him the evidence I taped tonight. And, if you're with me, you'll be fully informed of what's going on.' Not to mention he could keep an eye on her.

'My grandfather and I live here, of course I want to know.' Knowing Bree, she was probably planning some elaborate defence system already.

'Which is why I promise to tell you everything. But you need to do the same as well.'

She hesitated.

'Bree?' With his fingertip, he gently lifted her chin. 'It's a two-way street of communication between us. No more secrets. Okay?'

She narrowed her eyes, as if trying to get a read on him. He had nothing to hide.

'Deal.'

He grinned with relief. 'Good girl.' He kissed her forehead.

'You know, I'm not a good girl.'

'That's true.' His forehead rested against hers. 'Good girls don't kiss like you, my pretty little outlaw.'

Her cheeks heated. Was Bree blushing?

She turned away from him. 'I'm going now.'

'Want me to come inside?'

The look she gave him only made him grin wider. 'I can guard the cottage from the couch.' Which was right next to her bedroom.

She paused, her hand on the door handle, and turned back to him. 'I'm not going to tell Charlie what we found tonight.'

'Why not?'

'Because it'll stress him out and he may react one of two ways.'

'Which are?'

'Charlie might freak out enough to want to dig landmines around the cottage and organise hourly patrols with shotguns.'

Which was how Dex was reacting, and Ryder had yet to tell Ash and Cap, hoping to have a plan in place first to stop that pair from panicking.

But Bree had been unusually quiet the entire drive back from Starvation Dam. No interruptions. No smart-arse comebacks while he discussed with Dex about upgrading their property's security. For the moment, they had to proceed carefully, and that meant prioritising Elsie Creek Station's defences ASAP before they even dared to think about switching off the water pipe and upsetting Leo, the drug lord, who lived next door.

Yet Bree never said anything.

For someone as highly intelligent as Bree, who could have already nutted out over a hundred different scenarios, it was unusual. It worried him that she might go off on her own and do something risky, or let her temper flare—putting herself in danger.

'What's the second option?'

'Charlie will burn it all down and blame it on a bushfire out of control.'

He shook his head. 'Charlie's not like that, is he?' But it's something Bree would do.

'Where do you think I got my scheming temper from?' Surprisingly, she kissed his cheek. 'Thank you for keeping me involved. But you don't need to come with us tomorrow, it's a business trip. We'll have deliveries to make, too.'

'Nope, I'm coming. It's a date. I'll even shout you lunch at the pub.' Which didn't sound very romantic at all. But, then again, he'd never tried this hard for a woman when they normally bored him, or he just couldn't trust them. There was no one like the redhead closing the door on him.

The smile left his face and he headed back to his car, allowing that heat to strike deep in his chest. This was his backyard. His home. His family. And Ryder was going to do everything he could to get rid of Leo, once and for all.

Twenty-five

'**W**hen *were you going to tell us?*' Cap slammed his fist against the table, in between pacing the length of the boardroom, where Ash, Dex, and Ryder were seated calmly at six that same morning.

'I'm telling you now.' Ryder frowned at his brother, who was normally the level-headed peacekeeper. 'So sue me, if I wanted to let you two sleep.' Because he knew they'd be up all night, racked with worry, from here on out.

Cap leaned his fists on the table. 'You may be our big brother, but we're not boys.'

'I know that. Which is why you're each getting one of these.' Ryder slid three Glocks across the table, custom models from his personal arsenal—just a few of the many guns he'd legally designed as a registered gunsmith. 'You'll also get holsters, ammo, and two spare clips as backup for your rifles.'

'Nice.' Dex examined the weapon with a wry grin. Of course, Dex would be into them.

'I don't enjoy playing with guns.' Cap raised his hands away from the pistol as if it was diseased.

'Put it in the Tojo, do whatever you want with it,' said Ryder, reaching for his coffee cup. 'Listen, Cap. We're defending our home, and I know you never hesitated that time we had to defend our herd from a pack of wild dogs.'

Cap closed his eyes for a beat, as if to dampen his temper, before sitting heavily in his seat to share an even heavier sigh.

'Later today, when I come back from town, we'll do some target practice.'

'What else are we doing, bro?' Ash picked up the Glock, getting a feel for the weight in his hand. 'I've got my son and Harper to think about.'

'Dex and I have put more cameras along the border—don't worry, Ash, we left yours in your paddock.' Ryder pointed to the wall of monitors. 'We've also put in an electric wire along the eastern border to keep the livestock away, like that small herd of water buffalo. We do not want any of our stock breaking that fence line, forcing us to go in there.'

'So we're just gonna let Leo keep his crop while stealing our water?' Cap rubbed his wrinkled forehead as if fighting a migraine.

'When I take Bree and Charlie into town this morning, I'm going to see Marcus. The police need to be involved now, and I have no doubt he'll tell us that our job will be to do nothing. But we can defend our land. And I recommend we don't tell the other girls anything. There's no point in having them worry.'

'Even Bree?' Cap crossed his arms tightly over his chest while staring at the pistol on the table.

'It was Bree who discovered they were stealing our water in the first place, and she tracked the water pipe all the way to that crop,' said Ryder, leaning forward in his seat. 'Without Bree we would never have found it.'

'But we know where it is now.' Dex rocked in his chair, cradling his coffee mug in two hands.

'We also worked out how they've been monitoring us.' Didn't that make his blood boil, as he leaned closer to the table's set of maps. 'They've been using cameras, here, here, and here.' Ryder pointed to the map of their own station! 'It's how Leo has been ten steps ahead of us. Call me paranoid, but I even swept this room for bugs.'

The tech-nut, Ash, sat higher with his eyebrows knitting together. 'I didn't know you had the gadget for that.'

'Ryder's got a lot of fun toys, brother.' Dex matched Ash's

grin.

'Concentrate, boys...' Ryder's voice was low and loaded. His brothers were acting like cowboys in the schoolyard when he needed them to think like soldiers. 'We've set up surveillance on Leo's property as we need to learn the details of their operation, including their patrol patterns. Later, Ash, we'll use your drone to do a flyover, but it'll have to be high so they'll have no chance of accidentally spotting it.'

'What about the drone's noise?' Ash asked.

'Dex will do a drive-by in the grader with his stereo blasting. I want you to do a proper scan of his entire property to learn its layout. Look for any buildings, driveways, regularly used tracks, the lot.'

'Shouldn't you be leaving that sort of work for the police?' asked Cap.

'Marcus and his team won't have the resources we do, and he'll have a lot of red tape to trawl though before he can make a start. I don't want Leo to know we're onto him, but I want to know what that prick eats for breakfast. Where he parks his car. Who lives there. And how many men does he have working for him. Yesterday.'

'How long have they been doing this?'

'I don't know, Cap. That's the scary part. It's what ticked off Bree the most.' Ryder hated anyone upsetting his brothers or threatening his home, but what burred him up the most was anyone upsetting Bree.

'Why did Leo pick the station next door, of all places, to start his operation?' asked Cap. 'There are plenty of other places he could've grown his crop, with better water resources.'

'Bree mentioned we're not near any flight paths, major towns, or main roads. And the only thing that prick didn't get his lawyer to fight us on was our application to grow hemp.' He gritted his teeth. 'Leo's been playing us from the day we moved in. I bet the reason he only offered us the bare minimum to buy us out was a smokescreen. He needed us to fight him over water rights, so he had an excuse *not* to build his mine. It was all a cover for his money-laundering operation and dope-growing venture.'

'When did they lay down that water pipe?' Ash asked. 'It could have been anytime in the nine months since we rebuilt that dam.'

'Nah, it'd be much more recent than that,' said Dex. 'I would've dug it up when I extended that fire break after they let out those wild dogs to attack our herd.'

'I think they laid that pipe down around the time our cattle was stolen,' said Ryder. 'It fits Leo's MO. We all know he had something to do with those rustlers and he would've used them as a distraction. Leo's crew must have come in and put in that underground pipe when we were all so focused on finding our cattle on the west side that none of us were watching the east side.'

But now Ryder had an entire wall of cameras monitoring the boundary fence, including Elsie Creek Station's front gate, as well as Leo's front gate, and in particular that dope crop. It might be illegal, but Ryder was not going to sit around and wait. He had the equipment, he had the know-how, and he rarely slept, especially not when he had to protect his home and all who lived here.

'While I'm in town, I'll get some sensor lights and spotlights for around our houses. Do you guys need anything else? Or have any other suggestions for security?' Ryder was all ears.

'I hate living like this, with cameras, and spotlights, and guns.' Cap's shoulders sank as he dragged the Glock closer across the table. 'How long will we be living like this?'

Ryder wished he could give a definite time frame, but he couldn't. 'I'll talk to Marcus today...'

But Ryder wasn't going to wait for Marcus, either. Bree's idea of burning the crop sounded good, but it'd only engage the enemy, and that's not what he wanted until he was ready. 'If any of you see Leo, we act normal or ignore him. Cap?'

Cap scowled. 'I don't talk to the wanker. It's Dex you should worry about punching Leo out.'

'Believe me, I want to, brother. But as Ryder explained last night, we don't know who or how many men Leo has working for him. We have partners to protect now.'

'That's why we need to be smart about this and not rush in guns blazing,' said Ryder. 'We need to know what we're up against. We'll know soon enough, now we've got Leo under surveillance.'

'Are you going to tell Bree and Charlie?' Cap asked.

Ryder nodded. 'To stop Bree from running off and doing her own thing, I've agreed to keep her informed. But Bree has chosen *not* to tell Charlie.' Hoping his brothers did the same with their partners. 'Bree doesn't want to give her grandfather any reason to stress. Charlie has enough to worry about.'

'How is the murder investigation going?' Ash pointed at the floor to the outline of a body drawn in chalk.

'Bree and Charlie are going to see Porter this morning at the police station, and they'll be making arrangements for Harry's remains.'

'Are you going with them?' Ash asked.

'I told Bree I'd drive them into town.' Ryder glanced at his watch. 'I'd better jump in the shower, or Bree will take off without me.' He pushed the notebook into the middle of the table, along with two handheld radios, the same as the ones Dex and Ryder had clipped into their leather radio holsters. 'These radios are encrypted. We'll be using these handsets from here on out.'

'Do you think Leo is listening in on us, too?'

Ryder nodded. 'Monet mentioned her plane mechanic, Mickey, listens to the airwaves at the local airstrip and knew the police had come out here when we found those skeletons. I bet Leo is doing the same.' And they used their handheld radios like a phone, sometimes a group chat with Ash, Dex and Bree telling bad dad jokes.

'Won't it tip Leo off if he can't hear us anymore?'

'Leo won't hear anything. Not even static. These handsets operate on an encrypted frequency-hopping system, completely separate from standard channels. We can explain that it's part of the communications upgrade for our intranet… Lastly, we need someone watching the cameras to note the times and numbers of Leo's footmen doing their patrols. I know it might sound tedious—'

'I'll do it.' Cap dragged the pen and notebook closer. 'I'll take first watch.'

'Thanks.' Ryder was glad to see Cap had calmed down.

'I'll be in the workshop next door, doing a service on the harvester, if you need me,' said Dex, readjusting his radio harness.

'I'll have the satphone with me while I'm in town.' Ryder headed for the door. 'This is our home, and we have every right to defend it. And Cap…' Ryder landed a heavy hand on his brother's tight shoulder. 'Have faith that we will win this.'

Cap nodded. 'I know we will.'

Ash slipped on his radio harness. 'I'll go charge up the batteries on the drone. Mason will be awake soon. It's my turn to do brekkie.'

Together Ash and Ryder walked across the homestead's compound. The stars had faded, leaving the sky awash in soft pink and blue hues.

'You okay, Ash?'

Ash raked fingers through his hair. 'I don't know how I'm going to keep this from Harper, when I usually tell her everything.'

'Can Harper keep a secret?'

'Harper's better at it than me. Remember, she worked for the Australian Ambassador to Belgium, she would've had some sort of security clearance for that job.'

'Yet sometimes you need to hide things to protect those you care about, so they don't worry.'

'So you and Dex were up all night? I could have helped.'

Ryder patted his baby brother on the shoulder. 'You needed sleep. But you will be helping. Watching those cameras is a boring job.'

'I don't mind, I'll drag my games down and play while

watching those screens. I'll get Harper to hit the shops to stock up my sugar stash and get us some snacks for the boardroom.'

'Good idea. Won't the games distract you?'

'There is a pause button, dude.'

'I never got into those video games.' Then he remembered something. 'Hey, who is Ghost?'

'Ghost?' Ash cocked an eyebrow at Ryder as they paused at the front steps to the farmhouse.

'Last night Bree mentioned this Ghost. She said to ask you. He's some British Special Forces guy who wears a mask and goes by the name of Ghost. Is he a character in some movie or something?'

'Bree must be talking about Simon *Ghost* Riley from *Call of Duty*.' Ash scrolled through his phone as they entered the shade of the front porch. 'That's him. He's a legend in the game. A kick-arse SAS soldier who wears this skull-patterned balaclava and dark sunglasses all the time. No one has seen his face.'

Ryder took the phone and zoomed on the image of Ghost, who looked like a soldier of the hardcore, specialised military variety.

'You know…' Ash tilted his head at Ryder. 'Ghost is a hardened, no-nonsense soldier, who's fiercely loyal to those he cares about. He reminds me of someone I know, like a big brother who acts like he's got ice in his veins.'

Ryder grunted, passing Ash's phone back.

'You and Ghost share the same build. Any reason why Bree mentioned Ghost to you?'

'Hmph.' Ryder ignored him as he climbed the steps.

Ash skipped up the steps beating Ryder to the front door where he held it, wearing the boyish grin that his son Mason had inherited. 'Did you wear any of those scary masks like Ghost, when you were in the Army?'

'No. Face paint or black masks to not reflect any light.' But he was going to research more on this Ghost character if Bree had not only likened him to Ryder, but if she had some mask fetish. It'd be something to occupy his time while watching the surveillance cameras later. Dex had told him that Bree made swords and lances in the smithy's forge for customers who did live-action role-playing, and Bree had also mentioned cosplay. For a man who didn't know how to play, he was keen to learn more—especially after that kiss last night.

Twenty-six

After feeding the horses and checking over her list of orders that were packaged ready for delivery today, Bree headed back to the cottage for breakfast, keen to hit the road before Ryder showed up. The early morning air was still crisp enough for her to wrap Ryder's blanket around her shoulders.

'Was there anything else you wanted to take, Pop?' The warm scent of eggs and bacon greeted her as she cleaned her boots on the back doormat.

'Look who showed up for brekkie.' Pop served a fried egg from the heavy cast-iron frypan onto a plate filled with steak, bacon and greens.

'Morning, Bree.' It was Ryder, seated on the other side of the island bench, freshly showered, beard trimmed, in that tight black T-shirt that showed off every muscle in his torso. When did the guy work out?

'You're early.' *Bugger!*

'Didn't want to miss you.' His eyes shone with amusement over the lip of his tea mug.

'Dig in, son. We grew all that produce, except the mushrooms and the smoked bacon. It's what I call the stockman's breakfast.'

'Beats a drover's brekkie that was just a smoke and a sip of billy tea with an eye on the sunrise,' replied Ryder.

Charlie's face lit up with joy that someone else understood his lingo. 'And that's much better than a dingo's brekkie, which is just a drink of water and a look-see.'

The two men shared a grin and a nod on opposite sides of the kitchen counter.

'You look nice, Bree.' The timbre of Ryder's voice did something to her, as did the way his eyes travelled down her body, then back up again.

'Thank you.' She self-consciously brushed down her favourite dress—flowy, playful, and flattering for her full figure—which usually put her in a good mood.

After last night's escapade, she needed something to lift her mood and to stop worrying about Leo, her neighbour, who was a drug lord! She always knew he had that mobster vibe.

'I like that you're wearing that blanket.' Ryder gave her an intense stare, before attacking his breakfast with gusto.

What was the deal over this blanket? 'It was cool this morning...' Not now. The heat was creeping up her skin, that she removed the blanket as she took her seat at the bench. Charlie served up her plate. 'Did you get any sleep?'

'I rarely do... You?'

She shrugged. 'You timed that well.' She nodded at him, eating.

'I did, didn't I?' He grinned, loading up his fork. 'Best breakfast, Charlie, except for Bree's campfire brekkies. Your stockman's brekkie is worth the visit.'

'My beautiful Bea was never much of a morning person, so she made me promise to cook brekkie for her and our future children every morning—or she wasn't going to marry me.'

'You're kidding?' Ryder's chuckle was deep and short.

'Hey, I never complained, because I got to marry the most wonderful woman in the world. And my beautiful Bea got to sleep-in that little bit longer, and never complained about my cooking none either—even when the bread got burnt or the eggs were runny at first.' Charlie sighed, gazing at the wedding picture he proudly kept on the bookshelf among his many rodeo trophies.

'But I always made sure brekkie was better than what I got fed as a little tacker,' continued Charlie. 'My old man's version of a stockman's brekkie was freshly made damper dipped into the tin of golden syrup, washed down with some billy tea, while sitting around a campfire. I remember carting water in canteens, living off salty beef, and carrying carbide lamps. Every day, my father had us doing school by correspondence before sunrise. Spelling and maths we did in the saddle while droving, or in the truck driving to the next blacksmithing job, or some fencing contract we had to fill. If we were lucky, we'd have the radio to listen to at night. If not, we'd make up stories.'

'Ever regret any of it?'

'No, son.'

There, Charlie said it again. *Son*. It made her sit higher, carefully watching the two men for some reaction. But nothing.

'No matter how many miles of fencing wire I've tangled with, or outback dust I've swallowed, it's rotten rails and long snaking wire fences that still puts a smile on this old man's dial.' The many sun-hardened crinkles softened as he gave a dreamy smile. For Charlie, he could never retire, being a stockman wasn't a job, it was a lifestyle he lived and loved.

'What do you think is the worst thing about being a stockman?' Ryder asked.

'Well, um, lemme see...' Charlie scratched at his head of white hair. 'After eighty years working on stations, with plenty of bruises, cuts, lacerations and other painful experiences, including rodeoing...' He pointed to the large black-and-white image of him riding a bucking bull. 'Out of the top five for pain and discomfort, it'd have to go to that there bucking bull, Buckshot. Then I'd say it's the buffalo fly in the ear.'

'Really?' Ryder paused with his fork full of food.

Charlie shoved a thick finger in his ear as if cleaning it out. 'My old eardrums can't handle their wing beating frequency or something. That's when I'm looking for the nearest trough to sink my head underwater to drown the blighters.'

'I agree, those buffalo flies suck. But the horsefly is the worst for their bite.'

'Don't I know it. One bite is enough to make a sleeping pony leap in the air like it's been zapped.' Charlie slurped on his mug. 'Now, don't get me started on them pesky midges, mate. And with the wet season coming, I'm not looking forward to the return of them mongrel sticky black flies either...'

Bree ate fast, doing her best to ignore the men's gross conversation. Any second now, they'd start comparing scars as they bonded over breakfast.

Charlie had never been like this with her ex-husband, Finn.

Although Charlie behaved similarly with Cowboy Craig, who was the closest thing to a son for her grandfather. Charlie had taught Craig how to ride rodeo bulls and they shared a love of the sport. But Charlie never called Craig *son*.

'And I'm done.' She jumped off her stool.

'I've got this, kid.' Charlie took her plate, then turned to Ryder. 'So we'll be going in your ute, eh?'

Ryder used his toast to sop up the sauce on his plate. 'Yep, it's fully fuelled. Bree mentioned you had deliveries?'

'We've got the post office and the pub today.' Charlie again slurped from his banged-up enamel mug that he took everywhere. 'You've got no complaints about an old man taking his cuppa with him for the drive?'

'No, whatever you need, Charlie.'

'Why are you taking us into town?'

'Um...' Ryder hesitated, glancing at Bree.

'Ryder was going to visit his mate, Marcus. And I said we were visiting Porter at the police station—'

'So I offered,' said Ryder, finishing her sentence. 'Why waste fuel if we're going to the same place?'

'Too right, you are.' Charlie flicked on the kettle. 'You'd better get them orders into Ryder's ute then, kid.'

'I'll bring them down in the trolley.' Grabbing the blanket, she pushed open the back screen door. The cool outside air was invigorating as she headed past the silent patio area where her empty trough sat before her widescreen. It wouldn't be long, and she'd be dragging buckets of ice to fill the tub to cool down under an outback summer.

The irrigation for the vegetable garden brought a chill to the air, as a light hazy mist hung over the paddock, Drover's Rest, that spread to the fringes of Scary Forest. The back gate squeaked, and her boot steps echoed inside the blacksmith's workshop. She grabbed the small trolley to load the sturdy, boxed orders being posted today. The rolls of steel rods wrapped in bubble wrap were for the customers to collect from the pub.

'What are those?'

'What the hellfire!' She dropped her rolls that clanged on the ground but held one up like a sword. 'You could have warned me.' She was jumpy after last night. Why hadn't she heard the gate?

'Sorry.' Ryder leaned down to pick up her packages. 'Are these branding irons?'

'No. Some are fire pokers.'

'Fire pokers?'

'Yes, people like fancy fire pokers with their initials on them. It's the must-have gift for the person who has money to burn,' she said to the self-made billionaire who'd bought this cattle station with cash.

'Dex told me you make swords.' He wandered over to her workbench, where a sword waited for her to finish setting the faux jewels on the hilt and its matching shield. 'Is it true you go jousting?'

She shrugged. 'Not for a while.'

'Hmm… So where is *my* specialised fire poker? Because we both know your grandfather is holding Elsie Creek Station's branding iron to ransom in the caretaker's cottage.'

'That's between you and Charlie. And as you're not on my Christmas list for handmade goods, you should know there's a four-month waiting list. I'm a girl in demand.'

'Aww, that hurts.'

'We both know you're made of tougher stuff than that, Captain Cupcake.'

'Hmph. I see you extended the nickname,' he grumbled.

'Just because I pretend to be a grown-up, doesn't mean that I should stop expanding my vocabulary.'

He flashed her a grin, as he rubbed a hand over his jaw, his eyes all sparkly as they reflected the sunshine.

'Now that is cool.' He approached the back brick wall, charred from years of use from the blazing furnace. And on that wall hung a large, sculpted bull's head. 'Dex told me you made that for Charlie?'

Dex had a big mouth.

'How old were you?'

'Twelve.'

'Young. How old were you when you started on the tools.'

'Excuse me?'

'I had to help my dad and grandfather as a small boy. You?'

'Um…' Her brow ruffled, pulling back on her snarky attitude. 'Ever since I came to live here, I've been working in this shed after school and school holidays, learning the trade that very few people need anymore.'

'But you've found a way to be booked out for the next four months. Clever.'

'Ooh, that's high praise coming from someone like you. I'll be living off that compliment for a month, you know.'

'Better than you biting my head off,' he mumbled, walking around the blacksmith's shop. 'Can you make me one of those bull heads? A longhorn?'

'For where?'

'You left a big space on the boardroom wall, that'll be perfect for it.'

'I'm busy.' She grabbed the handle of the trolley, tucking the rolls under her arms.

'Here, let me take that trolley.'

'I can do it.'

'Listen, lady, I happen to have a particular way of loading up my ute, if you don't mind. I'm sure you're the same with your Kombi.'

She shrugged, readjusting the weight of the packaged rods where some of the bubble wrap popped in her hands.

'Here.' He tucked the blanket over her shoulders. 'I like you in this.'

'Why?' Her question made his eyes flare slightly. *Hello.* 'What is the deal with this blanket?'

'Um…' He focused on adjusting the trolley's load while she waited for a reply, with her arms full of fire pokers and branding irons.

'I can see you won't let this go.'

'Not now, I'm not.'

His fingers softly grabbed the edges of the blanket she had wrapped around her shoulders. 'If I tell you, will you keep using it?'

She shrugged. 'I'm not giving it back, if that's what you think.'

His grin grew into one of those sexy smiles that made her toes curl in her boots.

She swallowed hard, hoisting the bundles higher to create a barrier to any of Ryder's unprovoked kisses. Even if he was a good kisser, she didn't want him mussing up her hair and make-up. 'So, the story on the blanket?'

Ryder exhaled heavily. As a man who wasn't much for storytelling or conversations, she could tell he was struggling. But then, she'd never stood still long enough to hear his stories, so she waited.

The silence seemed long and empty.

'When did you get it?' If she asked questions, hopefully it'd make it easier for him to talk.

'Just before I started basic training in the Army.'

'Why the Army?' Considering the guy seemed happy as a stockman.

Ryder peered out to the paddock where their stockhorses grazed. 'With six younger brothers and sisters, always in my face, I wanted space… Don't get me wrong, I love my family.'

'I know you do.' The guy bought an entire cattle station for his brothers to call home.

'But I had to get out. My dad got paid to collect junk off the highway. My parents couldn't afford to give me the education I wanted, and I wasn't going to get it as a stockman, but I could in the Army. Unfortunately, some members of the family weren't happy about it.'

'Aww, they didn't want to see their big brother go.'

'So much so that they hid my mail, and I missed my date to show up for basic training.'

'Not possible.' Juggling the fire pokers in her arms, she tapped on her wrist, bare of any watch. 'You're a clock-watcher who is never late for anything.'

'Thank you for noticing.' He gave her a sideways grin. 'I think one of my sisters hid that letter from the Army.'

'That's kind of sweet.'

'Yeah, well, I was stuck in a strange city and had to wait for the next intake for basic training. That's when I met Miss Laurel Thomas.'

'The…' *Girlfriend*? Now why did that make her stomach churn?

'The spinster. Laurel was coming out of the shopping centre and dropped something off her trolley. I helped her. Next thing she insisted I push it to her car, where I noticed she had a flat tyre.'

'So you changed it?'

'Of course.' He shrugged with those big shoulders in that tight black shirt, hooking his thumbs through the belt loops of the jeans made for the man. 'Laurel asked what I was doing there, and I'd told her I was going to apply for a job at the supermarket, and asked if she knew of any work until I could start basic training.'

'And…'

'I've told no one this story.' He winced, pulling off his

stockman's hat to scratch nails though his hair. 'It's silly—'

'You can't stop now.' She stepped close enough to admire his masculine scent. 'Go on.'

He adjusted his hat that cleverly shaded his eyes. 'Well, to make a long story short, Laurel had very little, but she could offer me food and board for doing jobs around her house. Mostly to stop any of the local kids from hassling her, because her house looked like the scary witch house. It was that run-down.'

'Witch, huh?' Like Dex called her that nickname.

'Not like that. Few people realised Laurel cooked for the local homeless shelter. Even though she'd retired, she still did it a few days of the week.'

'Sounds like a sweet lady.'

'Anything but. She was a brandy-swigging, foul-mouthed woman who gave people hell with her comments. You would've liked her.'

'Why was she working there then, if she was giving lip to the customers?'

'Laurel's brother, Clyde, was an ex–combat vet. He wasn't coping too well back in society, and preferred living on the streets.'

'Where Laurel volunteered at this soup kitchen?'

He nodded.

'Did she—'

'She tried.' His chest rose and fell in a deep sigh. 'Laurel had a room for Clyde at her house, but her brother wouldn't accept it. So, she made sure Clyde had plenty to eat, clothes and blankets to keep him warm, while keeping watch over him.'

'And you stayed with her?'

'For a few months. I painted Laurel's house, fixed her plumbing, serviced her car, and tamed her garden, while scaring off some local kids who dared to hassle her. And Laurel also made me help her with her work at the soup kitchen.' Again, he rubbed the back of his neck. 'Laurel made me see the world in a different way. I was a broke kid from the bush who didn't know about city living.'

'Do you regret leaving your family?'

'No. It was my time. It might sound selfish, but I needed it. Like I told you, I never learned to play. I've always been too serious, too focused. I'm not like you and Dex, who know how to muck around and actually enjoy life. Now that I'm out of the Army, I wish I could let go a little—have more fun in my day.'

Why did that make her heart ache for the always serious and stern Ryder Riggs?

'And the blanket?' What was the connection?

'When I was getting ready to leave, Laurel gave me this handful of cash. It wasn't a lot. I knew she couldn't afford much, but she insisted on taking me shopping to get my recruit kit together.'

'What's that?'

'Toiletries, specific civilian clothing. I never had much. With no shopping malls anywhere near us, we were kids who shared clothes and lived off hand-me-downs. But Laurel insisted on helping, lecturing me on the difference between quality over quantity and to invest in something that would last. After living a life in the outback, in a house that never got cool enough in the summer, I wasn't ready for the southern winters.'

'I can relate.' Wrapping the blanket tighter around her shoulders.

'And, after having a chat with Clyde, huddled on a street corner, about his time in basic training, that's when I bought that blanket you're wearing now, and it went everywhere with me. Just like Laurel's brother, Clyde, carried one with him living on the streets... You see, in the Army, most of the personnel had photos of their family, a special book, a watch, or some keepsake. I grew up in a junkyard, well aware of what people threw away and didn't want much. Some of my bunkmates gave me a hard time being this dumb kid from the scrub carrying this blanket around.'

She bristled, with that blaze of protectiveness rising fast in her chest. 'That's not fair.'

He tilted his head at her with that grin growing. 'Look at you.'

Only then realising she was being protective of Ryder. *Nooo.* She had to step back. 'I hate bullies.'

He narrowed his eyes, his deep voice dropping lower, colder even. 'Were you bullied?'

She shrugged.

'Bree?'

'When I went to boarding school, somehow, they found out about my parents and some of them picked on me. But not for long.' No, she learned all about pranking those in the dormitory, and their weak spots, to ensure they never bothered her again.

'They obviously had no idea who they were dealing with.'

'No, they didn't. What about you?'

'I grew up being bullied. We were known as the junk brothers in school, until my mum decided we were all going to learn to box. After that we never got bullied again.'

'So, you took on the bullies in the Army?'

'No. Instead, I used it as a lesson.'

'How?'

'I learned quickly in the Army to never trust too fast, to quit no task too early, and to never expect too much from those around you. Most of all, to never talk too much.'

Well, that made a whole load of sense as to who he was now.

'But that simple woollen blanket was not some child's crutch, it was a small piece of home for me. It shaded me from the sun in the Afghan desert and sheltered me from the cold rains in Ireland. It was a beach blanket down in Mexico. The perfect pillow for a train ride through the Swiss Alps, and it was the cushion that saved my arse from getting burned on the ferry ride in Morocco. I thought I'd hang it up when I found a home...' Leaving that sentence hanging in the air for a moment. 'Yet, for something as simple as a blanket, it taught me the biggest lesson of all.'

'What's that?'

'To understand the true value in things, which has nothing to do with the price tag,' said the self-made billionaire who looked at her so deeply it unnerved her. 'And when you find something worthy, you do your best to hold on to it.'

'Here, take it back. It obviously means a lot to you.'

'No. It's yours, Bree.' He tenderly squeezed her arm. 'I want you to keep it.' He stared at her for a long time, as if trying to say something. It was a look that revealed how truly and deeply he cared about her.

No one had ever looked at her like that before, it set her heart hammering in her chest. 'We'd better get going.'

Twenty-seven

The front doors of the Elsie Creek Police Station slid open, releasing a brush of cool office air that blended with a rich coffee aroma greeting Ryder, Charlie, and Bree.

'Policeman Porter,' called out Charlie to the officer behind the large counter. 'Just the fella I came to see.'

'It's Senior—'

'Whatever. Have you solved the mystery yet?'

'No. Morning, Bree.' Porter came around the counter to give her a friendly peck on the cheek, shaking Ryder's hand as the security door clicked shut behind him. 'Look out, you two are in the same room together—you're not going to fist it out or something?'

'We're playing nicely,' said Bree. 'But I'll be selling tickets later if you want the sunset show. I'm sure there'll be fireworks by then.'

Ryder hoped not. With a clink of glass, he tucked the plastic bag he was carrying under his arm to remove his hat and straighten his hair. 'Is Marcus in?'

'Yeah, go on through.' Porter swiped his card to open the security door. Charlie bustled through, but Bree hesitated. Which was unlike her.

Ryder gently placed his hand on her lower back. 'Do you want to come with me or stay with Charlie?'

'How do I do both?'

'I'm all right, kid. I don't need a babysitter.' Charlie poked up the brim of his hat, to squint at the large table covered with assorted evidence.

Ryder recognised some of it from the cave they'd found after the landslide.

'Now, Porter, please indulge an old man and tell me what you've learned.'

'Um, well…' Porter gave Bree a pleading look for help.

Ryder could see she was torn. 'How about I fill you in later on what Marcus tells me and you tell me what Porter tells Charlie?'

'Deal.' She gave Porter a brotherly tap on his upper arm. 'Porter, did you say that Charlie needed to sign something?'

'I did.' Porter sighed with relief as he escorted Bree to the large evidence table.

Ryder left them to it, rapping his knuckles on Marcus's open office door. 'Morning.'

Sunshine streamed through the back window silhouetting the bulky body-building frame of the OIC, Elsie Creek's Detective Senior Sergeant Marcus Moore, seated behind his large desk. 'Hey, Ryder, this is a surprise.'

Ryder closed the door and shook hands with Marcus. 'Brought you something.' He dug around in his carry bag to pull out a bottle of bourbon.

'Jeez, you did not just put that on my desk.' Marcus didn't touch it, only raising his eyebrows at the bottle.

It was a bottle of Jack Daniel's Red Dog Saloon. It was one of the smoothest whiskies Ryder had ever tasted. 'One day I'll have a bourbon room, and I'd keep a case of that in there.' He slid it closer across the desk.

Still not touching it, the senior sergeant sat heavily in his large director's chair on the other side of the desk covered in paperwork. 'I know it's not my birthday. So, what's going on?'

'Well…' Ryder sat in the guest chair, producing his still images as he explained all about Leo's operation, ending his debriefing with the confession about his own surveillance cameras set in the heart of his neighbour's property.

'Oi, that's illegal, mate,' said the no-nonsense cop, wearing a scowl.

'I'm well aware. But I also know you don't have the equipment, and you'd be stuck under red tape, too. And the real reason I'm telling you this quietly is…'

Marcus arched an eyebrow. 'Go on.'

'Leo has deep pockets with lots of cash to splash with a lot of contacts. He had a mining official in the government send us a fake letter demanding access to our water. He's got his dodgy lawyers on retainer, and we don't know who else he has on his payroll. We must keep this in-house as much as possible. I can't risk someone tipping Leo off, when we both know how small the Territory is at times. Look, Leo may come across as a smooth-talking businessman, but he's not.'

'Tell that to the local mother's group who love him for the donation he made to the school pool.'

'Do you trust Leo?'

'Nope. He's too smooth for my books.'

'But he's smart. Leo has always been ten steps ahead of us. But not this time. This time we have him.'

'Any idea when Leo is going to start harvesting that crop?' Marcus tapped on the images showing Leo's dope field.

'Dex reckons it'll be less than two weeks.'

'And what are you and your brothers going to do in that time?' Marcus leaned back in his director's chair, like Dex rocked on his chair's back legs.

'Besides protecting our property, we're all taking turns to watch Leo's outfit.'

'Are you saying you have your neighbour under full surveillance?'

'That prick has been doing it to us, long before we even met him. Did you know he had one of his cronies strongarm Charlie, trying to get him to sign off on the caretaker's caveat before we bought the station?'

'He what?' Marcus sat forward in his chair.

'The only reason they stopped was because Bree shot one of them in the arse. Nothing beats a redhead with a temper who is very protective over her family.' He shook his head, admiring her for that. When he shouldn't. But Bree had no fear when it came to protecting her family.

'*She what*?' Marcus slammed his fists down on his desk, his voice rising as he leaned over the desk and scowled at Ryder. '*What sort of hillbilly, redneck outfit are you running out there?*'

As Marcus ranted about the many laws they'd broken, Ryder dragged out the second bottle of bourbon from his carry bag. This one was the Limited Edition Single Barrel bottle of Jacks.

The two bottles of high-end bourbon on Marcus's desk reminded Ryder of something Bree had said to him just yesterday while eating cupcakes: that she was open to bribery and corruption. But Marcus was different—not the corruption part, but a little gentle bribery… maybe. Still, he was someone Ryder had come to respect deeply, both as an officer of the law and as a friend.

'I'm sorry to put you in this position, Marcus, but…'

'Go on, spill it all, so I can really spit the dummy and start working on my ulcer.'

'There are some old shotguns at the station, too.' Even if Bree would give him an earful, he did promise Marcus he'd share any news.

Marcus sat back heavily in his chair, the scowl still there. 'Let me guess, you've found Price's illegal gun stash. How many?'

He shrugged, while trying to do his best to protect Bree. 'Will anyone get into trouble if I surrender those guns?' Bree may have asked about the need to surrender those unregistered shotguns earlier, but when it came to actually handing them over, he guessed it'd take some convincing. Knowing Bree, she'd argue her case for finders keepers instead.

Marcus glared long and hard at Ryder as he swung in his director's chair. His eyes then flicked to the closed door, where they heard Charlie's muffled voice from the other side.

Marcus let out a deep sigh while rubbing a rough hand over his face. 'If you can deliver those weapons to me, anonymously, no one will get into trouble.' He then reached out and turned the bottles around to read their labels. 'You know my wife owns a bar.'

'You'd be hard-pressed to find those particular brands of bourbon out here.'

'I know.' Marcus swivelled around in his chair and put them on the shelf behind him. 'I talked to Finn.'

'And?'

'You were right. Leo works for a fairly well-known crime organisation down south. They have their finger in everything: smuggling, racketeering, you name it. Normally they stay down south, but Finn discovered that Leo is branching out, with their blessings.'

'Which is who Leo must be supplying.'

'I'm assuming so, which would make sense with your theory about Leo using his property as part of some money-laundering scheme, too.' Marcus sat back in his chair, raking fingers through his hair. 'This is big.'

'I know.'

'I'll talk to my supervisor —'

'Do you trust him?'

'I do. Back in the day, I worked for the drug squad in Melbourne, and our biggest haul was for ten million. This...' he said, pointing at the paperwork, '... this makes me, and my team, look stupid.'

'How do you think I feel when the prick is right next door stealing my water and taking pot shots at my cousin in her plane. I will not let Leo get away with this. It's why I'm here telling you everything, to help you catch this prick. And I intend to share any information we learn, including tape footage to use as evidence.'

'I guess I'd better rustle up some paperwork to get around the illegal surveillance. Will we find any cameras that can be traced back to you when we make our bust?'

'No.'

'Good. I'll write this information off then as an anonymous tip.' Marcus began scribbling down some notes.

'Will you keep me posted?'

Marcus frowned, his pen pausing. 'You'd better keep me posted.'

'I said I would.'

'Good. And, once I've calmed down, I might come out and have a squiz at your surveillance set-up. Is it at the farmhouse?'

'No. Bree's made us a boardroom and a bar out there now. Said we needed to learn about work–life balance.' Although his world didn't feel very balanced.

'My wife does the same for me. It's what we agreed on when we got married, that there was more to life than work.'

It's what Ryder had hoped for at the station, his home, which was now in danger.

'Hey, does this new bar of yours keep the good stuff?'

'Only the lower-shelf stuff for my brothers. But I promise to break the seal on a few bottles worth tasting should you visit.' He owed Marcus that much.

'It'll take me a few days to organise things. Red tape will be slow, especially if we want to keep this as in-house as possible.'

'Do you trust your team?'

'Absolutely, or I would've transferred their arses out of here. If what you're saying about Leo having contacts in the government is true, we'll have to act fast once that search warrant is signed off.'

'How long will it take to get that warrant?'

'First, I'll need to legitimise your surveillance, that'll help me get a warrant. We don't want Leo getting off on some technicality, or have him coming back at you—'

'Leo doesn't scare me.'

'But he knows you have a family.'

The thought of his family in danger in his home only made his guts churn to hard concrete. 'If Leo gets busted, what'll happen to him?'

'By the sheer commercial volume, I'd say a minimum of fourteen years. But he'll lose all his assets, unless he proves he's made a purchase with legitimate funds, like his land.'

'There was no bill of sale for Leo's property. He never paid any stamp duty or land tax, nothing. But he's got his name on the property title without any mortgage to it.' Which clearly demonstrated the level of powerful contacts Leo had within the government system.

It made Marcus frown deeper. 'How do you know?'

'I had my lawyers do a property search when Leo tried to take our water, which he's now blatantly stealing from us. I'm putting a cap on this, Marcus. Two weeks, maximum. I don't think any of us will handle the pressure longer than that without snapping.'

'It'll be over before Leo can harvest, I promise you that.'

'Good.' Fourteen years didn't seem long enough for Leo, who was just slippery enough to escape prison time. Leo also had more than enough money to make bail and hire a private jet to skip the country.

Meanwhile Marcus had limited resources, with a small and somewhat inexperienced crew, looking after an area as big as a European country.

Ryder did not want Leo to get away with what he'd done to Bree and Charlie, and the fear he was now causing his own family. This was his home, he'd bought it specifically for his family, and he'd defend it to the death if he had to.

He followed Marcus out into the main foyer where poor Porter was being hassled by Charlie, while Bree picked over the evidence on the large table.

'There you are,' said Charlie. 'Are you done, son?'

'I am. Where to next?'

'The morgue. We were talking about walking over, but I like riding in that beast of yours. Makes me feel all important, you know.' Charlie grinned, wiping down his shirt as if wearing a fancy tie. 'But I gotta ask before we skedaddle, what's happening with that gold there, Marcus?'

'We've locked it up in the evidence safe until you're ready

to do something with it,' Marcus said, leaning his shoulder against the doorframe of his office. 'Legally, they're yours—but until we close the file on the case, it's safer in our hands. You know there were two boxes of gold ore?'

Charlie's grey eyebrows disappeared under the brim of his hat. 'Two boxes?'

'There was a bigger box the bodies were leaning against,' said Porter. 'It was a heavy sucker, too.'

Charlie scratched the back of his head, as if trying to remember. 'I only saw the first box… That must be my brother's nest egg he wrote about in his letter. It's what Harry was going to use to start his new life with Penelope Price.'

'Now it's yours, Charlie.'

'What will I do with it at my age? Might be a good little nest egg for the granddaughter.' Charlie winked at Bree.

'I'm fine, Pop. Spend it on yourself or donate it to your favourite charity.'

'Isn't that you, kid?'

She grinned, while angling her head at the photos spread out on the table. 'Porter? Was there a length of elastic in the evidence you brought in from archives?'

'Um, yeah…' The constable rummaged through the plastic bags to find the right one. 'Here. Don't know why that was there. But then again, they botched the entire investigation.'

'That's not a nice thing to say about the police department while wearing the uniform, with your boss standing right there.' With her phone, Bree took a photo of the elastic band, picking it up to feel it through the plastic as if trying to work out its dimensions.

What was up with that elastic band? Bree had pointed it out when they were going through the murder file only last night—although that felt like a year ago now.

'Back then, South Australia Police ran this investigation,' explained Porter. 'The officer in charge of the murder case had only been on the job for a week, I feel sorry for the guy. They didn't have the training or the tools we have today, and all this poor guy was given was a uniform, a set of keys to the station that was basically a room with a cot for him to sleep on, a police car that struggled to drive on the dirt tracks, and a phone line that kept dropping out. The poor guy had no support.' Porter shrugged, looking around at the modern police station.

'How do you know all that?'

'I went through his notes, and I can read between the lines. That constable was a lot younger than me, simply ordered to take photos, bag up everything, and send it down with the body. Even if my maths isn't the best, the measurements he made were all wrong.'

'I agree,' said Ryder. 'We were working on it last night.'

'Did you figure out anything?' Marcus asked.

'Only that the measurements were wrong. But at least that young officer took enough photos for us to work off the images. We're still working on it and haven't come to any conclusions yet.'

'Like I am.' Porter waved his hand over the table, filled with evidence.

'Which reminds me...' Bree looked up from the evidence table. 'Pop? You said Jack Price oversaw the munitions for the station? What sort of munitions?'

After talking about the missing cases of shotguns, her question had Ryder and Marcus standing very still to listen.

'Well, there were the usual rifles and shotties, as well as bullets and shells.'

'Was there anything else?'

'Gelly.'

'What?'

'Boom-boom sticks.' Charlie grinned wide. 'Gelignite.'

'Why would you have dynamite on a cattle station?' Porter asked.

'Jack Price was using it for the major excavations we had going on for Starvation Dam. It was back in 1961, during the first year of that drought, and Darcie's dad wanted the dam dug in deeper. We were all sick of using that ol' Massey backhoe, we called the widow maker, it gave us a heck of time. That's when Jack Price said he could blast it, and he did.'

'So how did that put Jack Price in charge of the munitions?' Porter asked.

'Back then there were no gun laws, but it was the head stockman's job to ration out the guns and ammo to deal with the wildlife and whatnot. You'd give a stash to the boundary riders, the bore runners, and even today I'm always carrying ammo in the saddle with me, just like Bree.'

'As Elsie Creek Station's head stockman,' said Porter, 'did you keep dynamite, Charlie?'

'Me? No. We only used it for Starvation Dam. Well, Price did. Only coz he knew his weapons, kind of like you there, son.' Charlie pointed to Ryder.

'Can I ask what happened to Jack Price's body?' Bree asked.

Porter flicked through some paperwork. 'It sat in the morgue for ages, because no one claimed him, no relatives, nothing. Which makes sense, now that we know it's a false name. Eventually, the local stockmen chipped in to pay for his burial, and the Salvos buried him in the Katherine Cemetery in the section designated for those without means or family.'

'Did you find any of Jack Price's family, now you know his real name?' Bree asked.

'I'm trying. Jack Price—or Jake Blackwell—had a younger sister who is proving to be a challenge to track down. But for Penelope Price's family I found one of her cousin's daughters.'

'What are they doing with Penelope's remains?' Charlie asked with sadness in his voice.

'Well, at first, they didn't care about the body and had no clue who Penelope was at all.' Porter slid his hands into the pockets of his police uniform and gave a meek shrug. 'It was only when I mentioned there may be a stack of cash to inherit that they volunteered to bury her down south.'

'How much cash did Penelope have on her?' Bree asked.

'Twenty thousand, in old bills.'

'Pop? How much was twenty grand worth back in 1962? I mean, compared to now.'

'Well, hard to say…' Charlie rubbed the back of his neck. 'Back then, if Penelope had that much tucked away, they would've had the means to buy a decent house, for sure.'

'A whole house, for twenty thousand dollars?' Porter blurted out.

'Ryder?' Bree looked to him for some explanation.

'Taking inflation into consideration,' said Ryder, 'twenty K back then would be the equivalent of over three hundred grand today.'

'Poor Penelope. No one to grieve for her for the right reasons. It's not right, you know.' Charlie held his hat over his heart. 'Do you reckon we can bury her here with Harry?' he asked Bree.

Porter shook his head. 'Sorry, Charlie, Penelope's family has already signed off on it, according to the morgue.'

'Which is where we're heading next. Thanks for your help, Porter. Let's go, Pop.' Bree scooped up her large leather bag from the floor, then hooked her arm through her grandfather's. 'Hi, Marcus. Bye, Marcus.'

Ryder recognised that look. Bree was on a mission, and nothing was going to stop her.

'Ryder?' Marcus mumbled quietly, grabbing Ryder's arm. 'I know you promised to keep me informed, and I trust you will. But what about her?' He nodded at the redhead, escorting Charlie to the front doors. 'Word is Leo has a thing for Bree. And she's never been shy to go toe-to-toe with him.'

Ryder's jaw clenched. The ice in his veins thickened, making every muscle in his body taut. For anyone watching, Ryder would only seem calm. Icy calm, with his voice low and controlled. 'Leo won't get near her.' Because he wasn't letting her out of his sight.

Twenty-eight

Hooking her arm through her grandfather's, Bree escorted Charlie, with Ryder following, down the deserted corridor, in the far forgotten corner of the small bush hospital, that ended at a glass door. There, Bree pressed the buzzer.

'Hi, Romie.' She waved at the middle-aged man in a lab coat, working inside the sterile room filled with steel benches. It was the morgue that doubled-up as the funeral home in this small town.

'Hey, Bree.' Romie opened the door. 'Are you here about Harry?'

'We are.'

'Come on through.'

'Do I have to?' Charlie hesitated at the doorway.

'We won't be long, Pop.'

'Are you comin' in too, son?' Charlie squeezed his hat, looking to Ryder to help him escape.

'I'll be right beside you.' Ryder was a cool customer who looked like he'd seen a few dead bodies in his time.

Even though she was dying to know about his meeting with Marcus, Bree was here for Charlie. Family always came first.

Romie rustled through the paperwork on his desk and pulled out a file. Flicking it open, he grabbed a pen. 'So, what are you planning for Harry? Cremation?'

'We're gonna bury him next to our father, with the rest of

the Splint family up at the local cemetery.' Charlie rolled his shoulders, clearing his throat. 'Take note, kid. I want the same. Don't forget, my plot is between my wife and daughter. Your…'

'I know, Pop.' Even if she'd known about his funeral plans for years, it still didn't stop Bree's stomach from spiralling at the horror of what her grandfather was saying. Sure, Charlie was an old man, with a heart condition, but she liked living under the fantasy that her grandfather was going to outlive her.

Bree needed to change this conversation. 'Romie, what's happening with Penelope Price?'

Romie flicked open another folder, dragging his finger down the page. 'Says here she's getting shipped out tomorrow. Why?'

'It's flamin' wrong what they're doing.'

Bree put her hand on Charlie's shoulder to silence him as she opened her bag and pulled out a bottle of her special homemade gin and put it on the table.

'Is that the cucumber-rose flavoured gin? My wife likes that one.'

'So you said.' And it was.

'How big is your handbag?' Ryder's eyebrows knitted together as he gawked at her large leather bag. 'No wonder Dex calls it the witchy sack.'

'Do you mind? Pop and I are negotiating here.'

'I wish you'd tell me what we're negotiating about, kid,' mumbled Charlie.

'Romie, I want you to swap wedding fingers on the skeletons.'

'Excuse me?' Romie blinked as Charlie's jaw dropped.

Ryder massaged one of his eyebrows, sharing a deep chuckle. It was rare to hear Ryder laugh.

'I'm serious.' Sure, it sounded ridiculous now she'd voiced her request, but the more she thought about it, the more it made sense. 'Penelope and Harry were lovers, who were going to get married, and they were buried together in a cave for over sixty years. Now they're going to be separated—it's wrong.'

'I agree, kid, but a finger?'

'I don't have a set of wedding rings on me, and I bet they took off all her jewellery. Amirite, Romie?'

'They had to. Its evidence.' Romie peered at the paperwork. 'Says here that Penelope Price wasn't wearing a wedding ring when they found her. But wasn't she married to that other fella, Jack Price?'

'It's complicated.' Boy, was it ever!

'Eh?'

'Look, they were going to get a sort of…' She shrugged, at a loss for the right word.

'Annulment,' said Ryder.

'That.' She gave the dark and broody male a nod of thanks. 'An annulment would have allowed Penelope Price to marry my Great-Uncle Harry, making her Charlie's sister-in-law.'

'Too right.' Charlie's head bobbed up and down eagerly.

'That's why I'm suggesting we swap their finger bones, where they would have worn their wedding bands as a symbol of their love—because they never got that chance to get married.' Was she making sense? 'Look, it might not be the most romantic gesture, but if Harry is going to be buried here, and Penelope is going to be shipped down south to be buried in some shoe box next to the pet cemetery—'

'I bloody well hope not!' Charlie's nostrils flared.

'Okay, Pop, this is the plan I'm proposing.' Bree held up her naked ring finger. 'If we swap Harry's wedding finger with Penelope's, her family won't know any different. It'll just be us and the departed lovers. That way they'll still have a piece of each other with them no matter where they go. They'll still be *together forever*. Just like the words they carved into that cave's wall.'

'I get it.' Charlie nodded. 'And I like it.'

Romie jabbed his pointer finger at his wrinkled forehead as if wrestling with what was right in the eyes of the law. 'I can't allow anyone to tamper with the bodies.'

'They're skeletons. How is anyone going to know that it didn't happen in that cave?'

'I could lose my job, Bree.'

'Fine. I'll give you a case of gin and swear to never tell a soul.' She looked at the others for confirmation.

Ryder dragged out his wallet and pulled out five crisp hundred-dollar bills. 'Here, Romie, why don't you go buy Charlie a coffee or something?'

It didn't take long for Romie to snatch up the cash. 'For the record, I know nothing.'

'You're a good man, Romie,' said Charlie, hooking his arm over Romie's shoulder. 'Why don't you show me where that smancy water fountain is?' asked Charlie, escorting Romie down the corridor. 'Did you see the footy on the tellie the other night? Didn't the Saints cop a hiding…'

Ryder closed the door wearing a smug expression.

'You didn't have to flash the cash. Romie would have taken the gin.' She snatched a pair of gloves from the box on the nearby shelf.

'Done this before, have we?'

'No. And if you'd told me this morning, I'd be doing this, I would have laughed in your face.'

'You are unpredictable, I'll give you that.'

She looked over the paperwork to find the right locker. 'Please, no icky stuff.'

'I've got you.' Ryder gently pushed her aside to open the cold storage locker.

Sliding on the plastic gloves, she took a steady breath as if bracing herself. Death wasn't new to her — come on, she'd grown up on a cattle station and had seen her fair share of it in the harsh outback. Still, this was different. 'You aren't afraid of dead bodies, are you?'

'Nope. You?' Ryder rolled out the large tray holding a long black bag.

'I've seen way more than I care to. But these were my first human skeletons. I've seen plenty of cattle bones in my times.' And the body on the tray was just that, bones. 'Which one is this?'

'Harry.' Ryder opened the next refrigerated locker and pulled out the other tray to read the tag on the black bag. 'This is Penelope.'

'At least they kept them side by side in the same freezer.' She unzipped Harry's black bag. 'You know, this should feel wrong.'

'It doesn't?' His tone was sarcastic as he unzipped Penelope's bag.

'No. It feels right.' Over time they'd just been left with a series of bones, allowing her to grab the bones of Harry's fourth finger. She then turned to Penelope. Her bones were smaller. Without clothing, or jewellery, it looked like a skeleton you'd see in any school science lab.

'For the record…'

'Hmmm…' Penelope's bone was so frail and light.

'I think this is a good idea.'

She gazed up at the stern stockman. 'I had to do something. They've been together for so long, it's not fair to separate them now.'

'But why the wedding finger?'

'Legend says there's a vein that runs from the heart to the fourth finger of the left hand.' She held up her gloved hand to trace along the finger. 'The Romans called it *vena amoris* — the vein of love. That's why most people wear their wedding rings there: to show their hearts have been claimed.'

'I don't see any rings on your fingers.'

She spread her fingers in the glove. 'I can't wear them. Working with hot metals means rings heat up and burn me. Pop's the same. He'll wear his wedding band if he went out, to show he belonged to someone.' Her voice softened as she glanced at the couple. 'I bet you don't believe in soulmates.'

He leaned closer, tucking one of her curls aside. 'I can see you do.'

'As much as I hate to admit it, I am a romantic.' She smiled faintly, thinking of her pile of romance books and all the times she'd helped Cap and Ash plan romantic gestures for their partners. 'I know this might not be the most romantic thing, but at least they'll have a part of each other, no matter where they end up.'

She placed the finger bones in their new spots. 'What do you think?'

Ryder stood beside her with his head tilted, his masculine aroma divine against the sterile room. 'No one will be able to tell what you've done. There's only a slight difference in the colour and bone length. Other than that, they look undisturbed.'

'But we'll know, and Charlie will know. Harry was family, and if Harry had married Penelope, she would be family too.' And it stopped part of that guilt for having ever thought wrong of Harry. Even if Harry may be accused of murder, his letter and his love for Penelope suggested otherwise.

'Harry and Penelope were going to elope. They were planning their happily-ever-after, it just got taken from them too soon—it's not fair.' Bree might not believe in love, but this couple did. And by doing this, maybe she would begin to believe in the beauty and power of love, too.

She went to zip up their bags and paused. 'I feel like we should say something.'

'What?'

'I don't know. It's not like I moonlight as a bone collector.'

'What's that prayer you say when you're about to eat cupcakes? That sounds like a wedding vow.'

'Hmm...' But was it right? 'Dearly beloved, we are gathered here today to join these two people in the act of matrimony...' Her voice bounced off the walls. 'It sounds lame.'

'Keep going.' Ryder nodded at her in encouragement.

'Fine.'

She took a deep breath, searching for some sort of inspiration for a couple who deserved so much better.

'Penelope, I may not have known you, but I learned about

you in Harry's letter, and I could hear the love he had for you in his words. When I first saw you in that cave, after my initial surprise, I saw a man and a woman. I saw a man sheltering his loved one, where you held on to each other, to comfort each other through the darkness, the way all those love stories say it should be. That even in death, you still never parted.'

'Harry, Penelope, in the short time you were together, you showed an enormous amount of love for each other. You showed love is about sharing fears and finding comfort in each other. You showed love for each other by working through the many challenges you faced, the painful times, and the hopes that had you planning your future together. You started your journey through life apart, and through the threads of time, you finally found each other to end your days together. I wish it had been different for you, but in the end, you chose each other because of love, because it was that once-in-a-lifetime kind of love.'

Placing her hands over their ring fingers she said, 'They say love is felt in the bones, where you truly become a part of each other, and I believe your love story will continue. Maybe you'll meet again in the afterlife, or in a new life where you'll meet for the first time, but know you were together to the end in this one. Rest in peace, Mrs Penelope *Splint*. Rest in peace Mr Harry Splint. May your souls be forever entwined. For you are his. She is yours. Always *together forever*.'

Ryder slid his arms around Bree's shoulders, and tenderly wiped the single tear trickling down her cheek. 'Together. Forever.'

It sounded like a promise that silkily glided over her skin to shift something inside her chest, spilling a gentle warmth from deep within her stone-cold soul. Was the fortress of granite guarding her heart, once reduced to ash, now stirring to life for Ryder?

Twenty-nine

'**D**o you want us to wait, kid?' Charlie asked from the front passenger seat of Ryder's ute, as he parked in front of the Post Office on Elsie Creek's main street.

'No, I'm good, Pop.' Bree unclipped her seat belt and quickly hustled out the back door, before Ryder could help. 'You can take the rest of the deliveries to the pub.'

At least Ryder could help her with the thin boxes that held her various branding irons, fire pokers, and swords. 'I'm happy to wait for you.' He didn't want her out of his sight. But it was daylight, on the main street, in a small town where Bree and Charlie knew everyone.

'I'll be catching up on the town gossip with Mrs Sternston for a bit.' She nodded at the sewing store next to the post office.

'Do you sew?'

'Steel and metals, sure. Needle and thread, no. However, I know some lovely ladies who'll happily do any sewing for me for a bottle of gin.' She gave one of her outlaw gin-maker grins that made her green eyes shine with mischief. Damn, she was pretty with her hair down and in that dress.

'Do you barter a lot with your gin?'

'Aw come on, cupcake, we live in the outback, it's the land of mates' rates. And I know you play that game, giving a certain senior sergeant two bottles of your top-shelf bourbon.'

'You saw that, huh?' But he bought those bottles, Bree

illegally distilled hers.

She ignored him as usual. 'I'll meet you at the pub when I'm done. Pop, please be sure to take all the branding irons inside. The rodeo is on next weekend, and a lot of our customers are coming in to collect. Mean Rene knows all about it. Be sure to give her a tip when you do.'

'I know what I'm doing, kid.' Charlie gave her a short wave, the grin growing as he rolled up the electric windows, then rolled them down again. 'Look, this car's so fancy the windows roll up with the touch of a button.' He was like a big kid in that car, rolling up the windows, again.

'Pop loves your car, almost as much as Dex's ute.' Bree took the boxes from Ryder's arms and stepped up onto the pavement.

'Are you going to the rodeo?' Ryder spotted the rodeo's poster on the Post Office noticeboard as he closed the back tray of his ute.

'Probably not. Ask Charlie. If he goes, I'll go.' With a twirl of her skirt showing off her creamy legs, her thick hair trailed down her back as she headed for the front doors of the post office. A stockman quickly jumped the steps to open the door for Bree, tipping his hat to her.

But then the guy tilted his head to perve on Bree as she disappeared inside.

Ryder glared with pure heat at the stranger.

'Sorry, mate. Didn't realise she was taken.' The stockman tapped his hat and hurried on by.

Even though he wanted to wait for Bree, Ryder drove Charlie to the pub. It was a quick trip to the building that towered over the one and only main intersection of Elsie Creek. An outback town so small it didn't even have a set of traffic lights, just a pedestrian crossing that he'd seen a pet water buffalo use more than the residents. 'Bree mentioned there's a rodeo on next weekend.'

From the front passenger seat, Charlie peered out the passenger window. 'Yep. Out the back of the pub.'

'Do you want to go?' He wouldn't mind taking Bree out.

'Bree said she'll go if you go.'

'I don't go anymore, son.'

'Why not? Is it an ex-rodeo thing?'

'It's a family thing.'

Ryder shrugged, not getting it.

'I'll go to the rodeo in Isa, Heartbreak, Katherine, Borroloola, Noonamah, and even the smaller rodeos across the Territory. Heck, I've even been to that smancy one on the Gold Coast for the national titles. But I don't go to the local one out 'ere at the pub.'

'Why not?'

'Because too many remember.'

Ryder parked his ute in the pub's dusty car park. Behind the pub stood a long stretch of green lawn with an empty rodeo ring at the far edge.

Surprisingly, it was a full-sized rodeo arena with an announcer's booth, the calf chute, two bucking chutes, turnout pens, even a small grandstand complete with empty stadium-style bleachers to seat a decent enough crowd. It had been a long time since he'd been to a rodeo.

But what he couldn't understand was why would Charlie, a retired national champion, avoid going to the rodeo in his own hometown?

Ryder unloaded the assorted brands from the ute's back tray. They were heavy. 'I'll carry these in for you, Charlie.' No wonder Bree was strong, if she worked with these daily.

'Did you help Bree do that thing with the fingers?' Charlie hitched up his jeans, and with that bandy-legged swagger he headed for the pub's doors.

'We did. Bree even said a nice prayer, too.'

'She's a good kid, that one. I know she did that for me.'

'I think Bree did that more for Harry and Penelope.' Especially those words Bree had said about love. He'd never heard anyone speak from the heart like that. It had been an honour for him to be there, to finally see that true inner beauty beneath the sassy redhead's outlaw attitude, to see the tender woman with a whole lot of love to give.

'Harry would have liked that, for sure.' Charlie gave a stiff sniff, with his grey eyes blinking as if ridding some grit that made his eyes all glassy. 'Come on, let's go have a beer and then skedaddle before the rodeo mob comes into town.'

Half an hour later, Bree made heads turn when she walked into the front bar. The din of conversation among the all-male crowd died down as she made her way to Charlie. A few stockmen nodded at her, a few even kissed her cheek, but more than a few of the younger male patrons watched her walk past with their heads tilted at the way her hips shifted with that outlaw swagger only highlighted by those long red tresses of a temptress in cowboy boots.

Bree was stunning as she leaned against the bar like she'd done it a thousand times, holding up her finger and with a nod at the barmaid she ordered her beer without saying a word. 'Pop. Did you do the deliveries?'

Charlie sipped on his cold schooner of beer, then wiped over his frothy lip. 'Yep. All done. Got Mean Rene looking after it. Even paid her a tip for her troubles. You were gone a while.'

'Mrs Sternston says *hi*. And Tess, and Molly, and—'

'Cor blimey, was there a sewing class happening?'

'It is a sewing store, Pop.' She took a sip of her beer, casually glancing around the room. 'Have you ordered lunch yet?'

'I'm not hungry.' Charlie then mumbled something over his beer, plonking his elbow on the bar. 'Rodeo mob got here early, they had a meeting on.'

'So?' She shrugged. 'You like Lenny's cooking.'

Charlie scowled, with his tone harsh. 'Order our meals as a takeaway, coz we're not staying, kid. And that's *final*.'

'Fine.' She cocked her head at her grandfather as if reading more than Charlie's foul mood. 'Do you want some lunch, Ryder?'

'I thought I'd shout lunch.'

'Bree will pay, son. It's only fair we pay for you driving us around today.'

'Back soon, I'll get us dinner too, because I'm not cooking when I get home.'

'Wait up, Bree…' Ryder followed her to the far end of the noisy bar. 'Where are you ordering?'

'From the chef himself.' She pushed on the side door to enter the quiet corridor.

'Well, if it isn't my favourite redhead.' It was Cowboy Craig, with his blond curls and cocky smile, strolling towards them, giving Bree a hug. 'Charlie here?'

'In the bar, and he's not happy. The rodeo crowd is here.'

'Damn, I didn't think of that. The committee were having their meeting about the rodeo next weekend.'

'Can you go keep him company, while I order lunch?'

Craig adjusted his white cowboy hat that only showed off his tan and blue eyes. 'Sure. But can I trust you to behave?'

'Always. That's why I brought my bodyguard.' She tossed her thumb in Ryder's direction.

'What?' Ryder had to be missing something.

'Craig…' She grabbed the cowboy's wrist. 'Before you go, we found Charlie's brother, Harry.'

'No way.' Craig listened intently as Bree explained the details.

She was giving far too much information away for Ryder's liking. Which wasn't like her, when Bree rarely told Ryder or his brothers the big picture.

'Thanks for letting me know. I'll go have a beer with Charlie now. Do you want me to come out home or something? It's a bit late for me to get you some cupcakes as my couch-surfing fee.'

Bree grinned.

Ryder frowned. Nobody should buy Bree cupcakes but him.

'Just buy the old man a beer.' Ryder cut in on this

conversation while putting his hand on Bree's lower back.

'I will. Hey, Bree?' Craig swivelled around on the heels of his fancy cowboy boots with their thick Cuban heels. His thumbs hooked into the belt loops of his jeans where his big rodeo champion belt buckle caught the light. 'Charlie should come to the rodeo. He is a legend, and he has a lot to share with the younger riders. They'd appreciate five minutes of his time.'

'As much as we both know it'll do him the world of good, it won't be long and word will get out that Harry's been found with another stockman's wife, which will stir it all up again.'

'I get it. I'll keep an eye on him in the bar. Ryder.' Craig tapped on the brim of his hat and pulled open the door to the front bar where the noise of voices mingled with the jukebox until the door shut behind him.

'Bree?'

'Hmm.'

Ryder grabbed her hand before she took off on him. 'Why doesn't Charlie want to go to the rodeo?'

'You should ask Charlie that.'

He spun her around to face him. 'I'm not going back to playing that stupid game of answering a question with a question where we end up snapping at each other.' He towered over her.

But the little outlaw only lifted her chin, sneering at him. 'You're snapping at me now.'

'Come on, we promised each other no more secrets.' Especially after she'd just been talking so openly with Craig only moments ago. 'Tell me the whole story, not drip-feed me information like some leaky tap I have to keep fixing!' He wasn't having any of that, not anymore.

'Fine.'

He gritted his teeth and waited. How is it that Bree could stir him up so quickly? 'And...'

'Jack Price taught Charlie how to rodeo and helped start the local rodeo here in town. He was head of the committee, where many of the original members—who are still involved—haven't forgotten Jack Price. It's those committee members who made it hard for Charlie to ride or even visit the Elsie Creek Rodeo, and the rest just followed their lead.'

'I see.'

'Do you? This is a small town, and the stockmen out here live to a code. Charlie has had to live with all that talk.'

'Because his brother ran off with a stockman's wife.' Which was a big no.

'Harry also stands accused of murdering a head stockman.'

He narrowed his eyes at the redhead. 'Do you believe Harry did it?'

'No, I don't. Not after re-reading that letter again at the police station earlier.'

Yet Bree was clever, so something else must have triggered her to make that assumption, compared to how she'd looked last night, when Bree wrote the words of a dead man on the floor of what she called the murder room.

'You have to see it from Charlie's point of view,' continued Bree. 'For the last sixty years, Charlie has lived with the consequences of his brother's actions.'

'How?' With four younger brothers it made Ryder step back with his brow ruffling.

'Even though Charlie has had a pretty full life, he was like Mia, hiding from her ex out at Elsie Creek Station. Charlie stayed out there to escape the looks, the frowns, and the fingers pointed at him whenever the local rodeo was on in town. Darcie told me that Jack Price had made some good friends out here. So, when their head stockman was murdered, people needed someone to blame, and Charlie became the easy target. Resentment like that tends to stick around here a lot longer than anywhere else.'

'It was hardly Charlie's fault.'

'I know. But with Harry missing, and that damning bit of evidence he drew in chalk—the one I didn't even know existed until yesterday—it was enough for some of the locals, especially those on the rodeo committee, to take it out on Charlie.' She gave a sigh, with her voice softening. 'It's why Charlie isn't having a funeral for Harry.'

Didn't that tug at Ryder's brow with concern. 'Why not? Charlie's been searching for his brother, he'd—'

'Because Charlie thinks it'll just stir up that bush telegraph into a feeding frenzy, and he doesn't want to be around to hear it. Would you?'

'No. You?'

That evil grin of hers showed she was ready to play dirty.

'I'd dare any of them to say it to my face. It's why Charlie doesn't want me here, because he knows I'll have a go at them.'

'And that's why I'm the bodyguard.' Because if anyone dared to say anything to Charlie, especially to Bree, he'd defend them. Without question.

But Bree would also complain that she could fight her own battles—which was why she was never shy in speaking her mind.

Pity that most of the battling going on these days was between Bree and himself.

She then looked him up and down, a subtle curl forming at the corners of her luscious lips, with her eyes flickering with a devilish shimmer, before turning and walking towards the pub's kitchen. It was a great view of her swinging those hips in that dress. 'Did you find out who Ghost is?'

'In between setting up cameras and arming my brothers with Glocks? Yeah, I did.' Ryder crossed his arms, eyeing her carefully.

Bree tilted her head, a smirk tugging at her lips. 'You armed your brothers with handguns?' From that look, she already knew all about it.

'It seemed like the right thing to do. Guess what else seemed like the right thing to do?' He leaned in slightly. 'I'm buying a Ghost mask so you can teach me how to play.'

Thirty

Late that night, Ryder took the night shift, kicking his brothers out to spend time with their partners. With his boots resting on the boardroom table, he kept one eye on the monitors, making a record of any activity happening on Leo's property. On the other side of him stood the creation of string lines showing the trajectory of the shot, with the murder file spread out before him, next to his bottle of bourbon and glass.

'Don't you sleep?' Bree stood in the doorway, carrying a jug of ice that he'd bet was filled with her homemade gin.

'Is this where I tell you off for sneaking around?' He tilted his head to admire the way she slinked into the room to peer at the wall of television monitors. Still in that pretty dress and boots that showed off her legs from town.

'Much happening?'

'Nope. But we worked out they do sentry rounds every hour—if they remember. I doubt they'll do much tonight.'

'Why?'

'Leo is away, back tomorrow. Left his—what do you call them?'

'Balding gorillas.'

He gave a quick grin. 'They're in charge, drinking beer, watching the football, tucked up inside the air-conditioned demountable they've got.' He pointed to the screen on the left. 'There's only four of them.'

'What's Marcus doing?'

'Trying to get search warrants as quietly as possible, which means getting the okay for our highly illegal surveillance footage, without anyone tipping Leo off.'

Of course, the outlaw would grin at that. 'Leo could have connections in the government, the courts, police, anywhere.'

'I know. But I promised Marcus I'd keep him updated.' Ryder sipped on his bourbon, his eyes following the length of that dress, the way it curved on her hips he itched to grip. 'Where's Charlie?'

'Asleep.'

'What brings you out here?'

'This does.' She dropped a scrap of material on the table.

He plucked it up, warm from being in her hand. 'Elastic? Is this why you went into the sewing shop today?'

Putting her jug of gin on the table, she shuffled through the many images of the original crime scene. 'It's been playing on my mind ever since I spotted it in the crime scene photos, yesterday. Mrs Sternston gave me the complete history of that type of elastic. Do want to hear it?' Her grin matched the shine in her eyes he'd come to recognise when she was being playful. And he liked her being playful. 'I promise to give you the hard and fast version.'

He preferred long and slow, but beggars couldn't be choosers, while pleased that she'd made the effort to come and talk to him. 'Hit me.'

'This is what they call braided elastic. It's used on waistlines, sleeve hems, or necklines commonly found in women's clothing, like the hem of a bodice. See?' She flicked over the curved edge of her top, giving him a beautiful flash of her hot pink lacy bra. Pinching the elastic between her fingers, she stretched it slightly. 'It has issues, like it will perish over time and lose its elasticity.'

'And?' Was he going to get another peek at that bra?

'It shouldn't be part of a murder scene, tucked into the far corner of a tack room.' She tapped on the image showing the elastic lying in the dust in the corner of the room.

'Maybe someone dropped it during the investigation? The

cop was a rookie. Who knows who else walked through the crime scene before the police arrived?'

'I get that. But still…' She shrugged.

'What did you see?' Because Bree had a knack of looking at things differently.

'Besides checking out the elastic band among the evidence at the police station, to get an idea of how long it was, I noticed the chalk piece found in Price's hand…' Again, she shuffled through the images of the sixty-year-old crime scene. 'It's not chalk. The police report says it's calcite mixed with limestone and sandstone.'

'I'm not a geologist, Bree.'

'That's the kind of rock that makes up the Stoneys.' She rolled a white rock across the table.

He sat up in his seat to catch it.

'How did Price, who'd been shot, happen to have that rock in his hand? There was no blackboard to write orders on the wall in this room. The photos also showed there were no other footprints, no blood trails, nothing to say he'd gone in search of something to write with. I've seen movies where the victim has written their killer's name in blood. But this…'

She was right.

Ryder scooped up the photo of Jack Price, holding the chalk as he lay on the ground. He stood to compare it to the drawing on the floor where Bree had written: *Harry Splint did this*.

'If you were shot in the back, bleeding to death, would you write that neatly?' She sounded so cold.

'The adrenaline could've kicked in.'

She arched an eyebrow at him. 'Been shot before, have we?'

'I know you've shot someone.'

'In the bum. He was hurting Charlie.' The fire in her eyes was both attractive and deadly. 'And I'd do it again, without blinking.'

'Okay, Bree,' he said, holding his hand up to calm her down. 'I'm not the enemy… Hey, how many were there that day?'

'Two. The one I shot had Charlie in a headlock over the bonnet of the car. I could hear the pain in my grandfather's voice.'

He gave her hand a tender squeeze. 'I'd do the same if anyone hurt my family.'

'Well, that idiot I shot wailed like a banshee. It was enough to scare away a flock of galahs grazing in the nearby paddock.' She pulled her hand free, to walk around the string line set-up. 'That guy was spilling blood through his fingers, with the help of his mate carrying him to the car. He was in no condition to write my name in the dirt out front of the homestead.' She pointed at her drawing of the body spread out on the floor.

She was right.

'What about you? I'm sure you have plenty of war stories about wounded people, considering you made weapons for them.'

'I'm not sharing them.' He scowled heavily, hands on hips. 'Don't ask.'

'But—'

'Bree.' His voice low, his teeth gritted. 'Don't.'

'I have one question.'

He closed his eyes, knowing it wouldn't be one question, because it'd lead to a dozen questions and so on.

'Jonathan told me it took ten years for you and your brothers to get back together, and that was due to you being in the Army for work.'

He barely nodded.

'But the Army would have given you leave. So why did you stay away from your brothers for that long? Then, when you finally do catch up, you end up buying them a station so you could all live and work together.'

He exhaled, not expecting that question. But when he gazed at Bree, there was no snarkiness, no playfulness, just concern of a different kind. 'I don't know.'

She tilted her head at him as if she didn't believe him. Yet, she never broke eye contact, as if to crack open his bones to the place where he kept his secrets. Some he never wanted to share because he didn't want to remember.

He raked fingers through his hair. 'With the patents, I had the means to support my family. I was investing it anyway, I just saw this place as an investment.'

'You might have at first, but…' She playfully poked at his chest, but he held her hand there.

'I needed my family more than they needed me.'

She double blinked at him, just like he couldn't believe he'd spilled that himself. Only this time it was his turn to step away from the redhead to take a deep swig of his bourbon.

'Go on.'

Of course she'd keep digging. Dex said she'd dig, Ash and Cap too. That Bree had a knack of digging for what hurt you the most. Great, now it was his turn.

If he told her, would she think differently of him?

'I needed to feel again.'

'Eh?'

'I was designing weapons, focusing on the damage they could do to armour plating, or through other obstacles. I wasn't looking at people and the destruction they could create. I'd lost my ability to be empathetic, or have any sympathy, and lost my trust in people.'

'Hey, I was a people person too, until people ruined it for me.' Her smile was gentle, soft even, and so was her tender squeeze as she held his hand. 'When did you realise this?'

'I didn't. My superior officer did. He told me to get out, get a life, and that any weapons I designed in the future should have patents on them before I shared them with anyone. Which I did—but waiting on patents to come through takes time.'

'So that's why you went to the mines?'

'A short stint at a diamond mine, until I got onto the oil rigs.'

'Why?'

'Because they offered food, accommodation, in a place

filled with other hard men, especially on a rig in the middle of the ocean.' He raked fingers through his hair, admitting this more to himself. 'I had to take the time to assimilate back into the real world, or I'd have ended up like Laurel's brother, Clyde, on the streets.'

'Ryder...' The way she said his actual name, it sounded like heaven spilling across her lips. 'I know all about those silent wounds that torment the mind and how they're the hardest to heal. I've also noticed how much you've changed since you first arrived.' She stepped forward to cradle his face in her warm hands, staring deeper into his soul than anyone had ever dared. And with her voice like soft rain falling from a lonely sky he fell for her all over again, with three little words: 'I get it.'

And he believed her.

He wanted to hold her, but she stepped back, her eyes dropping to his hands.

They were in tight fists.

He hadn't realised how wound up he was.

But it did nothing to scare the redhead standing before him. 'You may not have trusted people, but you knew you could trust your family—your brothers, who knew you back before you had money and would treat you that same way. You needed them to...'

'Defrost,' said the guy with ice in his veins.

'And to not hate the world but to see it as place of good. Elsie Creek Station has the gift of being the perfect grown-up's playground.'

'I thought it would be a world without enemies.'

They glanced in the easterly direction of Leo's property, the moment gone. Dammit.

'I have to ask. In your time in the Army, and with your experience dealing with weapons, is it normal for someone to move around after being shot—like in the movies, leaving a blood trail?'

Ryder nodded, realising where she was heading with her questioning. She was trying to figure out if the scene had somehow been staged. 'I've seen wounded soldiers do amazing things when filled with adrenaline. It's quite possible for Price to write that message.'

'He died with the stone in his hand, that wasn't chalk, and this…' She held up the elastic. 'This is part of it, too. Somehow. I know I might not be making sense—'

'It's okay, Bree. I'm listening.' After all, she'd listened to him without judgement. 'I'm open to any theory at this stage.' He took the elastic from her hand.

Bree tapped on the photo. 'Look at the end. You can't see it clearly in the photo, but when I checked it out today at the police station there's a loop, like this…' She knotted one end over into a loop then let the elastic dangle from her fingers. 'What would you use that for? Specifically this length, and with a loop at the end. It had to be attached to something.'

A creeping sensation ran over his scalp. 'Hold this end of the elastic and stay right there.'

'Where are you going?'

'To test it against the model.'

'You really got into the details of this crime scene, didn't you? I'm impressed. It's something I would do.'

'I'm impressed at your doggedness over the elastic and chalk.' But he had yet to digest the other part of sharing his soul with her. 'Keep holding it, I'm going to pull on it.'

She pinched the end with two hands as he pulled the band past the window frame to where he had the dummy-gun balanced on the drum, and right over the trigger.

'I'm going to let go from my end. Keep it taut. On my count… One… Two… Three.' He let it go as if pulling on the shotgun's trigger, the elastic band flung itself across the room, past Bree, and landed in the corner. Exactly like the murder scene's photo.

'The elastic was used from outside the room? But… why…' Bree's eyes widened. 'Someone rigged it? Or… did he do it to himself?'

'That's a huge leap, don't you think?' Ryder raised a brow, but her question had him thinking. 'Here, take this torch and follow me.'

'Where are we going?'

'To take a look at those oil drums. The images showed the lids were off those drums. There is nothing anywhere to say anyone did a check on those drums. And Charlie said no one touched this room in sixty years.'

'Er, hello, I came here a few times a week when I was cooking up a new batch of gin.'

'During that time, did you move any of those drums?'

'Not then, no. Darcie locked it up and told everyone not to come here. And I purposely left them there as a barrier to keep this space private. I only moved them to get to the window when I did the makeover of this room.'

'Which ones were they? I'm looking for fourteen.' He shone his torch over the two rows of oil drums they'd inherited when they'd bought the station. He knew Cap was trying to think of a way to safely get rid of them.

'That row near the outer wall.' On the far side of the long shed, she flashed her torch at the drums lined against the corrugated iron wall. 'Are you looking for a weapon or some clue after all this time?'

'We don't know. I'm just looking.' He grabbed a tyre lever from Dex's workbench for jemmying open the lids. The toxic fumes of the old sump oil forced them to stand back. He did not want to dig around in that gunk.

Bree rummaged around a stack of old tools inside the nearby shed and dragged out an old pitchfork. 'Here, use this.'

With the first drum he stirred the pitchfork around in the soupy thick oil as if it was a cauldron of gunk and found nothing.

The next drum held nothing but more gunk.

Under the outdoor spotlights, Bree opened the lids on more drums, where he'd give each one a poke and stir with the pitchfork, finding nothing but smelly old sump oil long past its use-by date.

But when Ryder jammed the pitchfork into the goo of

another drum, it clunked onto something halfway down. 'I've hit something.' He was able to wedge the tines of the pitchfork under the object, to drag it to the surface. It was a metal container.

'I got it.' Using a garbage bag she'd pinched from behind their outdoor bar, Bree picked up the box. 'It's heavy.'

'Put it down there.' Despite the passage of time and exposure to the oil, the protective seal on the metal container remained intact. However, it showed signs of corrosion, with some rust along the bottom edge.

Swapping the pitchfork for the tyre lever, he prised open the box. Inside, they found a sealed, canvas pouch that was completely dry. The durable canvas bag reminded him of something he'd used in the Army.

Inside, he found a few rolls of wax paper and carefully unrolled the package to discover a stash of thick cardboard rolls, like sticks.

'Is that—'

'Dynamite.' He swallowed hard. 'Bree, we need to move this stuff away. Considering their age, they'll be unstable.' Ryder went to return the dynamite to the box, only to discover the blasting caps used to ignite the explosives were at the bottom of the same box. *What the hell!* 'Move away, Bree.'

'No. You need me to help you.'

He hated her stubbornness at times like this—even if she was right. 'We'll put the dynamite sticks back inside the tin. But I need another container for these blasting caps. I won't keep them together like that. It's too dangerous.'

'I'm on it. Don't do anything silly.'

He shook his head at the woman known to do silly things. 'Why? Will you miss me?' It wasn't his first time handling explosives, but he knew the risks that could trigger an accidental detonation.

There was an almighty crash.

'What are you doing?'

Bree rushed back. 'I pinched the old coffee tin Dex uses

for his bolts. It's big enough for the blasting caps and it comes with a lid.'

'It's perfect.'

'Is this the part where I hold my breath?'

'You can leave and walk away.'

'Stop that.' She glared at him. 'Don't ask me that again. You just concentrate on what you're doing, Captain Cupcake.'

Even though he hated that nickname, he was grateful for her vote of confidence in him.

Taking a deep breath, he focused on the blasting caps and secured them inside the tin. He then carefully re-wrapped the dynamite sticks in the wax paper, sliding them back into the canvas bag, and then put them into the metal box and closed the lid.

Only then did he breathe.

'What do we do with it?' Bree asked.

'I'll put the box of dynamite in one of the ringers' rooms.' He nodded to the dark cluster of buildings on the far side of the stables. 'No one goes there, and it's well away from anyone. But I need you to store those blasting caps somewhere far away from here.'

'I'll store them in the old well.' Bree lightly jogged for the empty field.

'What old well?'

As per usual Bree didn't reply, her silhouette soon swallowed by the blanket of darkness.

That left him holding a box of dynamite.

Under a moonless sky, just after midnight, he headed for the dark buildings that stood on the far side of the stables.

He'd only peeked at these rooms once, when they'd first inspected the property. Like his brothers, he wasn't very interested in the dwellings, just the land and what they could do with it.

Behind him came the sound of someone running towards him.

'That'd better be you, Bree.'

'No, it's the billabong bunyip practising his line dancing

techniques.'

'Smart-arse.' Even if she was cute.

'Do you know where you're going?'

'No.'

Her white teeth showed off her smile. 'I don't mind playing tour guide, just this once.'

'If I knew that, I would've dug up some dynamite sticks a long time ago.'

Her giggle was light, defusing the heavy mood as she opened a door. 'There is nothing in this room, and it's the coolest one.'

'Good.' The temperature in the dark room dropped considerably, as he carefully placed the box on the patchy linoleum floor, then closed the door. 'No lock?'

'No. But we can slide this pallet piece through.' She slid the board across the handle, successfully locking it. Then she waved her hand over the door like an interior decorator. 'It needs a sign that says: *Open and die!*'

'You have the weirdest sense of humour.' He slung his arm over her shoulders.

But then she sobered as they headed for the shed's lights. 'Charlie said earlier today that Jack Price oversaw the dynamite.'

'I was there, remember?'

'But you weren't at dinner when Charlie told me that they haven't had dynamite out here, not since they finished excavation for Starvation Dam.'

'When was that again?'

'They started at the tail end of 1961, but they had to stop from the wet season, turning it into a massive mud pit, and they then finished it late in 1962.'

The year of Price's murder, and Harry's disappearance.

Deep in thought they walked side by side towards the lights coming from the boardroom and their outdoor bar.

'Do you think the cave-in, where we found Harry and Penelope, could have been deliberately set off with dynamite?'

Ryder gave a slow nod. 'It's possible, but we'll need blasting experts to confirm that.'

'If we tell the police we've found that dynamite, it might motivate them to steer their investigation in a new direction. Think about it, Harry and Penelope were trapped in that mine together. You saw that cave. It was so well reinforced, it's still holding up after two landslides.' She held up two fingers. 'First one was the original landslide that trapped Harry and Penelope inside. And the second landslide exposing the cave from the—'

'Stampede.' Again, he hooked his arm around her shoulders and neck to give her a comforting squeeze, hating how she'd been in danger then. 'Shall we look at the rest of the drums and see what we can find?'

'I'm in.'

Using the pitchfork, he stirred the goo inside the drums, a lot slower than before, hoping for no more nasty surprises. He dropped the tines of the pitchfork into each drum, where it disappeared in the sump oil soup of the dirty old 44-gallon drum. Rust and sludgy grease had formed on the bottom in thick clumps that he stirred like a witch over a cauldron, and chuckled.

'What?'

'If Dex were here, he'd be saying something about witches, cauldrons and midnight sacrifices.'

'Look at you, cupcake.' Standing beside him with her hand propped on her hip. 'Getting with the programme of finding that inner playful spirit. Or should I say, it's good to see you getting that broomstick out of your arse, babe.'

He rolled his eyes, but it didn't stop his grin. Bree had just called him *babe*.

The next six drums held nothing but more soupy muck. On the second-last drum, the pitchfork's tines hit something tall, that thumped against the side of the drum.

'I heard that.' Bree's eyes lit up.

'I felt it.' Whatever it was, it lay lengthways, making it hard for the pitchfork to catch. 'Can't get it.'

'I've got it.' With her arm wrapped inside a garbage bag, Bree reached into the black sludgy gunk. Her thick, fiery curls began to tumble forward, spilling over her shoulders in a wild cascade.

'Bree, your hair.' Ryder gently gathered the mass of hair, holding it back with care. To have her hair in his hands was one of those daydreams finally coming true, where the strands were heavy and soft in his grip, the red catching the shed's light like copper.

'Got it.' She pulled up the object by its metal tip, to reveal a shotgun.

Ryder instantly recognised it. 'It's a 1960 Winchester M12.'

'I know. I have twenty-two of these lying around the place.'

'You said sixteen before!'

'Only sixteen of them are working models.' She lifted the gun higher. 'This has to be the murder weapon, doesn't it?'

'It might be. But first, let's drain the oil out of it.' Ryder ripped the blue plastic tarp off Dex's workbench and spread it out over the gravel under the stars. From the top shelf, he grabbed some rubber gloves and snapped them on. 'Go get my phone, Bree. We need to document this properly for the police.'

She returned quickly, holding up the phone.

'Don't touch it,' he warned, carefully lifting the grease-covered firearm from the oil drum. 'If we're lucky, the oil might have preserved fingerprints or DNA.'

'After all this time?'

'Submerging it in oil provides some protection. I've seen it before during investigations.' Ryder raised the weapon on wooden blocks he'd scavenged from Dex's workshop, setting an oil tray underneath to let it drain.

'How do you know all this?'

'My old unit wasn't just about being weapons engineers. We worked like a JAG team, handling specialised investigations involving military firearms.'

Bree tilted her head, studying him with a curious expression. 'So that's why Marcus and Porter let you look at the case file?'

Ryder gave a short nod. 'Get ready to videotape the next part.'

'What are you doing?'

'I'm cracking the chamber to see if it's loaded.' Carefully, he worked the mechanism and pulled out a corroded shell casing. He held it up for the camera. 'This shotgun doesn't fire bullets—it uses shells loaded with pellets or slugs. These steel pellets might match what they found in the body.'

'When will we know?' Bree asked, keeping the phone steadily recording.

'We'll need a specialised forensic lab to confirm it. I can do the preliminary analysis myself, but it needs an independent review for transparency.'

'Aren't we technically tampering with evidence?'

'No, we're preserving it.' Ryder placed the shell casing and steel pellets into separate plastic bags, like he'd seen Porter do earlier. 'I'm not leaving a loaded firearm sitting on my property. And this will go to the police once the oil has drained.'

He washed his hands at the industrial sink, glancing at Bree as she filmed the last shot of the oil drum. 'Good work. I'll load these images to my PC and email them to Marcus in the morning.'

'Can you send them to Porter, please?'

He arched an eyebrow at her. 'Why?'

'It's Porter's case, and I know he's trying really hard.'

'Do you think he'll get upset over us...' *Finding all the relevant evidence.*

'If you call Porter, tell him what we found, then wait for those neurons to pop behind his eyes as he works it out for himself.'

'You know, I can't work out if you're being manipulative or just using the power of suggestion for good.' Bree had a knack for it—she'd done it to his brothers with the wildlife corridor set-up and other projects. All this time, she'd been the quiet instigator behind much of the station's management, where of course, Ryder was always the last to know.

It had irritated him to no end, even if he now understood it was for the good of the station. Still, being kept in the dark was one of the reasons he'd been angry enough to accuse Bree of cattle rustling. But she'd never explained why she did what she did. So he had to ask now. 'Why?'

'Porter is trying to get his detective's certificate. And he's been good to our family,' she said. 'He's never arrested Charlie once for driving without a licence.'

'How come Charlie hasn't got a licence when he drives the Razorback, and your horse truck around the property just fine?'

'Charlie got busted for drink driving, coming home from the pub one night. Porter found him parked on the side of the road, just outside of town, fast asleep behind the wheel, with the engine still running.'

'You would have been in a panic.'

'I was. I was in the Kombi, searching for him, when Porter flagged me down and told me what had happened. He had Charlie in the cells, sleeping it off before they could book him.'

'Did you lose your temper?' he asked the redhead.

'After being so worried, I was furious. Pop knew better that that...' She exhaled heavily, hands on hips as if to temper herself. 'But then I found the medical notes on the front seat of his ute. It was the day Charlie was told he had a heart condition.'

'Exactly what is wrong with his heart? Because Charlie acts like a healthy man to me.'

'Severe aortic stenosis. It's the narrowing of the heart's aortic valve that significantly reduces blood flow from the heart to the rest of his body. He gets chest pain, shortness of breath, and fatigue. And he does get tired, he just hides it from you guys.'

'Hmm...' That didn't sound good.

And neither was Bree's sigh that accompanied her sad eyes. 'They told Charlie he had a year, maybe less, if he didn't have the valve replacement surgery. But he refused.'

'When was that?'

'Five years ago.'

Damn.

'Anyway, the magistrate took into account Charlie's age and unblemished record, suspending his licence for twelve months along with a small fine. But Charlie was told to re-sit the driving test, which, of course, the old man refused. So, no licence. Not that he cares—he likes people driving him around now.'

'I noticed.' Charlie had been like a kid in the front seat of Ryder's ute today.

With her arms crossed over her belly, she stared at the gun. 'You did it, Ryder.'

His brow creased. 'Ryder, huh? Where's the Captain Cupcake?'

'Do you notice how Charlie calls you *son*?'

He nodded.

'Do you know when he switched to *son*?'

'After we found Harry. When I escorted him back from the cave, coming through Scary Forest, to call the police.'

'Charlie respects you.'

'I respect Charlie, too. Always have.'

'Even when you kick him out of the driver's seat of the Razorback that Charlie owns?'

'I drive better than Charlie. And I didn't hear you complaining today.'

She never sat in the passenger seat, always choosing the back. Bree never seemed entirely comfortable in his car—like she didn't belong in the polished, high-end world of showy wealth. Not that the redhead cared about money or status, it was the person behind the wealth that mattered to her, which only made her all the more precious to him.

'I should go.'

'No.' He grabbed her hand and led her to the boardroom. 'We deserve a drink after what we've done.' For a man who didn't like to talk, he wasn't ready to finish this conversation.

Thirty-one

Bree leaned against the bench in the Riggs brothers' boardroom, cradling her gin glass, staring at the string lines that reconstructed the scene. Even though it was late, her mind was racing, full of possibilities.

Yet watching the tall, dark and broody male, with muscles for days, who had somehow made this big room smaller—there was nothing like murder to kill a girl's desire.

'Humour me, okay… How was the gun set up?'

Ryder pointed to the string lines that led from the window to the pole, with one of those big hands that led to thick wrists, and strong arms with those Hollywood-hero-style biceps bulging as he pointed. 'From the photos and the shot's trajectory from the way it pierced his body…'

'Ah ha.' Since when did being a nerd become sexy on a stockman?

'Price would've used the open rims of the drum to position it in a way that allowed the gun to face into this room.'

Clearing her throat, she focused on getting back in the game of playing part-time detective. If their theory was right, and with what they'd found so far it seemed likely, it would be the best gift for her grandfather. But there were holes in her theory, bigger than a road train rolling sideways down a gully that she needed to fill before she got her grandfather's hopes up. 'How?'

'Price could have used the window ledge to hold it up,

and something else to chock it in place. Something that would have fallen on the outside from the pressure of the discharge.'

'The kickback?'

Ryder gave a short no-nonsense nod. 'A thin board, or a flat stick, wedged in behind the shotgun's recoil pad would have held it in place. Something tall to allow for gravity to help it topple outside of the drum. The elastic would've wrapped around that board, and then looped around the trigger. When the shotgun fired, the elastic was released, in turn releasing the board, so the shotgun fell into the drum. It's pretty diabolical.' Ryder stood next to her and pointed at the picture, his rich manly aroma teasing her. 'Even if that constable didn't know what he was doing, he did a good job taking photos to help us at least work that bit out.'

'If we're right... It means Jack Price pulled the trigger.' Once again, she checked over the string lines from the dummy gun to the pole to represent Jack Price's body.

'Seems like it.'

'So, Price staged the entire thing. That's wild.'

'It's really hard to get your mind around something like that. What would be his motive to go to the extreme of staging his own death to look like a murder?'

'I think that, maybe, Price killed Harry and Penelope. He might have been so livid that his wife was going to run away with another man that he set up the explosions to cause a cave-in, trapping them in there.'

'But would Price blow up the cave knowing all his cash was in there?'

She spun around to face Ryder. 'I bet he didn't know about the cash! I bet that once he discovered all his cash was missing, along with his ID and marriage certificate, he realised the only person who would've taken it was the wife he'd just buried inside a cave.' The pieces clicked into place in her mind, her eyes widening at the images on the table. 'Left with no money, no ID, no wife, with the bad guys after him for those stolen guns, and possibly the Army for his desertion, Jack Price would have lost all hope of escaping, so he framed Harry in his elaborate suicide-as-murder as revenge. What an arsehole!'

'If the evidence was laid out for the police, like Jack did by writing down Harry's name, they wouldn't need to look too hard for clues.'

'Which they didn't.' She grinned at the clever man with his dark eyes narrowed at the murder file on the table, with tousled brown hair, well-groomed beard, broad shoulders, and those jeans. No one filled out a pair of jeans quite like Ryder Riggs.

'What else have you got?'

'Well, according to Charlie's letter from Harry,' she said, rummaging through the file to produce his copy of the letter instead of looking at Ryder Riggs and those jeans. 'Those lovers—' *Wrong word!* 'The couple had been planning their escape but kept postponing it for months. They couldn't leave until they found the marriage certificate, because they needed it for the annulment so Harry and Penelope could get married.'

'But how did he know about Harry and Penelope, and that cave?'

'Well, he was a head stockman—and Charlie said Jack Price was a good one—head stockmen don't miss much, not when they're on the job with a station to run. And if Jack Price had people after him, he would've already been looking over his shoulder and could've noticed his wife was up to something and followed her—'

'Or their tracks.'

She nodded. 'I bet Jack Price found Harry's secret cave where they'd stashed their suitcases.'

'If he did, why didn't he take that gold?'

She shook her head. 'He couldn't have realised what it was. At first you guys weren't sure it was gold until I told you. They looked like rocks to you.'

'That's true. But I also don't want you getting ahead of yourself.'

Ahead, ha! She was about to break the land-speed record with her mind leaping off the edge of a cliff and into a paraglider's paradise. 'So, what if—'

'Bree?'

'Hey, you wanted me to talk, so I'm talking.' She was also quite impressed at how thick and fast this conversation flowed. 'My theories have been panning out so far.'

'True...' He leaned against the bench beside her to sip his bourbon while she drank her gin. 'You came up with the elastic—'

'And the rock that was used to write out his dying words. I bet if we found a geologist, they'd know about the rock type. We should also look for someone who knows about dynamite for mining.'

'Know of any?'

'Mia might know someone from her mining days.'

'Good point. I'll ask Mia in the morning.'

'Hey, about your cameras spying on the neighbours,' she said, pointing at the wall of monitors, 'you didn't see Mia's ex, by any chance?'

'The one you threatened to feed to the crocodiles?' Ryder smirked behind his bourbon glass. 'No. He's gone.'

'How do you know?'

'Because I had Marcus chase after Gavin on the highway.'

'To do what?'

'To make sure he escorted that mongrel out of town towards Alice Springs, so he had no excuse for coming through our district again.'

'Marcus agreed?'

'Porter had already filled him in about Mia and her bruises, back when he'd given up his dog, Willow. Remember, Marcus was there when Mia officially became Willow's owner at the campdraft.'

'Yeah, but—' It seemed weak to her.

'Marcus's pet hate is violence against women. Especially in his town.'

Okay, that sounded fair. 'What's your pet hate?'

He pushed off the bench to stand directly in front of her. 'Fighting with you.'

Her breath caught in her throat.

'Why do you hate me, Bree?'

'I don't hate you.'

'But you fight with me more than any of my brothers.'

'You called me a cattle rustler and were so close to calling me a liar, too.'

'I'm sorry. Jeez, how many times do I have to apologise?' Ryder raked a hand through his hair, frustration lacing his voice. 'I've felt guilty every damn day since I did that. I stupidly accused you because I was scared—scared of losing everything I've worked for, and I was scared of how much you already meant to me. I got it wrong.'

She stared at him for a long time.

His emotions were raw and unveiled, hiding nothing.

Whether it was the late nights, the lack of sleep, or the joy of finding something positive towards solving the murder mystery, somehow her shields were down, for the first time.

'Hating you was the hardest thing I've ever done,' she said, licking her lips. 'I've had to fight for everything I have, to just survive. So much so I'd come to accept that as a part of life, because I know to never get too comfortable. But fighting you, hating you, is like stepping into a fiery forge, only to be hammered on the anvil. I'm tired of fighting against you. I'm a much better person when we stand beside each other and fight side by side.' She pointed to the crime scene. 'Look at what we've achieved together. You and me, we're like some beautiful collision of some kind, that just keeps on clashing where that explosion is guaranteed.'

His large fingers tenderly gathered up one of her hands. 'I don't know why I upset you, or why I suffer with some block of emotions, foot-in-mouth, or whatever it is when it comes to you, but I am human, Bree. And I've never wanted to be close to anyone as much as I want to be with you. I-I—'

She pressed her free fingers across his lips. She couldn't let him say what his eyes were telling her. She wasn't ready for that. 'So don't put your foot in it now. Instead, do something positive with that mouth.'

'Like what?'

'Kiss me.'

Ryder didn't hesitate. His hands cupped her cheeks, and his lips were against hers in an instant, in the most tender kiss of her life.

He lifted her onto the side bench, while keeping his lips against hers, not breaking contact for a second. The heat of their kiss blazed into a furnace that had to melt all conventions of physics, effortlessly breaking down all those barriers that had protected her for so long.

But why did she give in now?

'Don't! Stop thinking and stay with me, Bree,' he murmured against her mouth.

How did he know?

But she did stop thinking, especially when his kiss deepened, pressing his lips harder against hers. Gripping the back of her head, with his fingers tangling in her hair as his tongue tangled with hers giving her a renewed thirst for more.

Her mind was in a losing battle as her body quivered under his touch. One of his hands was on her bare thigh, sliding higher over her hip to her chest. She moaned a breathy little sound as he clutched one of her breasts.

It should have snapped her out of it, but Ryder refused to let her go.

With one arm around her body, his mouth, tongue, and lips danced down her extended throat as they went lower and lower. His nimble fingers pulled down her dress, her bra exposed, and his eyes lit up.

'Gorgeous, just gorgeous.' He licked his lips, and his head dipped down to her cleavage.

Sweet sugary hot cakes, his hot mouth was as powerful and pleasing as the man. He suckled and licked one breast, while his fingers kneaded the other, somehow unlocking all her inner desires and deep need for Ryder Riggs.

Why was she fighting this man, who was doing everything right to please her? Why was she denying herself something good? To hell with the consequences, she could deal with all that tomorrow. She had to have some skin. And now.

Desperately, she pulled up his shirt.

His mouth broke away from hers, to rip the shirt off and toss it behind him, exposing that torso of perfection, only for his hot mouth to return its attention to her body with a vengeance. She groaned louder, her body moving from the impact he'd forced upon her as he worked from one breast to the other. His arm around her body keeping her in place, she had no choice but to hold on and enjoy the ride.

Her hands wandered down his chest, her nails scraping against his abs carved from warm smooth stone to that delicious light smattering of hair leading down to the waist of his jeans.

He came up for air, one hand cradling the side of her face like a love letter meant for her eyes only, his eyes locking on hers showing the depth of heat and desire he had for her. She completely forgot everything as her world filled with Ryder Riggs.

'We can stop.' His voice was deep, his breath ragged, combined with that look of his, it was as sexy as hell.

'Do you want to?' She knew what she wanted.

'Hell no.' Again, the assault on her lips resumed as he kissed her, bundling her closer as she sat on the steel workbench that ran along the wall.

There his fingers moved like magic. Gone was her underwear, her dress down to her waist, where her body wilfully arched into him.

He gave a hearty grunt of approval, pushing her thighs wider, the hand on her hip making her tilt for him, only spurred by her aching need to be touched. He had her body under his command. And no one had done that.

Without warning, he dropped to his knees, lifting one of her legs over his shoulder and all she had to hold on to was his head. His tongue, face, and fingers sent her to another heaven far beyond anything she'd ever felt.

If she wasn't pressed against the wall, she would've slid off the bench to the floor like liquid steel. One arm banded across her belly, fingers gripping her fleshy thigh, as he pressed his fingers inside her. Again, she all but melted away. Her eyes shut, as a thick moan escaped from her throat. It was unrecognisable as her own.

She had lost control, giving Ryder complete control, and he owned her!

Oh boy, did he own her, holding her open for him to play her with the fingers of a master fiddler at such a maddening pace she was whisked towards an edge that left her panting. A fine sheen of sweat coated her body that was rocking against his face as she started to tremble and whimper, with her nails digging into his skin.

That's when he stood to his full gloriously masculine height. Undoing those buttons on his jeans, he lowered them, exposing the full extension of his desire.

Dear Lord, it was beautiful. He was strong everywhere. With such a hidden power that forced the heat to rush up her inner thighs, with his hand skidding up her spine, to then trace her neck and her collarbone with one fingertip, while his dark eyes roamed over her face. There was nothing cold about this man who had ice in his veins, he was all molten heat and hunger. All for her.

He lined up, with a hand on her hip he lifted her chin. 'Look at me, Bree.'

She forced herself to focus on his dark eyes, as he slid inside her, filling her with a pleasure that she read so clearly on his own face as he withdrew to then thrust back into her.

He set the pace where the friction only made her want to cry out. Her body tightened around him, buried so deep, she had no choice but to surrender herself.

With his teeth running along her bare shoulder, his chest against hers, his pace became maddening as her body shattered. Breathy, choked cries that she was powerless to swallow back, rose from her throat as her world burst around her.

In her ear, he gave a harsh, sexy sound of satisfaction as she silently screamed against him. He then bundled her hair in his hands, the cool breeze a welcome reprieve against her hot skin.

Cursing under his breath, he plastered her back against the wall as another orgasm rolled through her, only this time he went with her, the hearty groan that came from his chest was deep, flowing freely towards her as he coated her womb with his seed.

They held each other, their skin slick with sweat, to the sounds of a ticking clock she couldn't see, and the hum of the air conditioner. He dropped his head in the juncture of her neck, and his arms snaked around her body, holding her close to his chest until their breathing returned to normal.

But there was nothing normal about what they'd done, or who she'd done it with. She was now in an internal wrestle with her awakening soul. A soul that she'd thought had been buried with her son—yet somehow, Ryder Riggs had just dragged it out of the pit of ashes, as if to claim it as his own.

Thirty-two

Ryder leaned against the fence as music blasted from inside the blacksmith shed. With her hair tucked under her black cap, Bree pulled a white-hot rod from the flames of the furnace. Swinging a thick hammer, she hit that rod, bending it, shaping it over the large anvil. The beat of metal on metal, hammer on anvil, was like an ancient drum, each metal clang in sync with the music.

She was beautiful to watch.

The shotgun-wielding, gin-making outlaw, was the queen of steel, and a sword-making magician of alchemy. She was the temptress of lust, strong enough to turn his cold, stony heart into a fire as hot as the forge she used to melt metal that she'd bend to her will. He could not stop watching the woman who had already placed her own brand on his heart.

In his peripheral view he spotted her grandfather coming down the garden path to lean his forearms over the gate's rail beside Ryder. 'The kid's been in a good mood lately.'

Ryder wanted to claim it was all his doing. Being with Bree had certainly put him in a good mood. He'd never slept better than when lying beside her. Even if they weren't letting anyone know what they were doing after dark, just being near her was a comfort.

Charlie pushed up the brim of his stockman's hat. 'What can I do you for, son?'

'We need to talk. With Bree.'

'Sounds ominous.'

With fingers to his mouth, Ryder let rip a whistle that ricocheted around the shed.

Bree spun around with a hammer in her hand. 'What was that for? Most people use words like *hello*, cupcake?'

He still hated that pet name, but she was wearing him down. 'I needed your attention.' And she had his, just by breathing.

'There are better ways to get a girl's attention than by bursting my eardrums.' She poked the hot iron into the water bucket. A hiss of steam curled in the air.

Leaving her latest creation to rest on the anvil, Bree tore off her thick gloves, they ran up to her elbows, made of the same thick leather as her full-bib apron. With the back of her hand, she wiped at the sweat glistening on her brow to brush back one of her curls.

Ryder wanted to tuck it behind her ear, then follow it with his lips down her slender neck to lick at the salty beads of sweat. But Bree was careful to never get too close to him when others were around.

She pulled down the heavy iron gate that closed off the blazing furnace, already hearing the flames fading in the forge for the day. 'Is there something you need, Ryder?'

Heck yeah, he had a list, a big one. But that was only for after dark when her grandfather had gone to bed.

She narrowed her eyes at him with a look that warned him to behave.

He didn't want to.

'Marcus and Porter are here. They want to talk to Charlie in the boardroom.' He then said to Charlie, 'It's to do with Harry.' It was all part of the plan.

'We shouldn't keep them waiting, son.' Charlie brushed past him, heading down the stone path that wound through the thriving vegetable garden.

'Is it time?' Bree asked Ryder quietly.

Ryder nodded. They'd elected not to tell Charlie of their findings last week, leaving it to the police. But Ryder made sure he'd sped up the process, calling in favours, hoping that what they discovered would fall in the right direction, for Charlie's sake.

'Are they here to discuss Leo's matter, too?' Bree dragged off her black skullcap that contained the long thick plait that rested over her shoulder like rich rope.

'Only after Charlie leaves.'

'Got it.'

'Hey.' He pulled her back to duck behind the wall of assorted bean varieties that grew thickly over an arched trellis, effectively shielding them from the house. 'I want a kiss.'

'My grandfather is just there.'

'I don't care.' Sneaking around had been hot, but he'd rather their relationship was out in the open. But he'd learned fast that wasn't what Bree wanted, so he took any chance he could, like this one. Wrapping that thick plait around his wrist to control her head, his lips met hers and kissed her like she was his air, his light, his life.

He'd never get sick of kissing her, especially when he watched her glassy green eyes shimmer to gaze at him as her body sighed against him.

She did that in those quiet moments, where the only sound was their breaths or heartbeats. Those moments just after he'd made love to her, and she'd gaze at him with wonder. In that small window of time she wore no shields, only pure open emotion showing on her face, filling her eyes, it was beautiful. All of her was beautiful.

But then she'd blink. And *bam*, reality set in and so too those shields that protected her heart.

'Why are we hiding this?' He hated how she retreated from him, starting down the path while untying the back of her apron. 'You said it was because of Charlie, but he likes me.'

She slid the strap of the welding apron over her head. 'Charlie would shoot you.'

'Would not.'

'He threatened to shoot Finn, and all the others.'

'How many others?' The fire burned in his chest.

'Don't judge, cupcake. It's not that many. Most men were either too scared of me, or not good enough to get an invitation past the front gate.'

So, Finn—that's definitely over? Because the weekend he was here it didn't seem like it.'

'Isn't it obvious already?' Bree rolled her eyes, the sigh exaggerated. 'Finn was a rerun, cupcake. Just because I revisited a chapter doesn't mean I'm rewriting the whole book. That story's done.'

Didn't that make him grin with pride.

'But Finn and I are still friends, okay?'

'Whatever. Just know, no one is good enough for you—except me.'

'Ah huh, and what brand of gun glue have you been sniffing today?' She rolled those pretty green eyes that contradicted the smile she was trying to hide.

'Come on, we're not children. We have no reason to keep hiding like this. I'm not ashamed to be with you, Bree.'

'I'm not ready. Okay?' She said it over her shoulder, while walking away from him. 'Hey, this is new for me, too. Why rush?'

He stopped to watch her disappear inside the cottage, where she hung her leather apron and gloves at the back door.

Even though he was ready to rush in with both feet, he'd forgotten how Bree had been burnt in ways he couldn't comprehend. He needed to exercise patience. He'd been patient with her this long.

He also knew Bree was scared of what was happening between them, when it felt so right. It was Bree who was holding back, making excuses to not trust her own feelings.

But if there was a way, or some gesture, to show her there was nothing to be afraid of, they wouldn't need to sneak around like teenagers after dark.

Ryder escorted Bree and Charlie to the boardroom, where two uniformed police officers were waiting. Marcus sat beside Porter at one end of the large boardroom table. Ash, Cap and Dex sat along the sides. All the monitors were turned off.

'Smell that coffee.' Charlie inhaled deeply as he took his seat at the head of the table.

'If you have a coffee now, you'll give your poor heart a workout it doesn't need, Pop.' Bree poured two glasses from the water cooler that stood by the door, and sat beside her grandfather, saying the usual hellos to the two policemen at the table.

'What's going on, lads?' Charlie steepled his fingers, with his elbows resting on the table he'd made by hand.

'Go ahead, Porter.' Marcus gave the young officer a nod.

Porter nervously cleared his throat as he flipped open a folder. 'Um, Charlie. We have news on Harry. It's about the cave-in, and the murder.'

The smile fell from Charlie's face as he leaned back in his seat. Bree gripped his hand and gave it a squeeze.

'We've discovered, that, um…' Porter tugged at the collar of his police uniform, clearing his throat again, to clutch his glass of water and drink deeply.

'Come on, Porter, spit it out, mate,' said Dex. 'The suspense is killing us.'

Porter's empty glass hit the table with a clunk. 'Harry didn't kill Jack Price, it was the other way around.'

'Come again?' Charlie cupped his ear like a horn.

'We've had forensic specialists go over the reports and the scene, and they concluded that the cave-in was deliberate, caused by a blast, trapping Penelope and Harry inside. That first blast made the area unstable, resulting in that landslide easily occurring after the stampede.'

'How do you know that?' Bree asked Porter.

'From a blasting technician who works for the mining companies. Using the images from Ash's drone, the techie was able to prove from the cave and surrounding debris layout that the damage was done with dynamite. On his PC, he showed me this really cool 3D terrain model that he uses to plan all his mine blasts. He was able to show me the likely points those dynamite sticks were laid and everything.'

'Dynamite?' Ash and Cap glanced at each other across the table.

'Last week, Ryder and Bree discovered a stash of dynamite and blasting caps in one of those old oil drums. We found Price's DNA on them. There's no way to prove it, but we think it's the same dynamite that was used to cause the cave-in, trapping your, um...' Porter cleared his throat, leaning closer to Charlie. 'On the evidence the original investigator had collected, we've been able to use modern forensic technology—'

'Like you said you would, when you first started this case, even giving it a new file name,' muttered Charlie.

'Operation Stoney Silence,' muttered Dex.

'Charlie,' blurted out Porter, shifting to the edge of his seat. 'There's more. There was also a weapon found inside one of the oil drums that was a part of the crime scene. There was one expended shell casing and one full.' He went on to explain all the evidence they had found, and the conclusions they had come to.

Charlie tilted his head, his brow ruffling. 'Are you saying Jack Price shot *himself* in the back?'

Porter nodded. 'I also believe Price deliberately caused the cave-in to trap Harry and Penelope. Then Price hid Harry's car in the Stoneys, where you found it after that sandstorm, hoping everyone would think that Harry and Pen had run away.'

'Is that how Price had that chalk piece to write that message?' Bree asked.

Porter nodded, flipping over pages in the file. 'It's a match for the same rocks collected from the area Harry's car was found.'

'Why would Price do this?' Charlie asked the police.

'Despair. Anger. Pride. Revenge. Who knows,' replied Porter, nodding at his sergeant.

'So Price decided to point the finger at my brother? I don't get it.' Charlie scratched the side of his head as if trying to make sense of this conversation.

Porter nodded grimly. 'Sorry, Charlie, but we believe Price blasted that cave as payback for Harry running away with his wife—who wasn't even legally married to Price. They could have blown his cover, and I think Jack suspected it even before the cave-in. But here's the thing: Jack didn't realise until after the blast that everything he needed—his money, his real and fake IDs, even his so-called marriage certificate—was buried in that cave. Without them, he couldn't escape the people who were after him. And with no way out and the promise of dying a horrible death at their hands, Jack decided to go out on his own terms. To make it worse, he blackened Harry's name in the process. It's sickening, really.'

'So my brother was innocent? Harry and Penelope were the ones murdered by Price, not the other way around?'

Again, Porter nodded. 'Penelope and Harry were the victims in all of this. Not Jack Price.'

'Struth.' Charlie ripped off his hat to run his fingers over his white hair.

'So, what happens now?' Bree asked the police, while rubbing her grandfather's shoulder.

It was the senior sergeant, Marcus, who answered, 'Since this case originally fell under South Australia's jurisdiction, Porter's findings will be sent to their regional commander for approval, after which the case will be officially closed.'

Porter closed the file, resting his hands on top, as if the matter was finally over. Case solved.

'Are you okay, Pop?'

'Yeah, nah, yeah…' Charlie blinked a few times, shaking his head slowly. Then he lifted it fast to face his granddaughter with his smile growing. 'Did you hear that, kid? My brother is innocent. Innocent, they said. Blimey, *Harry is* INNOCENT!' He hugged Bree, with his joyous laughter filling the room.

Charlie then rushed around the table to drag the young

constable in for a hug, giving him a hearty pat on the back. 'You're a good man, Policeman Porter.'

'It's Senior—'

'Whatever. Just accept my thanks for doing a bloody good job, mate.'

'You should thank Bree and Ryder, too. They found the extra evidence that allowed me to work it out.'

Charlie's smile faltered. 'Why didn't you tell me, kid?'

Bree shrugged. 'I didn't want to get your hopes up.'

'How did you get that DNA thingamabob stuff done so fast?' Charlie asked the police.

'You can thank Ryder for that.' Marcus pointed to Ryder at the other end of the table.

Ryder didn't want to say anything, but the way Bree was looking at him, he had to fess up. 'I told you I knew people. I just called in a few favours and had it rushed through.' The effort was worth it to see Charlie's reaction, and for Bree.

'You good man, you.' Charlie shook Ryder's hand, then gave him a hug with another hearty pat on the back. 'All you boys are good men.' Charlie shook Dex's hand, Ash's hand, then Cap's. His smile infectious. 'I reckon I'll load up the big beer cooler from the cottage and have a drink to Harry's innocence. Let's really put a dent in that bar of yours, boys.'

'Dex, do you want to give Charlie a hand?' Ryder suggested. 'I'll fill you in shortly.'

'No worries.' Dex followed Charlie outside, and Ryder closed the door. Ash grabbed the TV remote control then switched on all the monitors lining the wall.

'So, now that was the good news. I'm assuming you're about to give us the bad news?' Bree swivelled in her chair to face the police seated at the other end of the table.

'Have some faith, Bree. We are the good guys.' Marcus stood before the monitors with hands on hips, taking in the view of the huge cannabis crop. 'Leo's pretty brazen to grow his crop like that.'

'I know,' mumbled Ryder. It was obvious Leo was not threatened by anyone, especially the local police.

As the OIC, it was easy to see that Marcus was ticked, as he dropped a large envelope on the table. 'That's a copy of the paperwork asking for your assistance with the surveillance of your neighbour's property. But only from 0600 hours yesterday. However, I've sent some still images I scraped off your video footage for my supervisor, who has a warrant ready to get signed off for me to act. No one knows anything except the people in this room and my superintendent. We're being careful to not tip off Leo in any way.'

'Are you bringing in the drug squad from Darwin?'

'Can't. They don't have the manpower to spare.'

'They never do,' mumbled Porter quietly.

'So when?' Ryder asked, knowing his brothers were keen to put this nightmare behind them.

'It's the timing now.'

'What do you mean?'

'Tomorrow night, all my team are working at the rodeo. I don't have enough staff to do both. Even if I want to hit that prick today, we also have a town to look after, too.'

'So when do we get rid of that wanker next door?' Cap blurted out. The dark rings under his eyes were evident that this whole situation had hit Cap the hardest.

'We'll be raiding Leo on Sunday at seven am, to make full use of the daylight hours. You said that's when they have breakfast at their camp and swap patrol shifts?' Marcus asked Ryder, who nodded. 'Didn't you say Leo and his men are all going to the rodeo, too?'

Again, Ryder gave a short affirmative nod. 'Leo's shouting his men as a bonus. He's warned them they'll be putting in long hours for the harvest, which he's planning to start at the end of next week.' Burning it down and blaming it on a bushfire might be quicker. Ryder side-glanced at Bree, finding her staring at him.

Aw crap, she had to be thinking the same thing, no doubt already devising a master plan in the blink of an eye.

Ryder narrowed his eyes at the redhead, as if to say *don't do it!*

Of course, the little outlaw jutted her chin in that look of *you're not the boss of me*, then ignored him by returning her attention to the officers. She was so irritating!

'I promise you Leo will never harvest that crop. I just need you lot to steer clear of that area when my team go in there.' Marcus then dropped his elbow on the table and pointed at the redhead. 'You too, Bree.'

'Oh, hush now, officer. It's never been a part of my wish list to interfere with a police operation. Not when I'll be too busy creating a list of relatable songs to taunt Leo in prison for the rest of his life.'

Ash and Cap sniggered while Porter spluttered on his coffee.

Marcus leaned back in his seat. 'Are you guys going to the rodeo?'

Ryder and his brothers shook their heads. They were planning on taking turns to watch their surveillance monitors, like binge-watching a bad reality show.

'You should,' said Bree, 'as owners of Elsie Creek Station, it'll look suspicious if you don't attend. All cattle stations give their staff time off so they can attend race days, the campdraft, and local rodeos. It's a big part of our social calendar.'

'Bree's right. Everyone will be there,' said Marcus. 'Will you be going, Bree?'

'Charlie usually stays home—'

Ryder put his hand on her arm. 'He doesn't need to now.'

She moved her arm away. *No touching.*

He hated not being able to touch her in public. But Bree set the rules, and if he wanted to play, he had to behave.

'I'll talk to Charlie and see what he says.'

'I'm not going. Mia won't go into town either. We'll stay home,' said Cap, his eyes glued to the screens. 'I'm happy to sit here and watch.' Like he'd done most nights. It was Cap who had documented the neighbour's security routes, the names of the staff, their habits, and even knew the strains of cannabis they were growing, all from watching those monitors like some obsession.

In one way, Ryder wished he'd never installed those cameras, it hadn't been good for Cap's health. 'What about you, Ash? Do you want to go to the rodeo?'

'Harper's been on my case all week about going, she's never been to a rodeo. She's already bought our tickets, and a new hat.' Ash gave that boyish grin, defusing the heavy mood.

'How many hats is that now? She's practically lined the walls of the farmhouse hallway as it is.' The woman only had one head.

'It's Harper's money, bro, and if it makes her happy, that's enough for me.'

'Jeez, they're still in honeymoon mode,' mumbled Marcus.

'All my brothers are.' Ryder was jealous that his brothers could be like that. 'Bree, would you like to go to the rodeo?' *With me.*

'I haven't asked Charlie yet. But if we do go, I'll be too busy pretending I don't know you people in public.' Again, she had that evil shine in her eyes, damn it was sexy.

'I'm surprised you two aren't arguing,' said Porter, nodding at Bree and Ryder. 'But I'll give you both credit, when you two work together, you do big things.'

'Hear hear,' said Marcus, getting to his feet. 'Well, let's go before I drink Ryder's good bourbon. But I'll be back after we bust that crop to raid that stash you have for your bourbon room.'

'A what?' Bree asked.

This time, Ryder ignored her. 'Will you need our help, Marcus?' Ryder opened the door for the officers.

'No. I want you all to stand down while my team executes the warrant. We need a clean bust, so Leo can't worm his way out on a technicality. Are we all clear on that?' Marcus glared at everyone at the table. 'Bree? Can I trust you to behave?'

'Pfft. I'm always on my best behaviour.'

'For five minutes.' Porter gave Bree a playful wink, while tucking his paperwork under his elbow.

'And I'll see you mob tomorrow at the rodeo,' said Marcus, 'Where I'm sure you'll all be on your best behaviour.'

Thirty-three

In her soft bed in the cottage, Bree awoke to Ryder's arms wrapped around her, his warm chest against her back and his breathing deep and steady.

She rubbed her eyes, adjusting to the daylight. 'Hey.'

'Hmm.'

She nudged his arm. 'You need to get up.'

'Why? I'm comfortable.' His arms tightened around her, cuddling his naked body closer to her back.

'It's sunrise.'

'So?'

'Charlie.'

'Don't care.' His lips were on her neck, then up to her ear, making her squirm. One of his large hands, callused and rough, gently cupped her breast, his thumb kneading her nipple. 'Can't we just stay in bed? Charlie isn't awake yet.'

'How can you tell?'

'He's noisy. I haven't heard the telltale creak of the back door, or the bathroom, and I can't smell his bread.' But he was incredibly handsy this morning.

'Charlie drank a fair bit last night, and he danced.' She hadn't seen her grandfather dance like that in years, teaching Harper, Mia and Sophie how to line dance.

'You did too.'

She smiled the way you'd smile at a group of playful puppies. 'Charlie danced with everyone.' Whooping it up, celebrating the innocence of his brother, he had everyone involved, including little Mason. Except Ryder and Dex, who were busy holding up the bar.

'How about you dance with me tonight, at the rodeo?'

'How about you get out of my bed?'

'Not now, I'm not.' He turned her body over to press her back into the deep cushioning of the bed's mattress. His lips caressed up her neck as he rolled on top of her. His body weight was comforting, with a body length so much bigger, stronger, yet a perfect fit against hers.

She allowed her palms to skim over the warm muscles of his chest, shoulders, and arms. 'You are really making this hard for me.'

'Want to know what's hard? Shh—say nothing, just enjoy, baby.' And his lips pressed on hers, kissing her deeply, while his hands and slow fingers teased her body.

His lustful gaze made her shiver. That was soon followed by a sharp intake of air as he slid into her, giving that deep rumble of satisfaction that rolled in his chest as her body stretched to accept him.

She licked her lips, not with nerves, but with a hunger-filled passion, while arching herself to better accommodate him.

It must have flipped a switch inside him, with the way he grabbed her, crushing his mouth to hers, in a kiss that tasted way too good to be bad, bringing with it a whole new thrill of not allowing any of those noises threatening to escape her throat, as the bedsprings squeaked beneath her.

She moaned. It was loud. Desperate even.

His eyes flew open, to lock on hers, while trapping her on the soft bed. Above her, he went to move away from her.

She didn't want that!

Reaching up for him, keeping her body against him, she wrapped her legs and arms around his now-kneeling body, impaling him deeper, where he became the cure for her suffering and her escape from her past.

He pulled her closer, his large hands controlling her body as she grinded harder and their kisses grew more urgent.

She'd never been more turned on.

She knew he was going to make her scream as the white-hot pleasure threatened to steal her breath and her brain struggled to catch up. All she could do was surrender to those delicious feelings of this ride, the push, and the sliding grind of his body inside hers that was a potent combination of fireworks and fury.

She bit down on his shoulder to contain the scream. Her whole body trembled with pleasure.

But then his hands framed her face, where his dark eyes peered deep into her soul, as a fire began in her womb. Every stroke was so good, the fit absolute perfection.

'Don't stop.' Her body was already rolling into another storm.

He grinned against her skin and kept moving, the pleasure intensifying, the friction flawlessly fulfilling. When his thumb pressed over her sensitive nub, the sweet surprise of nerves exploding inside her had her coasting to the heavens, made even better as she felt him come with her, beneath her, inside her, to fully become a part of her, while she surrounded him. He had made her feel like a queen, with his embrace almost possessive, which surprisingly she enjoyed.

In that sliver of time, where the dust particles floated on a sunbeam illuminating her bedroom through the cracks of her curtains, the world was perfect. There were no horrors, no fears, just Ryder, raising his lips to meet hers in a kiss filled with such incredible tenderness while still joined as one.

Wrapping his muscular arms around her, he drew her to his chest, almost crushing her with the intensity of his embrace. It made her dizzy. If she was honest, all of him made her dizzy, like she was on an amusement park's merry-go-round ride, indulging in the infectious sugar rush of cotton candy that gave her the kind of giddiness that was a sweet ride indeed.

It made her feel safe.

And it had been a very long time since she'd ever truly

known that sensation.

With his fingers tenderly stroking her spine, her head rested on his broad shoulder, she enjoyed the rise and fall of his chest and the warmth of his breath against his skin. When she heard a door creak, her eyes flew open.

Oh no, Charlie was awake.

'I'm not sneaking out like I'm a teenager, Bree.'

'It is my grandfather's house, it's his rules.'

His lips brushed against hers, his warm breath making her skin prickle again with desire. 'Whose house?'

She pushed back, frowning. 'Don't you dare start playing landlord on me.' Jumping off the bed, she wrapped the bedsheet around her body. 'Get. Out.'

'Whoa, baby…'

'You can't buy me or own me. If you want me, you have to *earn* me—and not like this.' She threw his jeans at him. 'Go, before—'

'I'll leave in my own sweet time.' Ryder lay back on her bed, that grin both annoying and maddeningly sexy. When she didn't relent, he slid on his jeans, rolled off the bed, and slid into his boots before grabbing his shirt and hat. 'Tonight, you'd better not flirt with any cowboys.'

'What if I do? You're not the boss of me.' He didn't own her.

'Because I'll fight them all.'

'Why?'

'If you hadn't noticed, sweetheart, your ass is mine.' He gripped her butt cheeks hard, as hard as his lips pressed against hers in a blinding kiss of passion, to then let her go, and slip out the door.

With her fingertips pressing against her swollen lips still buzzing from his kiss, she tried to remain mad at him but could only bite on her bottom lip to stop her smile while watching Ryder slide on his shirt as he walked out the front gate.

She had to admit, this sneaking around only made it sweeter.

Why ruin it with relationship rules, which she knew he wanted.

But Bree wasn't ready. Not when she needed to focus on Charlie, because tonight would be Charlie's first time at the local rodeo in decades, fronting a lot of his peers.

She had a surprise organised for the old man. And a night off is what they all needed because they'd been living on the trigger's edge ever since they'd found Leo's crop.

In only one more sleep Leo would get raided, making tonight a dangerous time. A lot could happen in 24 hours.

Harry and Penelope had been planning to leave, with their suitcases hidden in that cave for weeks. Sadly, the day they made their move to leave, they never made it.

When Bree's mother had finally found the courage to leave her violent husband, she'd bought their bus tickets and packed their bags, then hid them in the back shed ready to leave in the morning. They only had to get through the night.

Yet Bree's mother never made midnight.

And Bree got to live with that memory forever.

In only one more night, if all went well, Leo would no longer be their neighbour. And so began the ticking clock to the final showdown…

Thirty-four

Hats on honeys were everywhere you looked, in assorted wide-brimmed hats brushed and bent just right, where dusty boots were even lucky enough to cop a polish. It was all part of a glorious parade of denim worn by men of various ages as they entered the grounds to the Elsie Creek Rodeo, with a line of utes filling the dusty paddock made into a car park.

'We should have gotten here earlier,' complained Charlie, in the front passenger seat of the Brookmere Green 1957 FJ Holden. It was Harry's car, once stashed in the Stoneys, now fully restored.

'You wanted me to drive Pandora.' Bree had helped Charlie polish this beast of a vehicle that rarely left the shed. But both Charlie and Harry had nothing to hide anymore, and Charlie was returning to the rodeo he hadn't set foot in over sixty years.

'Harry would've wanted it to be used. Me and my big brother had plenty of good times in this car...' The old stockman patted the dash like a trusty steed, his eyes distant as if picturing his brother in the car beside him.

Charlie sniffed, peering out the window. 'Where are we parking?'

'Ryder saved us a spot. Just look for his beastly vehicle.' Ryder had offered to wait around for them to leave together, but he had a carload, excluding Cap and Mia, who had elected to stay home and babysit Mason. 'We should have brought the Kombi van, then I would've had somewhere to crash, and I could've had a drink tonight.'

'I like my bed, thank you.'

'Are you still getting over boot scooting like a teenager last night?'

Charlie grinned in a way that shone brightly in his eyes. He looked truly happy. 'It was a good night, and I won't apologise for dancing. I don't do it enough, you know. As a lad, I used to get so embarrassed about dancing. Not much call for dancing out here. But then I plucked up the courage to dance with the most beautiful woman who took my breath away. My beautiful Bea. Boy, she loved to dance.'

'I remember.' She remembered the times she'd catch them dancing in the kitchen, or out the back under candlelight. Her grandparents lived a truly beautiful romance that had lasted for over fifty years. 'Does that mean you'll dance with me tonight, Pop?'

'And Harper, she said I had to.' Charlie pointed. 'There's Ryder's car. He got the good spots. But then they got here earlier.'

'You made me drive slow.'

'Because I didn't want dust covering the car. Not after we'd cleaned it.' He brushed some invisible dust off the dashboard. 'Pandora looks good. You know, Harry would have liked the name.'

Bree turned off the engine and paused behind the large vintage steering wheel, with the car key still in her hand. 'I'm sorry, Pop.'

'For what?'

'For naming this car for the wrong reasons, when I thought you were obsessed over Harry.'

'I was obsessed, kid. And if my beautiful Bea was still alive, she'd tell me off, just like you did.'

'I'm glad you didn't listen to me, and that you never quit.'

'No, I think fate had a hand in that, kid. How else would you have found Harry's cave like that?'

Still, that nagging guilt lay heavily in that place between

her shoulders, all for not supporting Charlie from the beginning. No matter what, Charlie had always sworn that Harry was innocent. And he'd been proven right.

Tonight, she was hoping to finally put that guilt to bed, once and for all.

She climbed out, calling to her grandfather over the roof of the vintage car. 'Don't forget to lock it.'

'Always forget that when I'm in town.' Charlie pushed the heavy steel door shut. Using his shirt's sleeve, he wiped some dust from the chrome. 'Have you given any thought to what to do with that gold, kid?'

'No. You?'

'Lenny knows a gold broker to smelt it down.'

'We could do that in the smithy's shed.' After all, she bent steel for a living.

'But this fella gives you some smancy certificate to sell it, keep it, or spend it.'

Bree checked over the locks in the back of the vintage car, before hoisting her leather bag over her shoulder, so much lighter with no gin bottles to carry, which she'd normally supply at an event like this where all her regular customers were attending. But tonight was for Charlie, who was looking extra sharp with his hair neatly trimmed, shaved, and in his good town boots and belt. 'What do you want to do with that gold?'

'I want you to spend it on that holiday you're always yakking on about. Then I want you to buy yourself a place. A home.'

Even though that had always been the plan when the caretaker's caveat ended, it meant losing not only her home but also her grandfather. The thought alone felt like an invisible, frozen hand was squeezing her heart.

'You'll want something with a decent paddock for the stockhorses, and a vegetable garden you can watch grow from the kitchen window...'

'Ah huh.' Funny that. It's exactly what she'd said to Charlie years ago, when Darcie first mentioned the caretaker's caveat. And again, when the station went up for sale, and again when Leo's men tried to strongarm Charlie into signing a waiver. But Charlie refused, determined to spend his last days at Elsie Creek Station, just like Darcie.

'You'll want to get yourself a pizza oven for baking bread in the mornings to not heat the house,' he said, 'and maybe a proper spa, instead of that watering trough you've got, to soak in at the end of a hot day on the tools.'

'Are you saying you want me to stay on the tools, Pop?' From a family of master brand makers, a tradition passed down from generation to generation, was she the last?

'You love it. Don't deny it, I saw you there yesterday. Me and Ryder were watching you, singing away as you made some new cattle brand. It's art for you, like it's always been for me.'

'A trade I have no papers for.' There were very few traditional blacksmiths around these days.

'Most people wouldn't understand, but back in the day you didn't need pieces of paper to do a job. You just had to show a fella that you had a good set of hands willing to work, and a set of ears willing to listen and learn.'

'Pity I did none of that.' She grinned.

Charlie chuckled, then held out his bent elbow to her. 'Stick with me, kid, and I'll show you a good time.'

She happily hooked her arm through his. 'You always have, Pop.'

From the day she'd arrived at Elsie Creek Station — homeless, motherless, fatherless, stepping off a bus in a strange town, with her name written on a paper luggage tag that was pinned to the same dress she'd been wearing when the police had found her — through everything, it was Charlie who'd helped her smile again. Seeing her grandfather smiling like this only made her smile more. It was like the rodeo champion was finally coming home.

Thirty-five

Inside the rodeo, Ryder leaned against the tall pub tables, alongside Ash, watching the many people coming and going.

Dex plonked three schooners of beer on their table and handed them out. 'Where did Harper and Sophie go?'

'To look around.' Ash sipped his beer.

'Any sign of Bree and Charlie?' Dex took a sip from his glass, with his eye on the shifting crowd. 'Pandora's here.'

'I think I spotted the redhead over there.' Ryder pointed to the crowd that shifted between the bleachers, the bar, or the stalls that were selling food, drinks, and assorted paraphernalia. It was busier than expected.

'I spotted Bree earlier,' said Ash. 'She's looking hot tonight. I'm so used to seeing her in riding gear or her blacksmithing gear that it's always a shock when she shows off her legs.'

Ryder grumbled behind his beer, keen to find her. But then she'd tell him to nick off, unlike any other women he'd met.

'What's going on with you and Bree?' Dex poked up the brim of his hat, resting his elbows on their beer table, his keen eyes taking in the details.

'Nothing.' Ryder shrugged.

'Nah…' Narrowing his eyes, Ash leaned in from the other side of the table as if to get a closer look at Ryder. 'I agree with Dex. Even Harper asked me if there was something going on between you two. You're being nice to each other, when normally you'd be bickering or complaining about her.'

'But *maaaate…*' Dex let rip that cheesy grin, pointing his beer at Ryder. 'Cap told me he spotted you this morning, putting on your shirt while sneaking out of the caretaker's cottage.'

'No way.' Ash raised his eyebrows at Dex. 'Gotta admit, our big brother did look like he'd just gotten out of bed at this morning's meeting.'

'So, you gonna share, brother?'

'Why? Are you going to give Bree some warning lecture?' He'd like to see them try.

'Like you gave Sophie and Mia.' Dex grinned behind his beer glass.

Ash shook his head. 'Don't forget what Ryder did with Harper, too.'

'I was only protecting you guys. You don't need to protect me from Bree.'

'So, there *is* something going on? How long?' Dex asked.

'Not long.' He hung his head, knowing they'd harp on him just like boys. Normally, he'd say nothing about any female because none of them had mattered enough. Yet, what he really wanted to do was shout out to the world that he was with Bree, and she was with him—especially with this crowd of cowboys. 'Bree's keeping it quiet for Charlie. Reckons he'll shoot me.'

'I'm surprised Bree hasn't.' Dex laughed. Only to lean in again. 'Did you notice Charlie calls you *son,* and us *lads*?' Dex missed nothing.

'Wait…' Ash wiped the beer froth from his top lip as he thought for a moment. 'Charlie does too. Is that because he knows you're sleeping with Bree? Which I struggle to picture.'

'Me too. Bree's like a sister.' Dex shuddered. 'But you look like you've finally been getting some sleep, brother.' Dex patted Ryder on the shoulder. 'And you look a lot more relaxed, even with the whole neighbour situation.'

'Best sleep I've had in decades.' And that was the truth.

'Oi, ten o'clock.' Ash nodded at some people behind them.

Ryder turned and scowled. It was Leo. 'Do not engage, Dex.' He could feel Dex's death look that was normally kept to the fighting rings. 'Ash?'

Ash was facing the other way. 'I'm looking for Harper. I'm not leaving her alone with that idiot in the same breathing space.'

'Hey…' Ryder grabbed Ash's arm. 'Don't do anything silly.'

'I won't.'

'And don't breathe a word about Bree to anyone.'

Ash grinned that cocky know-it-all grin. 'Oh, I'm telling Harper now. I keep no secrets from my lady, and she's going to love this.'

'Arsehole.'

Dex chuckled as Ash walked away.

'Well, well, well, look at what we've got here. I thought you boys would be busy stirring up spinifex fairies or something on the station.' It was Leo, with two of his men who Ryder recognised from their surveillance cameras.

'Leo.' Ryder was cold.

Dex casually leaned his elbow on the table, sizing up the competition. With the reflexes of a cat for fighting, Dex liked to lull people in, fooling them with his relaxed stance. While Ryder just glared.

'Are you here to try your luck at the rodeo, Leo?' Dex asked. 'They've got a sheep they save for the children, but it'll be a good start for your boys to ride.'

One of Leo's men scowled. 'I'll ride you in a minute, mate.'

'Sorry, slick, I don't swing that way. But we can get you downgraded to a billy goat's saddle.'

Leo grinned. The sick prick. 'Get us a beer and calm down, Gator. Bones go with him.'

'Yes, boss.'

Leo put his hands on his hips and surveyed the crowd. 'I saw that FJ Holden of Charlie's in the car park. Is he around?'

'Why?' Ryder asked coolly.

'Just wanted to say g'day. Being neighbourly and all. We could talk about musters, but we all know you have little to muster at that station of yours.'

'What's it to you?' asked Dex. 'Do you muster any cattle? Or do you just like to pretend you're a stockman, wearing that hat like the rest of the concrete cowboys in the city?'

Leo grinned again. 'We all know wherever Charlie is, Bree isn't too far behind. I'm going to ask her to dance with me later.'

'Leave Bree alone.' The growl was more heated than he'd realised, with Dex putting a hand on his shoulder.

'As Bree will tell you, she's her own boss. I'll let her tell me herself and make my night with her sassy comebacks that always make me smile.' With a chuckle, the smarmy bastard met up with his two men to grab his beer and join the crowd.

'Leo's right.' Dex nodded in Leo's direction.

'About what?' Ryder sculled down the rest of his beer. It didn't even touch the sides to control his temper.

'Bree will tell Leo to get nicked, she always does. But I think Leo's doing that to stir you up. You looked like you were going to rip his head off, which means you're in deep, brother.'

Ryder scrubbed a rough palm over his face. 'I am.' He wasn't going to deny it. He'd suspected that he'd been falling in love with Bree since the beginning, though he hadn't recognised it for most of that time—and once he did, he'd fought against it for as long as he could.

He spotted a rodeo rider, shaking hands and patting backs, with that white toothy grin and golden tan, highlighting that blond hair. The lights caught on his super shiny champion rodeo belt buckle, that went with the rodeo rider's vest, and chaps.

Dex swivelled around. 'Oi, look out, it's Cowboy Craig, looking all shiny with that belt buckle.'

'G'day, Dex.' Craig shook hands with Dex like old friends, giving Ryder a cordial nod.

'So why all dressed up?'

'For the parade they have on first, then the bulls begin.'

'Do you ride the bulls?'

'Nah. I've heard Charlie's story, and I've had my close call with a bull to know not to play with those horns.' Craig peered around at the crowd. 'I'm looking for Charlie and Bree. Have you seen them?'

'That way.' Ryder pointed to the bleachers.

'Are you two going to have a shot at the bulls?' Craig had a definite swagger, his leather chaps swishing with each step, along with the *tink tink* of his spurs on the dusty ground.

'The only bull I ride is the mechanical one,' said Dex. 'The one they have close enough to the bar.'

'Like my mate, Ryan, the vet. Except he'll only ride that thing if it's unplugged. If you guys want a shot at bull riding, they've got plenty of spaces available.'

'I'm good.' Dex rubbed his ribs, in particular the one that caused him lots of trouble a few months back.

'How is Charlie, after finding out his brother is innocent?' Craig asked, concerned.

'Good.' Ryder nodded. 'Charlie had everyone dancing last night, except me and Dex. We were holding up the bar.' It was the best spot to keep one eye on the monitors, and on Bree's smile as she danced. 'When did you find out?'

'Bree called. She wanted help organising something special for Charlie.'

Ryder never got jealous, and he trusted Bree. Even so, Craig was a single man. If it'd been Porter, it wouldn't have bothered him. But Cowboy Craig had the reputation of being a ladies' man. And why hadn't Bree asked Ryder for help? 'What sort of help did Bree need?'

'You'll have to wait and see. And there she is.' Craig pointed to the crowd that parted. 'Wow!'

Bree was turning heads among the rodeo crowd in a town where there were never enough women to go around.

Ryder's scowl darkened.

'Easy, brother.' Dex patted Ryder's shoulder. 'Craig's a mate. Bree and Craig are just platonic friends, since school, like a brother and sister. It's the same type of friendship I have with Bree.'

'Ah huh…' It still didn't make him breathe any easier.

But it was Bree that was making him feel things he didn't normally feel.

She was stunning, like a sunrise on the outback's horizon, captivating him with her colours that shone from her shiny thick red hair flowing past her shoulders, with her wide smile and green eyes. She wore a simple, strapless denim dress that not only showed off her legs, but accentuated her waist and hips, barely containing her generous cleavage. She was mouth-watering, even with her light and flowy jacket that barely brushed the tops of her sexy tall black boots, and her usual leather witchy sack that she never left the station without. How much gin was in that bag?

But seeing her like this, he had to do something big to show Bree and everyone else that they were together, and fast. But what?

Thirty-six

People were sucking up to Charlie, as Bree hovered beside her grandfather. Those who remembered the time of Jack Price's murder, and had blamed Harry, had come to apologise.

And so they should!

Bree had known word would get out, where plenty of Charlie's friends had come to offer their condolences—but not like this. They'd barely made it through the front gate and people were seeking out Charlie, when all she wanted to do was grab a drink and find their seats.

Then she spotted Ryder, being his usual grumpy ass, frowning at her, with Cowboy Craig and Dex on either side. What was Ryder's problem?

'Well, if it isn't my favourite redhead.' The blond cowboy grinned at her.

'Hey, Craig.' As she hugged Craig, Ryder glowered at her. While Dex bobbed his eyebrows up and down at her, glancing at Ryder then back at her.

Aw, man! Ryder had spilled their secret to his brothers. *The big mouth.*

'How are you, Charlie?' Craig shook Charlie's hand.

'Good. Better than good. Dying of thirst.'

'I'll get you a beer, Pop. You stay with Craig. I'll be right back.' She headed for the outdoor bar.

'You look nice.' Ryder's long, easy gait caught up with her in no time to escort her to the outdoor bar.

'Thank you.' She nodded at the barmaid as she held up two fingers. She was such a regular she didn't need to say what she drank.

Ignoring the busy crowd, Ryder stepped in close to her ear to whisper, 'You look good enough to eat.'

Didn't that send a wave of heat to flush over her skin? She needed air. Especially when trapped by his eyes slowly crawling over her body with a sort of primal hunger she hadn't seen before. 'What's with you?'

His open palm rubbed slow circles on her lower back. 'I want to stop hiding.'

'Listen, cupcake,' she said, adjusting his collar, and wiping some lint off his broad shoulders. 'What we do after dark is no one's business.'

'But I want to be able to be with you at any time.'

Saved by the barmaid and her beers, she freed herself. Call her crazy, but she enjoyed having power over the big man, who had power over everyone else.

The strange thing was he had power over her, too, and didn't even know it.

'I've got an idea.' He grabbed her elbow, stopping her from running away.

'Hmm…' She sipped her beer, taking in his shirt that was so well wrapped around his body in a good way, and those jeans. *Have mercy! Now that's how you wear a pair of jeans.*

'You like cowboys.'

'Why? Do you think I'm getting a little too cowgirl curious or something?' Cowboys, nah. It was an insult to stockmen. Besides, Ryder knew this.

'It is a rodeo. And you've got Cowboy Craig over there.'

'So? Charlie's an ex-rodeo cowboy, too.' She shrugged, clueless as to where he was going with this. 'Do you think you're tough enough to ride a bull?'

He dipped his head, keeping his eyes on her. 'Yeah, I do.'

'Pfft.' She rolled her eyes. 'Everybody wants to be a bull rider until it's time to be a bull rider.'

'Sweetheart,' he said in that rumbling tone, 'I'm willing to bet on it.' Ryder leaned in close with his eyes a warm, toasted hazelnut—which was such a contradiction for a man with ice in his veins. Yet, she'd seen behind that ice curtain, and it was changing.

'Not with me.'

'You make bets with my brother all the time.'

'You have nothing I want.' He couldn't buy her.

'Aww, that hurt.' He grinned, patting his hand over his heart, but there was a definite mischievous sparkle in his eyes.

Who was this man? It was a whole new side of Ryder she'd never seen before—he was being *playful*.

'If I ride a bull for the full eight seconds, we stop hiding from Charlie.'

'You told your brothers about us, didn't you?' She narrowed her eyes at him, playing that game of question for question, and no answers. 'Did you plaster it all over a billboard? Or did you pay your cousin, Monet, to do some skywriting in her little red plane?'

'They guessed.' But Ryder's lips twitched into a quick grin as he rubbed his jaw as if trying to keep a lid on his full wattage smile. 'But I'll take my shot on a bull ride.'

'Why? When you're the type of man who only knows about bull trading markets. Get in your lane.' She frowned and turned away.

But again, Ryder grabbed her arm, stopping her. 'Because your grandfather was a bull rider, and your mate Cowboy Craig is a bull rider.' He pointed to Craig in his rodeo leathers. 'Did Finn ride the bulls, too?'

'Yeah, Charlie taught him.' Then the penny dropped. Her eyes flared open as she spun around. 'No. Don't do it.' Because he was doing this to prove himself to Charlie. 'You'll get hurt.'

He stepped back, his voice deepening to match his frown. 'Don't you think I can do it?'

'It's dangerous.' She put down her beers at the nearest table to grab his arm, hoping to talk sense into the stubborn man. 'You should see the scars on Charlie's body after what that bull did to him. And Craig has had his own close call to never ride bulls again. Bucking bulls are —'

'If I win, we go public.'

'And if you lose, you'll end up in a pile of —'

'I have medical insurance. Have faith I can do this.'

'What is with you? You don't need to prove yourself to me.'

His smile ripped wide.

O-oh! She did not just admit that to Ryder, but also to herself that she cared way too much for this tall, hot and broody man, with his neatly trimmed beard highlighting his chiselled jaw, and lips good enough to bite—if this dark warrior-king wasn't acting like some child.

'Do we have a bet?'

'No.' She crossed her arms.

'You can't tell me what to do.'

The a-hole was now using her own words against her! 'You don't do spur-of-the-moment things.'

'Like you?'

She scowled at him. 'There's only room for one rebel in this family.'

'I'm not like Dex.

'No. You're thoughtful, dependable, and cautious even.' Traits she liked about him. 'You're that rock wall that stops someone from doing dumb things. And this is dumb. I can't believe I'm saying this, when it's usually me doing the dumb things. Not you.'

'Look, Bree…' He gently held her upper arms, lowering himself to meet her eyes. 'You have bets with Dex all the time. And you bet on him for his illegal fights while selling your gin.'

'This is different, you could seriously get hurt. For a smart businessman who doesn't play, this isn't like you.'

He stepped in closer. 'Because I have to do something bold to prove how much I care.'

'You don't have to.'

'I do.' He held out his hand. 'Do we have a bet?'

'I understand life is full of questionable life choices...' Hell, she had a long list of experiences in that department. 'And if you want to get stomped on by a land walrus to change your fairytale ending—'

'That's exactly what I'm doing.' He towered over her.

This man was chasing his happily ever after. With. Her.

She couldn't promise anyone that, certainly not herself.

Wait. Maybe he was bluffing? Which made sense. Kind of. 'Fine. Not like you're giving me any choice, I'll take that bet.' Because Ryder was going to do this with or without her consent. She shook his hand.

But Ryder held it, while sharing a wolfish grin. He pulled her close to kiss her cheek, then whispered into her ear, 'If I win, I'm sleeping with you tonight, in your bed and sleeping in late tomorrow, too.'

She pushed away from him. 'I'm not serving breakfast in bed, if that's what you think. It's not a hotel.'

'No, Bree. It feels like a home to me.' He gently smoothed down her hair, then winked at her. 'Back soon, babe.'

She watched him swagger off in the jeans that blessed that man. Only realising where he was going—to the working side of the rodeo grounds. He really was being serious!

She grabbed the beers, and hurried back to Craig and Dex, talking with Charlie. 'Dex, your brother has just lost the plot.'

'What's Ash done now?'

'I'm talking about Ryder. He's going to sign up to ride a bull.' She'd ridden plenty of bulls in the yards as a teenager, and she had a pet bull called Freckles, she'd hug like a puppy. But this was different, rodeo bulls could be dangerous. 'You have to stop him.'

'What the hell did you do to him, Bree?' Dex grinned at her.

'Nothing. Now go talk your brother out of this. This is your station's bank. You don't want him hurting himself.'

'You never did that for me.'

'This. Is. Different. Dex, you're a professional fighter. Ryder is a stockman, about to ride a professionally trained bull.' But Dex just kept grinning at her. 'Craig, you need to explain to Ryder how bad those bucking bulls are.'

'Nah, Ryder's a grown man.' Craig chuckled.

It did nothing to dampen her fear of Ryder getting hurt. 'Ryder knows nothing about rodeos.'

'Well, if he's that keen to ride a bull, I'll go give him the same tips you taught me, Charlie.' Craig patted Charlie's shoulder, sharing that bond of father and son. It's what Ryder was aiming for. Had to be.

'Pop?' She gave him a pleading look to stop this.

'Maybe I should give Ryder some tips myself.' Charlie snatched up his beer. 'Lead the way, lads. Ryder will need our help to survive.'

Thirty-seven

Ryder skimmed over the insurance forms, the ride and die forms, and the rules, then handed over his credit card and signed his life away on the dotted line.

'Have you ridden a bull before?' The middle-aged stockman's deep tan made his creases darken like shadows across his face.

'It's like riding a bigger horse, right?'

The man chuckled with a nod. 'Got any gear?'

'Nope.'

'We'll find you some. I'd recommend gloves.'

'I've got some in the ute.' He pulled out his phone and texted Ash: *Please grab my fencing gloves from the back of the ute, tucked in behind the spare tyre. I need them to ride a bull.*

Ash's response: *WTF bro! You for real?*

Ryder texted back: *Bring them to the back of the rodeo ring. ASAP.*

'We'll be drawing the bulls in a second, so stick around to find out your riding order. This is your number. Put it on your shirt, but I'd recommend you find yourself a vest to protect your chest.'

Ryder was given a number, like the one he'd given Mia when she represented his family at the muster dog trials. Ryder's had three numbers, unlike Cowboy Craig who wore the number 3, and in that display case that held Charlie's leather vest and chaps, it showed number 1.

'Bad luck on the number, son,' said Charlie, with Dex and

Craig approaching. 'Ya know what those numbers mean?'

Ryder didn't care. It just showed he'd paid for his spot.

'That's your ranking as a rider. And we all start somewhere, son.'

This is exactly what he'd hoped for. Bree was holding back for Charlie's sake, and what a better way to win over a champion bull rider, than to sit his arse on a bull.

'I can't believe you're doing this,' said Dex.

'Don't try to talk me out of it. I've already signed up.' He held up his number to Dex.

'Why?'

'I have a bet with Bree.' Bree was teaching him to play, and to be spontaneous. But he most enjoyed shocking the redhead by doing this.

My how the tables had turned, when normally he'd be the one trying to talk Bree out of doing something reckless. It's what made this all the more sweeter.

'Got any gear, son?' Charlie looked over at Ryder, but with approval.

'Nope.'

'I've got a spare vest, and chaps,' said Craig. 'I'll be right back.'

'I hope your medical insurance is all paid up, and your will is in order,' said Dex, shaking his head.

'Oi, leave off,' said Charlie. 'If the man wants to have a go, let him. I didn't see Ryder stop you from entering the ring for your fighting bouts.'

'I trained for those. But this is a bull. A properly trained bucking bull.'

'Hush now, you.' Charlie flicked his hand at Dex, then patted Ryder's shoulder. 'Do you know what bull you'll be riding, yet?'

Ryder shook his head. 'They said they were drawing the names out soon.'

'The rookie riders usually ride straight after the parade. You might like it.'

Ryder was only doing this once. It wasn't the first time

he'd been in a life-and-death situation. Yet, these guys did it as a sport. It took courage to get on a powerful beast like that, he had to respect the other rodeo riders around him, preparing to put on a good show.

'Why did you do it, Charlie? The bulls?' Considering the huge risk involved.

'Well, rodeo has always been a popular sport amongst the stockmen in the Northern Territory. We've got enough cattle stations with plenty of stockmen willing to have a go. As you'd know.'

'Sure, as a kid, I did the broncs, or just got my fill of rodeo breaking in stockhorses, or the occasional bull in the yards.' Ryder also remembered as a kid how he went with his brothers to see the local rodeo, where they got their first glimpse of the tough men that made them all want to be stockmen. He'd worked every school holiday on some station to gain the skills, even had a few decent muster seasons under his belt before he joined the Army.

'But it's more than that, son. Our local rodeo is a celebration of the tough, independent lifestyle that defines the Northern Territory's cattle industry. Very few people in Australia—certainly not those down south—live the way we do, with crocodiles and cyclones.' Charlie patted his heart. 'It's who we are as stockmen. And it's not about the trophies or showin' off either, it's about getting on that bull to prove you're tougher than the land we work on. It's about testing yourself, showin' you've got the guts to stand tall, even when the world is tryin' to buck you off.'

Those words hit home for Ryder, but also for his brother Dex. They'd been knocked on their arses plenty of times, as kids growing up in a junkyard, as men now trying to tame the wilderness that made the Northern Territory their home.

A stern man with a white hat stood on a crate. '*All right, you lot, it's time to draw the names…*'

The men's voices hushed as the adjudicator drew the names of the bulls they were to ride. The results written on a large board for everyone to see.

Craig rolled up with a load of black leather goods in his hands. 'I've got you this padded vest. It might be tight, but we can adjust the ties on the side. As your event is in the rough stock category, I'd recommend you wear these leather chaps, too.'

'The chaps will protect your legs from the bull and help with the ride,' explained Charlie.

It was a lot of fancy black leather, complete with tassels and stringy leather ties. It was kind of like the gear worn by the BDSM community. Hmm, Bree was certainly no buckle bunny, but she did have a kink for men wearing military uniforms and masks. Did she have one for leather-wearing bull riders?

'What about a ball cup to protect the jewels?' suggested Dex.

'I wouldn't recommend it,' said Craig. 'It's just plain uncomfortable and it'll throw you off balance.'

'I'll be fine.' Ryder slid his arms through the heavy vest. His Kevlar vest was lighter.

The adjudicator called out the bulls' names such as Dirty Harry, Evil Forces, Destroy, Holy Moly. There were no pet names like Coco, Fluffy, or Peanut. But if they had a bull named Cupcake, he'd pay to ride the thing just to show Bree he was no cupcake.

'You'll need some rosin, son. Ya got any, Craig?'

'Same recipe you gave me.' Craig lifted the lid on an old tin.

'What is that?' Dex dabbed his finger at the amber-like material. Sitting in the bottom of the tin, it was the size of a small bar of soap, that was a sticky mix between honey and super glue. 'It's gummy.'

'It helps your gloves keep a good grip on the rope,' explained Craig. 'When you're on the bull, you apply this rosin onto the riding rope. Then rub the rope repeatedly, to make the stuff hot to create a Velcro-effect. Listen, if you're only mucking around, I wouldn't recommend it, coz once it's activated, you're on for the ride.'

'I'll use it.' Ryder had a bet he was determined to win.

'Want a helmet?' asked Dex.

'Nope. It'd just get in my way. I don't want it slipping and blocking my view during the bull ride.' Ryder secured the chaps on his legs. They were heavier, compared to the pair he used to protect his legs when branding cattle in the drafting yards.

Ash ran up with the gloves. 'You're really doing this, huh?'

Ryder slid on his gloves. 'I'm not dressing up for fun, am I?'

'I don't believe it.' Ash looked at Dex, who shrugged.

'I'm sorry I haven't got a set of bull ropes to lend you, son.'

'I normally keep some bull ropes in the ute to lend, but I've only got bronc ropes with me,' said Craig.

'The adjudicator said he'd lend me some.'

'Good. I'll check them over for you,' said Charlie. 'Do you want to ride with a left or right-handed rope?'

'Left.'

'But you're right-handed,' said Dex.

'I still want to write, if something goes wrong.' Hoping not to tear his arm out of his shoulder socket.

'You'll want some spurs, son. They're an important part of the bull rider's kit.'

'Use mine,' volunteered Craig, unstrapping them from his boots. 'They're regulation, already checked by the judges. They're not too sharp to hurt the animal, but they'll help you get a good grip. Charlie gave me these.'

'That I did.' Charlie patted Craig's shoulder as Craig tied them onto Ryder's boots.

'Well, look at you.' Craig pushed back his hat and gave an approving nod. 'If I didn't know any better, I'd say you're ready to ride a bull.'

'The dressing up is the easy part,' said Dex, with his arms crossed over his chest, while Ash could only rub his neck wearing worry not normally seen on his younger brother.

'If you've got any tips on riding the thing, I'm listening.'

Charlie nodded with approval, patting Ryder's arm. 'I do.'

This is why Ryder was going through with this, just for that look. Now all he had to do was make the eight seconds to win his bet with Bree.

The adjudicator called out, '*Riggs. Riding Chainsaw. First ride out the gate.*'

The gathered rodeo riders murmured. Some shook their heads.

'Is that bad?' asked Ash.

'Craig, you know this crowd,' said Dex, 'what is wrong with Chainsaw?'

'Chainsaw is known as the widow maker. No one has ever lasted the full eight seconds on that bull.'

Thirty-eight

ree sat on the bleachers beside Harper. Sitting with them was Sophie, snapping away with her camera at the crowd, the bugs swirling high on the lights, the arena, and pretty much everything that moved. She was as happy as Harper was showing off her new hat.

'Oh, look. Ash texted me this photo.' Harper held up her phone screen, showing an image of Ryder all dressed up to ride a freaking bull.

The stubborn fool!

What's worse, Charlie stood on one side of Ryder, with Cowboy Craig on the other. As a man with a deep love for the sport, the retired rodeo champion seemed truly delighted to share his knowledge with someone like Ryder.

Maybe Ryder wasn't such a fool after all.

'Harper, can you send me that photo?'

'Sure.' Harper tapped away on the screen.

In a few moments, Bree's phone buzzed in her handbag. She dug it out, saving the image as her new screensaver. It'd been a long time since she'd seen Charlie back among the local rodeo crowd again, wearing a pride you couldn't buy.

Then the bank of towering lights became brighter, and the music died down.

'It's about to begin...' Bree sat higher. 'Get your camera ready, Sophie.'

A voice boomed over the speakers, welcoming everyone to the event, then introduced each rodeo rider into the rodeo arena as part of the opening parade. *'Cowboy Craig…'*

Craig came out, waving his hat in the air to a chorus of wolf whistles from the ladies in the crowd. He was clearly popular.

'Ryder Riggs.'

Bree tried to hide her smile, watching Ryder with that sexy, powerful swagger, his thick thighs flexing with each step as he stood beside Craig. No smile. No wave of the hat, just his usual grumpy arse.

She put her fingers to her lips and whistled super loud. It echoed, while making the people sitting in front of her wince. 'Sorry.' Not sorry. Because she got Ryder's attention, who patted down his vest like a proud peacock.

Bree blew him a kiss.

Finally, he found his smile.

Craig said something to Ryder, and they chuckled between them while standing in line with all the other rodeo riders. It was good they got along. Craig was a part of Charlie's family. As for Ryder Riggs…

'I can't believe Ryder is doing this,' said Harper. 'You know, he didn't talk to me for a month when I first came out here. He still barely does.'

'Me too. No, wait, Ryder gave me the big brother's speech.' Sophie then said in a deep voice as if to imitate Ryder, 'Hurt my brother and I hurt you.'

'That sounds nothing like Ryder.' But it had them giggling like teenagers on the bleachers.

After introducing all the rider's names, the MC tucked the clipboard under his arm, as he spoke to the crowd over the microphone that bellowed through the speakers surrounding the arena. 'Before we begin tonight…'

'Here we go,' said Bree, on the edge of her seat.

'I'd like you all to welcome a local legend. A three-time Australian Bull Riding Champion, with a trophy case full of awards to prove it. Please give a round of applause to our very own local champion, Charlie *Splinter* Splint.'

Hot tears peskily blurred her vision as she watched Ash

and Dex help push Charlie into the arena. With that bandy-legged swagger of a rodeo rider who'd lived in the saddle for most of his life, Charlie waved to the crowd.

Bree clapped harder and cheered louder for her grandfather as he walked past the younger rodeo riders who clapped for him, to stand between Ryder and Craig.

In Charlie's lifetime, he'd done many amazing things, and bull riding was one of his passions that he shared with many a rider over the years, many becoming champions themselves. But this moment, among his local peers, was priceless.

Again, the MC's voice boomed over the speakers. 'I only recently learned that Charlie's brother, Harry Splint, whose remains were found in a cave, was proven innocent in a sixty-year-old murder mystery—solved by our very own Senior Constable Porter.'

It was easy spotting Porter patrolling the crowd in his police uniform, and the way he dropped his head, getting all humble when his name was mentioned. Porter deserved the public recognition, especially among the locals.

The MC addressed the crowd: 'I'd like to extend our condolences to Harry's family, especially to his brother Charlie, and ask that you all to join us in a minute of silence to honour the passing of a fellow stockman.'

In an arena filled with wide-brimmed hats, the crowd rose to their feet and removed them in unison. Men, women, and children all took part, as their excited voices, cheers, and conversations all became silent.

Not even a horse nickered, nor a bull made a sound, as the seconds passed, and the entire arena bowed their head in silence for Harry Splint.

Charlie had never wanted to give his brother a funeral, in fear of the local backlash. This was so much better.

Bree sniffed, dabbing at the tears threatening to trickle down her cheeks and ruin her make-up, her heart glowing for those in the centre arena where her grandfather stood beside Ryder and Craig.

Charlie looked up at her and gave her a nod—his silent way of saying, *Thank you, kid.* The gesture filled her with a warmth that almost started a gush of tears. Her feeling of guilt for not supporting her grandfather over Harry had finally been put to rest, and her grandfather could lift his head proudly with their family name now publicly cleared.

But when Ryder caught her gaze, his nod communicated so much more. She felt it, deep within her chest, even deeper in her heart, and into her soul.

Then a much more terrifying thought charged at her like bull, leaving her both breathless and terrified over Ryder, in his rodeo rigging, preparing to throw his life away for an eight-second ride. It had every muscle inside her body coiling with tension.

She recognised that feeling all too well. It was the same fear that had haunted her nightmares when she was younger—the fear of losing someone you loved. Only this time, it was a thousand times stronger than she had ever felt before.

It was only then she realised... She was falling in love with Ryder Riggs!

Thirty-nine

The siren sounded, the crowd cheered, and the rodeo arena was soon cleared except for the rodeo clowns, where Ryder found himself in the chutes, sliding his legs over the large back of a big bull named Chainsaw.

'Slide your hand along here and heat the rope until that rosin clings,' Craig instructed, with Dex beside him.

'Got it.' The flat braided rope was smooth, solid, and his only lifeline.

'Now, son, listen up.' Charlie pushed his hat back, speaking close to Ryder's ear. 'You've gotta be quick from here on out. The longer you sit here, the longer the bull will read your feelings. And if it smells your fear, it'll have you.'

Ryder sat firm on the bull, feeling the beast's power beneath him. No fear, just focus. This wasn't combat, but it was a different kind of battle—one he was ready for. It wasn't about the ride, it was about Bree. He tightened his grip, the world narrowing down to eight seconds and one chance to win her over. 'Let's get on with it, then.'

'When you give the nod, they'll open that gate and the bull's gonna rear up.'

'Just be careful, mate,' said Craig. 'That first jump out of the chutes will be this bull's biggest. It's where Chainsaw has flicked off all his other riders with that first jump.

'Right.' Ryder heated the rope with the rosin until the grip became glue. He punched his gloved hand, doubling up the grip. And he was in.

'Use your legs, lean forward, using your arm in the air for balance,' called out Charlie. 'And for heaven's sake, son, keep that back straight. You get all hunched over, and Chainsaw will whip your spine around and crack it like a Christmas candy cane.'

'Is it too late to stop this?' asked Ash, with wide eyes.

'Like hell.' He was here now.

Charlie leaned down and tapped on Ryder's leg covered in thick leather chaps. 'Find his rhythm, son. Every bull has one. It's buck, kick, and rear, some twist at the same time. You find that rhythm and you'll finish the ride. Good luck, son.'

'Good luck, brother.' Dex also patted his shoulder.

'I wish I had my drone to tape this.' Ash giving him a thumbs up, while aiming his phone's camera at Ryder.

'You've got this, Ryder, give 'em hell.' Craig balanced on the rail nearby. 'Just give the fellas a nod when you're ready.'

Ryder checked his grip one more time. Then glanced up at the crowd and spotted Bree. She looked worried.

'Stuff it.' He nodded at the man.

And the gate swung open.

Forty

The crowd roared as Ryder entered the rodeo arena on the back of a bucking cross-bred Brahman bull named Chainsaw.

Bree was on her feet, her heart in her throat as the massive beast plunged, leaped, and spun in the air, stirring up the dust, with Ryder holding on with one hand, his other arm in the air, in the most dangerous sport on the planet.

Chainsaw snorted in fury, his eyes white and wild, twisting his body desperately to get that man off his back. The seconds seemed to trickle into hours as she watched on, horrified.

How on earth did her grandmother survive watching Charlie ride rodeo bulls, driving interstate for a simple eight-second ride, when there was nothing simple about this. Eight seconds he had to hold on for, and not touch the bull or himself with his free arm that he held high in the air.

Poor Granny Bea, watching those sharp horns gouge into her grandfather's chest, injuring him so gravely that it took Charlie a year before he rode a horse again. He was lucky to be alive.

And Ryder. Whatever possessed the normally sane, stern, plan-everything and do-nothing-spontaneous Captain, to ride a one-tonne bucking bull!

She counted down the seconds in her head. Three... Four... Five...

The crowd started counting. *'Six... Seven...'*

Bree couldn't tear her eyes off the scene, holding her breath with her fingers crossed.

A siren blasted.

And the crowd erupted in cheers. Some threw their hats in the air.

Behind the arena's fence, on the working part of the rodeo, Charlie, Craig, Dex and Ash all took turns hugging each other, jubilant for Ryder.

Ryder jumped off the bull.

He'd made it.

Only then did Bree breathe.

Ryder raised his hat to the cheering crowd as Chainsaw safely trotted away through the open gate.

Bree clapped her hands, the numbness swapped for the prickles in her fingers as she smiled at him. He'd done it.

But instead of returning to the back of the arena, with all the other rodeo riders, Ryder strode across the arena. He climbed up and over the railed fence that protected the audience, then hiked up the bleachers with the tassels shifting on his leather chaps, his eyes shaded by his black hat, heading straight for her.

'What are you doing?'

'This.' He took off his black hat and placed it on her head.

'You did not just do the cowboy-hat rule on me!' In front of the entire town!

'A bet is a bet, lady.' Bundling her up in his arms he brushed his mouth against hers, softly, slowly caressing her in a kiss that felt like more than just a kiss.

'I'm claiming my prize,' he mumbled against her lips.

She gripped his shirt with her fist. 'Promise me, you'll never do that again.'

He paused.

'I will not go through that again. Not like my grandmother did for Charlie. No more bulls.'

His smile grew, and it was slow and sexy, she was helpless to resist.

'I promise. Now let's seal that deal with a kiss.'

She should have fought against it, but the way he kissed her it was drugging her, as his strong arms cocooned her to lean her back in a Hollywood style–kiss, leaving her with no choice but to hold his shoulder, and his hat on her head, as he claimed her with a kiss that was long, slow and tender as the rest of the world faded away and it was just her and Ryder.

There was no hiding their relationship now.

Forty-one

'Did you have a good night tonight, Pop?' Bree hooked her arm around Charlie's as they strolled side by side across the dimly lit car park. She hadn't seen much of Charlie tonight, as he'd stayed on the working side of the rodeo. It's where her grandfather belonged, with his lifelong passion for the sport.

'I did.' He grinned back at the lights where the band was playing. 'I helped a few lads with their grips. Gave a few tips on the best way to ride them bulls. It helped Ryder beat Chainsaw.'

'Hmm…' She was waiting for Charlie to say something about Ryder, who, after he'd returned his rodeo gear, had sat beside her for the rest of the show. Ryder didn't care that he'd won nothing at the rodeo—except the adrenaline rush and their bet. Unlike Craig, who'd won another buckle for the best rider of the night, Ryder seemed content to keep his hand on her thigh and watch the rest of the rodeo as a couple.

It had been a long time since she'd been part of a couple.

'Did you organise that minute of silence for Harry?' Sadness filled his grey eyes. This is not how she wanted to end the night, when her grandfather had been on such a natural high.

'We never had a funeral for Harry, and he deserved something. Was that okay?'

'You've never made me prouder,' he said, tenderly patting her hand. 'Even though Harry never took part in any rodeos, he drove me there plenty of times. It's because of my rodeo money he could buy Pandora.' He pointed to the vintage car, catching the car park's spotlights. 'Harry and I emptied out our entire savings on fuel, hitting every roadhouse and outback pub on the way back to Elsie Creek Station. It was a hell of an adventure.'

'Sounds like it.'

'So…' Charlie cleared his throat. 'You and Ryder, eh?'

And there it was. She'd been waiting for it. 'You won't shoot him?'

Charlie chuckled. 'Well, kid, if anyone would've shot him, it's you. But, seeing as how you haven't, what am I gonna do?'

'Evening all.' It was Leo, their neighbour, coming up behind them. 'Bree.' He tipped his hat to her.

'Ugh. What a way to ruin the night.' She rolled her eyes dramatically, as always whenever she met Leo. 'Hello, Leo. I see you brought your balding gorillas with you. Isn't it past their bedtime at the zoo?' She tried to steer Charlie to the other side of the car.

'Aw, Bree, that hurts.'

'It would if you had feelings, but we both know you don't.' Pity it only amused Leo more, that was just a part of the game they played.

'Bree, that's not nice to talk to our neighbour like that,' said Charlie.

'Bree, listen to your grandfather.' It was obvious Leo wasn't offended at all.

She just glared at the man who always spoke with such precise pronunciation. 'What do you want, Spawn of Satan?'

'To say hello. I haven't seen you in a while and I always enjoy our little chats.'

She shook her head. 'I know you're used to dealing with overgrown children with the attention span of a goldfish,' she said, arching an eyebrow at his sidekicks, 'but I mean, why are you *here*?' She stood right in front of Leo. He was tall, lean, with an edge to him. He didn't scare her, never did.

'You don't do rodeos. You're not a cattleman. You're not a mining FIFO. And, as much as you love to create intricate word salads, I'd like the short and sharp version of why you came to Elsie Creek. You could have set up shop anywhere. It's a big country, with plenty of places that would have made lithium mining a lot easier for you, giving you a much bigger profit margin than the property next door that doesn't have enough water for that type of mining operation.' Even though she knew he had the dope crop, Leo could have set up his operations anywhere else but here.

Leo narrowed his dark eyes at her, he was always a cool and calculated customer, who had the power to wipe the smile off your face without even touching you. 'You know, you're the first person to ask me that.'

'It's none of our business, mate. Let's go, Bree.' Charlie tried to drag her away.

'No, the lady asked a question, and she deserves an answer.'

'I'm no lady. I'm a blacksmith with a poor attitude, in need of a jug of gin to take the edge off my bristling temper.'

'No, you're more than that. I've been watching you for a long time, Bree, to know how truly special you are.'

Didn't that send her inner alarm bells ringing. How long had Leo been watching her?

In the beginning, she'd been polite to the guy—nice, even. He was hot in his suits, with that mobster edge, effortlessly bantering with her as quickly as she dished it out. It was fun for a hot second, until she'd realised that he was trying to manipulate her. It's why she gave him so much lip, hoping to push him away.

Yet Leo would come back for more, always smiling at her, always asking her for that date, and she always said no. For almost eighteen months they'd played this game, ever since Elsie Creek Station went up for sale.

'I can't believe you'd settle for someone like Ryder Riggs.' Leo scoffed. 'You don't belong with someone like him. You need someone who'd truly appreciate your outlaw attitude, who could give you everything you desired.'

'Right, and you're expecting my ovaries to high-five themselves over you?' Someone like Leo would treat her like a possession, a piece of property to control.

She knew this much: Leo had made their life at the station miserable, until the Riggs brothers moved in at the beginning of this year's muster season.

Leo grinned. 'I'm much better than that cowboy. And you know it.'

'Firstly, Ryder is no cowboy, he's a cattleman. A stockman. Secondly, I don't know what you are.' She tilted her head at him, knowing there was more to Leo's story than he let on. 'I've never been able to work that out.' There had to be reason for all his twisted actions.

'Want me to explain?'

'No, thanks. We're going now.' Charlie tugged on her arm.

'No, I insist we have that chat.' Leo held his hand out to her. 'We're way overdue, Bree. After all, you've been knocking back how many of my requests for dinner?'

'Why can't you tell me here?' She'd always known her smart mouth would get her into trouble one day. But she'd also been told to be herself—if she didn't give Leo lip, he'd know something was up.

Charlie knew nothing about what Leo was really doing, because they hadn't trusted him to keep a secret. Sadly, her grandfather was the innocent bystander in all of this.

Parked beside Ryder's vehicle, Bree juggled Pandora's keys to find the right key, then unlocked the passenger door for Charlie.

'I can shout you a drink—'

'Inside the rodeo grounds. Sure.'

'No. If you want to know, you'll need to come this way.'

'I'm not going anywhere with you and your bridge trolls. Not when this Cinderella is over wearing her glass slippers for the night and is keen to go home and declare national pyjama day for the rest of the weekend.'

'Bree, I'm not taking a no this time.' Leo stepped in so close, his cologne sharp and rich. Just as tall as Ryder, but not as big in the shoulders, but Leo did have that lethal edge to him. 'You will come home with me. Now.' He nodded at one of his men, who lifted his jacket, to tap on his handgun, while the other one blocked any chance of escape.

'You don't scare me.' Leo might know how to invoke fear with the calmest of words, but not with Bree.

'I know.' His dark eyes sparkled in the spotlight, giving her a sly grin. 'It's one of the many things I admire about you.'

But poor Charlie, his face was pale, his confident stance crumbling as he backed away, with his eyes silently pleading for her to behave.

It was enough to create an icy dread that settled in her stomach. To protect her grandfather, she had no choice but to go with Leo.

She barely nodded.

Leo gleefully wrapped his arm around her and began a slow stroll under the stars. 'See, it's almost a romantic walk.'

But there was nothing romantic about this at all.

'I think you'll want to hear this. You too, Charlie,' Leo said, leading her towards his car with his armed cronies on either side of the wide-eyed Charlie. 'After all, we're practically family.'

Forty-two

Ryder strolled through the car park with the couples, Dex and Sophie, Ash and Harper, keen to get home and claim his prize for riding a damned bull. Never had he thought he'd do something like that. Yet, it worked out to be one of the best nights to go into his memory bank.

'Hey, I thought Bree was taking Charlie home?' Dex pointed to Pandora still parked beside Ryder's ute.

'She was.' But that was an hour ago. It had taken that long to drag his brothers out of the bar where they'd been celebrating with Cowboy Craig. Charlie had been with them, before he'd asked Bree to drive him home.

The old man had given Ryder the nod. There was no handshake, no lecture, just a nod, avoiding all awkward conversation of him kissing Bree in front of the entire town.

And he'd do it again in a heartbeat to win Bree over.

'Oops.' Sophie tripped over something on the ground.

Dex caught her. 'Careful, Soph.'

'What is that?' Sophie used her phone's torch to highlight the dusty paddock that doubled as a car park.

'Hey, that's Bree's witchy sack.' Dex retrieved the leather bag big enough to hide a bottle of gin.

'Ryder…' Ash pointed at Pandora's passenger door where the car keys were hanging in the lock, with the door slightly ajar.

His world stilled.

Bree would never leave those keys in the car, and neither

would Charlie. Bree would also never leave her purse in the dirt—but she was smart enough to leave it in a place where he'd find it, right by his driver's door.

His heart hammered in his chest as he peered across the emptying car park. 'BREE!'

Forty-three

'This way.' With four goons surrounding them, Leo led Charlie and Bree down a cracked cement path. The spotlight that sat on the corner of the simple demountable attracted a swirl of night bugs, as chirping crickets competed with the rhythmic sounds of commercial irrigation sprinklers that hissed as they pivoted, with their rhythmic *chug chug chug* water rotations echoing through the still night air.

'Cor blimey, what is that smell?' Charlie winced, with his hand over his nose and mouth at the sharp, almost oily scent, with a sweet undertone. 'It's enough to give a man a headache.'

'I agree,' said Leo, opening the door to the accommodations that reminded Bree of run-down rooms found at older mining camps.

'You can just let us go, Leo.' While pretending not to notice the whopping big field of dope, her mind raced through a set of escape scenarios, each one hitting a dead end. With Charlie as fragile as he was, he couldn't run or fight, so their chances of getting out were shrinking by the second.

She glanced at her grandfather—his deeply wrinkled face grew pale under the harsh spotlight, his eyes darting with worry. The sight was enough to trigger a crushing weight of desperation in her. But she had to be smart about this, as there was no way in hell she was going to leave her grandfather behind.

Leo's smile was sickly as he bowed at the door, sweeping his hand towards the inside. 'But I have something to show you. I promise it will answer all your questions.'

'We don't need to see it.' Her big mouth did this. *Idiot!*

'Boss said, inside. So inside you go.' The creep they called Gator gripped her arm.

'Listen here, liver lips, don't touch what you can't afford.' She ripped her arm free. Gritting her teeth, she spun around to stare down the imbecile, her temper bristling just under her skin. 'Touch me again and I'll save the planet from any chances of you breeding in the future.'

'Yeah, right.'

'I bend steel for a living, you concrete cowboy. Don't think I won't do it!' Gator was the creepiest. 'Which one did I shoot in the arse, Leo? No, not you, chicken legs.' She nodded at the one they called Bones. 'And I've never seen you two before. Brothers, right?'

The goofy one nodded. 'I'm Hammer and that's Wrench.'

'Tools!' She peered over her shoulder at Leo, even giggling. 'Which one is the sharpest tool in your shed?'

Leo laughed. He always understood her smart-arse cracks when very few people ever did. 'Bree, you do amuse me. Gentlemen, please play nice with our guests.'

Gator just sneered at her.

Bree refused to move. Even if the assorted night bugs landed in her hair, and a mosquito buzzed near her ear, she wasn't moving. Hoping that if she stood here long enough, under this spotlight, Ryder's cameras would pick them up for Cap to notice. After all, they were right next door—with only a few thousand acres between them.

'Bree, you did ask the question, and I'm only being neighbourly in answering them for you.'

'With guns and backup, like this one who smells like a split personality to me.' She narrowed her eyes at Gator. She was so close to waving her arms in the air, hoping that Cap was watching that wall of monitors in the boys' boardroom.

'Come on, kid. Leo's gotta show us something. If we behave, he'll let us go home.' Charlie tugged on her arm, leaving her with no choice but to follow her grandfather inside.

The door slammed shut behind her, closing her inside with five men and Charlie. She was unarmed, trapped, and outnumbered, right next to Leo's dope crop worth a few million dollars.

There was no way Leo was letting them go home now.

Forty-four

Ryder stared at Bree's bag, deliberately left behind, as a fresh wave of icy fear coursed through his veins. She'd been taken—he was sure of it. And there was only one thug who'd dare to do such a thing: Leo.

To be certain, he'd called Cap to watch the cameras back home and sent the others to search the rodeo grounds.

Back at his ute, his phone rang. It was Cap. Ryder answered immediately, his stomach clenching with a mix of fear and anger. 'Cap, did you see something to do with Bree?'

Cap's voice came through, grim and sharp. 'Bree and Charlie are with Leo. They're at his place.'

The words hit like a punch to the gut, echoing loudly in the rodeo car park. Ryder's fists clenched as anger surged through him, raw and unforgiving. He should have never let her out of his sight.

Ash and Dex ran up, their eyes wide with surprise. Behind them, Sophie and Harper, clutching each other's hands like sisters.

'No. Dammit.' Ryder's voice was tight, barely containing the storm of fear and rage brewing inside. His teeth ground together as he demanded, 'When did they get there?'

'Just now. Bree's giving them lip. You could see she's angry, she stood there for the longest time—'

'Because Bree knows where the cameras are.' *Good girl.*

'But Charlie looks terrified.'

An icy rush raced through his bloodstream, squeezing his

heart. 'Can you still see them?'

'No. Leo's taken them inside that demountable, and Leo's men had their handguns out. Does this mean that Charlie and Bree have been—'

'Kidnapped!' He gritted his teeth so tightly they were going to snap. 'Ash, Dex, take the girls home in Pandora. Cap, I want you to get the boardroom ready for everyone to hunker down. It's the most defensible place we have. Bree's stashed bedding and snacks in the cupboards just for this sort of situation.' A situation he didn't think would happen—but Bree had been paranoid over something. She called it a cyclone kit for the station, which he'd thought was strange when the cyclone season didn't officially start for another month. But with a new type of storm about to break, thank goodness he let Bree do what she wanted.

'Do we call the police?' Ash asked.

'They're all over the place, working.' Dex tore his hat off his head, raking fingers through his hair. 'I'll kill that bastard.'

Get in line! 'Cap, as soon as they arrive get everyone to the boardroom and put Sarge inside that room,' Ryder ordered over the phone, while facing his younger brothers. 'No one will get past that shepherd.' Sarge was a well-trained ex-police riot dog, who'd sat beside Ryder many times over many nights, like a good soldier. That dog would fight to the death to protect those he loved. He already had a bullet wound from protecting his previous owner.

'Do you want my dogs?' Cap asked over the phone.

'Absolutely. Let them out of the kennels, they can be our outdoor alarm system. And light the place up with the spotlights Dex and I installed.' *Only today.*

Dex's eyes widened at Ryder. Had they both picked up on Bree's vibe, aware that Leo's bust was happening in the morning. He glanced at his watch. It was just after eleven. The raid was set for seven.

But this play by Leo was something unexpected. What had triggered Leo to do this?

'Will Leo hurt them?' Ash croaked out, the worry showing on his face, but also on the girls.

Dex's hand landed heavily on Ash's shoulders. 'Not while Bree is there. Remember, Leo has always had a thing for Bree. I've seen it at the fights. He won't hurt her.'

'No, that prick wants to own her.' It was one of the things Bree hated, anyone owning her. But Leo—who liked to think he lived above the law—wasn't just going to own her, he was planning to keep her!

Like hell. Ryder's lip curled with his snarl full of heated rage.

'What are we going to do?' Cap asked over the phone.

'Everyone is coming home now, you lot all stay in that boardroom until I tell you otherwise.'

'What are you going to do?'

Ryder opened the back tray of his ute and dragged over his steel box. With a juggle of his keys, he unlocked the sturdy bolt and lifted the vacuum sealed lid. The car park's spotlight shone inside the large steel crate, filled with an assortment of weapons. The same ones they'd used on their midnight hike through Leo's land and more. 'I'm going to get them back.'

Forty-five

'Coffee? Tea? Wine? Beer? Bourbon,' offered Leo as he led them inside the simple demountable normally found on mine sites. For Bree, it reminded her of the ringers' rooms on Elsie Creek Station.

With the windows closed and the air conditioner on full blast, it was like walking into Antarctica, except it reeked of greasy sausages.

'How many times have I told you lot to not cook inside?' Leo ripped out the electric cord and passed the greasy frying pan to Wrench, who dumped it outside.

'May I?' Charlie pointed to the old dining chair, at the table that seated four. Other than that, they had a desk and a kitchenette in this sparsely furnished room. Behind her was the bedroom with bunk beds, and further along a small bathroom.

'Go ahead, Pop.' Bree pulled out the chair while glaring at Leo.

'Sorry, I forgot my manners.'

'You could show a shred of decency and let us walk home.'

'Charlie won't make it.'

'I'm a lot fitter than you know,' Charlie mumbled, pushing back the brim of his hat. 'What's this all about, Leo? You said you wanted to show us something. So show us and let us be on our way.'

Leo poured himself a bourbon, even pouring one for

Charlie and Bree. 'It's a nightcap then, or a peace-offering.'

Bree grabbed her glass and sipped on the hard liquor that was surprisingly smooth. No wonder Ryder liked it.

Right now, she had to think like Ryder. How would he size up this situation as a soldier?

Her eyes darted around the room as she leaned her back against the wall with Charlie in front of her. Gator and Bones lounged around on her left side. Opposite was Leo. To her right, bookending the door to freedom was Hammer, with his brother, Wrench. They were a ragtag lot.

While the AC was threatening to give her pneumonia, Leo's men were sweating, clearly not used to this outback weather. Hammer and Wrench were sunburnt, obviously showing their southern skin.

'Okay, Leo, now that you've brought us to your little house-warming party, can we get on with the show-and-tell? I already told you that this Cinderella's pumpkin has lost its puff hours ago.' She even feigned a yawn, mixed with weariness and boredom.

It didn't fool Leo, who only smiled with amusement. 'Charlie, I'd like you to tell me about your brother, Harry.'

'What do you want to know?'

'Tonight, at the rodeo, they had that one minute of silence for him. I was under the impression that Harry was wanted for murdering Elsie Creek Station's head stockman, who'd then run off with the man's wife?'

'But Harry didn't, you see.' Charlie fiddled with his glass where it rested on the table.

Leo, seated opposite Charlie, crossed one leg over a knee like a gentleman, cradling his glass of bourbon as if in some country club. 'Go on.'

'Harry was going to run off with Penelope.'

'The married woman.'

'Not legally. Jack Price wasn't his real name.'

'What was his name, then?'

'Jack Price was Jake Blackwell. An army deserter who'd pinched a load of shotties from them and done a runner to the scrub.'

'What else?'

'Well, I only knew the man as Jack Price. As my boss, he was a good head stockman, and before you ask,' said Charlie, raising his open palm, 'I had no clue what was going on with my brother and Jack's wife, coz I was out musterin'. By the time I'd come back, Price was dead, my brother was accused of murdering him, and run away with Jack's wife, Penelope.'

'So when did that story change?'

'The other week. We were out musterin' and there was a stampede. Bree cut 'em off. You should have seen it, riding her horse with the reins in her teeth, pumping the shotgun in one hand, while cracking her whip to stop them.'

'Pop, they don't need to hear that.' She internally cringed with embarrassment. But Charlie always loved an audience, even if it was at gunpoint.

'Leo wanted to hear this, and I don't mind tellin' a tale now and again.' Charlie then swivelled around to face Leo, but he also included the other men in the room speaking to them just like he did to the crowd at the rodeo earlier. 'Anyhoodle, with the ground shaking from over a thousand head of cattle, it started a landslide.'

'Hey, we felt that,' said Hammer, with Wrench nodding beside him. 'We thought it was an earthquake.'

'I'm not surprised. It happened just on the other side of Cattleman's Keep there.'

'Any damage to the property, or the cattle?'

'The cattle bolted back the way they came, along with Bree and Ryder. But once the dust had settled, it revealed this old mining cave.' Charlie scooped up the glass, his hand shaky as he swallowed a mouthful of liquor. 'And... Well...' He glanced back at Bree to finish for him.

'That's where I found Great-Uncle Harry's skeleton, holding his lover, Penelope. They'd died in each other's arms.'

'No way.' Wrench pulled out a chair and flipped it around to sit on it like a horse's saddle. Even Bones sat on the edge of the kitchen bench, with Hammer sitting on the desk. It was Gator, as the watchdog, who hadn't relaxed his stance. 'From the cave-in?'

'Lack of oxygen.' Charlie nodded. 'We didn't even know the cave existed. But there it was. And according to them geo-whatnot mining specialists, they'd been trapped alive by dynamite blasts.'

'Did they know who did it?'

Again, Charlie nodded. 'Jack Price did it. Murdered his own wife, he did.'

'How?' Leo's look shifted from one of amusement to something else entirely.

'Jack Price used the dynamite to get back at his wife for leaving him for another man. The police reckon some bad people were after him for skedaddling with his stolen shotguns, that he'd been trying to sell as fast as he could. But when he went to grab his cash and passport so he could leave, it was all gone.'

'Where was it?' This time Bones, on the other side, asked the question.

'His wife, Penelope, had his ID and all that dosh. The thing was, Price didn't know it, only realising *after* he'd buried her behind tons of rock and rubble.'

'Jeez...' The brothers Wrench and Hammer looked at each other, both raking fingers through their hair. It had Bree wondering if they were twins.

'Now them coppers reckon, based on the evidence Ryder and Bree found—'

'What was that?' Leo asked her.

She shrugged. 'The murder weapon and some dynamite.'

'How did the police—'

'Oi.' Charlie raised his hands at the men who were holding them hostage, as if trying to control the conversation in the pub.

Bree grinned, shaking her head. 'Sorry, Pop, the floor is yours.'

'Right, where were we?' Charlie pushed back his hat, the

light catching on its unique hatband made from the crocodile that had dared to bite him. 'Oh, yeah…' He cleared his throat. 'Now, according to them copper's findings, they reckoned Jack Price was so devastated that he had nothing left, and with them bad guys after him, he set up his suicide to look like a murder and pin it on Harry. Which is what everyone had thought these past sixty years.' Charlie shook his head. 'But according to the forensic whatnot and the DNA thingy they scraped from the gun, the dynamite, the clothing, and stuff they dragged out of archives, they matched the DNA to Jack Price. He not only murdered my brother and his own wife, but he also hid Harry's car in the Stoneys, letting everyone—including me—think that he'd absconded with a married woman. But I never believed my brother murdered anyone. He just didn't have it in him.' Charlie sighed, picked up his glass and raised it in the air. 'Either way, it's a sad tale… May they all rest in peace.'

Everyone raised their glass in a toast before taking a sip, even Leo.

Charlie rested his forearms on the table opposite Leo. 'So why do you want to know that story, eh?'

It then clicked, and Bree's eyes flared. 'Are you related to Price?'

Leo nodded. 'Jake Blackwell was my uncle.'

'Blackwell Mining Company!' It was the name of Leo's mining company. Why hadn't she seen this sooner?

'My mother picked out the company name. She was Jake's sister, who believed your family killed my family, making her suffer. And where I come from, we believe in payback. An eye for an eye.'

'But we had nothing to do with Price's death. He killed himself,' said Bree.

'So, I've just found out. Honestly, I'd only recently learned about my uncle.'

Bree leaned closer to Leo over the table. 'This is about those stolen guns, isn't it?'

Leo didn't nod, but his cold eyes grew darker. 'My uncle

was supposed to settle his gambling debt with the organisation by giving them those stolen guns. But he never showed, leaving my mother behind.'

'They didn't hurt her, did they?' Charlie's concern was genuine. Even Bree stopped looking at Leo like a villain for just a moment.

'My mother was forced to marry a lower-ranking member of the family as a way to repay that debt.'

'Did you know?' Bree asked.

'I always knew my mother was part of an arranged marriage, just not the reason why. And my father always treated her well.' He stared long and hard at Bree.

'Go on,' urged Bree

'I never knew I had an uncle, or what he'd done, and how it affected my mother, until my mother spotted an article about his death in some obscure newspaper and demanded justice.'

'Those news articles were written over sixty years ago. Why only now?' Bree had seen the articles that Charlie had kept in a scrapbook, piled on their table with the rest of her grandfather's notes in his search for Harry.

'My mother is part of this charity that helps save the archives in libraries and stumbled upon an article written about the head stockman. It had a picture of Jack Price, and she knew who it was straight away. She then hired a private detective to find out where her brother was buried, where the station was, and how he'd been murdered. That's when my mother learned that Elsie Creek Station was up for sale. Only then did she explain the entire story to me, demanding some sort of family justice.'

It sounded lame to Bree. But then again, if anyone dared harmed a hair on her family, she'd cut loose. 'Is that why you wanted the station?'

'I never wanted to buy it. Not when I got this property so easily. And I knew the caretaker's caveat was watertight, so there was no way Charlie was going to sell to us.'

'What about your lithium mine? Was that ever going to

happen?'

'Nope. It was something to keep the Riggs brothers busy chasing their tails.' Leo's smirk irritated Bree.

'Hey,' she said with a sneer, 'you burned down our crops, making me play drover to feed our cattle for months. You destroyed Starvation Dam, poisoned our dogs, and made us sick from lead poisoning, Charlie had to go to hospital for a few days. Not to mention that idiot I shot in the arse...' She gripped her glass as a random thought popped into her head. 'Did you have anything to do with Darcie's death?'

'No. But I have been wearing down the defences of a certain old man,' he said with a cold smile, nodding at Charlie. 'Call it settling the score for what your family did to mine.'

'You prick.' She threw the glass at Leo. His arm deflected it to smash against the far wall, as she dragged her grandfather out of his chair and used her body to shield him. 'You leave my grandfather alone. Charlie had nothing to do with any of this.'

'So I found out only tonight.' Leo motioned his hand to his men who'd pulled out their guns. 'Calm down, all of you. *Sit down, men.* I mean that. Bree is only doing what I'd do for my family.'

But Bree wasn't giving Leo the satisfaction of agreeing with him for being protective over what little family she had left.

Leo angled his head towards her, the light deepening the sharp shadows of his cheekbones, and the sinister shine to his darkening eyes. 'You know, Bree, I wish it could have been different. I honestly believed it would have worked out with us.'

'In your nightmares, demon seed. I don't know why you'd even want me, I'm just the caretaker's granddaughter, a simple bushie's blacksmith.'

'Oh, you're far more than that, Bree. You have that rare outlaw quality, and bucketloads of mobster wife attitude that is rare for women in my world. With your level of cunningness, matched with my financial backing, we would have become very rich together without the need for getting our hands dirty.' Leo glanced around the hovel with a level of disdain.

That was never going to happen, not least because this man had hurt her family and was holding her against her will. 'What do you want? You know we had nothing to do with your uncle's death, so let us go.'

'Well…' Leo licked his lips as his eyes crawled over her.

She answered it with a sneer.

It only made him chuckle. 'I want to show you something.' Leo swiped up a remote control, turning the monitor around on his desk and hit play. 'Our cameras caught you finding our hidden pipeline.'

She remained expressionless, while watching herself on the screen at Starvation Dam, where she tracked that hidden irrigation pipe, with her black stallion dutifully following her to the border.

'You were about to jump the fence,' said Leo, fast forwarding the video, 'but something spooked you and then once you mounted your horse, something spooked it too.'

She watched as Black Hand reared up as she tried to control him, before turning to gallop away and fast.

'When was this, kid?' Charlie asked.

'A while ago.'

'Must have been something bad to spook your horse, when Black Hand never once flinched when you cracked that whip as he raced ahead of that stampede.'

'I agree,' said Leo, pointing the remote at Bree. 'You are fearless. It's one of many qualities I admire about you. So when you found that water pipe, I was expecting you to jump that fence. But you never came back. And you never cut the water line. What was it that spooked someone like you?'

'Ever hear of the Travellers?' she asked, completely deadpan.

'Noooo.' Charlie dragged off his hat, shaking his head, with his voice full of doom and gloom. 'That's bad news of the worst kind if you've got Travellers, boys.'

'What's a Traveller?' Hammer leaned closer from his seat.

'Ancient spirits that guard the outback. They're bad omens for some. You don't muck around with the Travellers, even the animals know to steer clear of 'em.'

'Yeah, right,' scoffed Gator. 'Next you'll be telling us it's drop bears and bunyips.'

Bones shook his head with a low chuckle. But Charlie had Wrench and Hammer listening for more.

'Well, we don't just have the Travellers in this region, we've also got the Billabong Bunyip to deal with, too. He's a legend in this area.'

Bree shuddered. 'It's the story every local bush kid gets told from the time they can walk.'

Leo narrowed his eyes at Bree while scratching his cheek, unconvinced. 'Bree, how about you tell me the truth? What was it that scared you off enough to not come back?'

She peered at his men spread around the room. 'You didn't tell him?'

'Tell me what?' Leo shrugged.

She feigned a gasp. 'Your men are keeping secrets from you.'

'What secret?' Leo leaned closer to her, with only the table between them. 'What did they do?'

'They shot at a plane.'

Leo spun around to face his men. 'What plane?'

'It was a red one, boss. It was getting too close. We had to do something,' said Hammer with his hands out as if to calm down a lion. 'We didn't hit it, did we, Bones?'

'No, boss.'

'Oh, yes, you did.' Bree was having fun stirring the pot. 'They clipped that plane's wing, the pilot had to land next door. And guess what?'

They all looked at her, the air crackling as she paused for dramatic effect, just like her grandfather did in his storytelling. But this pause was ticking off Leo more.

'Bree...' he warned her.

'That pilot, of the plane your boys shot at? She's a cousin to the Riggs brothers.'

Leo's face said it all as he stared at her for the longest time, as if the air had been sucked into a vacuum. Due to the actions of his men—shooting at that plane—they had drawn the worst kind of attention, and Leo knew it. *'You idiots!'*

'Boss?' All his men stood.

Leo paced the floor, the anger darkening his features. 'Wrench, Hammer, burn the crop, now. Bones pack up our gear and get ready to torch the rest of this place. We leave no evidence behind.' He picked up the laptop and ripped out its cord. 'Gator, tie those two up. They'll be coming with us.'

'Just let us go.' Bree scowled at Leo.

'You're a smart girl, you know I can't do that, not until we're safely out of the Territory. But if you behave, maybe I'll let you go. Or I'll use that time to convince you to be with me. But I'll let my mother decide Charlie's fate.'

'Not gonna happen!' Shielding her grandfather, she grabbed a chair, ready to use it as a weapon. She may not have been able to protect her mother all those years ago, but she was a grown woman now and she'd do anything to protect her grandfather, no matter the cost.

That's when something exploded on the other side of the door, forcing them all to duck for cover. The noise was deafening and so was the flash of light.

Bree pushed the table over and dragged Charlie behind it, as the windows smashed, sending shards of glass across the room, as the upper walls of the demountable were peppered with bullets turning it into Swiss cheese.

'Bree!'

It was Ryder.

Forty-six

Using his tactical military knife, Ryder slid back the window lock, pushed the window open and climbed inside the bedroom.

'Bree!'

It was his own voice, recorded on his phone, followed by a spurt of gunfire, but on the other side of the building.

Dex wasn't very subtle. But Ryder *had* asked his trigger-happy brother for a diversion using his favourite toy, the woodcutter.

And it worked.

Everyone else was distracted, facing the front door while he entered the room behind them. 'Hands up.'

He was ready for it. The two men on his left drew their weapons, and he shot them without blinking. The other two fled through the front door, where Dex shot them in the legs, they crumpled onto the cracked concrete path.

Dex ran up and kicked their weapons away, aiming his new lethal toy at their heads. 'Please move. Go on, I dare you.'

They weren't going anywhere, flat on their stomachs with their hands out in surrender.

But it was Leo who was an issue.

The prick had Bree, while Charlie was trapped in the corner, too close to Ryder's line of fire.

'Let go.' Bree struggled against the enemy.

'No. I wish I could. But we both know Ryder won't shoot,

not you.'

That prick was right. But it did nothing to deter him from aiming at Leo.

'I would have used that crop to buy Elsie Creek Station for you, Bree.' Leo's cheek pressed against Bree's, his handgun pressed against her ribs, wrapping his other arm around her while watching Ryder. 'I know how much that place really means to you, Bree. Not him,' he said sneering at Ryder. 'He has no clue how much you sacrificed for that station, how much you care about that land of red dust. I know, because I've been watching you for a long time.'

'Stalker much!' Somehow Bree got free, enough to spin around to face Leo. Even though Ryder's heart dropped, Bree was using her body to shield Charlie. 'Charlie, go. Get outside. Now!'

Ryder grabbed the old man. 'Dex is outside. Go.'

'Not without—'

Ryder pushed Charlie out the door, then spun around for Bree, who was again being held by Leo. 'Police are on their way.'

'I have no doubt,' replied Leo, who was eerily calm. The same way Bree had been mega mad at Ryder for accusing her of being a cattle rustler. It was the kind of anger that made you want to watch your back, making Leo a thousand times more dangerous.

With his pistol raised, Ryder had the prick in his sights, but Leo had his gun aimed at Bree. 'I will not give you a warning shot. Let Bree go, and I won't kill you.'

'I knew you were a killer.' Leo then said to Bree, 'You could have done so much better with me.'

'And you're such a prize? You didn't exactly shower me with flowers and chocolates, did you. No, you became our tormentor.' Bree's anger hit a whole new level. She stamped the heel of her boot against Leo's foot, then slammed the back of her head into Leo's face.

Ryder took his shot.

As the bullet passed through Leo's right shoulder, Ryder

grabbed Bree's hand, dragging her away from Leo. Leo landed on the floor where Ryder pressed a boot against his neck, forcing his head down as blood leaked out from the non-fatal wound. 'You deserve to die.'

'I can pay you whatever you want.'

'You'll have nothing left when the police seize your assets.'

Bree grabbed Ryder's spare handgun, clicked off the safety and pressed it to Leo's head.

'Bree? Let Marcus deal with this.'

'No.' She got lower to Leo. 'Your uncle killed my uncle. You poisoned Charlie's dogs. Held that old man in a strongarm hold, hurting him, to try and make him sign some papers like a bunch of bullies. You tormented us for almost two years. You made constant legal threats against the Riggs brothers, poisoned Cap's dogs at the campdraft, and organised for their cattle to be stolen so you could steal their water. You know what happens to cattle rustlers in the outback? I'd be happy to show you.'

'Don't do it, Bree.'

'He kidnapped us!' She pressed her gun into Leo's temple.

'Babe, he'll go down for his crop.'

Leo's eyes flared at Ryder.

'Yeah, arsehole. We came back that same night your idiot sidekicks shot at the plane, and we found your crop.' Bree gave an evil grin. 'And the Riggs brothers have been watching you, just like you've been watching us.' Her anger was pure fire. She lashed out and kicked Leo's wounded shoulder.

Leo groaned in pain, gripping his bleeding shoulder as he writhed on the floor.

'Don't you know we could have been friendly neighbours to you? The old-fashioned kind that baked bread and shared excess vegetables and beers over the fence line.'

'I'm sorry, Bree.'

'No, you're not. I know you're not.' She leaned closer to Leo. 'People may think I'm a horrible person. I'm loud, I'm mean, and mouthy, but I've seen evil, Leo. I watched my father murder my mother after taunting her for years. Which is exactly what you've been doing, taunting my grandfather, hoping to send him to the grave, and you're never going to stop, are you?'

'He what?' Ryder glared down at the mongrel. He'd known about the damage Leo and his goons had caused, but he hadn't realised the full extent of Leo's handiwork, especially how it had been targeted specifically at Charlie — until now.

Bree peeked back at Ryder.

With her distracted for just a second, it was all the opportunity Leo needed. He pushed Bree towards Ryder where they collided into each other, falling back onto the floor, as Leo scrambled to his feet, holding the gun he'd dropped.

Rolling away from Bree, Ryder turned his gun towards Leo.

But as he pulled the trigger a round was already shattering Leo's chest. He was dead before he hit the floor.

'No one hurts my family,' Bree growled, with the smoking gun in her hands.

Forty-seven

'Hey…' Ryder's arms snaked around Bree's body, holding her closer as he snuggled up to her in bed, early the next morning. 'Are you okay?'

'You?' Of course, she didn't answer.

'My hand is sore from signing all that paperwork for the police. At least we can sleep in.' Why move? He didn't have to sneak out like he used to.

She sighed into the pillow. 'You don't hate me or think I'm weird?'

'Sure. But for which part.' His lips curled against her soft skin, that was warm like summer morning, soft like silky cream, and smelled of heaven.

'For shooting Leo.'

'No.' He rolled her over to brush away her hair, to read her eyes. 'You don't scare me. You never did.'

'But I shot Leo. I think we broke the rules of murder club.'

'It wasn't murder, Bree, it was self-defence. Leo would have used that gun if he'd gotten the chance, he kidnapped you, and he would've been slippery enough to get away with what he'd done to you, Charlie, and my family. You said he'd never stop.'

'That's true.'

'But you stopped him, and you slept so well you snored all night.'

'Pfft, I don't snore.'

'You do. Which means you have no guilt for your actions.

You understand that feeling of guilt, right?'

'I do. I used to feel so guilty over not believing Charlie about Harry.' She paused, with her brow ruffling. 'Is that why you were always walking around the homestead at night, worrying?'

He rolled onto his back to stare at the ceiling. 'I used to suffer nightmares. Snatches of things from missions I'd hoped to forget. I haven't slept well in years, not until I began sleeping with you.' He tenderly stroked her nose, her worry and the open vulnerability so clear.

She sat up, tucking in the surrounding sheets. 'Are you sure you want to be with someone who shot a man?'

'Hey.' He tapped her thigh, sitting up beside her. 'I get why you did it.'

'Are you sure? Because I'm having trouble trying to work out why I'm not upset over it.'

'Because you never got the chance to protect your mother. But you are protective of Charlie, even me and my brothers. You're very protective of your family, Bree. It's one of the many things I love about you.'

Her eyes flared.

'Yes, I love you. You weren't the only one who shot him. I'd do it again in a heartbeat if anyone dared to harm you. But right now,' he said, kissing her forehead. 'I need the bathroom. I've never used the bathroom in this house before. Where is it, again?'

'It's the last door on the right.'

He wasn't expecting a response from Bree for saying he loved her, because she would need time. But he'd do it again just to keep her safe. Although he'd give Dex some training on guerrilla warfare for the future. With Ash the late-night gamer also keen to learn more, it wouldn't hurt to build a firing range one day.

From inside the bathroom, he heard the kettle whistling in the kitchen.

At the sink, he splashed water over his face, taming down his hair that was everywhere. Drying his face on a towel, he checked out the showerhead. It was massive compared to the outdoor shower he used, avoiding the farmhouse bathroom for fear of disturbing Harper's various bottled products. Dex had told him that Bree had made this shower herself, with a tub big enough to hold two people, which had a grand view of the garden and paddock. Now that's a bathroom! One he'd love to share with Bree.

'Morning, son.' Charlie was at the island bench, the aroma of his billy tea warming, blending with the other herbs hanging from the kitchen window.

'Charlie. How are you?'

'Can't complain. How's Bree?'

'She's a little unsure about what she did yesterday.'

'Killing Leo?'

Ryder nodded.

'Bree was the same when she shot that mongrel in the bum, that time. Warning them fellas she'd aim for their heads, before you mob bought this place.' He finished pouring out his billy tea into three cups. One was his battered enamel cup that went everywhere with him. One was Bree's. Charlie pushed the third cup across the wooden counter to Ryder.

The gesture made his day.

'You're a good man, Ryder. But you'll have your hands full with that one.'

'I know.'

'Nah, I don't think you do. Bree's had to fight for everything. At school, the kids picked on her when they found out about her parents. Of course she fought them, but it became that thing her and Finn had in common.'

'They met in school?'

'Boarding school.' Charlie sighed, hands on his hips, with his head slowly shaking from side to side. 'I wished she'd finished school, but when my beautiful Bea passed away, Bree quit to come home and take care of me. None of us expected Finn to show up looking for work soon after. And, well, you know the rest...' Charlie gazed at the locked door.

'Is that Liam's room?'

'It is.' Charlie sighed. 'All I want is for Bree to be happy. As a kid, she was happy, then lost her parents. As a married woman with a family, she was happy, then lost everything. All that heartache does something to a person, that she's learned not to get close to anyone. But then you came along, son. You took her brassiness and showed her it was okay to be herself and not change. I liked that about you. Hell, son, you shot up the neighbours to rescue us, and for that...' He held out his hand to Ryder. 'You have my respect, my gratitude, and I'd like to welcome you to the family.'

He shook Charlie's hand, grateful for it. 'You don't need to be so formal, Charlie. The cuppa is enough.'

'It's what Bree wanted.' Charlie gave a coy wink as he tapped the side of his temple. 'I know you two have been sneaking around.'

'You do, huh?'

'Back in the day I would have chased you out with the shotgun, but then I saw how much Bree smiles with you. It's like there's this weight lifted off her shoulders, like she's finding her happiness, again.'

'I hope so.'

'You'll know it when you see it. Coz when that girl opens her heart, Ryder, it is a beautiful thing. That's when she'll tuck you under that protective wing of hers, where no matter what, she'll always have your back. But if I know that girl, she'll be wondering if she's scared you off.'

'She hasn't.'

'I hope not. There aren't too many men strong enough to handle a strong woman like Bree. Finn had his shot and lost it. Leo thought he could, but he would have taken her down a dark path. For you, it's the other way around. It's Bree who is bringing you out of that darkness, and she's just hitching a ride that's helping both of you.'

What the? Ryder double blinked. Was Charlie right? Bree had not only been teaching him to play, but she'd also softened up a lot herself since they'd first met, bickering with each other.

'I'm not gonna ask, but I'm guessing it's something you did in your army days, coz, son, you didn't even flinch shooting Leo. But then, neither did Bree. Never be afraid of her, Ryder, coz that girl has a bucketload of love to give.' Then with cup in hand, Charlie pushed open the back door. 'Be sure to give my granddaughter her cuppa. It's a rare thing for her to have a cuppa in bed.'

'I will.'

'Well, I'll get out of your hair, boss. You have a station to run where that to-do list never ends.' Charlie slid on his well-worn stockman's hat, tapped the brim, and walked out the back door carrying his tin mug.

Ryder carried the other two mugs into the bedroom to find Bree getting dressed. 'What are you doing? I thought we could stay in bed.' He held out the tea mug. 'Charlie made me a cuppa.'

'I see that.'

'And he welcomed me to the family.'

'Really?' Her eyebrows lifted as she sipped from her cup.

Outside the big shepherd barked, and Ryder pulled back the curtain to spot the police car rolling in.

'Marcus is early,' murmured Bree over his shoulder.

'Or he's stopping in on his way home. I'll go see. We'll be down in the boardroom. Come find me later?'

'Pfft. I'm not running after you. Not when I have horses to feed, and Charlie will cook breakfast soon.' She gave a coy grin. 'Now you've got the welcome, that old man will save you a plate, you know that.'

'Well, I'll be back to join you then.' And wasn't going to miss it.

He kissed her cheek, then tenderly stroked her hair. 'You don't scare me, Bree. In fact, I respect you, admire you, as well as love you more each and every day.'

She gasped slightly at his words.

But it had him smiling, as he threw on his shirt, and left the cottage through the front door, heading down the stone path. The fragrance of the flowers in the front garden was invigorating as they greeted the sun.

Looking back at the stone cottage, at the way the sunlight spread its warm buttery light over the quiet and peaceful homestead, made last night seem like a nightmare. Leo was gone, Elsie Creek Station was secure, and Charlie had welcomed him into the family. After everything they'd been through, it felt like the dawn of not only a new day, but a new beginning to this place they all called home.

Forty-eight

Ryder had told Bree he loved her.

If she was honest with herself, she knew he'd felt that way about her for a while now—she just hadn't let him say it. And she'd never wanted to hear it.

Yet…

It was enough to fill her with heavenly sweet, feel-good giddiness as she sipped her tea at the kitchen sink, glancing over the brimming vegetable garden.

Normally on a Sunday morning she'd prepare a roast, ensuring they had enough leftovers to carry them over for a few days. But with her grandfather accepting Ryder, the guy had earned his seat at the table, so she'd have to double up on everything.

Grabbing her basket and snips to harvest from her garden, like she did most mornings, she spotted Charlie through the kitchen window, at the far end of their yard. It's where he stood in the same place, every morning, leaning against the fence to raise his tin mug to salute the sunrise as if to say, *I made it another day.*

It was Charlie's favourite spot to watch the sunrise spread its large sunbeams over the lush green fields of Drover's Rest, that stretched to meet the Scary Forest where birds fluttered in clusters above the treetops, under the shadow of the mighty escarpment known as Cattleman's Keep.

With the murder solved, Leo gone, life could go back to normal, and Elsie Creek Station could get back to being a cattle station again.

Then Charlie collapsed to the ground.

'*Pop*?' She dropped her teacup in the sink with a splash. The screen door whacked against the house as her bare feet slapped against the cold flat stones that made up the path.

'Pop?' She rolled him over. 'What's wrong?'

His breath was raspy, his face red as he struggled for air.

'Take a breath, Pop, a slow one.' She loosened his shirt's collar. 'It's just the stress of the past few days, and the late nights, Pop. We'll get you in the house and back into bed. I'll put your favourite movies on and—'

'Hey…' He grabbed her hand, his face twisted in pain. 'It's time.'

'No. Keep fighting this.'

'My beautiful Bea is waiting for me.'

'No. Don't leave me.' He was supposed to outlive her. All of them were.

'It's time, kid…' His voice dropped, his breathing laboured, with his left hand squeezed into a fist, as the beats of his heart beneath her hand grew slower, and more erratic.

'Pop, I can—' He had a no-resuscitation order in place. As much as she wanted to, he'd been adamant about it, leaving her powerless to do anything.

'Lift me up, kid. I wanna see that sunrise one more time.'

Oh hellfire, no!

Even though she didn't want to, she'd always done as he'd asked.

She sat close, propping him up to her chest. He was so heavy. 'How's that?'

'Good. Really good.' Charlie sighed, but it barely made his chest move, his breaths were getting fainter as she held him against her, as he watched the sun barely breach the horizon to warm his skin. 'You did good, kid. Don't ever forget that I'm proud of you…' His frail hand brushed her cheek, his dulling grey eyes full of love and admiration. 'I love you, kid.'

She cupped her mouth to stop blubbering, with the thick

hot tears against her cheeks.

'Say it back, kid. Come on.'

'I love you too, Pop.'

He nodded, satisfied, then slumped against her chest, lying on the stone path, in the garden he'd built with his wife, on the edge of the stock school he'd created, on the land he loved. His body became heavier, his eyes became still on the soft blue summer sky as his last breath left his chest in a whisper on an outback sunrise, and the world became silent.

Forty-nine

The days merged into one—sunrise, sunset, then sunrise and sunset, stuck in a cycle of light and dark. Bree ate food she didn't taste. She drank but wasn't thirsty. She listened but didn't hear, all while completely and totally numb.

The doctor said Charlie's heart had given out. Those last few days had been too much of a strain for his heart.

Even though they said he'd proved them all wrong, lasting an extra five years past their diagnosis, Bree had always hoped her grandfather would outlive her, just so she didn't have to do this on her own.

She thought she'd be ready for the funeral, but nothing could prepare her for the deep-seated level of loneliness, where grief became a long road without sunshine and flowers.

When the lawyer gave her a letter from Charlie, it gave her something to hold on to, to see her through that ugly haze created by grief.

In true Charlie style, it was simple:

Hey, Kid,

Don't grieve too long. We always knew this was gonna happen. Unlike other people, we had warning enough to plan my funeral and everything.

But I decided to find a blinking pen and write down the extra bits I might forget to tell you. This is the fifth time I've rewritten this letter. I think the lawyer's getting sick of me doing it.

Anyhoodle, after recent events, finding Pandora, and the cave with Harry and that gold, I had to. So this is why you've got this letter, when I haven't written one in decades. So, here we go...

Someone said to me once, dunno who, but they reckoned I should look at this whole tricky heart thing as a gift, coz I'd been told when my time was up. And I did.

The way I see it, kid, we're all given a ticket of time in this world. We never truly know when that ticket gets called up, which is why I got to live every second of every day like it's my last, living a life with no regrets. And I tried hard to have none.

So, this is my last list of things I want you to do for me, kid. You'd better do it, too.

It's not a big list, but it'll help you grieve, and also to move on with your future. So, attached is a list of things I want you to give to people, like Cowboy Craig. He gets my rodeo ropes and spurs, coz I know he'll treasure them.

Don't sell Pandora to anyone, even if she just sits in the shed. I enjoyed watching you smile when you drove her, and Harry would want it to stay in the family. Just don't let Dex turn it into a hot rod, okay?

Sadly, the caretaker's caveat is over, and according to that contract, we've got this grace period to move all our gear out. Don't get mad at them Riggs brothers because this is what Darcie and I negotiated. So, it's an ironclad deal, kid.

First up, I want you to clean out my room. I know it might seem cruel to do it so soon, but it's what I want. Then you're to clean out Liam's room, too. The clothes and stuff you don't want are to go to Mrs Sternston at the sewing store. She'll send it to a friend in Queensland, who runs the Goodwill there. That way, you won't see anyone wearing our clobber round town.

The Station Hand says he's got room to store the blacksmithing gear for as long as you need, and for anything else you want to store for a bit, including the stockhorses. Although Cowboy Craig has some stables at his place, if you need. And I'm sure there are plenty of people who'll volunteer or offer to buy them. They're good stockhorses.

If you haven't already, see Lenny about Harry's gold you found, and he'll take it to the gold broker and sell it.

Then I want you to use the gold for that holiday you've always yakked about, then find yourself a home. As much as I would have loved having the means to buy Elsie Creek Station, which has always been a home for us both, I can't. So get your own, kid. Find that place perfect for you where you can work on the tools, with one eye on the weather and a view of your own paddock.

Just know I'll always be watching over you from the long paddock of eternity with the rest of your family, so you know you're never alone.

Until then, may your seat sit well in that stockman's saddle with that stockwhip whirling like the wind, and be sure to raise your cuppa as you keep an eye on that outback sunrise every day forward until we meet again.

All my love, your grandfather,

Charlie 'Splinter' Splint (Your Pop)

Bree had read it enough times now that the paper was wearing at the creases. Wiping at her tears, she tucked the letter safely away in her pocket, nearing the last of the entire funeral process. After this, the packing would start, but first she had to get through today.

The morning was warm, the breeze barely shifting the fine layer of red dust over the hazy, desolate outback highway. Strong hooves clashed on the black top as the rumble of the horse-drawn carriage led down the asphalt road towards the tiny outback town of Elsie Creek.

On the back of the flatbed horse cart lay a simple wooden coffin. On top lay a well-worn stockwhip.

Dressed in black, Bree walked behind the open carriage. She held her grandfather's hat to her chest, as she walked Charlie's grey stockhorse, Slim, with its empty saddle signifying the loss of the rider.

As the sun climbed higher, her shadow blended with that of the horse and the carriage, as the start of a stockman's funeral.

It had started with just her, the horse, and the carriage driven by the Station Hand himself, continuing a long and proud tradition unique to the stockmen in the Elsie Creek region.

But then they came…

The Riggs Brothers, all five of them—Ryder, Dex, Cap, Ash, and their youngest brother Jonathan—rode their stockhorses, alongside Cowboy Craig.

But then more came…

Men, women, old, young, riding on worn saddles, with wide-brimmed hats bent to shade their eyes, their stockwhips slung over their shoulders, with their proud stockhorses forming sturdy lines like the Light Horse Brigade. Rows and rows of stockhorses and their riders followed the carriage as it travelled down main street.

The town's stores had closed, and more mourners lined the street as the sound of over a hundred sturdy and sure-footed stockhorses' hooves echoed off the shopfront windows.

The long line of stockmen rode past the pub that towered over the town's corner. They rode past the train line, and the empty stockyards of the train station, following Bree, who walked behind the carriage, leading an empty-saddled stockhorse to the small church on the hill.

The service was brief, just how Charlie would have liked it. And was laid to rest beside his wife, near his brother and Bree's mother, and among the other relatives she'd never known.

With the formalities over, it was time to move to the pub where they told stories about the stockman and master brand maker they all knew. There Bree shook hands, smiled politely, just as her grandfather would have expected of her, and when it was over, there was silence.

The cottage was silent. The pizza oven cold. The Razorback had dust on its seat. The tools her grandfather had hand-forged were lying in the shade, his leather apron hung on the hook, and time had stood still once again.

This place had too many memories now. Always expecting her grandfather to wander down the garden path and open the back screen door, to wipe his boots at the doormat, while poking up the brim of his hat to share some news.

But now the caretaker's caveat was officially over.

Fifty

Ever since that stockman with the bandy-legged swagger had passed, there had been a big gaping hole in the lives of those who lived at Elsie Creek Station. Charlie had been so full of life, happily dancing with the ladies, giving bull-riding tips to the next generation of rodeo riders, or telling scary stories around a campfire.

Ryder truly missed the old man who always had a story to tell, missing the aroma of baking bread that greeted him in the mornings, or that robust cup of billy tea.

Following the smell of coffee brewing, Ryder walked into the boardroom where Ash and Cap were already seated at the table to begin their regular morning meeting. 'Morning.'

'How's Bree?' Cap asked.

'Quiet. In the shed this morning.' Even though she'd been up long before dawn, it was a good thing. Ryder had tried to comfort her, but it was like Bree had completely switched off. All that playfulness, that sassy spark, was buried deep behind her hollow eyes. But he'd refused to let her go through this alone.

'This is for you lot.' He dealt out the large manila envelopes like dealing a pack of cards.

'What's this?' Ash spun his envelope around on the tabletop.

'I want you all to work out your wills.' Ryder was doing what he always did, prepare for the future.

'You're kidding.' Ash's jaw dropped. He was young, and

still had that ten-foot-tall bulletproof bravado that Ryder remembered at that age.

'With Charlie's passing and what Bree is going through, I think we owe it to ourselves and our loved ones to make it as easy as possible for those we leave behind. I've updated mine. You guys have dependants now that you need to take care of. Ash, you will need to do one for your son. Cap, you've got dogs. And you've all got live-in partners.'

The sounds of hooves trotting towards them stopped, a horse snorted, and in a few moments, Dex strolled inside carrying a large rolled up package the length of a shotgun. 'Morning.'

'How was the ride?'

'Great. I thought our stockhorses were good, but Bree's horse is a beast.'

'You rode Black Hand?' Ryder's jaw tightened. Bree loved that horse.

Dex nodded. 'He's having a drink in the trough by the bar.'

Bree still fed her horses daily, but she hadn't ridden them since Charlie had passed.

'Unless you can get Bree to start riding again, I'll be riding Slim tomorrow.' They all knew the stockhorses were used to being ridden on a regular rotation.

'Good idea. I'll get Bree back on Black Hand tomorrow, and I'll ride Slim.' Even if Bree may argue with him, Ryder would carry her to that saddle if he had to. He'd rather she'd get mad at him than continue in the catatonic state she'd been in lately. Grief just sucked.

'Cool, I'll go back to running in the mornings then. Can't wait until we get our first station hand to care for the horses.' Dex poured himself a coffee, carrying that long roll on his shoulder.

'And they can clean the troughs,' mumbled Ash.

'Oh, and the fencing, don't forget the fencing,' said Cap, peeking inside the large envelope.

'Did I miss much?' Dex dropped into his chair and

dumped the roll on the table with a heavy thud.

'Just that I want you to make out a will.' Ryder dropped the envelope in front of Dex. 'I want it back in a week to lodge them.'

'Swap ya. I found this package on the bar.' He slid it across the table.

Ryder peeled back the bubble wrap, the same stuff Bree used for her customer's packages. Only this time it revealed a green blanket, the one he'd given Bree when he'd fixed her shotgun. It was his blanket!

Was she giving him her shotgun back?

'What's that?' Ash asked, with Cap leaning forward.

Ryder rolled open the blanket to reveal a branding iron.

'Is that the Elsie Creek brand?' Ash was on his feet to pick up the branding iron, with Cap scooting around the table to stand beside him.

Dex plucked up a note tucked inside the blanket and read out:

As per the final request of Charlie Splint, this is for the Riggs brothers.

Please take care of it, boys, and all that this brand represents as the owners of Elsie Creek Station.

Bree.

Ryder gathered up his old green blanket, releasing another slip of paper that fell to the table. 'It's the brand's registration. Bree's transferred it into our name.'

'We finally have it,' said Ash, passing the branding iron to Cap.

Yet none of them felt like celebrating ownership of the brand they'd argued with Charlie about from the very beginning.

Cap passed the iron to Ryder, who cradled the rare legacy branding iron as if it were forged from more than metal. It held the weight of this station's history, that was part of the stories of every beast and every hand who had ever marked this land.

He passed it on to Dex, all of them solemn as it exchanged hands. It wasn't merely an iron rod passing from one owner to the next, it was the station's soul, entrusted to Ryder and his brothers to carry forward.

Ryder then carried it to the vacant space on the wall, where he'd asked Bree to make him a bull's head when she did this room's makeover. Of course she'd refused, yet kept this space blank, complete with the special hanging hooks. He'd never understood why she'd left this space empty, until now.

It was the perfect place to hang their legacy brand for all to see, as all four brothers stood in a row and stared at it in heavy silence. It felt official now, as owners of Elsie Creek Station, with the torch being passed on from the caretaker, and longest serving head stockman, to the next generation of stockmen.

Then they all heard the familiar rumble of the Kombi van.

'Where is Bree going?' Dex peered through the wall of windows.

Ryder shrugged, yet there was a tingling sensation at the base of his neck. Something wasn't right. Bree could have given him that brand personally, there was no reason to leave it on the bar like that. And she had Dex riding her horse, Black Hand.

'When is Bree going on that holiday? What was it?' Cap asked. 'Some beach…'

'To drink gin on a beach with no crocodiles while she waited to go watch the Stanley Cup,' said Ash. 'Bree's got Harper watching ice hockey now. I had no idea how brutal and quick that game is.'

'Does anyone remember where Bree's first stop was?' Cap asked.

'To drive to the nearest international airport and catch the first plane out to Tahiti.' Dex grabbed Ryder's arm. 'Brother, Bree always said she was going to do that as soon as Charlie's affairs were in order.' Dex pointed to the branding iron that hung from the wall. 'That looks like finished business to me.'

The yellow Kombi van puttered down the long driveway.

'Bree wouldn't leave without saying goodbye, would she?' Ash headed to the window.

'She'd better not.' Tossing the green blanket over his shoulder, Ryder stalked out the door to find Bree's horse, Black Hand, patiently standing by the water trough. Without a second thought, Ryder swung into the saddle and gave chase after that yellow Kombi van disappearing in a cloud of red dust.

Fifty-one

Behind the steering wheel of the yellow Kombi van, Bree drove towards the main gate, while busily skipping through the songs on her playlist, searching for something loud to drown her thoughts.

'*What the hellfire!*' She slammed her foot on the brakes as Ryder galloped up on Black Hand, the stallion rearing in front of the vehicle. 'Are you crazy? I could've hurt my horse.'

'Where are you going?' Ryder leaped off the saddle. With the green blanket in one hand, he tied the horse's reins to the front bull bar.

'Town.'

'And?'

'I'm going through Charlie's to-do list.'

'No, you're being sneaky is what you're doing.' Ryder tossed that green blanket over his shoulder, then ripped open her driver's door and snatched the keys out of the ignition. 'Get out.'

'Why?'

'Because I'm scared that you're about to disappear out of my life forever and go on that holiday.' He peeked into the back of the Kombi full of suitcases and assorted boxes. 'That's what you're doing, isn't it? You're leaving me.' Pain etched across his face. It was heartbreaking.

'Listen, the caretaker's caveat is over,' she said, slinking out of the driver's seat. 'I will not take advantage of you.'

'No, Bree. Dammit.' He ripped off his hat to rake fingers

through his hair. 'The caretaker's caveat is not over.'

'It is—'

'No!' He grabbed her hands. 'The reason I nominated Drover's Rest as my paddock and the cottage as my house was to give them to you.'

'Excuse me?' Did she hear that right? Or was her foggy brain still stuck in the grief cycle where she chose to shut off completely. It was easier that way than to deal with what life kept throwing at her. It would have been easier if she'd never met Ryder, too.

'It's yours.'

'Nooo.' Oh, she was wide awake now.

'I haven't told my brothers yet, but I have gifted you that area, so that no matter who owns the station, it's yours as part of the *new* caretaker's caveat.'

'Why?'

'Because we were never your bosses. You never worked for us. You worked *with* us, always for the good of Elsie Creek Station. You were more than an overseer, more than a head stockman, Bree. You are Elsie Creek Station. And if you leave, not only would it break me, it would break all that is good and worthy about what we've been fighting so hard to protect in this place.'

Yet, she'd been fighting so hard to leave. This was her chance. Her responsibilities to everyone were over. 'This is not my home. It was Charlie's.'

'That is simply *not true!*' His words echoed around them as he stepped in closer. 'You've fought bushfires to protect the crops, you drove the herd not only along the long paddock, but to the hidden lands of Wombat Flats, and hid another herd in Scary Forest, that you'd check on regularly. You've ensured all the water was safe with the water filters in our houses to keep not only us but the muster dogs safe within their kennels. You captured and made us relocate a salt-water crocodile into the wild not only to preserve its life, but to protect the freshwater crocodiles in our waterways that are an endangered species. As well as orchestrated the preservation of certain wildlife corridors for the native animals who share this land.'

'Nah. I—'

'I know, Bree,' he said, taking her hands. 'I was there when you sang lullabies to the herd after midnight, while protecting them from a pack of wild dogs. You grew up playing games as a child at stock school, always looking out for the stock, and I've seen how you've helped my brothers and what you did for their houses.'

'They needed somewhere.'

'To make it feel like home, like it is for you.' He lifted her chin making her stare into his deep brown eyes. 'Don't you get it, Bree? You *are* Elsie Creek Station. You are the heart and soul of this place and if you leave, I leave too. Because I love you. You are everything to me.'

He stepped back, the frown returning enough to stop her from saying anything.

'And this stupid, crusty, worthless blanket,' he said through gritted teeth, squeezing it in his fist. 'You know why I gave you this. I told you not to give it back, especially after I told you the story! Only you would see its true worth!'

'It's why I wrapped the branding iron in it. I know what it means to you.' She couldn't keep it. And she didn't want this confrontation either. Sneaking out to go drink on some beach to not feel, to not remember, had always been part of her plan. Not this.

'When I first gave this to you, it was to show you how much I cared about you, but also to tell you that you are my home, you are my everything. It's the same way I can see how much this place is your home. And that's why I've made the caretaker's caveat a permanent fixture as part of Elsie Creek Station not only for you, but for your children or whoever you see fit to stay with you.'

She swallowed. The words he spoke weren't real. It couldn't be true. 'What do you get out of it?' What was the catch?

Fifty-two

'I just want to see you happy, Bree.' With the back of his fingers, Ryder captured the small tear trickling down her cheek. She'd been crying too easily ever since Charlie had passed. It broke his heart seeing her like this— but she was going to break his soul if she left him.

'Maybe I don't want to be happy right now. Maybe I just want to find some corner of the universe to scream my lungs out at the injustices it keeps dishing up to me.'

'Fine. I'll go with you.'

'It won't be pretty. And it won't be perfect.'

'But it will be real. And being real is so much better than being perfect.' He exhaled as heavily as she did, as if they were both reining in their tempers.

'I've said it before and I'll say it again, Bree: you do not scare me. I can handle your cranky moods and your temper. Your sass has always amused me, even putting up with that stupid pet name.'

There was a slight twitch in the corners of her lips. It gave him hope he was getting through to her.

'I love you, Bree.' He cupped the side of her face, his thumb brushing over her cheek. 'I love how you have this special smile that reaches your eyes when you finish a job in the shed, that self-satisfaction you have as the steam curls over the water that you use to cool off your latest creation. I loved watching you ride during a muster, that didn't involve stampedes or landslides. How your hair blows in the wind when you're driving the Razorback. And how you're never scared of anything.'

'I am scared.'

'Of what?'

She dropped her head.

He lifted her chin. 'Tell me.'

'Of being alone.' Her voice was so soft, so frail.

'You're not alone, baby, I'm right here.' He gathered up her soft hand and held it against his heart. 'And if you'll have me, I'll marry you in a heartbeat.'

She blinked as if her eyes were full of grit, but the spark was there as if waking up to the world. 'Is that a proposal?'

'Sure. Why not? This would be the best place to do it.' He pointed at the intricately handcrafted metal sign that read *Elsie Creek Station*, hand-forged by Bree's grandfather and great-grandfather, that towered over the main entrance. Its long shadow reflected across the red dirt that made up the driveway that doubled as an airstrip. 'Unless you want something fancier?'

'I want nothing.'

'Yes, you do, Bree. You want a family. I know you do.'

She shook her head 'I lost them. All of them.'

'No, not all,' he said, stepping in closer. 'I'm right here, and there's my brothers and their families. We're all part of the package. Don't you see that?'

Again, she shook her head.

'Through you, I learned to play, but also to live a life by enjoying those small moments found each day with you. I want to go riding with you in the mornings to greet the sunrise as we check over the herd, and help you haul in those crab pots before dawn. I want to share breakfast with you, and to sit beside you at a campfire under the stars. I want to explore every part of this land with you, hearing all those stories you've learned about our home, with you by my side as my wife. I want us to be *together forever*.'

Her eyes sparked to life, to stare at him fully for the first time in days.

He then pointed to the cases in the back of her van. 'Were you leaving me?'

'I—I… was letting go.' She sighed heavily as she peeked back at the van. 'It's Liam's, my grandmother's and Charlie's stuff, to go to the Goodwill.'

'Why? And don't say it's because of Charlie's list.'

'It is on Charlie's list.' Bree lifted her chin feistily, her eyes blazing with the stubborn fire Ryder had once dreaded, but was now grateful to see it again. 'I was cleaning out the house because it needed to be done.'

'To help you move forward, not leave me behind. So, what were you planning on doing today? The truth. No games.'

'I'm taking this stuff to town, then collecting my gold from the police station and delivering it to Lenny to sell for me. Charlie wanted me to use that for my holiday, then to find a home to live.'

'You've been very specific about that holiday.'

'I've never had one.'

'Excuse me?' He stepped back, tilting his head at her.

She shrugged. 'I've always had to take care of someone or something…' She nodded at the land that surrounded them and the road that led to the homestead. 'I've never regretted being a carer, not for one second, but I promised Charlie that I'd take a holiday when he left, because I'd been the carer for Darcie, Charlie, and this place for years. I wanted a break, somewhere that is free from deadly wildlife, like crocodiles.'

'Like Tahiti.'

She nodded. 'And I've always wanted to see a live ice hockey game. We don't get many games out here…' She gazed at the sunburnt land that made up the remote outback.

'Save that gold, invest it, and I'll take you on that holiday, and then we'll both come home to where we belong.'

'You can't buy me.'

'Don't you think I know that by now? But I can spoil you, if you'll let me.'

For once she looked at a loss for what to say.

'Look, I told you I was missing something and bought this property for my brothers.'

'For family.'

'Correct. What I didn't know—until I'd met this sassy redhead, so fiercely loyal to her loved ones, who fought with me every inch of the way and is still fighting me when I know we belong together—is what I was missing. Bree, we've been through so much together. We've fought for this family, and for this station, side by side. When we did the muster to Wombat Flats, hiding from the sandstorm in the cave. Then we shared moments mustering the herd together by moonlight, just you and me. We sat side by side in the hospital when my brother was on that breathing machine. We fought against Leo, swapped wedding fingers in a morgue, discovered dynamite and solved a murder mystery at midnight. In case you hadn't notice, Bree, I'd walk through fire for you, to be with you. For you are the fire that helped melt the ice that used to run through my veins.'

She gazed at him, listening silently. It gave him hope she was really hearing him.

'I love you. And the way I love you, there's nothing you can do about it, and there's nothing you can do to make me stop loving you, and there's nothing you can do to make me change my mind.'

'Oh, hellfire...' she murmured under her breath.

'I know this is the most I've ever said to anyone, except you. I'm only like this with you.' He then took a deep calming breath. 'Now, tell me, what do you want from me that'll make you happy again?'

She stared up at him with her beautiful green eyes, where, for the first time in what felt like forever, a twinkle broke through, with a mischievous shine even. 'Yes.'

Did he hear that right?

Fifty-three

'**W**here's the no?' Ryder stood so close, his head tilted, gazing at Bree in one of those unreadable expressions. 'You're always saying no to me.'

She gave him a shrug, biting back her smile. 'Well, now I'm saying yes.' She liked this game of surprising Ryder.

He stepped back, running a hand over his bearded jaw as if trying to read this right. 'Is that a yes you'll live with me?'

'Mmm, technically, if I own the cottage—'

'Bree!'

'Yes.'

He swallowed hard and licked his lips. 'Is that a yes to marrying me?'

The air just got thicker and heavier.

'Is that a yes that we'll be together forever?' He froze as if holding his breath.

She didn't move, but her heart was hammering at a bazillion beats. 'Yes. But know you'll be in for a helluva ride.'

'Is there any other way?' He held her so close she felt his heart beat against her hand. 'Now you have to tell me you love me. I know you do.'

'I just said yes. What more do you want from me?'

'Bree.' He let her go, the frown returning.

She matched it. 'Don't start telling me what to do, cupcake, you're not the boss of me—'

He pulled her close and kissed her, long and deep,

pouring everything into that one kiss, leaving her tingling throughout her body.

Still holding her close, he murmured, 'I'll take you to Tahiti and to watch the Stanley Cup as our honeymoon.'

'If we can elope, you'll have a deal.' She grinned, fisting his shirt.

'We'll leave today.' He let rip that full smile like he'd gone and swallowed the sun. 'First, tell me you love me. Go on.'

'Well…'

'Bree!'

'Fine. For the record,' she said, jutting out her chin, 'I've always loved you. I just fought it because I didn't want to lose you, too.'

'I'm not going anywhere without you. This is our home, it's where we belong.'

Strangely, she believed him. The overwhelm wasn't there, the fright wasn't there, and the fear that had been holding her back was gone as she whispered, 'I love you, Captain Cupcake. I've loved you for a very long time.'

He gently rested his forehead against hers, tenderly holding her hands. 'Say it.'

'We will be *together forever*. For you are mine…'

'And I am yours…'

Together they said, 'And we'll be *together forever*. Always.'

And she believed it.

For Charlie, who will always be that legendary stockman to me.

Read The Extended Epilogue!

Learn about:
Elsie Creek Station
The family tree
Behind the scenes
Plus more.

Free & Exclusive!
Simply go to:
https://melarowe.com/the-stockmen-series-gifts/

Want more from the Elsie Creek World?

Binge-read the bestsellers found in:

- The Elsie Creek Series

- The Station Duology

- The Stockmen Series

- The Stock Squad

Find them at your favourite online bookstore.

ACKNOWLEDGEMENTS

It's always bittersweet finishing a series. So, I won't say this four-book journey is truly over, because some of the characters from the Elsie Creek World will undoubtedly pop up again in the future—I'm sure of it.

In the meantime, thank you, dear reader, for joining me on this adventure. I also extend my gratitude to everyone who helped bring this series to life, starting with the many retired ringers, stockmen, boundary riders, cheeky chopper pilots, fencers, and rodeo riders. So many trades, jobs, and personalities inspired me and shaped this outback adventure into something I'm proud to say has roots in real-life experiences.

A special thanks to the retired Acting Sergeant Tania Smith for helping me work through that non-murder scene. Again, a big thanks to the Aunties of Larrakia Nation for your cultural assistance. And the Handbrake, as always for being there.

So, to end this series using the words of the Elsie Creek Stockmen:

May your seat sit well in that stockman's saddle, with that stock-whip whirling like the wind. Be sure to raise your cuppa as you greet that next sunrise, from every day forward, until we meet again in my next book series,

A. ROWE

ABOUT THE AUTHOR

Australian bestselling author, Mel A ROWE, creates romantic escapes for today's busy readers to enjoy from the comfort of their home.

Delivering stories with a dash of drama, witty humour and quirky family units, Mel is known for reinventing romantic versions of home, taking her common characters on uncommon journeys that lead from boardrooms to billabongs as they try to find their own HAPPILY EVER AFTER.

Living in Australia's Northern Territory, Mel enjoys random outback road trips, fumbling with her camera, annoying her family with her bad singing, and making new friends in the middle of nowhere—except for water buffalos. She's been chased by a few.

Find Mel at

MelAROWE.com

Receive exclusive insights, book gifts, and news
of upcoming releases by joining:
https://melarowe.com/newsletter/

Also by MEL A ROWE

ELSIE CREEK SERIES:
The Art of Dust
Diamond in the Dust
Caked in Dust
Xmas Dust
Muster in the Dust
Rolled in Dust
Written in Dust
Doctoring Dust
Buffalo Dust

OASIS OF THE OUTBACK DUOLOGY:
The Station, Volume One
The Station, Volume Two

THE STOCKMEN SERIES:
Stockman's Sandstorm
Stockman's Stowaway
Stockman's Stormcloud
Stockman's Showdown

THE STOCK SQUAD:
Rough Stock
Cold Stock
Wild Stock
Prime Stock

STANDALONE STORIES:
Avoiding the Pity Party
Unplanned Party
The Football Whisperer
Winter's Walk
Run Beautiful Run
The Sister Trip

For more visit MelAROWE.com